Clare Connelly was rai[...] among a family of avid [...] of her childhood up a tr[...] hand. Clare is married t[...] and they live in a bungalow near the sea with their two children. She is frequently found staring into space—a surefire sign that she's in the world of her characters. She has a penchant for French food and ice-cold champagne, and Mills & Boon novels continue to be her favourite-ever books. Writing for Mills & Boon is a long-held dream. Clare can be contacted via clareconnelly.com or her Facebook page.

Rachael Stewart adores conjuring up stories, from heartwarmingly romantic to wildly erotic. She's been writing since she could put pen to paper— as the stacks of scrawled-on pages in her loft will attest to. A Welsh lass at heart, she now lives in Yorkshire, with her very own hero and three awesome kids—and if she's not tapping out a story she's wrapped up in one or enjoying the great outdoors. Reach her on Facebook, Twitter (@rach_b52) or at rachaelstewartauthor.com.

If you liked
Harden My Hart and *Losing Control*
why not try

The Rebound by Stefanie London
As You Crave It by J. Margot Critch

Also by Clare Connelly

Guilty as Sin

Her Guilty Secret
His Innocent Seduction

The Billionaires Club

The Deal

The Notorious Harts

Cross My Hart
Burn My Hart

Also by Rachael Stewart

Mr One-Night Stand
Mr Temptation
Naughty or Nice
Getting Dirty

Discover more at millsandboon.co.uk

HARDEN MY HART

CLARE CONNELLY

LOSING CONTROL

RACHAEL STEWART

MILLS & BOON

First Published in Great Britain 2020
by Mills & Boon, an imprint of HarperCollins*Publishers*
1 London Bridge Street, London, SE1 9GF

Harden My Hart © 2020 Clare Connelly

Losing Control © 2020 Rachael Stewart

ISBN: 978-0-263-27763-0

MIX
Paper from
responsible sources
FSC® C007454

Printed and bound in Spain
by CPI, Barcelona

HARDEN MY HART

CLARE CONNELLY

MILLS & BOON

To Steph, who has loved the Harts
right from the start.

Thanks for your support and many discussions
about hero hotness at school pick-up time.

PROLOGUE

'THIS ISN'T OPTIONAL, BRO.'

I close my eyes, wondering what time it is and, for a moment, where I am. Ibiza? Madrid? Rome?

I was on a yacht at some point—the lapping of the water is at the forefront of my mind—but was that last night? Or days ago? I train my eyes—so bleary it's as if they've been acid-washed—on the side table. There's a half-empty bottle of rum—apparently I drink rum now—my sunglasses, a pair of keys. Further into the room there's my jeans and a shirt, thrown over a chair.

New York? Am I in New York?

'What?' My voice sounds like it's been acid-washed too. All gravelled and deep. My mouth tastes like an ashtray. I push up, lifting a hand towards my hair to get it out of my eyes on autopilot before remembering I shaved it a month ago. It's grown out a little, but it's still short enough not to bother me.

'Grace had the baby weeks ago. You have to go see them.'

Something pulls at my gut—something that momentarily makes breathing impossible. I have an almost irresistible urge to tell Theo all the things he seems to have forgotten:

Jagger's your brother, not mine. I'm not a real Hart. That baby isn't my niece. She's yours.

But we've had all those conversations before, enough times for me to know he'll never understand how it feels to wake up at twenty-nine thinking you're one thing, only to have a meeting that pulls everything out from under you. To have no earthly idea who you are nor where you came from. To have lived your whole life with an inexplicable but no less real belief that you were different. Wrong somehow.

I'm not a Hart.

I never was.

I was raised by a Hart, raised to be a Hart, but the blood in my veins isn't theirs. I don't belong and never did—everything I've believed in my life is based on fraud. Even as I think that, I catch myself. Did I really feel like I belonged? Shards of memory slide through me, sharp and unrelenting.

'You're not like your brothers. You've gotta work harder, be better.'

Or, *'I know your mom was prone to outbursts but in this house you keep a grip on how you're feeling. Tears are for babies.'*

That last one was a week after I'd moved in with the Harts—I was just a kid. My mom wasn't coming back for me, I'd had a bad dream and all I wanted was to be held by her, to breathe her in, to feel her arms wrapping me tight.

'*You live here with me now. The sooner you ac-cept that, the happier you'll be.*'

In some ways Ryan, the man who raised me, mas-querading as my father, was right, but hearing it just made me want to break down and cry. I was terri-fied and miserable.

'Holden?' Theo's waiting for me to say something. I shove the memories aside; they're not helpful.

'I will.' I grip the phone, pushing out of bed on one wave of reluctance, forcing my feet to carry my naked body across the room. Something makes a noise. I turn around to see a woman in my bed.

Hmm.

Who is she? I frown, trying to piece together the events of last night, of the last few nights, with no success.

I grab my jeans, almost tripping over my feet as I step into them, zipping them up halfway then strid-ing out of the bedroom and into the kitchen.

Los Angeles. The sun beats a path through the windows in a way I find offensive. I want to tell it to fuck off. Instead, I pull the curtains shut but the rough motion hurts my head.

'Go there today.'

There's half a bottle of beer left on the bench. I lift it, take a drink then pull a face. It's room tem-perature and flat. 'Why?'

'Because. You're being a dick. Your brother and his wife have had a baby and you've dropped off the face of the earth. Pull your head out of your arse and get there.'

I grip the phone tighter. Theo's the baby of the family but he's never pulled any punches with me. With anyone. I like that about him generally, but right now it makes me want to reach through the phone line and shake him.

'I've got stuff on today.'

'Don't be such a shit. I'll make the arrangements. Just get your butt to LAX by midday or I'll fly over there and drag you to Australia myself.'

CHAPTER ONE

Five hours out of Sydney

I'M USED TO flying in luxury. It only took me a couple of years to work my way out of economy and into premium cabins. Up until recently, until I handed in my notice after eight years' of criss-crossing the globe, I was working first class cabins. But even those are nothing compared to the unrivalled grandeur inside this Hart jet.

I'm talking a huge plane, like a commercial jet, that more closely resembles a penthouse apartment. Leather sofas, reclining armchairs, a cinema, bedrooms fitted out like the nicest hotels I've ever been in, bathrooms with proper spa baths, and a boardroom fitted out with a bank of computer screens, printers, everything you could need to run an empire from the air. I don't know what I expected, but definitely nothing quite like this.

'Please, Cora, I need your help. I've never been so sick. I literally can't even get out of bed. There's no way I can fly today. We weren't meant to be going

anywhere; this is completely unscheduled. Besides, you've quit now, haven't you?' I hesitated. *'It's a luxury long haul. Maybe a domestic flight or two once you're there. And I'll owe you. Big time.'*

I press my lips together, wondering when I became such a soft touch, shaking my head a little from side to side. The induction was brief but thorough. A nice man—Edward—who'd been managing Hart jet crew for eight years, he explained as we boarded the steps, ran me through the basics. It was, in theory, as Amy had said, much easier than commercial. No regularly scheduled meal service and instead of looking after a cabin full of passengers who expected me to jump when they snapped their fingers I had only one passenger.

Holden.

Hotter than Hades.

Hart.

And though there's only one of him he's sure intent on making me feel as hectic as if I had a full complement of guests to care for.

I look at the dim light in the galley, compressing my lips. There are four flight crew members on board, plus four pilots. I was nominated to do the overnight shift but I don't care. The truth is, I love flying through the night. There's something magical about it—contrasting shades of darkness that only the trained eye can pick out. Purples and blacks blend differently depending on the atmosphere and whether we're flying over ocean or land. I'm used to this, but I'll never tire of it. I've tried to capture the phenomenon on film without success. It's one of the few things that are better in reality, rather than captured as a photograph.

The other crew members are sleeping. They presumed Holden would sleep and that I'd be left to my own devices. It is, after all, two in the morning LA time. But no, he's wide awake, and when I push into the cabin his grey eyes—the colour of the ocean on a stormy day—are fixed on me in a way that provokes an involuntary and unwelcome reaction. I want to photograph him. The idea comes to me unbidden but I can't help imagining what a striking portrait he'd make. He's handsome but there's a contrast with his easy good looks and his manner, which is somewhat forbidding.

My stomach pulls and my pulse heaves. I ignore the unwelcome physical response, keeping a professional expression locked to my face.

'Can I help you, sir?'

He turns his attention back to the papers in front of him. They bear the 'Hart Brothers Industries' insignia in the corner.

'Who are you?'

I frown, not immediately comprehending why he's asking me that.

Impatience flickers across his face; my pulse trembles. 'It's not rocket science. I'm asking your name.'

'Cora.'

'Cora what?'

'Cora Andersson.'

He nods, then drops his attention to his papers once more. Distracted by his work, I have a moment to observe him unawares and I take advantage of it before I realise what I'm doing. I've heard of him, I've seen his photo in the papers, but up close he's all kinds of distracting. Handsome, sure, but not in an ordinary way. His complexion is tanned, his hair dark, his features broad and symmetrical. A square jaw, a straight nose, lips that are almost rectangular and a divot in his chin that is the one softening part of his whole expression. His physique is just as impressive. I couldn't help but notice as he boarded the plane and lifted his backpack off, so his shirt pulled apart at the waist to reveal a flat, toned stomach, that he's fit.

Really fit.

My mouth goes dry and after a few seconds I realise the absurdity of what I'm doing—standing in the cabin, staring at Holden Hart until I can hardly think straight.

'Is that all, sir?'

'Sit.' He waves a hand towards the armchair opposite, not directly answering my question.

'I—'

I what? It's not like I can make the kind of excuse I ordinarily would when a passenger tries to keep me hostage, taking advantage of the fact we're there to make their journey as pleasant as possible.

He knows I don't have another call button awaiting my attention.

'It wasn't an invitation.'

That goads me. 'It was what? An order? A command?' I think of Amy and regret lashing out. She trusts me. She recommended me to take over for her. I shouldn't risk doing anything that could hurt her job. But seriously?

Something changes in his expression. I can't say what—it's a tiny shift of his lips and eyes so he looks—for barely a millisecond—amused. Then, nothing. He drinks his beer, his eyes on mine so I know I can't drop my gaze to his Adam's apple, despite the fact I have a strong impulse to do just that.

He replaces the beer on the table in front of him, his expression contemplative. 'I don't know you.' The words are said simply, yet I feel like there's an undercurrent to them I can't possibly comprehend.

'No, that's true.' I don't sit down, but nor do I move.

'I know everyone who flies with me.'

I relax a little. He's a control freak, that's all. 'I see.'

'So? What are you doing on my jet?'

There's a simple answer to this. Why do I feel like I want to tease him a little, string this out, make him worry? The urge is completely unprofessional.

And yet… 'Flying to Australia.'

He frowns, and then his eyes spark to mine and something changes in the air between us. I want to take the words back, so too my teasing—okay, flirty—tone. What the hell's got into me?

'You're some kind of sky hitchhiker?'

My smile is involuntary. This time when he gestures to the seat opposite him I take it with only the slightest hesitation. 'Yep. Thanks for letting me jump aboard.'

He lifts a brow but it takes me a second to hear the unintentional double entendre to my words. I wonder if he's going to say something. To tease me back. He doesn't. His face is like stone once more. Grumpy, cross. 'So, Cora Andersson, how did you come to be wearing a Hart uniform?'

I look down at the navy suit, glad Amy and I are basically the same size. She's a little less endowed in the bust region and, okay, she's slimmer at the waist too so I'm wearing a T-shirt beneath the shirt of the suit, just in case I pop a button.

'I'm filling in for someone.'

'I see.'

'Amy.' I dart my tongue out, licking my lower lip, then stop as soon as his eyes drop to the gesture, following it lazily so heat flicks at the soles of my feet.

'Hancock.'

I'm impressed by his instant recollection. Then again, Amy's pretty memorable with her flame-red hair, eyes like emeralds and creamy, flawless skin.

'Right.'

'Where is she?'

'Sick.'

He doesn't react except for the slightest narrowing of his eyes. 'So why you?'

'What do you mean?'

'We have other staff.'

I compress my lips. 'She said something about a training weekend.'

He lifts his brows then nods, slowly. 'Right. Every quarter our flight crew are sent for retraining.'

'Every quarter?'

He nods, his eyes scanning my face. After a moment—a moment that scatters heat across my flesh like sunbeams—he drawls, 'You have thoughts on that?'

'Should I?' I'm a study of wide-eyed innocence.

'Whether you should or shouldn't has no bearing on your thoughts.'

I dip my head forward, concealing a small smile at his quick retort.

'So? What are they?'

I lift my gaze, fixing him with a steady look.

'Quarterly retraining seems…somewhat excessive.'

His eyes narrow and I feel every bit of his multi-billion-dollar CEO strength. It makes my tummy loop.

'Why?'

It's a little hard to think straight under the intensity of his stare. 'Well, not a lot changes in three months.'

'People change.' His voice is low. 'The training isn't just to teach. It's to test.'

I consider that. It's true, people can become lazy, or distracted. I've had a few occasions in the sky that have caused me to have a mid-air freak-out because one of my fellow crew failed to properly secure something or double-check a switch before take-off.

'Only the best fly with us.'

I'd smile if I thought he was making a joke, but his expression is deadly serious.

'I can assure you I'm across all the safety features of this plane. In fact, it's the same model I ordinarily work on.' It's hard to think of past tense in relation to my job, despite the fact I've officially hung up my uniform.

He relaxes back in his chair a bit, his ocean-grey eyes lingering on my lips even though my tongue is now firmly planted in my mouth. 'So you're flight crew?'

I nod. 'I was.'

'For a commercial airline?'

I name one of the biggest. 'I started working the European routes but then I switched to mainly transatlantic, which is how I happened to be in the States when Amy called.' I don't mention that I've recently resigned. After eight years of flying, almost entirely without a break, I'm pretty sure I was sailing close to the burnout wind.

Or maybe it's just the dissatisfaction that comes from realising you chased down the wrong path in life? I've felt that a lot lately—dissatisfaction with my choices, like I'm waking up from a strange dream and discovering I'm not where I thought I'd be. The one passion I've had since childhood has languished and failed to find expression, but I'm determined to change that. I think of the course I've applied to and excitement stirs inside of me. Why shouldn't I follow my dreams?

His eyes are watching me, a hint of disapproval at the corners.

'What's the matter, sir? Are you worried I won't know what to do in the event of a crash?'

His laugh surprises me. It's thick and coarse, deep like the rumbling of thunder in the middle of the wet season. For a moment my breath catches in my throat.

'In the event of a crash I don't imagine anything you do will make much damned difference, Cora.'

His cynicism is both amusing and refreshing.

'I presume you signed the relevant employment forms?'

I shake my head. 'There wasn't time.'

His brows shoot up. 'Then you need to stop working immediately.'

'What? Why?'

'For litigation, for starters.'

'Worried I might fall and sue you? Bankrupt you even?'

He's fighting a smile. Why does he do that? Why not just let it take over his face? He draws on his beer, long and slow, his eyes holding mine just like they did last time.

'Who knows?'

'Fine. I promise not to sue.'

'Did you at least sign a confidentiality agreement?'

'No.'

He swears. 'For God's sake. Were you dragooned into service this morning or something?'

I don't have the same hesitation he does when it

comes to smiling. I let one spread across my face and his eyes drop to it, his expression hard to read. 'Actually, yeah.'

'For God's sake.' He goes to press the button in his armrest but I reach across, my hand on his, shaking my head.

'Everyone else is asleep. Don't wake them. Whatever you need, I can get it.'

'I can't believe Edward didn't cover this.'

I liked Edward. The idea of him getting in trouble because of an administrative oversight makes me panic a little. 'It's not his fault. It was all very rushed.'

'That's no excuse.'

'Actually, it is. Do you have any idea how much work goes into getting a plane ready to fly on the spur of the moment? You should be grateful Amy managed to find a replacement, that Edward was able to get me up to speed on how your flights are run. So I didn't sign some papers. Is that really such a big deal?'

His eyes spark with mine. Lightning flashes between us and for a second I remember that I was supposed to be circumspect for Amy's sake, but that doesn't come naturally to me.

'I'm not grateful. I'm pissed off.'

'I can tell. But you shouldn't be.'

'You're saying I'm wrong?'

'Yeah.'

Silence. It crackles and hums.

'Do you know what this is?' He gestures to the papers in front of him. I spare them a glance then lift my shoulders. I wish I hadn't when the shirt strains a little at the front. I resist crossing my arms.

'No.'

'I'm in negotiations to buy out Roosevelts.' He names a famous burger chain in the States.

'So?'

'So, it's highly confidential. It's an example of why everyone around me signs a confidentiality agreement. I need to know I can trust and rely on each person I work with. I don't want to have to be guarded with what I say in your presence.'

'First of all—' I lean forward unconsciously '—I don't work for you. I'll only be around you for another five hours or so. Secondly, you just told me about your deal. I wouldn't be any the wiser if you hadn't blabbed it.'

'Blabbed it?' He half smiles once more and my heart rate kicks up a notch.

'Revealed it,' I correct with a shake of my head, but my own smile is lifting across my face.

'You'll need to sign an agreement before you disembark.'

I have no problem with that and yet I say, 'And if I don't?'

His eyes hold mine for several beats. 'Then I'll keep you on board as my prisoner.'

Something dances down my spine. Anticipation? My mouth's dry again. My pulse is heavy. 'You wouldn't dare.'

'I've recently learned that I can never rule anything out.'

It's like a switch has been flicked. He focuses on the papers in front of him and doesn't look up again, so I wonder if he even knows I'm here. It's like I've been dismissed and for no reason I can fathom. I was actually enjoying our sparring.

Hell, I even enjoyed his 'threat' of keeping me prisoner on this plane—though I wish I didn't. I suspect it's some kind of betrayal to the sisterhood, but I don't think I'd be human if I didn't look at Holden Hart and have a few fantasies running through my brain. I'm kind of comforted by my physical response, actually. It's been a long time since I've had any interest in a man, so it's nice to feel something, even if it is inconvenient and inappropriate.

'Are you done with me then, sir?' I infuse the words with snark even when I know I shouldn't. Jeez, he's my boss! Okay, not my boss, but Amy's boss, and how I act is going to reflect on her and I don't particularly want her getting chewed out because I couldn't curtail my responses.

He lifts his eyes to mine and now there's something very dangerous in their depths. Something that swirls from him to me and shifts deep into my blood. He leans forward, bracing his elbows on his knees, his gaze never dropping from my face. My breasts tingle, my nipples tightening against the soft cotton of my bra, so all I can think of is how long it's been since a man's touched me there. I look at his hands— big, long-fingered hands that would be capable of...

Oh, God. Stop it!

'Do you want me to be done with you?'

The heat that threatened to fill my cheeks floods my whole body now, and it's most powerful and full of intensity between my legs. My sex throbs, my insides churn.

'I—'

Where's my snark gone now?

His smile is knowing. Mocking. Sexy. My stomach rolls.

He reaches for his papers, shuffling them into a neat pile and placing his pen on top. 'You're still sitting there.'

I am. I need to move. My knees are heavy.

I force my body into action, standing, my mind running at a thousand miles an hour, no way of discerning what I feel and want. It's clear that I've been weirdly bested by this guy though.

That's highly unusual. I always, and I mean always, hold the upper hand. With guys, sure, but with passengers too. I don't second-guess myself.

'I'm going.'

I take a step past him but he reaches out, grabbing my wrist. He's looking at his phone, not me, but his thumb rubs across my inner wrist so heat is a literal lava stream in my body.

'Ask the captain for a confidentiality agreement.'

'Is that really necessary?'

He looks up at me, his eyes grey like storm clouds. 'Sign it, Cora. It's non-negotiable.' He drops my hand and returns his focus to his work; my wrist burns like crazy the whole time I walk away from him.

CHAPTER TWO

Three hours out of Sydney

TWO HOURS. THAT'S some kind of record, given I've had a hard-on since she left the cabin. I wanted to press the call button again almost straight away, but I have this sick obsession with testing myself.

'You're showing yourself to be weak-minded. Grow a backbone.'

My father's words—no, not my father. The man who raised me. I make the mental correction with a grimace. He said that to me when I was thirteen years old. I don't even remember what my supposed offence was now, just that, yet again, it was something I'd done wrong. I test myself often and that habit has its birthplace in Ryan's little pearls of wisdom. I'm doing it now, as though waiting proves something to myself. As though waiting to see how long I can go before drawing Cora back to me proves that I'm not weak-minded.

Cora.

It's an unusual name, not one I've heard often,

but it suits her. Cora with her shimmering dark hair, eyes that are the clearest shade of brown, almost like caramel, skin that's got the hint of a tan, but nothing like mine, and a body that is…

What?

So different to what I would classify as my usual 'type'. I've dated a lot of models—and by date I mean fucked—in my time. I'm talking women who are almost as tall as me, lithe and slim, no breasts, no hips, and Cora definitely isn't that. I had to use all my will-power to stop staring at the way the button-up shirt pulled across her tits.

I lean back in the chair, closing my eyes, imagining what they'd feel like in my hands, the weight of them, the roundness of them, the softness…they'd be soft because they're real. I mean, without inspecting them closer I couldn't be one hundred per cent sure but they're in proportion with the rest of her body. Nice, rounded hips and an arse that swayed as she walked away. A neat waist and a face that is…beautiful. There is no other word for it. Something about her pushed through me until I wanted to drag her out of the chair across from me, pull her into my lap and pop all the damned buttons to save her shirt the hassle.

I had to get rid of her before she realised how close I was to acting on that impulse.

But she didn't want to go. She stared at me and I realised: I wasn't alone. She wanted me too.

Which brings me back to the whole 'deserving a medal' thing, because I've sat here on the one damned beer, checking the valuations for Roosevelts when honestly I just want to find wherever Cora's hiding.

In the end, at precisely the two-hour mark, sufficiently tested, I press the call button. This time I stand up, preferring to be on my feet when she enters. She only takes a few seconds to appear, which tells me she hasn't been sleeping. I guess she's used to flying through the night, but it's almost dawn in LA. She must be exhausted.

She doesn't look it though. Her eyes lift to mine and there's that same insouciant challenge in them that flared in her features before.

'Yes, sir?'

Businesslike, crisp. I wonder if she has any idea how sexy I find that.

'How do you know Miss Hancock?'

The fingers of one hand fidget at her side. She doesn't strike me as someone who'd fidget.

'We used to work together.'

I frown. 'She's been with Hart for six years.'

'Right. Before that.'

I nod. 'And you're still close enough that she'd call you to fill in for her at a moment's notice?'

Her frown is a little quirk of her lips. Her face is so expressive; I can read her like a book. 'Why wouldn't we be?'

'Six years is a long time. Presumably you fly a lot? I know she does.'

'Hmm, then again, there's email, Facebook—you know, ways to keep in touch when we're not in the same city.' She winks, and a little dimple digs itself into her cheek. My cock strains at my pants. I want her.

'Did you need something?'

It's like she can read my mind. 'Yes: company. Sit down.'

She doesn't move. 'Another order?'

'If you like.'

Her eyes flare wider, just by a few degrees, but enough to make me wonder if that's exactly what she'd like. To be told what to do, to be commanded.

'You haven't slept all flight. Aren't you tired?'

I take a step forward. Her eyes widen further still. 'No.'

The pulse point at the base of her throat shows a fine throbbing. I stare at it for a moment, transfixed. I want Cora; it doesn't occur to me that I won't get her.

'You know, I never get involved with people who work for me.'

She's quiet. I move closer. She stands her ground, her eyes holding mine.

'I break a lot of rules, but never that one.'

Her breasts move sharply with each intake of breath. My fingers ache to catch them, to weigh them in my palms, to feel them.

'Why do you break rules, Holden?'

Not Mr Hart. Holden. It's so hot on her pouting lips. I want to make her scream my name. Grateful my hangover's dissipated—beer helps with that—I take one more step. Two more and my chest will be against those soft breasts of hers.

'It's a lot of fun. Haven't you heard?'

She swallows, her throat moving convulsively with the effort.

'And you?'

She frowns, fine lines forming between her brows. 'And me what?'

'Do you break the rules, or play by them?'

'I—'

Another swallow, her frown deepens. 'I think rules serve a purpose. They're there to guide us.'

I make a throaty noise of approval even when I disagree.

'Anyway…' She clears her throat and moves backwards infinitesimally.

I'm enjoying this way too much.

'Anyway,' I murmur, smiling. Her breath catches in her throat; her eyes drop to my mouth. Her fingers fidget a little more.

'Sir…'

It's a pleading sound. Satisfaction envelops me.

'I'm glad you didn't sign the official employment forms.'

She swallows. 'Are you?'

'It'd be a waste.'

'Of what?'

Another step.

'Of this.'

Her chin lifts, her eyes defiant. 'What?'

But I know she feels it. One more step and I have to bite back a groan when my chest presses to the tip of her breasts so I feel her hard nipples against me and want to devour her whole.

'You don't feel it?' She has to tilt her head to look up at me. Up close, she smells like summer. Coconut, vanilla and sea spray. 'I expected better from you, Cora.'

Her nostrils flare a little as she expels a breath; it's warm against my throat. I want to kiss her. I want to fuck her.

Okay, I *need* to fuck her. And I know it has nothing to do with her and everything to do with me and my headspace right now, but I don't give a shit. She's here and if I can get her into bed maybe I'll stop my damned head from thinking just long enough to get some peace.

'Well? Are we ignoring this or not?'

I look up at him, my body at complete odds with my brain. I can't think of a single reason to say no to him. I don't actually work for the Harts. And it's not like I'm going to get Amy in trouble. This isn't fooling around with another crew member or a pilot. This is Holden freaking Hart. There won't be any repercussions for Amy if I decide to sleep with him.

This is all about what I want, and what he's offering.

My heart punches within my chest. I stay where I am but God, I want to push forward. My breasts are tingling from the light contact with his chest. My body is on fire. I haven't been with a guy in over a year.

Yeah, I've been lonely, and the idea of having

sex with someone catches me unawares. I'm beyond tempted.

Not because it's Holden Hart, not because he's incredibly hot, but because I want to remember what it feels like to be kissed, touched, to be human. It's been a long time since I've felt that.

I wonder if there are reasons I'm missing, reasons I should walk away from this, but I really can't think of one. All I know is that if I get off the plane without following through on this impulse I'll regret it. I've made a few decisions in my life that I wish I could do over, and I don't want him to be one of them.

I want him, and I want to do this. There isn't a shred of doubt in my mind.

A thrill of pleasurable anticipation ignites in the pit of my stomach. I smile slowly, my eyes meeting his. It's madness, but I don't care.

'Cora?'

There's impatience in his tone. I like that. Or, rather, how much he wants me is a bit of a power trip, even when I feel exactly the same strength of desire for him.

'I'm thinking,' I say, tilting my head to the side to consider this.

'Maybe there's something I could do to help you make up your mind?'

My heart steps up a beat. 'Such as?'

His grin is the last word in sensual promise. I can barely stand. 'Let's see.' He moves his hands to the button at the waistband of my trousers. He holds my gaze, a droll challenge in his expression as he flicks it open then slides the zip down. A tremble of want moves from the base of my stomach to between my shoulder blades, but I stay right where I am.

His fingers catch on the elastic of my underpants, pulling at them gently, pushing them down a little so I hold my breath as his hands connect with my bare flesh. I have to bite down on my lip to stop from moaning.

I know I could stop this if I wanted to, but I don't. God, I really don't. Suddenly, I can't believe it's been a year since I had sex. And how long before Grant? Another year? I deserve this, damn it! I almost laugh, so excited by the prospect of what's about to happen, but any hint of amusement is strangled in my throat the second his finger moves lower, sliding deep into my underpants and probing my flesh.

'What if I told you I could make you feel better than you've ever known possible?' The words are husky with sensual promise.

I close my eyes a second, needing to remember how to breathe—something which feels easier when I'm not looking at Holden Hart. 'I'd say you're full of confidence in your abilities.'

'With good reason.'

His finger pushes inside of me and I groan then, unable to stop myself, unable to think. I'm all instinct and reaction.

'Open your eyes.'

I don't comply immediately. I still need help to breathe. But after a few seconds I do, groggily, slowly, to find him staring down at me.

'I want you to look at me when you come.'

Something flickers inside of me. Disbelief, excitement. His finger probes my sex and I arch my back, tilting forward a little, surrendering to this. His other hand cups one of my breasts through my jacket—I didn't realise how badly I wanted him to do that until he holds it in his hand and I feel like I've come home.

My eyes flutter closed of their own accord.

'Open,' he grunts, dropping his head closer to mine, moving his finger in and out of me then finding my clit and circling it slowly at first, so the teasing is a form of agony. I blink up at him. There's fierce determination on his face but a dark determination too, as though making me come is the single most important thing he's ever done. Hey, who am I to complain?

'Good.' His nod of approval unpicks something else inside of me so I feel my surrender washing over me like a wave. He moves faster, his eyes heavy as they watch me, but I don't look away, I don't close my own eyes. I stare at him and I feel a thousand and one things. Breathing becomes frantic. His fingers move and my body responds until I'm so close it hurts.

I lift a hand, curving my fingers around his shoulder, my eyes pleading.

'You're nearly there, baby,' he murmurs, the words low and dark.

I nod desperately. 'Show me.' He moves harder and I buck my hips forward until my release grips me and won't let go. I dig my fingers into his shoulder and then I explode, his name just a groan against my teeth. 'Holden…' It tumbles out of me without my consent, again and again. I have no idea how this happened, but I'm so glad it did. His hand drops from my breast, curving around my butt instead, bringing me against his rock-hard cock. He moves his hips, pressing himself against me, so if it weren't for our clothes he'd be taking me right now, I'm sure of it.

'Have you ever had sex at forty thousand feet?'

I shake my head.

'Eight years as flight crew and it never occurred to you?'

I'm still struggling to breathe, let alone form words. I shake my head. It's not that it didn't occur to me. Nor that I didn't have opportunities, invitations. I've just never given into anything like this before. I've never felt anything exactly like it.

'Then I guess it's about time we remedy that, huh?'

God, I want to do this. Briefly, I think about the other crew on board—all fast asleep. I think about Amy, the friend I owe it to not to screw this up. And I push those thoughts away just as quickly as they came to me because I want, more than anything, to go to bed with Holden Hart. To hell with the consequences.

'We've got some turbulence coming up, Mr Hart. If you fasten your seat belt I'll come back and let you know when we're above it.'

I could punch something. I'm so hard, I need Cora

with a passion that surprises me. I had sex last night with whatever the blonde woman's name was. It's not like I'm desperate. But Cora is…what?

I don't know. Different.

Fascinating.

'You heard the captain,' I murmur resignedly. Her cheeks are pink with passion. Her eyes hold mine. I grab her hand and pull her beside me towards one of the sofas—not the armchairs. Too much physical distance there. I wait until she sits down, watching as she buckles in, smiling a little as she also refastens her pants. I resist the urge to ask her if there's any point to that and take the seat beside her, loosely fastening the belt over my hips.

'So you don't buck the seat belt rule then?'

I study her thoughtfully. 'For myself, maybe.'

Her eyes flare a little and she looks away, as if surprised by my answer, and I'm surprised by my reaction to that realisation. Like the fact I care about her safety is unexpected, which makes me wonder about the dropkicks she ordinarily hooks up with, or the dropkick she thinks I am, and a surge of something like anger blasts through me. I'm surprised to feel that but, then again, I'm angry about every fucking thing these days.

'You're still our brother, man. I don't care what a DNA test says.'

Easy for Jagger to say. Easy for Theo to say. They're not like me. All my life I've known I was different to them—wrong somehow. I used to think it was just because Ryan was angry he didn't know about me for the first few years of my life, angry at my mother for keeping me secret. Now? I guess he knew I was different too. That's why he pushed me, why he separated me, made things harder for me, isolated me in many ways.

I grind my teeth, not wanting to think about my messed-up family—except they're not my family. I'm alone. No mother. No idea who my biological father is. The man who raised me is dead.

Silence has fallen in the cabin without my realising it. I angle my face to hers, pulling myself into the moment fully, relieved to focus on Cora. She's awkward—shy almost—and I find that fascinating for how unusual it is.

The plane bumps a little, and then some more.

Neither of us reacts—we both fly too frequently for a bit of turbulence to cause a stir.

'How about you?' She angles her face towards mine, her eyes sweeping across my face thoughtfully.

'What about me?' The question is a little gruff.

'I gather you're a card-carrying member of the mile-high club?'

I wonder at my hesitation to admit that. 'Does that bother you?'

Her smile shifts something beneath my ribcage. 'Nope. Not at all. I'd expect as much from someone like you.' I wonder why that bothers me. She leans a little closer, reaches for my wrist and turns it over so she can see the time on my watch. 'Besides, in about two hours and forty minutes I don't ever plan on seeing you again.'

There's something perfect about that. I love one-night stands. I love the impermanence of it, I love great sex, I love knowing there are no expectations to follow. Two and a half hours sounds like just about enough of Cora for me.

I grin, reaching across and pulling her shirt out of the waistband of her pants. 'Seeing as you don't technically work for me, I really think we should get you out of this uniform.'

Her laugh is soft, like leaves on the breeze. 'I don't have any problem with that, but I'm going to insist on a little privacy.'

I look around. 'Do you see someone I don't?'

'No, but I'm very aware there are other people on this flight and they're likely to walk in at any point. Public sex isn't really my thing.'

In truth, I don't want to share this with anyone else either. I'd prefer to know we're not going to be interrupted.

'And we're stuck here until the captain says otherwise,' she says, pretending to ponder this.

I make a gruff noise of agreement.

'So how do we keep ourselves busy?'

Her smile shows me she has her own thoughts on this, and a second later she's moving her head closer, her lips seeking mine. I freeze, instantly rejecting what she's doing.

I don't kiss. I mean, ever. It's too... I don't know. Too something. But she doesn't realise and I don't react quickly enough so her lips press to mine, her tongue flicking tentatively into my mouth, explor-

ing, wondering, questioning, and I'm frozen, my lips
her willing captives, my body tense, but gradually
relaxing as bit by bit her proximity and her kiss eat
away at my usual boundaries so—to my surprise—
I'm kissing her back, tasting her sweetness in my
mouth and, miraculously, wanting more.

I groan, lifting a hand and gripping the back of
her head, holding her right where she is, my tongue
duelling with hers, my body pressing forward so that
even with our seat belts I'm close to her. Somehow,
the fact I can't pull her on top of me like I want to
only serves to enhance the eroticism of this, like
she's forbidden fruit or something, frustratingly out
of reach. I want her, I know I'll have her, but being
kept at a distance is a strange form of torture—only
torture's never felt so good.

I can't remember the last time I just kissed a guy. I
mean, really kissed him. Like made out in that teenager way of just exploring each other's mouths, feeling each other's responses, breathing someone deep
into your lungs so they take over your body cell by
cell. It's so easy to get straight to sex but kissing
Holden is stirring me to a fever-pitch of wanting.
Our hands are barely involved. He's holding my head
like he doesn't want me to move away from him but,
other than that, we're not touching. It's just our lips
melded together, our mouths moving with the same
ferocity, the same urgent need.

I barely hear the captain's announcement over the
PA—that we've cleared the turbulence—but Holden

must because his hands reach for my buckle, undoing it and then freeing his, before pulling me onto his lap so my legs are straddling him and his cock is right where I need it. Inwardly I curse Eve and her naked shame, because clothing seems like an impossible cruelty now and I wish it had never been invented.

'Let's take this to the bedroom.'

I'm so hot, so wet. I push up to standing, my knees unsteady, straightening my shirt on autopilot, even when I anticipate being naked any minute now. His eyes catch the gesture and his lopsided smile shows he's thinking the same thing I am.

'Good morning, Mr Hart. I've got a coffee here for you.'

My heart moves to my throat. I whirl around, sure my face must show a thousand shades of guilt when I see Edward standing looking at us both.

His eyes reveal not a thing, but how could he not realise what we've just been doing? My cheeks flame pink and, despite the thousand and one reasons I had for not caring about what we were about to do, suddenly I feel a dizzying sense of relief that common sense interrupted—in the form of Edward—before I let things go too far.

'Excuse me.' I barely blink in Holden's direction before striding from the cabin, my blood rushing so fast it's all I can hear.

CHAPTER THREE

Two hours out of Sydney

'HE'S NOT A BAD GUY.'

Edward's in the galley, putting fruit on a plate. I reach over and take a strawberry. It's sweet, courtesy of the beautiful summer we've been having.

'Usually, anyway.'

'Oh?' I pretend no interest but I'm still troubled by the way I fell into Holden's arms. There's nothing wrong with that, it's just not in my nature to be so spontaneous, and I have no idea what kind of voodoo he used, or spell he cast, to make me go weak at the knees without so much as dinner first.

'Don't get me wrong, he's hardly Joe Civil but he's decent enough.' He lifts his face towards mine, his hair greying at the temples, his face pleasingly lined—proof of a life filled with smiles. 'But he's not the kind of guy you'd want to get involved with.'

Heat floods my face. I'm sure I must be as pink as the berry I've just eaten. I don't say anything in response.

Edward's smile is awkward. 'I mean, he entertains on the jet often.'

My stomach tightens for no reason I can think of. I have no right to feel annoyed. He's trying to give me a kindly warning and, besides, Holden hasn't said or done anything to contradict what Edward's saying. It's not news to me. I shouldn't care. I *don't* care.

'I'll bet.' I smile to show I'm not offended or bothered.

'Amy mentioned you recently broke up with a guy?'

I still, frowning. Grant's a long way in my past, our break-up was over a year ago, but that's not why I pause. It feels disconcerting that Amy would have discussed me with a colleague, until I remember that she's been seeing someone lately.

'Oh, my God. *You're* Eddy?'

He grins, but shifts his gaze towards the curtain. Suddenly, a lot of things make sense. Why he's being so kind to me, why he cares that I was about to go to bed with a man-whore like Holden.

'We're keeping it on the down-low. It's not exactly smiled upon and neither of us wants to risk our job.'

'Of course.' I nod. 'I understand that.'

'So she's mentioned me?'

Bless him. His probing question is charming. I lift my shoulders. 'Amy doesn't kiss and tell.'

He laughs. 'Okay, but at least you know who I am.'

I reach for another strawberry.

'Anyway, he's a nice guy like I said, a great boss, but he's not someone I'd ever recommend getting involved with. Unless you're after one night of mad sex—no guarantee he'll remember your name the next day.'

'Got it.' I stand up, wiping my hands on a paper towel before discarding it in the bin.

'I mean—'

I lift a hand, stalling him. 'Eddy, we don't need to talk about this any more, okay? I get it.'

'Okay.' His breath whooshes out in relief. 'You don't need to see him again. You've been working all flight. We'll take over now.' I nod distractedly. Is that what I want? To not see Holden again?

Chicken, a little voice inside my mind taunts. As if running away is what I want to do.

What's so wrong with a one-night stand anyway? Nothing.

That's what I wanted.

I'm not interested in dating, and I'm definitely not interested in dating a guy like Holden, so Eddy's revelation shouldn't have changed a thing for me.

What does that mean? I look towards the curtain uncertainly, doubts plaguing me.

Wanting someone is one thing.

Acting on it quite another.

And yet… I make a tea and try not to think about it. Instead, I focus on the fact I'll be in Sydney again, my future a blank roll of film waiting for me to mark the image of my future on it as I see fit. That's what I need to focus on, not the fact Holden's chest felt like it would be filled with rippling abs.

'He's asking for you.'

I jolt at the interruption. One of the other flight crew walks in—a girl, Belinda? I smile, even as my heart is erupting. 'Says you were halfway through an interesting conversation before and he wants to hear the end of it?'

A smile curls the edges of my lips. Does he indeed?

'Do me a favour?'

Belinda lifts a brow and says nothing.

'Just tell him I'm busy. I'll get to him if I can.'

Her jaw drops. 'Mr Hart won't like that.'

'No, I don't think he will.'

Busy? I glare at Belinda but that's nothing new. Since I found out I'm not a Hart I've pretty much had one setting: scowl.

Busy.

Busy doing what? It's my goddamned jet.

'Oh? Can you take over from whatever it is she's doing?'

'Um…' Belinda casts a glance over her shoulder. 'I'll see.'

'He's kind of pissed off.'

I sip my tea, flipping a page of the magazine.

'Is he?'

'What were you two talking about?'

I catch Eddy's eye over Belinda's head and suppress a smile. 'Nothing important.'

'Yeah, well, he seems to disagree.'

'Tell him I'll get to him if I can.'

'Seriously—' Belinda shakes her head '—no way. He'll shoot the messenger.'

I sip my tea again. 'Last message, I promise.'

'For God's sake. Where is she?'

'In the galley, sir.'

'Tell her if she doesn't drop whatever the hell she's doing I'll throw her out an emergency exit.'

Belinda's jaw drops. I'm not surprised. It's too much, even for me.

'I—'

Now. I turn my attention to the paper but the throbbing in my cock makes it impossible to concentrate.

I laugh. Belinda looks like she's about to pass out. 'Just don't go out there again,' I say quietly.

'I don't get it. What's going on?'

'I just think it won't do him any harm to wait, that's all.'

'Yeah, well, I'm not the one he's threatening to throw out of the airplane.'

I grin, flipping the page of my magazine, pretending to read whilst stilling my beating heart.

'What the hell are you playing at?'

I tap my fingers on the armrest, watching as she walks towards me so slowly it's a form of torture in and of itself. She blinks her huge caramel eyes, her lashes long, her smile a master class in enigma even the Mona Lisa could learn a thing or two from.

'I don't know what you mean.'

'Like hell you don't.' I stand out of the seat, moving towards her, stopping just short of touching her. 'Why didn't you come in here?' The words emerge as a petulant growl.

'I'm on a break.' She lifts her shoulders, her eyes fixing on mine. 'In fact, I've been working all night and now I need to have a rest.'

'A rest?' I repeat, completely confounded.

She nods slowly, a single finger lifting to the top button of my shirt and flicking it. 'Know somewhere I could lie down?'

Relief pours through me. Whatever game she was playing before, she's stopped.

'Yes.' I lace my fingers through hers and pull her after me, through the cabin, past the boardroom, into one of the bedrooms. I drag her into my arms as I kick the door shut, kissing her again—apparently I've forgotten that I don't ordinarily kiss. 'Will this do?'

She doesn't break the kiss, nor does she look around the room. 'Perfectly.'

'Great.' I push at the blazer she wears, angry with it for no reason I can think of, needing it off her body, needing everything off her body except for me. There is a compulsion driving me, a literal need, as though without her I will expire. She is my breath and my all in that moment, just for this moment, for the next hour or so.

I drop the blazer at our feet and push her forward at the same time, my fingers fumbling for the buttons of her shirt. When I can't open them quickly I growl and push at the fabric so it's fisted in my hands and a couple of buttons pop off.

'Jesus…' She laughs, a husky sound that draws across my throat. I don't even notice. She's wearing a cotton shirt over her bra but I can see the fabric, I can see the indented valley of her breasts and I rage with a need to feel her in the palms of my hands, just as I have since almost the first moment I saw her— really saw her.

I push at her shirt, my hands expressing my desperate need, so she laughs and shakes her head at the same time. 'What's your rush?' But she lifts her hands over her head, her lips parted, so I feel her own hunger is as powerful as mine.

I discard the shirt and then unhook her bra, making an audible groan of relief when it's dispensed with and her beautiful, full breasts are before me, so round and pale, the dusky aureoles calling to me.

'Fuck me,' I mutter, my eyes almost accusing as they flick to hers before I give the full force of my attention back to her breasts. I lift my hands, savouring this moment, warm and full in my hands, my fingers finding her nipples, running over those sensitive points until her breath catches and her hips sway forward, my fingers moving a little harder, tracing circles at first and then squeezing her nipples until she pants my name, pushing her hips forward, seeking more, needing more relief than this. So I drop my head, pulling one of her nipples between my teeth, stretching it then rolling it with my tongue before sucking on it until she's crying out and I can barely take another moment.

I've always been good at this. Sex. Fucking. I've had a lot of practice—since the first time I lost myself in a woman. I was fifteen, she was eighteen, and I was less than spectacular. Fortunately, she let me practice that whole summer and by the end I knew I was good. And I like it. But not just because coming is the closest thing to whole I've ever felt. I like making women come. I like watching their faces. I love pleasuring them and hearing a goddamned woman like Cora screaming my name is pretty much what I live for.

Sometimes I rush it. Sometimes fast, and once, is more than enough. I can do the job in ten minutes. But I don't like to. And with Cora what I'd really like to do is draw this out. I don't know why but she spurs something in my gut that makes me want to tease her and torment her. She made me wait before, when I was horny as fuck, and now I want to make her wait.

I reach for her pants, pulling them down her legs, holding them as she steps out of them, but leaving her underpants in place. It's a simple black thong, hardly the last word in sophisticated seduction, but it gets my heart galloping inside of me anyway, or maybe that's what the thong's concealing, what it's doing to her thighs, her butt. I need to hold that too. I reach around, curving my hands over her rear, feeling her roundness, drawing her towards me and burying my head in the curve of her neck, breathing in her soft hair, letting my tongue shift forwards to lick her flesh, to taste her, to savour her.

'Enough preamble.' Her words are throaty. 'I came in here to sleep with you.'

I feel a burst of something like amusement because her directness is somehow surprising, and yet it's not. Maybe that's what I like about her? In our first conversation together she showed she wasn't intimidated by me, nor was she particularly impressed by me.

'Really? I came in here to talk about global warming.' I curve my hands into the elastic of the thong.

She pushes at my shirt now, her own curiosity overtaking her, or perhaps she wants to speed this along, with no idea she's fighting a losing battle there because I don't want to be rushed. Cora is an experience best served long and slow.

'I'm going to fuck you,' I promise as she strips my shirt then turns her attention to my jeans. 'I'm going to fuck you so slowly you can't bear it. I'm going to let my cock ride you bit by bit until you're begging me for more and I'll give it to you, but only when I'm good and ready. I'm going to make you whimper for the release I can give you, baby.'

I feel her shiver against me and grin and as she pushes at my jeans, freeing them from my body, I let my hands push aside the fabric of her underwear, my palm pushing over her sex, just like I did before. 'You're so wet.' I run a finger over her seam, her heat pulling a drop of cum from my tip, so when her hands find my boxers and push them down she must feel it.

'I'm not the only one.'

'Damn straight.' And I step forward, tumbling her onto the bed, but I don't follow with her. I stand above her, looking down, my eyes devouring the feast that is Cora Andersson naked. Her body is creamy pale with the exception of her rosebud nipples and the ash hair at the apex of her thighs, her skin soft like a rose petal. Her breasts, when she's lying down, are soft—definitely real. Her hair, dark like the night, contrasts with her skin and the sheets and all I can think is that I have a real life X-rated Snow White in my bed.

The plane bumps a little, but I barely feel it. Finally I get rid of her underpants, then grip her thighs, pulling on them just hard enough to draw her to the edge of the bed. I kneel between her legs, my intention clear. She makes a little sound of surprise but I don't let go. I haven't shaved in days, not by choice so much as I've been pretty much drunk since Wednesday of last week.

I run my stubbled face over her inner thigh but when she jerks her legs in response I hold her completely still, her beautiful pussy in front of my face, and I stare at her perfection because I'm a connoisseur and she is something else, but a second later her hands are in my hair, pulling me towards her clit so I grin, and even though I'm desperate to taste her, to make her come with just my mouth, I still want to tease her, to make her pay for making me wait, so I resist her guidance and turn my face, nuzzling her thigh some more, holding her legs wide for me even as her ticklish response has her jerking her legs away. I position my face between her legs and expel a long, slow breath so she stills, waiting for me to give her more of that. I do, another breath, but no touching.

'You are so beautiful.' I grin, kissing the soft flesh of her inner thigh, letting my tongue trace circles there. She's not pulling away from me now. Her breathing is so loud I can hear it over the jet engines.

'Put your money where your mouth is.' There's a hint of complaint in the words.

'My mouth is here.' I bite her inner thigh, just lightly, but she squawks. 'And here.' I transfer to the other thigh. She moans this time, arching her back. She's desperate for me, her sex so pink, gleaming, begging for my touch. But tormenting her is way too fucking fun.

'Do you want me to touch you?' I ask, my hands on her thighs moving in circles, my fingers massaging her flesh so she mumbles something incoherently.

'Do you want me to taste you?'

'God, yes, please!'

The desperation in her voice almost breaks me.

'Tell me what you like,' I suggest almost casually, like I'm not desperate to get my mouth on her.

'I like— I like—'

'Mmm?' I lick the fold of skin at the very top of her thigh, so close to her vagina that she twists, trying to push herself into my mouth.

'Do you want me to lick you? Suck you?'

'I don't… I don't know.'

I move to the other leg, tracing the fold of flesh there, letting my tongue drift low, towards the curve of her buttock, and her hands push over my scalp, her nails scratching my shoulders, her desperation so fucking hot.

'I don't know,' she says again, shaking her head, trying to move thighs I have resolutely clamped in place. 'I don't remember the last time a guy was down there.'

That pulls me out of what we're doing. I lift my head so I can meet her eyes, but she's staring up at the ceiling. 'Why not?'

No answer. I flick my gaze back to her pussy, my cock jerking painfully. This is a vagina that deserves to be worshipped.

'Just…because.'

'You don't like it?'

'I think I will,' she groans then pushes up on her elbows and fixes me with a stare that I barely notice because I'm so busy with the flush of her cheeks and the fullness of her lower lip, like she's been torment-ing it with her teeth. 'Show me what you're made of and I'll let you know.'

'So I've got the pressure of all mankind on me now?'

'Yeah, you're officially an ambassador for oral sex so show me what you can do, Holden Hart.'

She is weirdly unique and fascinating. I push my face further forward so my lips are just touching her flesh. I can feel the frantic rushing of her blood; my thumb, on her inner thigh, is so close to her pulse point. I run my hands down her legs, finding her ankles and lifting them to the bed, pushing her legs wider so I have full access to her, and then I let my tongue—finally—part her seam slowly, lightly, tormenting her even now with the insufficiency of this. My tip follows her curves, her dips, mapping her terrain, finding what excites her, my fingers working at her thighs, and then I press my tongue to her clit, running it in circles, slowly at first and then more urgently so she's crying out, my name filling the cabin, her desperation everything I needed.

I close my mouth over her clit and begin to suck, pulling it into my mouth then releasing it, moving my tongue lower, letting it sink inside of her so she bucks sharply then drives her hands through my hair, her legs lifting of their own accord and pressing to my face, holding me where I am—not that I'd go anywhere, anyway. My hands have let go; they're seeking their own exploration. My fingers follow my tongue's path, separating her seam, pushing inside of her while my mouth returns to her clit. She tastes like heaven. I move my fingers in and out, gently, slowly. Her sex is so tight I've got no idea how I'm going to fit inside her, but I will.

'Shit, Holden, don't stop. Whatever you do, please, don't stop.'

'Come, baby.' I move my fingers faster and right as she's on the brink I drop them, taking over with my tongue, moving furiously, fast, so she explodes against my mouth and I feel every single damned reverberation of her body as she rides the orgasm, pleasure making her shake, her body heaving with the intensity of what she's just felt.

I stay where I am, my mouth wringing every last drop of pleasure from her before I kiss my way up her stomach to nuzzle between her breasts. Her hands are softer on my head now, patting me like I'm a dog and I've done a good job for her. I grin, shifting to one of her nipples and pulling it into my mouth.

She makes a little noise but her eyes are closed, her cheeks pink. I pull myself up so I'm level with her face, and only then does she turn to face me. Her face is pink, her eyes fevered, her breasts moving with each puff of air she draws into her lungs. 'That was…unexpected.'

I move my finger to her hip, idly tracing circles there, my eyes following my finger's path.

'Are you…' Her voice carries a frown, so I lift my eyes to her face to find her watching me with an obvious expression of confusion.

'Am I?'

My hand wanders higher, to the gentle curve above her hip, then higher, to the side of her breast.

'Done?'

A laugh is trapped, deep in my throat. 'Done? I haven't even started, Cora.'

CHAPTER FOUR

One hour out of Sydney.
Thirty minutes before descent is commenced.

IF IT'S AT ALL possible for a human being to leave the mortal coil whilst remaining alive, to explode from any constraint of body and bone, to break free from the cells of their existence and morph into something else, then I am doing that. I am no longer Cora Andersson. I am a part of a star or a piece of flotsam in the orbit of earth, filled with colours and sensations and feelings but no earthly inhibitions. I feel my body in a way I never have before. I feel each breath, not as a breath that serves purely to inflate and oxygenate, but as a weight travelling through my windpipe and into my diaphragm. My blood is solid, tangible, pulsing inside of me so I'm aware of it passing through each of my cells and veins. Every organ is brighter and more intense, my heart, my stomach, my lungs, my eyes. There is a vividness to my surroundings that I cannot explain but which sustains me.

And yet I'm drowning too, dying and desperate, needing Holden to take full possession of my body in a way his body has been promising he will for so long that I cannot put a time on it. There is no time in this abyss I've moved to.

I've lost count of how many times I've said his name, of how many times I've cried *'Please...'* without any real idea what I'm asking for, knowing only that I need something he's uniquely placed to give.

I'm barely conscious. A combination of exhaustion and now the kind of sexual satisfaction and tension I could never have conceptualised have made me heavy with the weight of feelings. And I'm more alive and alert than I've ever been, my awareness of every pump of blood through my body makes me feel poised for action.

The plane dips. I feel it in my stomach, as always. I'm programmed to feel every shift, noticing is instinctive to me, even before this insane hyperawareness kicked in.

'I want...' The words trip from my mouth. I push up onto my elbows to find him watching me, his grey eyes like steel, so something shifts in my gut. This man is...what? I can't find a word to describe him. I am losing all my words; maybe even my mind.

'You want me to fuck you,' he prompts, his voice gravelled, his cheeks stained a dark purple, his cock as hard as it was when I pulled his pants from his body a very long time ago. Since then he has dragged his mouth over every inch of my body, making me come again and again, with his fingers, his mouth, with the promise of his cock.

I nod, my hand curling around his arousal so his head whips to face me quickly.

'I wouldn't do that if I were you.'

Fascinating.

'Why not?'

He pushes up on his elbow so we're side to side, matching bookmarks, and his eyes bore into mine with a look of sheer determination.

'Because I won't be able to fuck you if you make me come.' He leans forward and presses a harsh kiss to my mouth, driving me back against the bed. A moment later he pulls away, but only for a second; he's back with a condom, which he tears open and slides over his length, his eyes holding mine. There's a challenge and a question in them, as though even now, after the way he's driven me to the edge of sanity, I might not actually want him, want this.

'Don't even think about changing your mind,' I say firmly, reaching my hands up as he leans forward, bringing his body over mine.

'Do you think that's likely?'

I shake my head and hold my breath, because his tip is between my legs, his possession so close I'm incapable of anything but waiting, of needing. Longing has overtaken me. My body is marked by his touch. Red on my breasts from his beard, between my thighs, purple bruises from where he's kissed me and sucked my flesh until blood has discoloured the surface.

He presses forward but only by degrees—it's in no way enough. I am hungry to feel all of him. Every single part of him. I lift my hips, taking him deeper, but he pulls back, his eyes clashing with mine, strength and warning in every line of his face.

I get the message. He wants to do this. It's his game. And while he's been playing it in such a way that I'm the winner, it goes against the grain to surrender completely. I like to run the game too. So I lift my hands to his chest, pushing him. Surprise is the only advantage, the only reason I'm able to topple him onto his back. I grin, my eyes meeting his with a matching challenge, and before he can question what I'm doing I straddle him and move down his length. But, Christ.

I have to go slowly too because he's huge and it's been a long time since I've been with anyone, and the feeling is somewhat foreign at first. I take my time, aware that he's watching me, his breath hissing out from between his teeth, and I get comfortable bit by bit, then move lower until finally I'm sitting on his hips, his cock buried inside of me. I stay like that, giving my body every opportunity to adjust to this, then he flicks his hips so I laugh, but the noise quickly transforms to a moan. I lean forward, my breasts crushed to his chest, fingers digging into his shoulders—I have marked his body in all the ways he's marked mine. Scratches abound. There's a bite mark on his hip.

I find his lips, kissing them slowly as I move up and down, not quickly, just gently—this is an exploration more than anything else—but it's not enough for him and I have to remind myself that I've come several times while he has been all that is attentive and patient. His hands grip my hips and he's moving me easily, guiding me up and down his length so my already sensitive body, my overstretched feelings ring like wind chimes in a storm. I drop my head to his shoulder, kissing him, biting him, tasting his salty flesh and then he rolls us so I'm beneath him, the weight of his body atop mine instantly delightful.

Like this, he's so much deeper and his thrusts are harder so I'm crying out in seconds, digging my heels into the mattress to get purchase, pushing my hips up as he drives into me. My nails run down his back and then his mouth is crushing mine, his kiss dominating every single one of my senses.

Heat fills my veins; my eyes are laced with stars. His name fills my mouth, pushes to his mouth and he kisses it right back into my soul. 'I'm coming,' I whimper, because the fiercest orgasm of them all is gripping me, and this time I'm not alone.

'Hell, yes,' he groans, and he drives himself into me, tipping us both over the edge so I hear my name deep in his chest and then on his lips and I capture it with my mouth, tasting it, feeling his absolute and complete surrender to me. He pumps and my muscles squeeze him, his body racked with the force of his orgasm; my legs wrap around his waist and hold him tight to my body and my hands work slowly up and down his back as though I'm calming a raging human. There is a beating of a faraway drum like the metronomes I remember from music class, but I don't listen to it. I hear only this. My heart, his heart, pleasure, release and, yes, relief because finally we are freed from this madness, our obliteration mutual and complete. There is no further need to torment ourselves with this utter desperate want.

It's like the bursting of a dam, the freeing of a tsunami. I lie there, my back pressed to the sheet, his tortured breathing filling the room, the plane moving steadily closer to earth, my pulse settling, my body aching and throbbing and pulsing with impossible pleasures.

I feel as though I boarded a flight and got sucked into some kind of hurricane, the current dragging me into the atmosphere, away from everything I thought I felt and knew, swirling me around so my limbs are spread and then spitting me out somewhere almost unrecognisable. That is to say, I barely recognise myself. Before Grant I dated Shawn, but he was the first guy since Dave—with good reason. Dave took me a long time to recover from. Not just Dave but what we lost together. I've been hesitant to get involved with any guy because of Dave, and definitely hesitant to let my body have full throttle at its desire.

But here I am, windswept by a hurricane I didn't see coming, and not even a little bit sorry I didn't seek better shelter.

This was amazing. But also it was enough. There's perfection in uniqueness. One experience, one memory, one time.

'Good morning, Mr Hart.' The disembodied voice

of the captain crackles into the room. Holden doesn't react. I lie there, eyes open, heart thudding, and listen.

'We're commencing our final descent into Sydney. If you take a seat and fasten your seat belt, we'll have you on the tarmac in twenty minutes.'

He doesn't move but my well-trained ears clock the shifts that are taking place. The flaperons being lowered, the clicking away of galley furniture, all the operations that make it possible for the plane to land safely. He shifts a little, giving me breathing space, and I take full advantage, wriggling out from under him, separating our bodies with genuine regret, and taking the briefest moment to steady my still-rushing pulse before I stand at the side of the bed.

I don't look at him as I scout the room for my clothes. There's a very clear path of destruction. I pull my thong on first, then my bra, but, before I can get my shirt in place, he's standing behind me, still naked, his body warm, his hands lifting to cup my breasts, his mouth dropping to niggle at my ear.

My stomach twists.

I want—what?

I spin in the circle of his arms, looking up into his face, and I smile. It's all I can think to do.

His eyes move from one side of my mouth to the other, a frown on his face, as though he's not quite sure how to interpret the gesture.

'Thank you,' I say simply. 'That was incredible.' And it was. I pull away from him, dressing quickly. I feel him watching me, which makes my fingers fumble. Then I walk towards the door, double-checking I haven't forgotten anything before I leave.

'Where are you going?'

I press my fingers to the door handle, lowering it before turning to face him briefly. 'Back to work. Enjoy your stay in Sydney, Mr Hart.' I wink, give him one more grin and then slip out of the room, my pulse hammering so much harder than my casual departure would indicate.

Sydney glitters beneath us as we come in to land. The famous Opera House sparkles like a pearl against the moody darkness of the ocean, the lights of the city casting a shimmering glow across the water. I take a crew seat, buckle in and refuse to think about Holden Hart and what we've just done. Not because I'm ashamed, not because I regret it, but because I know it can only be a one-time thing and if I'm not careful I'll want to push out of the crew seat, stride back to where he is and beg him for one more night.

And then what?

Another? And another?

That's not Holden's speed and nor is it mine. Or, rather, it's not on my agenda right now. For the first time in a long time I'm facing the truth of what I want in life. I'm not running any more.

It's time to settle down and let myself be who I am—and that's going to take all my focus. I'm not interested in getting involved with any guy—not even one as sinfully hot and undoubtedly talented as Holden Hart.

* * *

The baby is a baby. Little with pink skin and tufty black hair, eyes that are dark—when they're open, which isn't often.

'She sleeps a lot,' Grace says almost apologetically, but then I look at my sister-in-law and see the smile on her face and I realise it's less apology and more doting.

I nod, try to smile, because it's expected of me, and wonder when I can leave. Perhaps Jagger senses my mood because he brings me a Scotch, handing it to me before stepping over to Grace and wrapping an arm around her, drawing her to his waist. I look away, my eyes hitching to the view of Sydney beneath us. Their obvious joy is weird to observe, but it's not because I resent their happiness. Here, in the midst of their domestic bliss, I feel the most like an outsider, the least like a Hart, that I have since I learned the truth.

The baby—Felicity, named for the happiness she brings to their lives—makes a noise, then another, and Grace reaches for her, lifting her out of the bassinet and drawing her against her chest, breathing her in as though Felicity holds the meaning of life in the fluff on top of her scalp.

'Want to hold her?'

It's one of those questions people ask when they think the answer is a foregone conclusion. Grace is walking towards me, holding the baby out. I stare at her, momentarily lost for words, then lift my Scotch glass by way of explanation. 'I'm good. Hands are full.'

Grace pulls a face and her voice is gentle, encouraging. 'She's tougher than she looks. You won't hurt her.'

I shrug, turning away from them, striding towards the balcony.

'Don't worry about it,' I hear Jagger murmur. 'It's just Holden.'

I stiffen for a moment, contemplate saying something, or doing something different, but hey, he's probably right. This is really just what I'm like, now more than ever.

Sullen.

Cross.

Antisocial.

Except with—

Don't do it.

I don't want to think about Cora. It's been three nights since I got to Sydney and, thanks to the Roosevelts deal and a major commercial lease agreement with my Sydney casino, I've been working too much to let my mind go back to the flight. To remember the way she came, moaning my name over and over, the way she straddled me and took me deep, burying me inside of her.

Sex helps me feel whole again, it helps me forget, but sex with Cora did more than that. It temporarily obliterated my sense of time and place so I barely remembered I used to be a Hart, let alone that it was all a lie.

Cora is like a drug, the hit from being with her every bit as heady as any ecstasy could render.

And I'm in hardcore withdrawal right now. I want more of her. Not because of her but because of how she makes me feel, which I'm pretty sure makes me a douche for even thinking about calling her.

I'd be using her. Using her to get high. Using her to forget.

So?

It's not like she wouldn't be getting anything out of it. I know how much she enjoyed being with me. Why wouldn't she sign up for another night or three? What's the big deal?

Or could I get the same rush from someone else? If I went into the casino tonight and spent some time in the bar, found someone else to take home?

I frown, catching my reflection in the mirror. I do this a lot. Frown. Stare. Brood. Ordinarily, sex with a random woman would hit the spot, but not right now. It's specifically Cora I want to get high on, Cora I want to see again.

And before I can second-guess myself I pull my phone from my back pocket and type out a message to my head of security.

Find out where Cora Andersson is staying. She was working as flight crew on the way over to Sydney.

Then, as an afterthought:

Thanks.

CHAPTER FIVE

Three days after landing

BOX UPON BOX upon box. Here in this unassuming storage container in Bankstown is all that remains of my Old Life. I stand on the precipice looking in—as though there's danger within, as though I'll have to slay a dragon if I move any further.

The dragon—if in evidence—has been here for a long time, since I locked the sliding door eight years ago and haven't been back since. Even when Dad died I stayed away. It was all too much, too hard. I was too angry and I knew that wasn't appropriate. Grief was called for, but I'd grieved already. His death was a mere formality; he'd cast the die a long time ago, positioning himself for a state of decline that nobody could drag him from.

I shake my head, fully aware of the damage these thoughts can do, and pull my scarf more tightly around my neck, buttoning up my jacket as though it's some kind of shield, before moving into the small space. There's a light to my right. I turn it on, sneeze a couple of times as my nose adjusts to the dust, then stand still, right in the middle of the remnants of who I used to be. Boxes to the right are easy—clothes. They can go to a charity shop. I don't think I'd fit into any of the things I wore as a teenager, nor do I think I'd still like them.

Schoolbooks are beneath them. I run a finger over the corrugated cardboard, then move deeper. A small grey box brings back a rush of familiarity. I pull it from where it sits, wedged between a shelf and another box, and liberate the lid.

My breath catches. My fingers fumble. I pull the photos out, a visceral ache spreading through me.

Dad.

His eyes look back at me, so alive, so bright, it's impossible not to remember every detail of the day I took this photo. It was morning—he was always at his best in the mornings. We'd had our first rain of the wet season, but the storm had begun to clear overnight.

'Come on, kiddo. Let's go see if there are any frogs about.'

I was no longer a 'kiddo' but the name had stuck. Or perhaps he simply hadn't realised that I was growing up. Eighteen and convinced I was on the precipice of serious maturity.

I'd been waiting to tell him. About Dave, about the baby we'd conceived, about the fact we'd decided to get married and rent a little house together on the outskirts of town.

But the morning had been so perfect, and perfect

mornings with Dad were so rare. I hadn't wanted to ruin it.

I took the photo spontaneously. I always had my camera with me back then. I made a joke and he laughed and, before he could realise what I was doing, I opened the shutter and snapped this picture.

I run my finger over the edge now, slowly, reverently, wondering how many photos you could take of someone to reconstruct them completely? I feel as though, in this photo, he's so very real, I can almost hear his laugh reverberating across the fabric of time.

I place the picture on top of a different cardboard box and keep sifting through the images. I was in a black and white phase—moody, angsty teen pictures, clearly the work of someone who loved listening to Hole and Marilyn Manson. I shake my head, a wry smile touching my lips.

Photos of Sundown Creek knot my stomach with nostalgia. I sit cross-legged on the cold concrete floor of the storage shed, not really feeling the iciness. I'm not here in Bankstown; I'm back in the town where I grew up. I can hear the birds flying over the creek, the low hum of farm machinery, the distant whirring of the mysterious airplanes that used to fly overhead, gracefully bringing themselves down over Sydney.

Dave.

I find his photo right at the bottom. Dave, with his shaggy blond hair and freckles across his nose, aviator sunglasses and the air of someone who was older than his years. As a high school kid he looked more like a uni student, and he acted like it too. He was the first one of his year level to get a driver's licence, first one to get a car.

I was so impressed by him. I place the photo with the one of Dad, and then add one of our old home too, but there's a heaviness within me as I do that. Because home is still there. Dad's gone. Dave's gone. Our baby's gone, but the home is there and sooner or later I'm going to have to face the music and go back—even if just to clean it out and get it ready to sell.

My throat knots at the thought of that. I haven't been back since that weekend.

Of their own accord, my eyes shift sideways.

Don't Open

Dramatic nineteen-year-old me scrawled the warning to my future self, as if knowing that the loss would never get easier. The little bags of baby clothes, perfectly clean, ready for our child, were all there, waiting to be filled out with chubby arms and legs. But they never had.

I couldn't bear the idea of donating them, even though I should have. Good clothes like that needn't have gone to waste. But they belonged to our baby and it seemed to me that if we couldn't give him life we could at least honour his death and keep something—some tangible proof of his existence, even when everyone else, even when time itself, moved on.

I stand up, wiping my hands on my thighs, and

get to cataloguing the rest of my stuff. If I'm going to stay in Sydney I need to know what's here. Most of it will go. Not all.

Apparently twenty-seven-year-old me is no more inclined to part with the clothes our baby would have worn, had he lived, than nineteen-year-old me was.

The photos, my old film cameras and film, that will stay with me too.

I spend a couple of hours in the storage shed, but leave with just a small bag of things. The photographs I singled out, a couple of books I remember loving and, at the last moment, a teddy bear I slept with as a child. I don't know why: the nostalgia's apparently getting to me.

I'm staying at a friend's apartment. She's doing her PhD in Egyptian Archaeology and is outside of Cairo for a year on a dig. Her place is in Surry Hills, a suburb lined with terraced houses, leafy trees and wrought iron balconies; it's far nicer than I could justify being able to afford right now. The course I want to do is going to be an investment and it's not like starting a photography business is going to be easy.

Not only has she loaned me her apartment, but she threw her Vespa into the mix as well. *'Seriously, it has to be driven or it will die. Helmet and keys are in the laundry.'*

I step over the seat, kick the stand and rev the engine. On the first day I could barely start the thing and now I weave it in and out of traffic as though I've been riding motorbikes all my life.

It's winter but beautiful, with a blue sky, crisp

temperature, shining sun. I take the Vespa off the highway, turning towards Surry Hills, retracing the roads I drove along earlier today. A few minutes from where I'm staying, I pull over and grab a champagne bottle on a whim—it feels like a day worthy of marking. I've been dreading going to the storage shed for years and now that I've done it I feel like I deserve a pat on the back.

I tuck the champagne into the bag that sits on the side of the Vespa then slide the helmet into place, dipping my head forward as I drive the rest of the way.

I can't miss the plane that flies overhead, the trail white against the immaculate blue sky, and something fires inside of me. Memories I've been working very hard not to give in to. Memories of the Hart jet, the bed, of Holden Hart. Memories of the way he touched me, kissed me, worshipped me as though I were some kind of idol and he a devout follower, brought me over the edge of pleasure time after time after time after time.

And, beyond those memories, acceptance.

He's probably gone by now. I didn't ask what he was coming to Sydney for, nor how long he intended to be here, but I doubt someone like him stays anywhere for very long.

Whatever we shared on the plane, neither of us intended for it to be more than that, otherwise we would have swapped numbers, made sure we had a way to speak to each other, to arrange another...

Stop.

It is what it is. He's so much a part of my past he might as well have his own dusty little box in the living museum of my life that is that storage shed.

I pull the Vespa into its space and cut the engine, but I don't move. I sit there, lost in thought, giving myself a moment before I unhook the helmet and head inside.

Cora Andersson in the flight crew uniform that didn't quite fit was sexier than I have words to describe. Cora Andersson in my bed, naked and panting with need for me, was hotter than hell.

But this?

I shift a little in my seat, glad for the darkly tinted windows that allow me to observe her without being noticed. Astride a small motorbike she looks wild and free, sexy and untamed. I strain against my pants, my cock recognising its mistress is right across the street. A few moments pass and then her hands—hands that curled around my length and held me tight—undo her helmet. She keeps it in one hand whilst lifting a bag off the bike in the other.

Curious, I watch her a moment and try to imagine how this will go down. What the hell will I say to her? Will she be happy to see me? Or freaked? Like I'm some kind of stalker or something?

It's a sign of how hooked on her I am that I can even think like that. Women usually throw themselves at my feet, but not Cora.

Cora was different.

Before I can second-guess the wisdom of this, I open my door and step out. 'Stay here,' I direct the driver under my breath, closing the door behind me and doing a cursory inspection for cars before I step across to her.

Perhaps she sees me in her peripheral vision because she pauses, midway to a dark green door, and turns around.

I see the moment she recognises me. Her eyes flare wider, her lips part and she lifts a hand to self-consciously brush her dark hair back from her face.

There's something different about her—something I instinctively recognise because it moves within me. A darkness. A sadness. I pause, a frown creasing my brow.

'Holden?'

She's dressed for the weather. Jeans, a jacket and a brightly coloured scarf that picks up the pink tones of her cheeks.

I close the distance between us, my body only an inch or so from hers—close enough that I imagine I can feel her warmth, close enough that I can taste her familiar scent on my tongue.

'Hey.' My voice is low, drawn from deep inside me. I briefly wonder what I'm doing—once is always enough. But I know myself, and I know that, despite that, I want Cora again.

'You're still here?'

I lift a brow. 'I just got here ten minutes ago.'

She shakes her head so her chestnut hair lifts with the breeze. 'I mean in Australia.'

Oh, right. 'Yeah.'

She nods slowly, her brow knitting like that tells her pretty much nothing.

'And you're…here why?'

As soon as she asks the question I realise I'm here partly because of her, and this. Because I needed to see her again. Sure, there are meetings I need to have, but I could have Skyped those. And I've seen Felicity now, ticked that box. There's no reason for me to still be here in Australia—except one.

Cora.

'I've got some business at the casino.' The words give away nothing of my realisation; they're dutifully laid-back and noncommittal.

Her smile is enigmatic and so familiar it's like being punched in the gut. I have this sense that she's laughing at me.

'I mean here, where I'm staying.'

I look towards the building, but I feel her eyes stay on my face as though she's touching me. It's a nice place. Old, probably late nineteenth century, possibly early twentieth, with distressed bricks, a little Juliet balcony and several pot plants boasting geraniums, lavender and a bonsai lemon.

'Holden?'

I angle my face towards her. Cora is the first woman I've ever wanted more than once. I don't know what it is about her but I want to fuck her out of my system.

'Why do you think?'

Her pulse races. I see the flesh at the base of her

throat tremble. Her eyes widen, her lips part. I take a step forward so our bodies are just an inch apart.

'I—' Her tongue traces the outline of her lower lip. I want to suck it into my mouth.

'Have you been thinking about me?'

Her eyes drop—all the answer I need. At least the fever is not mine alone.

'I've been… You're not…'

Another step forwards. Now our bodies touch. I feel her soft, sweet breasts crush to my chest and stifle a groan. 'Yes?' The word is dragged from me, demanding and raw.

'Yes.' She lifts her face to mine, staring at me so I feel a sharp stab of relief. 'I never do that—sleep with guys I barely know. Of course I've been thinking about you. Wondering why it happened.'

My smile is a cynical twist of my lips. 'And did you work it out?' I lift my hands to her hips, holding her there for a second before letting them slide around her back, pushing them inside her jeans, curving around her arse and dragging her against my cock.

'Holden!' The word sounds aghast and laced with needs all at once. 'People will see.'

'And you don't like public sex,' I tease, remembering her saying that on the flight.

'I…' Her cheeks flush pink and I suspect she might be warming to the idea.

'Then invite me in.'

A soft groan escapes her mouth. I drop my head, catching it in my own, my lips colliding with hers, my tongue teasing her tongue, my hands staying right where they are, cupping the naked flesh of her butt, only I grind my hips forward, pressing my cock against her clit, clothing no encumbrance to showing her pleasure. She whimpers in my arms. I smile against her mouth but it's a grim smile because, in the back of my mind, I told myself I wouldn't use Cora like this. She's different, and she deserves better than to act as a form of lobotomy.

My cock disagrees.

'Where are your keys?'

Her hand comes between us, so close to my cock I pause for a second, wondering if she's going to touch me right here on the street. But she's feeling around for her keys. I hear them jangle between us. Relief shifts through me.

I pull my hands out of her jeans only so we can move. There are a few steps—paved with black and white tiles—that lead to the front door. She jams the key in and turns it. The big timber door opens with a low creak. No sooner has she stepped inside than I move behind her, kicking the door shut in the same movement I reach for her, dragging her back to me.

My kiss is now heavy, demanding, my body no longer held at bay by doubts about whether she'd be happy to see me or not. I need her—I need this—and I'm not going to think about that for a second longer.

I push at her jacket, freeing it from her body. She drops a bag to the floor to let the sleeves fall—there's a bottle of champagne inside.

'Celebrating?'

'Apparently.' She grins, and light explodes in my chest because it shows she has no doubts about this, and I'm glad. This doesn't need to be messy or complicated.

I palm her breasts through the fabric of her shirt, marvelling at their softness and size, stepping forward, leading her through this apartment, not caring where we end up, just needing to get there fast. Her hands push at my pants, apparently the same urgency driving her. I step out of them as we walk, kicking my shoes off, and my socks, until I'm fully dressed up top and wearing only boxer briefs below.

As we walk her hands slide into my pants, pulling my cock out and gripping me so hard I see stars for a second. It's too much. With a gruff sound I kiss her hard enough to push her backwards, against the stairs. She sits on one and I bring my body over hers, knees pressing into the timber, my cock at her sex seeking fulfilment. I came prepared. I pull a condom from the pocket of my jacket, roll it over my dick at the same time I push properly out of my boxers. Her jeans and underwear take seconds to remove.

She's panting, her voice making small, staccato bursts into the hallway.

'Ever fucked on the steps?'

She laughs, an uneven sound that makes me realise how completely blindsided she is by this. She shakes her head, shifts her hips, inviting me to take her. 'But there's a first time for everything, right?'

'Right.' I don't hesitate a moment more. I drive myself into her, deep and hard, swearing as her soft, wet core squeezes around my length. Stars are in my eyes once more. I thrust hard, then pull out, then take her again, my arm curving behind her head to save her from hitting it against the tread.

Steps is new for me too but hell, I can get so deep like this, my body is perfectly positioned to feel every little part of her. I push up for a second, staring down at her, my breath thundering through my body.

'Too many clothes.' The words are angry, accusatory almost. I soften them with an attempt at a smile then push at her shirt. She sits up, just high enough for me to push the clothes from her body, her sex squeezing me harder at the small movement. Her bra. Damn it. I drag it downwards so her breasts fall from the lace cups, her generous, pale, soft breasts, and I fill my hands with them, shaking my head at how goddamned gorgeous they are as I begin to push into her again, hard and demanding, needing to take over, needing to make her completely mine. Without my arm her head hits the steps and she laughs, wiggling forward a little, propping up on her elbows at the same time.

It just makes her breasts look even better. I fantasise about all the ways we could use these stairs— her kneeling on them, me taking her from behind, her wrists strapped to the banister, me sitting, her on top of me. Fuck. I feel a little cum leak out but I'm not ready.

I drop my mouth to her breasts, drawing a nipple between my teeth and rolling it hard, flicking the sensitive tip with my tongue until she's almost screaming with pleasure. I drop a hand to her hip then run it around to her backside, separating the roundness there and finding her seam. I push my fingers against her, my cock so deep inside of her, my fingers tracing the rim of her anus, pushing her upwards, hard against me.

She cries my name out again and again, thrashing her head from side to side, so I push a finger in a little, just a hint, enough to make her swear and buck her hips, her muscles tightening everywhere. I move my mouth to her other breast and next time I push my fingertip into her butt I bite down on her nipple in time with it so she explodes, her orgasm so hard and intense that she almost cuts off circulation in my dick.

Her face when she comes is perfect. I stare at her, my breath tortured, my dick harder than I've ever known it.

I want more. I want this, her, all of it, all of her. I need... I don't know. I watch as her breathing slows and then, before euphoria seeps completely from her, I pull out, staring down at her with a feeling of resignation.

'What are you—'

I grip her hips, lifting her as I move to lie down on the steps. She straddles me, understanding, taking me inside of her with a soft moan, her eyes drifting shut as she processes this. I buck my hips but she presses a hand to my chest, stilling me.

'My turn.'

I watch as she begins to move, up and down, her

body doing everything I need, slowly first, then fast, as her moans become louder. Pleasure builds within both of us until it doesn't—crash is inevitable. We surrender to it in unison, our release silent save for the sound of our breathing, frantic in its intensity, desperate and hungry.

When I leave her place ten minutes later—just long enough for me to throw my clothes back on—I feel as though I've been slammed into by a truck. And yet a grim smile lifts my lips because it was the best feeling I've known in a long time—the most authentic and genuine, the least complicated.

    I could get addicted to that.

CHAPTER SIX

Five days after landing

'I'LL CALL YOU.'

He said that as he left. I was too shell-shocked to respond. Holden Hart showed up at my door like some kind of grenade. Gorgeous, sexy, and he kissed me so damn fast and hard that I didn't have a second to draw breath, much less wonder what the hell he was doing at my place.

Except it was obvious.

From that first kiss I knew he hadn't come to chat.

He wanted me with the same ferocity I'd felt from him onboard. No, it was more than that, stronger. On the flight he'd been restrained, showing me pleasure after pleasure after pleasure, showering me in multiple orgasms before he'd finally taken possession of my body.

This was different.

He fucked me as though there was a stick of dynamite that would explode unless he moved fast. It was urgent and overwhelming, and then he shifted, lifting me from him easily, and smiled—that smile of his that almost looks like he's in pain rather than genuinely happy—and he moved back down the stairs, pulling his clothes on as though what we'd just done was normal and expected. Ordinary.

I watched for several moments before doing the same, but we moved like two separate, parallel weather systems circling the eastern seaboard. At the door he offered that same smile. 'Thanks. I'll call you.'

It was on the tip of my tongue to tell him not to bother, then to point out he didn't have my number, but a second later he was gone, striding across the street to an SUV with darkly tinted windows. He climbed into the back and it pulled out of the kerb almost immediately.

He must have had my number though—on the same paperwork I'd filled out for Edward, I presume, he'd obtained it.

No number came up when he called so I almost didn't answer, except I'm waiting on a call from the university regarding my application.

'Cora, it's Holden.'

He needn't have said anything beyond the first syllable of my name. His voice is like a fingerprint, so unique, so him.

My blood almost burst free from my veins.

'Oh.' Surprise flared inside of me. I really didn't think he would call. 'Hey.'

'Are you free tonight?'

My pulse burst to life faster. Harder. 'I'm— Why?'

A pause. My stomach twisted. Why did I think? To take me to dinner? To go to a show? I rolled my eyes at the naivety of my question. Holden Hart has made it abundantly clear what he wants from me.

I swallow and close my eyes for a second. 'Never mind.' The thing is, I want the same from him. I can't get distracted right now. Sex is fine but a relationship isn't. Sleeping with Holden is amazing and uncomplicated. A smile lifts the corners of my lips.

'I'm at the casino.' His voice is smooth, deep and husky. My nipples are straining against my bra, remembering the perfection of his touch last time—the perfection of his touch *everywhere*. Heat stains my cheeks as I remember the way his fingers teased my ass, his cock inside of me, his lips on my breast, so I felt as though I existed purely for Holden, purely for pleasure.

'And?' I couldn't resist prompting.

'Would you like to come over?'

But something about his manner makes me want to goad him a little. 'Is "come over" a euphemism for "have sex"?'

I can almost hear his grin. 'Would you like it to be?'

I roll my eyes. 'Begging for compliments?'

His laugh spins something inside of me. 'I'll beg for you if I have to.'

It makes my gut clench because, even though he just laughed, I hear something else in his voice. Something serious and gruff. Urgency.

'Not over the phone. It's much more fun in person.'

'I couldn't agree more.' A pause. 'I'll send a car.'

But I like the idea of having my own wheels, my own escape. 'That's fine. I can drive.'

'Your Vespa?'

I grin at his obvious surprise. 'What's wrong with that?'

'Nothing.' Another gruff sound. 'It's just incredibly hot, that's all.'

That brings a smile to my face. 'I'll wear the helmet up.'

Another laugh. 'Don't. You'll likely be arrested.'

I laugh softly.

'Come to the front entrance. Valet will take care of the bike.'

I'm about to hang up.

'Cora?'

I wait, breathless.

'The fewer clothes you wear the better.'

Hart Casinos are everywhere. There's literally one in every big city of the world. This isn't my first time stepping into one, so I'm familiar with the luxurious fittings. Burgundy carpet with gold details, dark wooden furniture, enormously high ceilings marked with ceiling roses and crystal chandeliers— every single one is a testament to old world glitz at the same time as boasting state-of-the-art technology.

I've been to Hart Casinos before, but never like this I think as my Vespa is taken care of by valet attendants. I push into the doors and almost immediately a woman walks over to me. 'Miss Andersson?'

I'm startled by her recognition.

'I—yes. How did you know?'

Her smile reveals nothing. Her tone is curt and professional. 'Mr Hart is waiting for you.'

She's wearing sky-high heels and her stride is long. She cuts across the gaming floor so I have a brief impression of roulette wheels and then catch a glimpse of an opening door that shows poker tables beyond it. We cross a threshold and carpet gives way to marble. Two security guards in full black military-style fatigues and holding impressive guns flank a golden elevator door. The woman swipes a card she wears at her hip and the doors open.

Her manicured hand gestures for me to precede her into the elevator. I do, and she follows, the faintest hint of Dior perfume reaching my nostrils. None of the buttons have numbers; they're just discreet brass circles. She presses one then flicks me another smile, curt, just as the first.

'How did you know who I was?'

'We have security measures in place for any of Mr Hart's guests.'

It's a reminder of Edward's warning aboard the flight: '...he's not someone I'd ever recommend getting involved with. Unless you're after one night of mad sex—no guarantee he'll remember your name the next day.'

Well, he remembered my name. He remembered it well enough to come to my apartment, to make love to me against the hardwood stairs, and he remembered it enough to call me earlier this evening.

Sure, it's a booty call, plain and simple, but that's everything I want. Sex with Holden Hart and no hope of anything more.

The doors ping open and we're in what looks like a very high-tech office space and, despite the lateness of the hour, it's full of people sitting at desks.

'I'll just get you to walk through that arch, please.' She nods to a security scanner and disbelief halts my breath.

'Security?'

'It's protocol.'

I compress my lips, reminding myself that Holden Hart is worth over one hundred and fifty billion American dollars. This kind of rigmarole is part and parcel of his life and, as insulting as it is on one level, on another it's impossible not to understand the necessity for the precaution.

Besides, it's hardly a strip search.

That will come later.

The thought heats my cheeks so I'm worried the X-ray will show my elevated heart rate as I step through the scanner. It doesn't. Nothing untoward is in evidence, apparently.

'This way.' She gestures to another elevator and this time, when the doors ping open, she doesn't follow behind me. Instead, she simply swipes her card and presses a button then offers one more brittle smile as the doors clip shut.

I hold my breath, feeling like I'm spinning on some kind of merry-go-round.

The doors open and the merry-go-round speeds

up because, whatever this place is, I feel as though it's a palace high up in the sky.

I step off the elevator, my eyes moving quickly through the space. Double height ceilings, more marble here, white and glossy, world-class artwork, designer furniture and views of Sydney that are unlike anything I've ever seen.

One whole wall of the penthouse is constructed from glass and as I stare at this incredible apartment a door opens and Holden steps in.

My heart begins to hammer, slamming into my ribs like it has some kind of vendetta against the rest of my body.

Now, in the middle of his penthouse, I feel all kinds of uncertain. It's one thing to know a guy's a billionaire, and sure, he had the private jet, but somehow this just feels so much more *real* because it's a language I speak. I know what property costs. I know what Sydney costs.

I process all those thoughts in the space of a few seconds, but when he steps into the room and closes the door I can think of nothing but Holden.

First of all, it's winter and he's just been out on the balcony wearing only a pair of jeans and a white T-shirt. Is he crazy? Secondly, he looks good enough to eat. Tanned and virile, his short dark hair serving to emphasise the strength of his face, his eyes locked to me in a way that heats my blood.

'Cora.' He says my name like it's an incantation. Or maybe he says it with disbelief, like he didn't think I'd actually come. I move deeper into the apartment, looking for somewhere I can put my clutch down and deciding on a little side table. I lay it on the edge then unravel my scarf and place it there too. I'm conscious of his eyes on me the whole time and my body responds predictably.

'The security to get up here's kind of intense.'

He nods, his expression unchanging. 'It's necessary.'

'But why here? You didn't have a bodyguard on the flight.'

He moves closer, his hands reaching for the shoulders of my jacket, holding it so I can shrug out of it. *This* is familiar. Slower than last time, but no less urgent. If anything, there's a sort of restraint about him, as though he's willing himself not to pounce on me.

'My jet is a safe space. Staff are rigorously screened. Ordinarily.'

Was that why he was so surprised at how easily I'd got on board? A pang of something like remorse shifts through me. 'I didn't realise.'

'Generally, I can operate beneath the radar, which makes this kind of security unnecessary. But here in the casino there's a chance of being targeted.' His hands linger on my shoulders, his touch like heaven. 'I hope you weren't offended.'

'Not at all. Just interested.'

His thumb begins to stroke my collarbone, moving over the dress so it pulls a bit and somehow the added tactile experience of the dress underneath his thumb on my skin makes my body tremble. My stomach squeezes and my nipples pucker almost painfully.

'Interested, huh?'

I feel his subtle shift in conversation and nod. 'Very.'

'Me too.'

Needs wash over me. I close my eyes for a moment as if I can brace for this, and when I open them he's reaching for me, lifting me over his shoulder so I can only laugh.

'I can walk, you know.'

'Yeah, but I can walk quicker.'

It speaks of a breathtaking urgency—familiar, once more—and I stop smiling because I feel it too, I feel this desperate need pushing me to him, just like last time we were together. I flush as I remember the stairs and the way we made love there.

I'm barely aware of the layout of the penthouse. The enormous entrance way and living room I stepped into feeds into a long, wide corridor. Marble underfoot, white walls, the frames of world-class paintings. We pass several doors, some shut, some open, none easy to see through, before he rounds a corner and enters a darkened room. I'm conscious of another glittering aspect of Sydney, this time looking back towards the CBD, so it's all high-rises and lights.

Just inside the door he eases me to the ground, but the second my feet hit the carpet he's reaching for the bottom of my dress and lifting it up my body, his impatience igniting a fierce volcanic eruption within me because I can't say I've ever needed anything like I need Holden.

But maybe he was right this afternoon. Perhaps it's not him I need so much as the wilful obliteration of memories that feel so much more real now that I'm back in Australia.

The dress is a caress as he drives it up my body. I'm not wearing a bra. *The fewer clothes you wear the better.* For both of us.

'Jesus.' He groans, dropping his head and burying it between my breasts so I tilt my head back to give him better access. His hands grip my hips, holding me to him, and then he's undressing himself with the same desperate hunger, pushing his jeans down, stripping his shirt over his head, stepping out of his socks so he's completely naked.

I take a step back because one thing I haven't done yet—either of the times we were together— is properly *look* at him. I was so caught up in what we were doing both times, in the excitement of it, that my observational skills were off kilter, but now I want to see and recognise every damned detail I can.

His chest isn't just broad and muscled, it's marked with layers of ink, so many tattoos that I could spend hours decoding them, asking about each, because I'm as sure as anything that there's a story there.

One in particular stands out and sends a shiver down my spine. Letters in what I imagine must be the Greek alphabet and, above them, a picture of some kind of mythological god. I press a finger to it but he winces, as though it's fresh ink when it's not. It's like I've hurt him.

And before I can ask the significance of the tattoo he's pushing me across the room with his body, his powerful frame guiding me to the bed so we stumble onto it together and all thoughts of artwork flee from my brain. There is no space for them when Holden Hart is on top of me, pressing me into the mattress with his powerful frame. I kick my shoes off—he's forgotten them—then wrap my legs around him, silently drawing him towards me. At the same time I push up onto my elbows, moving my mouth towards his. He hesitates for a second, looking at me with a question or a doubt in his eyes, then shakes his head gruffly, makes a growling noise and takes complete possession of my mouth, the pressure of the kiss pushing me back down into the bed.

I writhe beneath him, my body needing more than he's giving me, my pulse firing for some kind of absolution from this delightful torment. His cock is between my legs and I ache to feel him inside of me, just like last time, but he doesn't move and he doesn't answer my repeated attempts to bring him towards my sex.

I swear into his mouth and shake my head, breaking our kiss.

'Fuck me, Holden.'

His eyes flicker to mine, something travelling between us, unspoken but important, and then he stands, staring down at me as his chest shifts with each breath he draws in. I watch as he strides, long-legged, across the room, disappearing through a door for a moment then returning with not just one condom but a line of them.

And lightning strikes through the core of my being because I was so very close to forgetting about protection completely. I'm not even on the fucking pill! What the hell? Didn't I learn my lesson with Dave? But of course I did! The few guys I've been with since Dave have had to listen to my lectures on safe sex *ad nauseum* because falling pregnant is a consequence I'm not willing to entertain, ever.

'Crap.' There's an apology in my curse. 'I was just so—'

'I know.'

He rips one foil square open and pulls the rubber out, positioning it over his length while he's watching me.

'I *never* don't use protection,' I say urgently, needing him, for some reason, to understand, as if that can assuage the torrent of panic which engulfs me.

'I don't either. It will never happen, Cora. If you forget, I won't.'

I swallow because it's not really good enough, but there's no point belabouring that point now. I can reprimand myself later.

'Please…' I reach for him, knowing he'll drive those thoughts from my mind too, that forgetfulness is within reach. 'Now.'

He nods, understanding, dropping on top of me so I laugh. He doesn't. He's so serious. So sombre.

But in this—sex—we connect, so I wonder what it is in his life that makes him how he is, and I reject the idea of asking him because it speaks of something other than this.

His nudges my legs apart and drives into me. Not like last time. Not tentatively, not slowly. He drives himself into me in a way that tells me he's been craving this, needing me, just as badly as I have him. I moan as he fills my body, my muscles rejoicing to welcome him back, my back arching. No sooner has he entered me than he begins to move, and he drags his mouth to my breasts, tormenting my nipples in a way from which they're yet to recover.

I hold him tight and I mirror his movements, my mouth seeking his shoulder first then migrating lower, nipping his collarbone before kissing the top of his pectoral muscle and then, out of nowhere, a mind-blowing orgasm bursts through me, ripping me apart at the seams, obliterating sense from soul. I explode on a rushed wave, all the more potent for how surprising the orgasm was to me. It came out of nowhere and it burned me alive.

I shout his name, uncaring if anyone hears, uncaring if I deafen him, because he deserves it in a way, for being so good at this.

He makes a low rumbling noise, not exactly a laugh but something close to it, and then he's standing up, grabbing me to follow, kissing me as he grips my hips and turns me over, his hands fondling my breasts, pushing me towards the bed so I'm bent at the hips and then he enters me from behind, his possession absolute, his cock so deep that I feel another orgasm building already. One hand pushes down my body, finding my clit, and he strums me there while his other hand is clamped vice-like across my breasts, driving me towards heaven… God, another galaxy, I don't know! Except I'm floating out of this room and far from this earth.

Every time he pushes into me my body reverberates and his hand at my clit doesn't let up so the orgasm that's building crashes over me and this time he's with me, his own release marked by the sound of his voice joining mine, a groan forced out of him as he holds me still, both of us allowed to experience every shift and vibration brought on by this. I stay there, my elbows propped on the bed, my eyes focused on the view of Sydney, stars in my eyes and a lightness inside of me.

A happiness and euphoria that must somehow be biologically programmed.

There is no other explanation. Sex releases happy-making hormones and I guess I've never really known great sex before because I've definitely never had such a palpable shift in my mood as this.

I don't know how long we stay like that. Long enough that my breathing slows and my heart steadies and then he's pulling out of me, and I have to use all my willpower to stop from crying out at the loss.

I bite my lip to stop an actual sound of complaint. Two orgasms in ten minutes? I don't think

I have anything to complain about, actually. But nonetheless…

I push up from the bed, schooling my features into a bland expression—so as not to give anything away—and force a cool smile to my face. I'm pretty sure my eyes are fevered and my cheeks are red from pleasure but when I turn to face him I offer only the smile.

He's looking at me as though he wants to say something. But what?

I feel that shift inside of him, the seriousness that I first noticed on board his plane. I wonder what's behind it, what's lurking beneath the surface with him.

Uncertainty threatens to engulf me. Should I go? I feel like that's the sensible thing to do. His invitation was for sex. Nothing more. So?

'That was great,' I say, annoyed that the words emerge a little breathlessly. I don't want him to know how affected I was by that pleasure. But I was. I am.

He nods, rubbing a hand over his stubbled jaw. 'Stay for a drink?'

Something trips inside of me. Because it confirms what I'd just been thinking—that he's expecting me to go away now we've slept together. And I hate that it bothers me because I came here expecting that.

But there's something else, because he doesn't actually want me to go right now, hence he's offering me a drink. Unless he's just being polite.

I tilt my chin, refusing to second-guess his intentions. What do *I* want? That's what I should be focusing on.

The problem is, I really don't know. On the one hand, I want to stay. On the other? Something feels wrong and I don't know what. I'm no good at this.

'That's fine.' The words are brittle and, unconsciously, a frown shifts over my face.

My frown is reflected on his face.

We stare at each other, a strange awkwardness between us, given what we've just shared. There is intimacy and there's intimacy, and while we have plenty of one, the real intimacy is something neither of us wants, and it's nowhere in evidence anyway.

'I'm glad you came over.'

A smile shifts the frown, just a small lift of one corner of my lips. 'So am I.'

His brow furrows and then he moves towards me again, his body warm, his masculine fragrance tickling my nostrils and making desire stir lazily back to life.

'Stay for a drink.' This time it's not a question. I look up at him, knowing I should go, that staying is futile, and yet my feet don't move.

I want to stay. I want to have a drink with him, and I want to ask him about each and every tattoo that scores the smooth flesh of his body. And that's the main reason I know I have to go. Because asking questions leads to knowledge and knowledge is a very dangerous commodity. Knowledge of a person can create affection for them, and I will not feel that for Holden, or anyone. Not now. Not when I'm on the brink of a new life, and new possibilities abound.

I shake my head, forcing a smile across my face.

'Thanks, but I got what I came for.' I soften the statement with a wink, returning the mood between us to light, fun and flirty, then lift up and press my lips to his. 'See you later.'

CHAPTER SEVEN

Six days after landing

I SCAN THE DOCUMENTS, only half listening to the meeting progressing around me. I barely slept last night. After Cora left I changed into a suit and toured the casino. It's the only way to get a proper feel for how a place is running and I make it my business to play a few hands of poker at each of my casinos, every time I'm there. I stayed on the floor until four in the morning, then threw back a few Scotches before finally dropping into bed a little before five.

It smelled like Cora and sex. It made me want her, so the couple of hours' sleep were punctuated by memories of her, of all the ways I want to fuck her— so much more than ten minutes would ever satisfy.

My mind replays every minute of the night before, specifically the time I spent with Cora. I see her eyes when I asked her to stay for a drink, the realisation that buried within that request was an expectation she'd go away again, soon.

Did I hurt her feelings? Did she think I meant for her to spend the night? No. It was obvious why I invited her over. And that was obviously why she came.

'I got what I came for.' We're on the same page. This guilt is misplaced. So too is my desire to prolong the time we do spend together.

Spend together?

I scowl, scanning the documents, analysing that. It makes it sound like I want this to become a regular thing. I imagine not seeing Cora again and my body practically jerks in revolt. What the hell? Once is enough. Twice? More than.

But it's not.

What I need is to get her out of my system— properly. Not ten minutes. Not necessarily even one night. A proper fuck fest so I can say goodbye and mean it next time.

'The numbers don't stack up.' I interrupt my Australian director of operations, fixing him with a level stare. 'The returns don't justify the investment.'

'But we're seeing strong growth—'

'Not strong enough.' I stand, sweeping my gaze around the room, letting my eyes land on each person in attendance. 'I'm not going to waste my time for numbers like this. Show me a plan for improvement and then I'll consider it.' I move towards the door without a backwards glance. I'm bored with meetings. I'm bored with business.

I'm bored with everything except Cora. I pull my phone out to text her right as it starts ringing. My brother—no, not my brother. When will I get used to that? Theo's face flashes up on the screen. I swipe it to answer.

'You're there?'

'What?' I'm testy.

'You're in Australia.'

I compress my lips, stalking away from the board-room and into the office I use here in our Sydney headquarters. The trees of Sydney's Hyde Park are just visible from here, buffered by a few glass build-ings between.

I fight an urge to ask Theo what the hell it is to him.

'So?'

'I'm glad. Did you see Felicity?'

It takes me a second to realise who he's talking about. The baby. Jagger and Grace's child, the little Hart. My eyes sweep shut and my breath chokes a little. What I've lost stands before me, a monumen-tal, epic, indisputable pain. Everything I believed myself to be is gone.

I am alone.

No parents. No family. No pink niece with fluffy hair. Just me.

'Yeah.'

'And?'

I press my palm into the desk to stop myself from swearing. 'And what? It's a baby. What do you expect me to say?' I try to cover my anger with a laugh but it comes out as derisive.

Theo's silent. I hate this. I hate hurting him. I know if we were having this conversation face to face he'd be looking at me with pity—the kind of pity I came to resent as a child. He and Jagger were sorry for me then, sorry for how hard Ryan was on me, for how he pushed me not to show my emotions, not to cry when I was hurt, pushed me to 'man up'. And they're pitying me again now. But I'm not some kid any more, thrown away by his mother. I'm a grown ass man and I have every right to feel the way I feel.

I shake my head roughly, brushing a hand over my short hair.

'Are you seeing her again?' For a moment I think of Cora but he's talking about Felicity, not my sex life.

'I hadn't planned on it.' I close my eyes and see the little girl, who possessed Jagger's eyes and nose, and feel the strangeness of my blood and features. I never looked like a Hart, not like Felicity will, and now I know why.

'For God's sake, man.' His breathing is rushed down the phone line. 'I know what you've been through and I'm trying to be sympathetic, but how long is this Holden Hart pity show going to go on for?'

I slam my palm into the desk again, harder this time. There's no satisfaction in that. No satisfaction in anything except alcohol and sex. Cora.

I grip the phone tighter, staring out at Sydney.

'I've got work to do.'

'Like you give a shit,' Theo snaps. 'You've been drinking yourself into oblivion for the better part of a year—'

'I've still been working,' I bite out because it's bad enough to have inherited a fortune from Ryan Hart, it's another to know I have no rightful claim to it. The only solace is that I'm great at what I do, that thanks to me the value of our casino holdings has trebled in the past decade.

'Fine. I'll concede that—'

'That's big of you.'

'Just stop being such a pain in the arse.' He makes a groaning noise. 'I'm sorry Dad lied to you. I'm sorry your mom lied to you. I'm sorry every fucking person who should have known better didn't do you the courtesy of telling you who your biological father is. I'm sorry you had to learn the truth from Barrett Byron-Moore—for both him and you.' I wince as I remember that distinctly uncomfortable conversation with one of our oldest family friends, a guy who's almost like a fourth Hart brother. 'But don't you get it? Ryan chose to raise you. He chose to bring you up as a Hart, and Holden, he loved you, as much as he was capable of loving anyone. More than he loved me, more than he loved Jagger. He *chose* to love you. How long are you going to torture yourself with this?'

Anger shreds me and I doubt even Cora can obliterate these emotions completely. That doesn't mean I don't want her to try though.

'You have no idea what you're talking about.'

'I've had a front row seat to this for a year now. Don't speak to me as though I don't know...'

'You don't know anything.' The words are torn

from me. I stride across to the windows, my breath heavy in my lungs. 'You don't know a damned thing.'

'I—'

'Listen—' I interrupt, searching for words to make sense of this '—you guys are trying to help me. I get it. You think you can say something that will make this better, but you can't. You don't have to keep calling me, checking on me, trying to fix this. He was your dad, but you're not responsible for his fucked-up choices. You don't need to worry about me any more; I'm not your problem.'

'You think you're my *problem*? That that's why I'm checking up on you? You're our brother.'

I hate this. Fighting with my brother—with Theo—is like poison. 'Just because you say that doesn't make it true. I'm not biologically and I'm not legally. The truth is, Theo, I have no idea who I am.'

He's quiet, absorbing that. Finally, he sighs. 'I'm not an idiot. I get how hard that would be. I'm not expecting you to just let it go. But just let me say this: I'm here for you. So's Jagger.'

I close my eyes for a second, nodding stiffly. 'I know that.' I disconnect the call, jam the phone into my pocket, staring at the trees and the way they shift in the afternoon breeze, but all I can think of is the man I thought was my father.

Ryan Hart.

Why did he take me in? Why did he raise me? My presence ruined his marriage to Jagger's mom— we're only three months apart in age, so it was obvious I was the product of an affair.

Jagger's mom, as it turns out, is now a raging alcoholic and from time to time I've had to go to LA to help her out, to get her into rehab or out of prison if her disorderly behaviour gets too extreme—for Jagger's sake. And only then, when blind drunk and off her face, does she tell me what she really felt about me.

'Who was your mother anyway? A whore. A stupid young whore.'

I don't know if that's true. My mother had a lot of boyfriends. I was young when I went to live with Ryan Hart but not so young that I don't remember all the men who came to visit before that. Still, I don't think she was a prostitute—she slept with rich men and benefited from that. There's a fine line between, but Jagger's mother will never see it that way.

And I get it.

Who wouldn't hate the kid that's very existence ruined your marriage?

I wasn't conceived as a result of their affair, but he did sleep with my mother. I don't know how long it went on for, I don't know if it meant anything to him, or her. But now I know I'm not his son.

My gut clenches and I turn my back on the view.

There are two reliable ways to forget. One is sex, and right now the idea of sex with anyone other than Cora is less than appealing, and I have the self-awareness to appreciate that I'm not in the right headspace to call her.

The second is alcohol. I grab my jacket, pulling it on and barging out of the office. There's a bar around the corner, and I intend to go there and not leave again until I'm falling-down drunk.

I stare at the back of the camera, zooming in on the picture I've taken. It's okay, but not much better than that. Sure, it captures the geometric shapes of the Opera House, but none of the drama. It's just like any other photo of this well-known landmark.

I flick through the camera, scrolling past the dozen or so images I've taken today, to the last time I used it. New York. I was practising portraits. There's a shot of a little boy, about six or seven, his eyes heavy with things he's seen, his mother beside him, her hands outstretched. He's grubby and yet there's a spirit in his eyes that I've captured in the photo.

I move my finger over the buttons again, scrolling forward until I reach a young woman who'd just stepped out of the subway. The lights of Times Square shimmer in the background, but in the foreground it's just her. She's looking up, as if for directions, and a rucksack is hooked over one shoulder. There's such optimism in her expression, such naïve hope, as though in New York she'll find everything she's ever wanted.

On a small breath of exasperation I switch the camera off and sit down on a park bench. Tourists mill around me, unmistakable with their loud voices and selfie sticks. Seagulls flap at their feet, looking for morsels to eat.

And a sense of dissatisfaction grips me because

I'm thinking of Holden way more often than I'd like. How often wouldn't bother me?

Not at all?

That's not possible. Not after what we shared, what we did. But I have a sense of dissatisfaction at the way things finished between us the other night—two nights ago.

I try to blank my mind, to simply sit, but my hand hovers on my camera, as if ready at any moment to flick it on and capture a moment in time, to translate an emotion onto digital film.

That's what I do.

I trap moments like someone might a butterfly, pinning it as though that can bring it back to life.

A busker begins to play his guitar, singing an acoustic version of a song that was on the top of the charts a few years ago. I listen, and I watch, and I forcibly remove every hint of Holden from my thoughts because having him there doesn't serve any purpose.

I shouldn't be here.

It's about the tenth time I've admitted that to myself since my driver pulled up outside Cora's place. I shouldn't be here and yet I have been for the past hour, looking up at her place, waiting for lights to switch on to indicate that she's home, or waiting until I see her walking home. Something.

I tried to forget with alcohol, but this time it didn't work. Drinking made me angrier, so I contemplated throwing my phone into the harbour so Theo and

Jagger would stop calling me, feeling sorry for me, wanting to heal me somehow.

I also contemplated getting on my plane and leaving Australia, leaving Jagger and Grace and baby Felicity, and Cora, just disappearing for a while. But I've tried that too. After I first learned the truth I lost myself in Europe for months at a time. Jagger and Theo kept loose tabs on me but otherwise they let me go, as if they understood I needed that time.

So why can't they understand that I still do?

Another ten minutes pass. I lift my phone out and think about texting her. I hold it in my lap. Another five minutes go by and then I hear the sound of the Vespa before I see it. A moment later, it zips around the corner and my gut kicks me into action. I wait until she's parked and lifted the helmet off and then I step out of the car, crossing to her before she can see me, so I'm almost touching her before she realises and looks up.

Her lips part in recognition and then something else—concern?

I register it and realise I must look like shit. I showered a day or so ago, but since then I've consumed my body weight in liquor and barely eaten. Maybe coming here right now, like this, wasn't my best idea.

'Holden?' My name is swallowed inside of her. She shakes her head, like I'm some kind of ghost or something. 'You're still here?'

It's what she said last time, like she keeps thinking I might have flown right out of the country. 'I'm still here.' My words are unintentionally gruff. I don't have a problem with Cora—she doesn't deserve my wrath, even the overflow of it. I have to get a grip on this, and I can see only one way to do that. Assuming a more nonchalant tone, I shrug. 'I'm here for another week. Seven days.'

Her eyes flare and she swallows, her throat moving beneath my focused inspection. 'And then you go back to the States?'

Relief bursts through me. A week is good. A week to do some work with the manager of the casino floor, a week to see Felicity and get Theo off my back and a week to have a bit more fun with Cora—if she's amenable. Going by the last time we were together, I'd say she will be.

'So, why are you here?' She gestures to her house and there's no misunderstanding now.

'I came to ask you to come over.'

A frown shifts across her expression. 'Why?'

My look is sceptical and her cheeks bloom with colour.

'Why not just call me or send a text?'

'Because I wanted to make sure you said yes.' None of this is her fault and yet the power she holds over me fills me with resentment. 'Because I didn't want to wait for your answer.'

She closes her lips, looking beyond me, towards the limousine at my back.

'Damn it, Cora,' I say when she doesn't respond. 'Either invite me up or get in my car.'

She bites into her lower lip, and her eyes are so

awash with confusion that I could drown in their depths. What am I doing? What right do I have to come here and draw Cora into my messed-up life?

She expels a soft sigh and I feel it. The battle she's waging. The fight she's locked in—like me. Knowing what we should do, knowing what's inevitable. She looks towards the house, a little furrow on her brow, and then back at me.

'Wait here. I just need to grab something.'

She thrusts the bag she's holding towards me then hesitates, and I hold my breath, wondering if maybe she's going to change her mind after all.

But she doesn't.

She walks inside and a moment later, carrying a larger handbag, she's back, her eyes meeting mine. She doesn't smile. There's a look of determination on her face and I wonder if she has the same ambition I do—to have sex until we can begin to forget this, each other.

It's then that I realise my method of forgetting has bred within me a new addiction. A new need, a new dependence.

But I don't need to worry about that. In a week I'll go back to America, back to the way I was before Cora, and that will be the end of this.

With Holden at my side there's no need to go through the same security protocols. We take a different elevator, this time straight to his penthouse. Neither of us speaks as it lifts us into the heavens, and that's a problem because it gives me ample time to think. To wonder what I'm doing.

And the thing is, I don't know but I can say with absolute certainty that being here is one hundred per cent where I want to be right now. Being with him is what I need.

'Have you eaten?' His question seems louder than it is by virtue of the fact neither of us has made a sound since getting to the casino.

'I had a burger a little while ago.'

'Good.'

Our eyes hold for a second and then he gestures inwards.

'After you.'

I step into his penthouse, seeing it with different eyes now, eyes that are less wowed by the grandeur because they've seen it already and therefore more able to take in details. Two of the pictures I recognise. One is a Van Gogh, the other a Seurat. Originals? Undoubtedly.

'This place is amazing.'

He shuts the door behind himself and strides across the living space towards a kitchen I barely clocked last time. It's large with shining white pantries, a marble bench top and windows at the back of it that frame another picture-perfect view of the city.

'Do you spend much time here?'

My fingers itch to lift my camera from the bag and snap a photograph of that view. Night lighting is hard to do justice to; I need practice.

He opens the fridge door and pulls out a couple

of beers but, before he can crack the top off mine, I shake my head. 'I'll just have water, thanks.'

He pushes the beer back into the fridge and grabs a glass for me, filling it with filtered water from the fridge. I notice he still cracks the beer and memories sear me out of nowhere. My dad, the smell of beer, the ever-present bottle. I push those thoughts aside.

I've mentally dealt with Dad's alcoholism, and the waste his life became. I don't need to think about it now. Besides, I don't know Holden well enough to know how much he drinks, nor how often.

'I'm in Australia several times a year. This is where I stay.'

There's nothing to say in response to that. I presume he travels a heck of a lot, given he has a private jet. It makes sense he'd stay in his own casino. These are conclusions I could have reached for myself.

'I'm glad you came with me tonight.' His voice is serious, and I wonder if he truly doubted that I would. Did he actually think I might say no?

Something heavy shifts in the air around us.

I nod, try to smile, but it doesn't quite work.

'I should apologise, for last time.'

Surprise makes my heartbeat quicken. 'Oh?'

'I was more abrupt than I intended.' His words are a growl.

I shake my head a little. 'No, you were fine.'

'I didn't want you to stay.' The words are like little arrows, darting into my body and zipping through my blood. 'In fact, I wanted you to go after we had sex because that's what I do.'

I ignore the barbs of jealousy.

'But that's always the end of it.'

I nod, even when I don't quite understand.

'Always. I prefer not to think of the women I've slept with again.' Our eyes are locked, and just holding his gaze is making my blood surge.

'So why can't I stop thinking about you, Cora?' He says my name deliberately, to show not only does he remember it, it's haunting him in some way, not touching me, drinking his beer as though in doing so he'll be able to contain a need to reach for me.

But I can't analyse it because pleasure is zipping through me now too. Intense pleasure at his admission, at realising that for every ounce of determination I've had to bring to my mind to stop from thinking about him, he's dealing with that too.

'I don't know,' I say, but the words are lighter, happier, because this feels like good news. It doesn't change what I want from him but it makes me feel as though I'm not alone in that. We're both out on a limb, navigating this strange dependency simultaneously.

He moves towards me, his purpose clear, and I stay where I am, waiting, needing, wanting.

'Why can't I stop goddamned thinking about you?' His words reverberate with frustration, so I gather he's really been trying—and failing—to put me from his mind.

'I don't know,' I repeat, lifting a hand to his chest, letting my fingers splay across his pectoral muscle so I can feel the strong beating of his heart beneath my palm. My eyes latch to his and there's promise in their depths, as well as my need.

'But I've been having the same problem.'

He lifts one brow, curving his hand around my wrist and lifting my hand to his lips. He kisses my palm then moves it to my side, so his body can touch mine, so we're toe to toe.

'I want you to stay the night.'

My heart trips because the way he says that, it's not just an invitation. It speaks of a visceral need, like I hold the key to his survival in the palm of my hand, as though my answer alone will determine his fate.

I stare at him, my pulse galloping through me. I wonder if I should fight this harder, control it better, but ultimately, if the last week has taught me anything it's that I'd be waging a futile battle.

I want Holden. I need him in the same way he needs me.

And so I nod slowly, just a small shift of my head but it's enough. For as long as he's in Sydney he's mine and I'm his, and that's that.

CHAPTER EIGHT

Seven nights left in Sydney

'I LIKE THIS ONE.'

Her fingertips move over my chest, tracing a tattoo I had done a long time ago.

'Yeah?' A gruff sound. I let my fingertips undertake their own exploration. There are no marks on her skin; it's flawless. Fresh, beautiful, unmarked, undamaged, except by the ravages of my lovemaking, which was thorough and has wrought changes on her flesh, changes that will fade as the day goes on. To be replaced by me next time?

I catch the thought, spinning it over in my brain, because it's unusual and odd. Then again, I've accepted that this is unusual. I've accepted the ways in which she's different to my usual lovers.

'It's...pretty.'

That almost makes me laugh. I tilt my head to look at her. Her eyes are trained on my chest, beautiful eyes, a shade I've never really seen before. Deep and golden, like trapped sunrays and honeycomb.

'You know what I mean. Delicate.' She flicks those eyes towards me. I look away, towards the tattoo again, my frown instinctive.

'What is it?'

'A rose.'

'Yes, I should have said, "Why is it?"'

My gut clenches. 'No one's ever asked me that before.'

She lifts a brow, a small smile curving her seductive lips. 'I suppose you don't stick around long enough for them to ask.'

That's true. I find myself hesitating when the answer is simple. 'I got it young. I was stupid and... just a kid. I liked the idea of it.'

'Hmm,' she says. 'There might be an answer in there somewhere, but I'm afraid I can't decode it.'

When I close my eyes I can see the roses that my mother grew. I can smell their honeyed fragrance, intoxicating. I can hear the bees that flocked to the blooms, filling the garden with a background hum, especially in the sun-filled afternoons.

'How old were you?' she tries again, still tracing lines over the rose—to the left of my belly—her light touch mesmerising.

'Fourteen.'

'Fourteen?' She pushes up on one elbow, alarm in her eyes. 'That's illegal, right?'

'No charges were pressed,' I drawl, amused at how scandalised she is.

'But you were still a boy.'

'At fourteen, I was definitely not "still a boy".'

'Okay, but didn't the tattooist or whatever check your ID?'

'I didn't have any ID. I was fourteen.'

'You know what I mean.' She presses her hand to my arm, a light slap, designed not to hurt so much as to gently chastise. But I catch her hand, lifting her fingers to my lips, sucking one deep into my mouth then releasing it, biting the tip on its way out. Her eyes flare to mine and the familiar sense of desire begins to unfurl.

She is naked against my side, her legs tangled with mine, her breasts crushed to my chest. I like her like this. I have lost all concept of time but I think it's past midnight. There is a part of me that seems to be dreading the fact she might go at any point. And that dread forces realisation—I want her to stay. Only so I can enjoy this, her, as much as possible on this night.

Maybe I'll wake up tomorrow without this insatiable craving for her.

Maybe I'll be over her in the morning.

'Is it a secret?' she prompts, dropping her head and rolling her tongue over my nipple, her smile filled with cheek and query when she flicks her eyes back to mine. My harsh breath is involuntary.

'No.'

It's not. But, at the same time, only Jagger and Theo know. My brothers. My heart thumps painfully at the word *brothers*, and how long I took its usage for granted. How easily I believed what I was told. As a child, that's our purview, but why didn't I question it as an adult? Why didn't I wonder?

Perhaps I did. I knew I was different. The black sheep of our family, different, wrong somehow.

Perhaps that was my instincts telling me something was wrong. That I was being lied to by people I had come to trust.

Acid fills my mouth and I crave Cora, I crave beer, I crave obliteration.

'What's wrong, Holden?' Her hand presses to my cheek, the look of amusement gone completely.

I feel the darkness stirring in my eyes when I look at her.

'Nothing.'

It's a lie. We both feel it. She frowns, the flicker across her lips pleasing me. This is what I'm good at. Destruction, misery, grief, ruination. My special gifts, those I hold in abundance.

Her frown deepens. 'You're lying.' She scrambles up, and my chest cleaves in two because she's going to get out of bed and leave after all, and I'll be alone with the thoughts and memories she's invoked.

But she doesn't leave. She straddles me, leaning forward so her generous breasts are crushed to my chest and her mouth just an inch over mine. But it's her eyes that hold my full attention in that moment, eyes that are beautiful and magical and they completely enthral me.

'You don't have to tell me.' Her smile is gentle, like she's trying to coax a child out from under the bed after a nightmare. 'I was just curious, but it doesn't really matter.'

It doesn't matter. None of this does. The marks

of my past, scored across my flesh, are not important. Not to her, and no longer to me. The childish whims that led me to etch my feelings in my skin, almost as though I could ink them rather than experience them.

And the reasons for my tattoos don't matter to Cora, because I don't matter to Cora. We barely know each other. This is sex. Her curiosity in my tattoos is simple—she presumes they're pretty decorations, each one chosen for its aesthetic appeal. Her question was light because she expected the answer to be.

'I thought about getting a tattoo once,' she says, her voice casual, but there's a brittleness beneath it that has me pulling myself out of my own self-obsessed thoughts, wondering if her flawless skin carries invisible marks nonetheless.

'You didn't?'

Her smile is a flash, wiping away whatever I imagined I saw or heard in her voice, whatever complexity I intuited. 'Too painful. I don't like needles.'

She kisses me and I let her, surrendering to the sheer physicality of this, letting it push everything else from my mind.

I didn't mean to fall asleep here in his incredible bedroom in this penthouse above Sydney, but I was exhausted. Now the sun is rising, streaking hesitant colour through a bleak winter's sky, and instincts I have carried within me from childhood stir. I push the sheets back quietly, sparing a glance for Holden that becomes so much more, because a glance is never enough.

It's the first chance I've had to observe him properly. He's asleep, no likelihood that his intelligent gaze will shift and catch me like this, so I linger, my eyes scrutinizing his face first, the tension and hardness in it lessened by sleep. Like this, his features are still chiselled, stone-like, but his expression is relaxed. Vulnerable. Something in my chest shifts.

Vulnerable? Holden Hart?

I'm being delusional. Too much sex. I let my eyes drop to his body, circling across the tattoos, landing on the rose and then, last of all, the Greek word beneath that quite frightening-looking picture.

Reluctantly, I push away from the bed, grabbing a shirt of his rather than my own clothes—which are tangled in the sheets and beneath the bed—sliding it over my head and inhaling unconsciously, breathing him in so my nipples tighten and my insides warm. It's a freezing cold morning—his shirt won't be enough. Fortunately, there's a blanket on the edge of one of the leather sofas. I lift it up as I go, grabbing my camera backpack last of all.

The photos I took the day before, attempting to grab the shadows of the Opera House to show the juxtaposition of light and dark, manmade structure versus untamed ocean, are insufficient. I can't say why, but they don't work.

I click the doors open softly, moving to the edge of the balcony and opening the collapsible tripod first, extending each leg and snapping them into position before locking my camera in place. Then I wrap the blanket around my shoulders and I wait. It's still too early. Night is winning the battle, reluctant to surrender supremacy of the sky. I wrap the blanket more tightly around my shoulders, contemplate making a coffee—except the noise might wake him and I don't want to do that—and I wait some more.

Curiosity has me looking around this penthouse balcony—every bit as palatial as the inside of this place. It's enormous, of course, and looks to wrap around the building, which I hadn't noticed before. There are several areas set up—sitting areas, a barbecue zone, and as I continue to look I notice a hot tub and a pool, so it really does have everything you could ever need. There are even potted plants— lemon trees and some kind of vine that's growing over a gazebo construction near the pool.

It's a shame he doesn't live here full-time.

The thought bursts into my brain, surprising me, so I physically freeze, staring towards the harbour again, trying to make sense of that.

For *his* sake, I mean, relaxing. It's so beautiful, surely nowhere on earth could offer what this does? Here, high in the sky, you could forget you were above a casino, forget you were in the middle of a bustling city. It's a kind of bliss, far removed from that, beautiful and striking and peaceful and pleasurable.

The sun is getting stronger. Rays of insistent light penetrate the night, and I return to the camera, switching the viewfinder on, looking at the way the lens interprets what I'm seeing. I have to make some adjustments to the settings in order to more closely capture the truth of this day's break. Changing the ISO and aperture, I set the timer—I left my remote switch at home—and press the button, waiting for the timer to count down and snap the image. I'm impatient—as I always am—to see the result.

I move back to the tripod, covering my eyes to remove any additional shade and replay the image. My heart thrills because yes, it's close. Not quite perfect but almost. I try again, going through the same motions, a few additional tweaks, and then snap.

I don't know how long I stand here doing this, long enough for the sun to rise higher in the sky, for the light to get brighter, for night to capitulate entirely, leaving only a smudge of grey on the horizon as a reminder that the fight is merely delayed, not lost. And I lose myself in this perfection—rendering the magic of something like a sunrise onto film is one of the reasons I became enamoured of photography, and it's one of the reasons I'm sure it's what I want to do for the rest of my life. I'm ready to stop running and start living.

I lose myself in the act of photo-taking and forget almost everything else.

I reach for her instinctively when I wake. My body thunders with needs and my mind isn't alert enough to stand in my way, to fight against that dependency and craving.

But she's not there.

Her side of the bed is cold, no hint of her sweet body remains in the sheets so I could almost wonder if I dreamed that night, except no. I feel her jeans tangled at my feet.

It doesn't guarantee that she's still here. In fact, it could simply mean she didn't want to speak to me before she left.

Something like panic flashes in my gut because I wonder if I deserve that. Did I say or do anything that could have hurt her? I wasn't exactly sober when I went to her place. Could I be forgetting something?

But no, I don't think that's it.

I push out of bed, pausing only to drag on my jeans. I button them up as I stride down the corridor, checking rooms as I go, until I reach the living space. No sign of her. My sense of foreboding increases.

I look towards the view, uncertainty within me, and then pause.

Because she's out there, wrapped in one of the mohair blankets from the lounge. I can see her bare calves and ankles, bare feet, hair loose and tangled, wild in the morning breeze. And there's something else.

What's she doing? I frown, moving closer, and then pause. A camera?

Curiosity propels me the rest of the distance. When I open the door she turns to face me, her lips lifting in that ready smile of hers, so I try to dredge one up in response.

'Good morning,' I say instead, moving towards her.

'Hi.' She looks towards the camera almost apologetically. 'I hope you don't mind. The sunrise was just too beautiful to miss.'

'Mind?' I lift my shoulders, conscious of the way her attention drops to the gesture. 'It's a free country.'

'Yeah, but it's your home.'

'Not my home.' The rejection is swift. I look away from her, acid burning the insides of my mouth. I don't have a home. Not really. I'm not being melodramatic. A home is a place you feel comfortable, that you want to be. It's been a long time since I've felt that, if ever.

'Right. You know what I mean.' She's casual, as though the distinction doesn't matter. And perhaps it doesn't, to someone who knows their place, who doesn't question it.

'Where are you from?'

She turns back to her camera and I breathe in deeply before I realise what I'm doing—inhaling the sweetness of her hair as the wind breathes it my way.

'Australia.'

'Obviously.' Her accent was one of the first things I noticed about her. 'Here, in Sydney?'

'I spent some time here.'

It's a very vague response, the kind of answer that tells me more than she intends. 'And before that?'

I can't help myself. I move to stand behind her, wrapping my arms around her waist and drawing her back to me. She comes willingly, her body moulding perfectly to mine.

'Before that,' she says consideringly, her voice

quiet in a way it hasn't been before, 'I lived a few hours north, in a place called Sundown Creek.'

I drop my head forward, nudging the blanket aside with my chin so my lips can press to the bare flesh of her neck, tasting the curve of skin there, my tongue running over it reverentially.

'Why'd you leave?'

She stills. I feel it. I feel every part of her grow tense and, out of nowhere, something stirs within me. Anger. A protective instinct. Something foreign and impossible to translate into rational comprehension.

'I wanted to do something else with my life.'

That's not it. 'Something else? As opposed to?'

She turns in my arms, her face serious, more serious than I've ever seen it. I can feel a war being waged within her and I sympathise because I'm almost constantly at loggerheads with myself.

But I don't relent because I want to know, and I'm not good at subjugating my wishes.

'Cora?'

She bites down on her lower lip, the act a little distracting, and shifts so the blanket moves and I see she's wearing a shirt of mine. She's mis-buttoned it so her neck is exposed, and I have to concentrate not to groan because if I really look I know I'll see the generous swell of her breasts and all thought will evaporate from my brain.

'It's boring.' She waves her hand through the air and flutters her eyes, smiles, but it's not an open smile, it's a smile designed to shut this conversation down. 'Anyway, I lost track of time. I should go.'

Frustration is unmistakable. 'Should you?'

I don't want her to. That much is obvious, to me, and surely to her. But, more than that, I don't want her to close me out of this conversation. I'm genuinely curious about her life. It makes very little sense, and yet I feel it.

'Are you keeping secrets from me?' I aim for teasing but I think the words emerge as a little mocking.

'Never, Mr Rose Tattoo.'

She has a fair point. I clearly put an end to her questions the night before; she's returning that, but not in a tit-for-tat way so much as reminding me of the boundaries that we never discussed but are both observing.

Her finger moves to the tattoo, swirling around it, and I close my eyes for a moment, something unlocking within me. I shift a little, my body moving closer to hers, my free hand lifting to her hair, and then I open my eyes, look right down at her and find myself speaking.

'I got it when my mother died.'

Her finger stills, as if snagging on my skin, then begins to move again, more gently, kindly.

'Oh.' A soft exhalation.

'I hadn't seen her in a long time. Years. She'd been sick and I was very angry with her. I barely knew her in the end.'

She nods thoughtfully. 'So the tattoo is a tribute?'

I frown. 'That's one word for it.'

'You have another?'

'Not really.' I shake my head. 'Show me your photos.'

She frowns, looking towards the camera. 'In a moment.' She catches my hand, lacing her fingers through it.

'I'm really sorry about your mum.'

I tilt my head, my expression grim.

'Why the rose?'

Jesus, she's really not going to let this go. 'She had roses in her garden, where I grew up, before she sent me to live with the Harts.' The words are flattened of emotion, just like Ryan taught me.

'How old were you when you went to live with them?'

'Young. Why?'

'Was she sick? Is that why you were sent away?'

I stiffen. *'Your mother is not a person I care to discuss.'* 'No.'

Her eyes probe my face; I keep my expression neutral. 'Did your dad sue for custody?'

Nausea almost winds me. 'No.' She's not going to let this go. I turn to face her properly, meeting her eyes as though it doesn't cost me. 'She didn't want me any more. I wasn't particularly conducive to her lifestyle.'

'What lifestyle was that?'

'She liked to entertain. She was glamorous and I was a hindrance.'

Her eyes narrow, as though she can't make sense of this. 'So she sent you to live with your dad and... what? Had you on holidays? Weekends?'

My heart shifts. 'I only saw her a few times after that, never for long. The first I knew she'd got sick was when she died.'

Cora's expression shows an abundance of pain and sympathy. She moves towards me and puts a hand on my chest, her features soft and beautiful, stirring something to life inside me. 'And that hurt.'

It's not a question. I can remember every detail of that afternoon so vividly. My mother taking me to a huge building, a skyscraper with offices, leaving me sitting in a waiting room filled with expensive leather furniture while a nice woman, Mrs Adams—she was one of my father's assistants—ferried lavender short-breads and sweet tea to me, in between waiting on Ryan Hart and my mother. I remember the exact taste of those biscuits, the smell of the sun-warmed leather furniture, the sound of the air-conditioning humming, the sheen of the polished tiles beneath my feet. I remember the boredom that seeped into my bones right before shock took over. I push the memories aside.

'I was a child. Lots of things hurt. I grew out of that.'

She lifts a finger, tracing the rose, her eyes troubled, showing that perhaps she disagrees with me. She doesn't speak, though, and I find myself—strangely—filling the silence.

'She loved roses.'

Her expression is sympathetic. I don't want sympathy; I hate it. I change the subject abruptly.

'Are you hungry?'

Her eyes widen a little, her brows lifting. 'I can grab something later, on my way home.'

'No.' I press myself against her, my mouth finding her earlobe and drawing it in, wobbling it between my teeth so I catch her small groan, I feel it against my body. I can't say why it matters to me, but I want Cora to stay longer—I feel that I need her in this moment. 'You'll stay and eat with me first.'

She lifts her face to mine, something shifting from her to me. 'Are you trying to boss me around again?' A smile is quirking the corners of her lips.

'Yes.' And then, because she's making fun of me and I hear what I sound like, I say, 'Okay?'

She lifts her fingers, walking them up my side then twisting them behind my back, rubbing the flesh between my shoulder blades. 'Maybe.'

'Maybe?'

'What's for breakfast?'

That's easy. 'Whatever you want, baby.'

CHAPTER NINE

The sixth to last morning

'So, Sundown Creek?'

I pause, midway through lifting a corner of waffle to my mouth, shooting him a look that's part exasperated, part impressed—that he remembered, that he's interested. I can't really work out why the latter is true, but an hour after we came in from the balcony he's brought the conversation back to the question of where I used to live.

'Uh-huh.' I resume the waffle's trajectory, biting it and watching him as I chew, inwardly amused by his obvious discontent. Holden Hart is not a man who likes to be made to wait.

I wonder if that's because he's who he is—as in, a guy who was raised with a silver spoon, knowing his billionaire fate awaited him, and so from a very young age he's been worshipped and adored, with an army of servants to undertake all his bidding.

Or is it just him? There's a latent authority that moves within him. I felt in from the moment he

stepped onto the jet and, unobserved, I watched him.
I feel it now.

'What was it like?'

That's an easier question. General, non-specific.
'It was quiet.' I lean back in the chair a little, thinking of my hometown. 'It's a small place, well off
the beaten track. Miles in from the coastline, just a
small creek to irrigate the crops, and the creek dries
up completely through winter—we get our storms
in summer. I was bored a lot, as a child.' I look towards my camera backpack, on the edge of the sofa.
'I think that's why I got into photography.'

'Yeah?'

'I found an old camera of my grandma's and
started playing around. Grandpa had a darkroom,
and taught me how to develop the films.' My smile
is laced with nostalgia. 'I hate to think what kind
of chemicals I inhaled as an incautious seven-year-
old. And what it must have cost them to sustain my
hobby.'

'You were passionate about it.'

'Yes, but a lot of the photos were terrible—' I
laugh '—I had a lot to learn.'

'So this is your hobby still?'

'It's more than a hobby. It's a...' I search for the
right word. My eyes fall to him and it's easy to remember. 'A compulsion.'

'Why?'

I consider that a moment. 'A photo is a snapshot
of time. But it's so much more. In a photo you can
capture an extra layer of reality, things you can't

fathom or don't recognise in the moment are there to be understood later. Lines around eyes, hopes, dreams, wants, needs.'

'So you prefer portraits to landscape?'

My smile is whimsical. 'I think landscapes can have secrets of their own too. I like juxtaposition and contrast.' I stand up, moving to grab the camera, flicking up the photos I took the day before. 'See what I mean? The sharp tips of the Opera House, the gentle lifts of the tiny waves in the harbour? The shadows here and the sunlight there? Contrast makes us care; it intrigues us.'

He studies the photo. 'This child with her ice cream cone and eyes so full of hope and the old lady on the bench, enjoying the sunshine.'

My heart bursts because I noticed exactly the same detail—I intentionally framed it that way. This is why I want to be a photographer. It's a form of art and information. 'Yes.' Just a small breath sound.

'This is very good.' He clicks into another photo and another, then places the camera down.

I feel as though I've trapped a beautiful butterfly in a glass jar. These dreams of mine have been secret for so long, kept that way by my own certainty that they're laughable and fanciful, and yet, with Holden, I want to share them with him.

I tilt my head to the side, trying to find the words, and end up blurting it out. 'Actually, I'm hoping to pursue this as more than just a hobby.' My cheeks infuse with heat. 'I mean, I know it's hard to make a living from something like photography, but I have a little capital, enough to pour into this, and it's what I've always wanted to do.'

I've piqued his interest. He leans forward a little, his eyes assessing. 'What does that entail?'

'To start with, a course through the National Photography Institute. It's here in Sydney, so kind of a no-brainer.' I lift my shoulders. 'I'm nervous, you know. I love photography and I'm worried—'

'Why?'

'Well, there's a chance I might suck at it. And then what? I mean, I quit a great job for this, because I wanted to chase the dream I had when I was just a kid. That's stupid, right?'

'You don't suck.'

I push his praise away. 'But following my dreams?'

'People seem to say you should pursue your dreams.'

'But you don't?'

His smile is hard to analyse. 'I don't believe in dreams, no.'

Something chips at my heart. An ache for him, pain, deep inside of me.

'But you're talented. This isn't a whim.'

Pleasure at his praise warms me.

'And what then, after the course?'

'Well, it's a year long. Then, there are some great opportunities to shadow renowned photographers, depending on area of interest. Finally, the business part, but I can't even think of that yet.'

'And your career as a flight attendant?'

'It served its purpose.' The telling phrase is out

before I can stop it. I lift some more waffle to my mouth.

'Which was?'

I chew, fingering the lip of my coffee mug. 'To see the world.' It's a version of the truth. 'Sundown Creek is beneath the flight path for a lot of planes. I used to stand in our garden, looking up at the sky and watching those white trails track across the deep blue and I wanted, more than anything, to be on board. To go somewhere. I wanted to leave Sundown Creek, even as a girl.'

'Why?'

He doesn't fall for the romance of exploration. His question is more probing than that.

'Lots of reasons. Haven't you ever wanted to get away?'

His laugh completely lacks humour. It's a gruff sound that makes my heart ache for him for a reason I can't comprehend.

'That's how you felt?' He refocuses the conversation to me with effortless ease.

'I wanted—yes. I wanted to get away.'

'From what?'

My heart slows. It almost stops. I feel tempted to talk to him, tempted to tell him everything, and I wonder at that, because holding this inside of me is habit. It's been a long time since I've spoken to anyone about anything important. I'm an expert in shallow, meaningless social engagements.

But talking to Holden is like talking to nobody, in the sense that I won't know him in a week or two, and he won't know me. Maybe that's why I find this strangely seductive. Or maybe it's because I've been more physically intimate with him than anyone else and there's a sense of connection that comes from that act, whether wanted or not.

'Everything, I guess.'

He leans forward. 'That's kind of vague.'

'I know.' I run my knife over the top of the waffle then put it down, because I'm fidgeting for the sake of it.

'But it's the truth,' I say, shaking my head, my smile heavy with sadness. 'My dad. My boyfriend. My life.' The last word is heavy with grief, because by 'life' I mean 'loss'.

'You don't get on with your dad?'

'He died.' The words are said without emotion, but that doesn't mean I don't feel his loss. 'A year ago.'

'I see.'

I like that he doesn't offer a platitude. I realise I did when he told me about his mum, but I'm glad he leaves it be.

'We weren't close, in the end.'

He's quiet, like he knows that if he doesn't interrupt I'll keep going.

'He wasn't abusive or anything. But he was—'

He's still silent. I search for a word.

'Self-destructive. It was hard to watch.'

He doesn't move, except for the small, almost imperceptible, shift in his eyes.

'How so?'

'Oh, you know. A raging alcoholic. One beer after

another after another until he could barely stand. Which made him, from time to time, mean. Angry. Unsafe.' I shake my head, frustrated at my inability to help him coiling through me like a fresh wound. 'It was just him and me. It's hard as a kid not to take that on.' I lift my shoulders. 'Over the years I've come to realise it wasn't my fault, but it felt like it, a lot of the time.'

'Where were your grandparents?'

'My dad was in his fifties when I was born, so they were older, you know? They died before I was ten.' I shake my head slowly. 'Up until then, it was okay because I had somewhere else to go, but then, nothing.'

'And your mother?'

'I never knew her. I gather she was a lot younger than my dad. Didn't feel like she could cope with being a parent. She stayed around just long enough for me to be born then split in the middle of the night. He never found her again. She never reached out to me.'

There's an eerie watchfulness in Holden's expression. He's so still, almost as though he's carved from stone.

'And that doesn't bother you?'

'No.' I purse my lips. 'She's an abstract to me. Being a parent is about more than biology. Like your mom, I guess, she just didn't want to be a mum, so I don't think of her like that. She gave birth to me, full stop. Dad raised me. And he wasn't the best dad in the world—not by a long stretch—but he loved me and he was there for me.'

His stillness persists. His eyes don't quite meet mine. I feel as though he's lost in thought, contemplating what I've said, imbuing it with more weight than I intended.

'Anyway...'

'You still wanted to escape him, though?'

His question shifts the focus back to our conversation, when I was about to wrap it up. 'It's more complex than that.'

'How so?'

I hear it. The silence. The hospital room filled with equipment, the beeping, the gentle throbbing of pulse monitors. The quiet nothingness of all the staff as the baby was pulled from my body, not breathing.

'I had some personal stuff. It was easier to move on from it when I wasn't in town.'

'Your boyfriend?'

'He was part of it, yes.' I can't smile dismissively like I want to. My memories are making me heavy. 'It's not something I like to discuss.'

'Why not?'

'Because it's difficult and sad.'

'Try.'

I sip my coffee, my eyes shifting to the view. The day is turning grey, the sky thick and leaden. Maybe keeping our baby a secret is part of the problem. Perhaps I would have recovered from that grief more quickly if I'd been open to discussing it.

'I had a baby.' I fix him with a stare that conceals the trauma of that. 'A stillbirth.'

I swallow. The lump in my throat won't shift.

Great. I'm going to cry. I dig my nails into my palms beneath the table, trying to hold the emotions at bay.

'It was the hardest thing I ever went through. I felt alone and bereft and like an abject failure, and there was no one I could talk to, no one who'd understand, and I just wanted—needed—to escape. Every moment I spent in Sundown Creek made me feel like I was drowning. We had a funeral service, a small one, and spread his ashes over the creek bed.' Salty tears fill my eyes. 'I left town the next day.'

'How old were you?'

'I'd just turned nineteen.'

He's silent. I feel the weight of my confession, I feel his response, even when he doesn't frame one. After a moment he stands, putting a hand out to mine, silently urging me to echo his movement and stand. I do, his touch a comfort no words could offer.

'I'm sorry.' I don't knock the platitude back. I need it. He drops his mouth, kissing me slowly, and it's only after a moment I realise I can taste salt in my mouth; I'm crying, unchecked, my tears joining with our kisses. His arms wrap around my middle and lift me, his lips never leaving mine as he carries me, body to body, through the penthouse and into his bedroom.

I'm still wearing his shirt. He pushes it up, over my head, without bothering to undo the buttons. It's not necessary. The shirt is too big. It comes away easily. I'm naked beneath. And as if he understands my need for obliteration he kneels before me, his mouth seeking my sex, his tongue tormenting me as his hands hold my hips, keeping me where I am, so the warmth and power of pleasure begin to drum through me, rolling like waves I can't resist, dragging me away from the pain of my memories into an ocean that is clear and forgiving, an ocean where there's no blame, no hurt.

I hold his shoulders, my orgasm coming gently at first, tingling the tips of my toes and the edges of my fingers, before tearing me apart with its blinding intensity. I hold onto him as though he's an anchor of sorts, and perhaps he is, or maybe it's this gift of pleasure that's tethering me to an earthly certainty I didn't even know I needed.

My breathing is tortured, my body spent in the same way as when I ran a half-marathon a few years ago. He stands slowly, tangling his fingers in mine, his stare direct. And he does that, simply looks at me, for a long time, his jaw clenched so a muscle throbs at its base and I stare right back at him, as if hypnotised or something.

I once heard that intense pain understands intense pain, that there's something innately bonding about it, and I wonder, briefly, if there is a shared experience, something between us that resonates on a level we can't understand, as though my consciousness and his consciousness are communicating beyond our spoken words.

How else can I explain this? I feel like he gets it, gets me, and I haven't felt that in such a long time.

'I want to fuck you.'

The words are incongruous if taken at face value,

but the tone in his voice fells me at my knees because it's hoarse and deep, like he's hurting because I'm hurting. I stare at him, my stomach in knots, my mind spinning, as though I'm about to step off the edge of a cliff.

'Please.' Like he needs this as much as I do. I bite down on my lip and I nod, surrendering to this heady rush, knowing it will obliterate the pain of my confession, knowing it will push my memories back into the recesses of my mind.

I have no words for her, afterwards. I can't say anything, but that doesn't mean I'm not thinking it, that the feelings aren't there, demanding I let them in, just this once. I stroke my fingers over her naked back, appreciating the softness of her skin, the indent at the base of her spine before her body swells to form her buttocks.

I am filled with a sense of guilt. Not because her grief is my fault in any way, but because I've been so wrapped up in my own shit storm of a life that I failed to realise she was navigating her own sadness.

I think of the teenager she would have been, pregnant, and then suddenly without a baby, and I wonder at the boyfriend who got her pregnant. I wonder if he supported her and helped her with her grief. I wonder if her dad, in his alcoholism, was capable of providing words of support.

'Will you miss your work?'

She props her chin on my chest, her eyes drugged

by satiation. My ego swells. I like seeing her like that and knowing I'm the reason for it.

'The cabin crew stuff?'

I make a small shift of my head that passes as a nod.

'In some ways,' she says quietly. 'I wanted to see the world as a kid, and my job's enabled me to do that.' She walks her fingers over my chest, capturing my hand in hers, holding it as though it's an object of value, stroking it gently.

'Where in particular?' It's small talk, but I feel like she needs it. Or maybe I do. It's casual and easy, which is what I probably should have kept this all along. Knowing things about her, important things, makes me uncomfortable, like she's trusted me with something I can't deliver.

'The pyramids.' Her smile is sweet, self-deprecating. 'As a child, that was the "ultimate" experience. I ticked it off my list two years into the job.'

'What else was on your list?'

'Oh, everywhere. I've been to so many places.'

'Such as?'

'Morocco, Rome, Paris, Tokyo, New York, London, Singapore, Cairo, Belgium—just about everywhere.'

'And where have you missed?'

'The Northern Lights,' she says with a sigh. 'I went to Canada once, thinking I'd see them, but I didn't time it right. The night wasn't clear enough. That's definitely something I want to experience at least once.'

'They're spectacular.'

'You've been?'

'Mmm.' I shift my hand out of hers, lifting it so I can reach for the glass of water on my side of the bed. I take a drink then rearrange myself, propping up on one elbow so I can see her better.

'And are they breathtaking?'

You are breathtaking. The words swirl through me but I don't say them. Instead, somewhat gruffly, I admit, 'Yes. As you would imagine.'

She sighs, flopping back on the bed. 'I'm jealous.'

'You'll get there.'

'I know. It'll be harder now I'm not flying. As cabin crew, it wasn't such a big deal to jump on a crew seat and travel wherever I wanted.'

'Is that why you took a job doing this?'

'I didn't take a job doing this.' She gestures to our naked bodies and smiles at me, a smile that sparks a clunky reaction inside of my chest.

'No?' I return it, and the feeling is so spontaneous and so overwhelmingly natural that I swallow it almost immediately.

'Nope.' Her own smile shifts, and a small sigh escapes her lips. 'It seemed like the easiest way to see the world.' She nods. 'I had a friend who'd got a job for Australian Air, and she recommended I apply. I did well at school, and I had a lot of hospitality experience. I was fortunate to get a placement straight away, doing domestic routes during my training and then onto international.'

'I doubt "fortune" had anything to do with it. You strike me as someone who'd be excellent at your job.'

She laughs. 'I slept with you when I was working for you.'

'It's different.'

'Is it?'

'You were temping.' I lift my shoulders. 'So you've quit?'

'Yes.' Her expression is serious. Her face is so expressive I feel I have an unfair advantage, like I can read her as one might a book. 'After my dad died I was entitled to take some time, and I didn't. I came back for the funeral—' her voice shifts a little '—but there wasn't much point sticking around. I wasn't ready to pack up his house or anything. I just feel like there's all this stuff I need to get on with. Photography, my life, responsibilities. Grown-up stuff.'

'So the house is unoccupied?'

She nods. 'I had it locked up for Future Cora to deal with. Unfortunately, that's now me, so I'll have to get back at some point soon to sort it out. I can't leave it there indefinitely.'

'Why don't you want to do it?'

'It's just hard.' Her eyes meet mine, and I feel her struggle and her honesty. 'It's like stepping back in time and, honestly, to a time I'd rather forget. Everything's like it was before. My room. The kitchen.' She shakes her head. 'But so much more rundown. He drank himself into an early grave. I couldn't stop him. I wasn't enough of a reason for him to stop.' She bites that full lower lip and I lean forward, pressing my forehead to hers, breathing her in, not particularly wanting to think about the fact I've doused my organs in liquor daily since learning the truth about my own father.

'I tried. I really did. Before…the baby. But afterwards, the fight just left me.'

'That's understandable.'

'Is it?' A crease forms between her brows. 'I don't know. I feel like he deserved better.'

'We all make our own beds, Cora.'

'Maybe.' She sounds unconvinced.

'And your boyfriend?'

'Dave?'

'That was the father?'

'Yeah.'

'Do you still speak to him?'

She pulls a face. 'He was kind of a waste of space.'

'Yeah?'

'Oh, yeah. The sort of guy who was a legend in his own lunchbox. You know the sort. Small community, great at football, much adored, parents owned half the town, so he had a bit of money behind him, and he was drop-dead gorgeous. I fell head over heels for him and I think he liked the attention. What he didn't like was the idea of monogamy, only I didn't realise that until I was six months pregnant with his baby.'

I bite back a curse. 'I see.'

'Mmm. Walking in to find him in bed with someone else wasn't exactly what I'd been planning on. It sounds stupid but I honestly thought he loved me. We were young; I was naïve.' She frowns. 'I think I probably wanted to be loved, you know? I wanted someone the opposite to my dad, someone who'd…

I don't know. Would make me feel part of a family. And he had a great family, big and happy.'

Her words feel accusatory when I know they're not, but it's a reminder that I can't offer her what she wants—and I don't plan on offering her anything more than this, anyway.

'Maybe he did love you. Maybe the cheating was a mistake.' The excuse surprises me. I don't know why I make it for him. Perhaps to make her happy, to relieve her of some pain.

'It doesn't matter. Dave was a lifetime ago. I feel like I dodged a bullet in some ways.' She pales. 'Not because of the baby.' Tears fill her eyes and that ache, right below my ribs, is back. 'But because I found out he wasn't being faithful and the stars fell from my eyes. It made it easier to leave, after—'

Her voice trails off into nothing.

'I get it.'

And I do, but I also hate it. I don't understand why, but I want to reach into Cora's past and erase all this pain, I want to make things better for her. But I'm hardly anyone's saviour. My path in life right now is bent on self-destruction and little more.

'Do you ever hear from him?'

'I hear *of* him, from time to time. Last I heard he was working on an oyster farm out of Broome.'

'Married?'

'Not that I know of.' She shrugs. 'Anyway, that's all ancient history. I'm just focusing on my future now, trying to write the life I want for myself, you know.'

I can't imagine having that kind of attitude, but I

nod because I want Cora to have whatever she wants, and the new life she's planning sounds pretty perfect for her. 'I'd like to see more of your photos.'

'My portfolio?'

'Sure. But I meant the ones you took this morning.'

'Right.' She smiles, but there's a sense of reserve in her expression. 'They're rough. I was just practising.'

'Show me.'

She moves her hand towards my belly, running her fingers up towards my chest, then lower, following a line of dark hair that arrows towards my cock. Her eyes lift to mine, and there's a silent challenge in them.

'Soon.'

And in that single word I feel a rebirth of my needs and wants, so I jerk my head in a small sign of approval.

'Soon will be fine.'

Her smile is pure sexiness. 'I'm glad to hear it, Mr Hart.' And her head drops to my chest, then follows the same path as her finger, so I suck in a deep breath and prepare for what she's about to do.

There's no preparing for it though. The moment she wraps her mouth around my length I feel the strangest sense that I've come home. I refuse to analyse it—I don't have the brainpower right now, anyway—but that doesn't change the fact there's perfection in this moment. Sheer, undeniable perfection…six more days of it.

CHAPTER TEN

Five nights left in Sydney

THEO'S LOOKING AT ME in that way I'm now very, very used to. Like he doesn't know if he wants to shake me or hug me. Pity is in his eyes, the same pity I've come to know often, that I resent with every fibre of my being.

'How's Asha?' The question is calculated. If anything can relax him, it's talking about his fiancée. I offer him a beer from the fridge. He takes it, shifting his gaze to the view and, sure enough, a smile moves over his face when he thinks of the woman he's going to marry. 'Busy. Amazing.'

His happiness should make me happy but it doesn't. Much like Jagger and Grace, I feel like my brothers both exist in bubbles now, completely self-contained and separate from me. They have these lives—rich, full lives—and even if it weren't for the fact I'm not a real Hart I'd still feel on the outside.

'The new product line's going well?'

'She's killing it.' His pride is tangible. 'She knew

it would be huge but it's dominating sales in its demographic; they can barely keep up with demand.'

'She must be thrilled.' I think I sound normal. It's a normal thing to say, right? So why does Theo whip his head around to look at me, a frown settling over his face.

'Yeah. How's the casino?'

I shift my shoulders. 'Good. The development's coming together well. The Roosevelts deal's almost completed.'

'And you?'

I drain half of the beer before I can answer, then cradle it in the palm of my hand. Here we are, at the crux of things. 'Is that why you came out here?'

His eyes narrow. 'Jagger says you're not returning his calls.'

Something hollows me inside. It's true. Twice a day, every day, Jagger's been calling, and I've been ignoring them. Ignoring him. I close my eyes and see their beautiful daughter and feel…the opposite of Felicity. I'm happy for him, theoretically, but seeing that biological connection and knowing myself to be completely alienated from anything like that fills me with an inexplicable rage. Not at the baby, not at Jagger, not at anyone I can think of. It's just a free-floating anger that's eating me alive.

Except when I'm with Cora.

Or drunk.

I should have left Australia by now. Being here isn't good for anyone. Europe beckons. Or South America. Somewhere far from this, them, my life.

But Cora… I told her a week and I don't want to walk away from that. I'm not stupid enough to think we can sleep together longer than that without it getting messy. Not messy for me—I'm an expert at keeping my feelings removed from my day-to-day life, but Cora isn't, and I don't want to hurt her just because she makes me feel good.

'I got his calls.'

Theo's eyes narrow. 'You should make an effort. Go see them, and the baby.'

I'm silent. He's moving towards shaking me, I think. The hug prospect seems like a distant memory.

'Grace has been asking about you.'

Guilt spears me. Grace is incredible. Even though I've spent the last year and a half in a drunken, self-pitying fog, I'm not blind. I see what she's like, what she's done for Jagger. Perhaps what she's even done for Theo, because I don't think a relationship was on his horizon at all until he saw how happy Jagger was.

'Yeah?'

'Yeah, man. I think she's hurt that you're here in Sydney and you've only been over once.'

I finish the beer, placing the bottle down a little heavier than I'd intended so it makes a cracking noise in the silence of the room. 'Fine. I'll go see them. Happy?'

He doesn't rise to the bait. 'I'm here for the rest of the week; we can go together. How's tomorrow?'

Something snags in my throat. I feel like I'm being pressed against a wall by a huge rock. I hate this feeling, I hate it. 'Fine.' I shrug with assumed nonchalance, contemplating calling Edward and having the jet fuelled. Maybe Cora could come with me—we could have the next six days somewhere different, somewhere better, without my brothers and this mess. Maybe we could go to the Northern Lights. The idea of making love to her beneath the stars makes Jagger, Theo, Grace, Felicity, Asha, all fade into nothing. But Theo is right here, staring across at me, waiting for an answer.

'Tomorrow?'

I want to tell him to get lost but instead I nod.

His eyes sweep through the apartment. I don't know what he expects to find. The place is immaculate, courtesy of the twice-daily maid service.

'Amanda mentioned you've been seeing someone.'

I still, the idea of my casino's head of security speaking to my brother about my personal life making me furious.

'Has she? That's not invasive at all,' I snap sarcastically.

'I asked.' He holds a hand up to silence me. 'In fact, I pretty much interrogated.' He grimaces. 'Come on, man. You've shut Jagger and me out. Do you think I want to go to the casino staff to find out what you're up to? How you're living?'

More guilt. I want him to go. I want to be alone. No, I want to be with Cora but hell, I don't know if even Cora would be able to pull me out of this.

'I'm living fine.'

'Sure you are. You're getting wasted every chance

you get, travelling non-stop, and fucking anything that moves. You're *completely* fine.'

I pace to the fridge, wrenching the door open, pulling out another beer, cracking the top off it before I answer him. I know I should calm down. I know this is coming from a good place. I know he's worried—that he's been worried about me since I told them both about Ryan.

'Listen—' he sighs, slows his voice down, and I know Theo well enough to know he's trying to 'manage' me '—what Dad did—'

'We'll never know what Dad did. He let me live with you. But why? For what reason?'

'Maybe we'll never know,' Theo says, and something inside of me snaps but I don't give in to it. I've said it often enough—the not knowing is what's killing me. I hate it. I hate that I have no anchor to the reality of my being.

'He raised you as his son. He wanted you.' After a slight pause, 'He loved you as much as he loved anyone: as much as he was capable of loving.'

'Do you remember what he was like with me?' I pierce Theo with a dark stare and feel the truth of my deepest-held feelings slipping through me, falling inexorably towards the surface, towards a light I want to ignore.

Theo, at least, has the grace to nod. 'He was a bastard to you a lot of the time.'

'You say he loved me? Honestly, half the time it felt like he hated me.'

'He expected a lot of you because he knew you were capable of it.'

'I was taught not to cry, not to get angry, not to care about anything other than his damned business. I was taught not to *feel* anything.'

'But now you feel everything and you have no idea what to do with that. You think you're the only one he screwed up? Jesus, he had no time for any of us. You're lucky you got any attention from him at all.'

'Lucky?' The word is wrenched from me.

'Fine.' Theo holds his hands up appeasingly. 'Not lucky, but we can't rewrite the past. We can't wake Dad up from the dead and ask him what the hell he was thinking. You've hired an investigator and maybe one day he'll have the answers you need but you can't keep freezing us out until then, man.'

'What do you want from me?' The words emerge deadpan. Calm. But the kind of calm that's like the eye of a storm. I can feel it raging inside of me, I can feel how close it is to bursting.

'You have to get a grip on your emotions, Holden. Don't let your feelings control you, block them out. Think only with your head, not your heart.'

My head though is the problem. I work in facts and logic and I can't make sense of any of this. I lock my gaze to Theo's, wondering if he has a sense for how overwhelmed I am by this.

'I wish you'd just leave me the fuck alone. Just let it go. Let *me* go.'

He stares at me for several seconds then shakes

his head. 'You're such an ass. I'll pick you up in the morning. Be ready and be sober.'

My temper explodes. Not immediately. No, immediately I concentrate on getting drunk. I'm halfway through a bottle of Scotch before my anger rises, unstoppable, a force that is unending, unconquerable.

I'm a child again, being left on the doorstep of Ryan Hart, my life changed for ever with the realisation that my mother doesn't want me. That I'm too much for her, that I interrupt her lifestyle with my needing food and conversation, my endless barrage of questions.

I'm a child again, breaking up a marriage, breaking up a family. I'm a child, and then a Hart, raised alongside Jagger, then Theo.

I'm twenty-nine, sitting opposite Barrett—not just a close family friend but also a lawyer who handles our family business. He's frowning, and suddenly saying words that make little sense.

'There seems to be some dispute as to your parentage.'

There was no dispute in the end. Only a lie. A lie that my father perpetuated until the day he died. Why? Why in the world would the most selfish bastard on the planet take in a kid that wasn't his? Raise that child. Lie to me.

I am left with a thousand questions and no answers, no answers within reach. Even the investigator I engaged when this first happened can't help.

Month after month he sends me a small statement. 'Still digging. Nil so far.'

Who's my biological father? Why did Ryan take me in? Why didn't he tell me the truth?

Did my real father know about me? Or did my mother lie to him? Did she lie to Ryan? God, the not knowing is the hardest thing of all.

I think of Cora out of nowhere, of the way she dismissed her own mother so easily. *'Being a parent is about more than biology.'* Is she right? Should I only care about the fact Ryan raised me? Should I ignore the fact he also lied to me? That the only chance to know any damned thing about my parentage died with him.

I can't.

I'm glad, for Cora's sake, that she can make her peace so easily with a mother who didn't want her. I'm glad she's not being eaten alive by it. I wish I could be more like her, in more ways than one.

Hours later, when I collapse into bed, I see my phone on charge. There's a message from her.

I'm halfway to drunk. I can barely read it. But I lift it up anyway, staring at the screen until the letters make sense.

Goodnight. x

On the one hand, the smart thing to do would be to ignore her. Goodnight text messages with smiley faces and little kiss marks are sweet and kind and I don't want that.

But I do want Cora. I *need* her.
I lift the phone closer and open a reply.

What are you up to?

Her response is immediate.

Going to sleep.

Send me a photo?

A pause, and then...

Of me in bed?

She adds a little flame emoji.

Yes.

I wonder if she'll do it and I practically hold my breath waiting, wondering in the very back of my mind why it matters to me so much.

My pyjamas are incredibly sexy. I don't know if you're prepared for this.

A grin slips across my face. A second later it grows broader. Cora's wearing pyjamas that bear the logo of the airline she used to fly with—the type handed out to first-class passengers.

Beautiful.

She sends back an eye-rolling emoji.

I load the photo up again, zooming in to her eyes. They're beautiful eyes and even like this, trapped in a photograph, I feel so much warmth coming from her it makes my gut tense.

Do I get a photo?

I think about snapping one, but don't. If I can see only warmth in her eyes then she would easily see coldness in mine and I don't want to show her that right now.

I take a picture of the view instead, and add a caption.

Wish you were here.

She doesn't reply, and in the morning, when I re-read our exchange, I'm glad for that. My comment was too much, given what we are. I load up the photo of her and find myself staring at it while I make my morning coffee, safe in my ability to do so because in four days I plan to be on my jet and winging my way away from this place.

'We have to talk.'

It's Jagger this time, drawing me out of the living room onto his penthouse balcony. From here, I can see the casino. I can see all the way to my balcony. If I squint, I can see where Cora was standing, wrapped in a blanket, taking photos of the sunrise, just two days ago.

'What's up?' My voice is deep, my tone cold. I see Jagger's frown. My gut twists.

'Nothing's up, man. We just haven't seen you in a while.' He comes to stand beside me, staring out at the harbour. We stood like this at the funeral—Dad's. Ryan's. Not talking, silent, side by side, shoulder to shoulder.

'Listen—' he sighs, drags one hand through his blond hair, curves the other around the balcony and leans forward a little '—Theo's worried about you.'

'No shit.'

'We both are.'

Guilt, I'm experienced with. It slices me like a blade.

'There's no need. I'm fine.'

He makes a sound that is so familiar. A sarcastic laugh; I've heard it often. From him, from me, from Theo. It's one of those traits we share, traits I now realise have more to do with environment than biology, because we are biologically distinct.

'You're all torn up, and I don't know how to fix it. Theo says time, but I don't know. I feel like enough time's passed but you don't seem to be dealing with it at all. If anything, you're getting worse.'

'I'm fine,' I reiterate, glaring out at the harbour. 'Look, man, just drop it.' I look over my shoulder. Theo's inside with Grace, doing a FaceTime call with Asha so she can see Felicity. Perfect, happy families.

I grind my teeth, looking back at Jagger. 'It doesn't matter.'

'It matters to me. You're my brother—'

I feel an insane urge to punch him. I don't. 'I'm just some guy you grew up with.'

'For Christ's sake, stop it. We both know that's not true.'

'Bullshit. I know it's true. I've always known it was true.'

'What?' He stares at me and I realise what I said, shaking my head.

'I don't mean that. I just mean...' I search for the words, my mind not quite catching up. 'I've always been different to you. I felt different and, deep down, I think I knew I *was* different. Ryan was way harder on me than he was on you guys—'

'He knew you were smarter than Theo and me put together. He wanted you to make the most of your potential.'

But I see it so much more clearly now. 'No, he didn't want me to end up like my mother.' My eyes narrow. 'Or maybe he didn't want me to end up like my father. Maybe he knew who my father is—was— maybe he knew something about him that made him ride me extra hard. I'll never know, but at least the way he treated me makes sense now. He always set me apart from you guys, made me feel different, and I was.'

Jagger's face contorts with emotion. He stares at me for several beats and then shakes his head. 'You're making yourself feel like this. I'm standing here right now telling you you're our brother. I don't care what some DNA test says. It doesn't change anything for me.'

'That's great for you, but for me everything's different. I wish you and Theo would just accept that I have a right to feel this way.' I straighten, fully aware I'm being an ass, torching every bridge I can see. And even though I might say I don't care, I do, because I don't want to stand here and fight with Jagger.

'Look… I've got to go.'

'Go where?'

'Anywhere but here.'

Cora.

'Nice,' Jagger snaps, but he reaches out and grabs my arm, jerking me around so I instinctively react, lifting a hand to push at his shoulder. His eyes spark with mine and years of frustration—frustrations with me—come to the fore.

He lifts his hands—both of them—and shoves them at my chest. I react on instinct again, this time lifting a fist and bringing it down on his face. He lunges backwards and then lurches forward, his own fist lifting. I dodge his first hook but he lands another, this one crunching against my cheekbone so I taste blood in my mouth and I'm so glad—glad for the pain, the blinding shock.

He lunges for me and I grip his arms but then Theo is there, pulling at me, shouting at Jagger, separating us, and I hear a baby's crying and Grace's voice, panic and pain, and I stop immediately, stepping back as if waking from a nightmare. My brother's face is bruised—I did that. I lift a finger to my own cheek and it comes away bloodied. Jagger's nursing his fist in the palm of his hand and Theo's looking from one of us to the other as though we've lost our minds.

It's on the tip of my tongue to apologise because, deep down, I know this is wrong. But I don't. I can't. I don't want to look at Jagger or Theo right now. I stalk towards the sliding glass doors but as I reach them I pause, my eyes reaching Grace's. 'I'm sorry.' She doesn't deserve this.

Her features show sympathy. 'It's fine. Don't go. Let me get you some ice.'

I shake my head.

'Please, Holden. Just stay a minute. Let me make sure you're okay.'

I make a hollow, sarcastic laughing sound, so like Jagger's that I wince. 'Okay? I will be.' And then, because I see hurt in her eyes, I reach out and touch her wrist. 'I am sorry.'

'I know.' Her eyes shift, moving to Jagger, and their connection hits me. Their uniqueness, their understanding.

Feeling like an outsider—and deserving that—I move away quickly. I don't look at Felicity as I pass the crib. I don't think I can bear that today.

I need to see you.

My heart speeds up a notch. I sit down on the windowsill, basking in the afternoon sunshine and the dust motes that are visible along its path, reread-ing his text.

I smile without really meaning to and load up the keypad.

Really?

Yeah. I'm downstairs.

My heart races now. I shift a little, looking over my shoulder and, sure enough, there's a black Range Rover parked just a few car spaces down. The win-dows are tinted jet black but as I watch he lowers the window by a crack.

I look around the apartment, my pulse throbbing. It's been two days since I was last at his place. He's not the only one with needs—mine are here too, threatening to engulf me.

I hesitate for the briefest moment and then:

Want to come in?

He doesn't type a response, but I see the door open and a second later he steps out. My heart stops rac-ing and just thuds to a halt in my chest. Holy mother of everything I hold dear, he looks...so good I could faint. I mean, seriously. This guy is...black jeans, black leather jacket, dark sunglasses, hair longer than when we first met and a bit messy, like he's been run-ning his hands through it. He doesn't look up as he crosses the street, his stride long, and a second later he's at the front door.

I move quickly, wrenching the door in and staring at him for all of two seconds before he sweeps in and pulls me into his arms, dragging my body against his. He takes like rum and cigarettes, so I pull back, look at him again. His eyes don't meet mine but his mouth does, searching, seeking, kissing, possessing—a harsh kiss, a kiss born of need and some kind of desperation I can't fathom.

But I don't question it because I have needs too, remember, and I hear the ticking of a stopwatch all the time—he's leaving soon. And he's stirring everything up inside me so I can't think straight, I don't want to think straight. He lifts me, holding me against him—always making me feel like I weigh nothing when this is so not true—carrying me deeper into the apartment.

I push a hand behind us. 'Bedroom.'

But he ignores me, stepping into the lounge and moving to the sofa. His hands are fumbling with his jeans, pushing them down before he's lifting my skirt, finding my underpants and lowering them as he kisses me back into the sofa.

'I need you.' It's a statement. A sexy, dark, gruff statement but I hear a question in it too and I nod because I need him as well. I need him but not, I think, in the way he needs me.

I push that thought away because it's confusing and deep and not what I want to focus on. There's only this. Him and me.

He pulls on a condom and a second later takes me with a guttural groan, pushing into me so I cry out, arching my back, welcoming him, the speed of this, the urgency. He thrusts hard and I dig my heels in at his back, and neither of us says anything else. There's the sound of my breath rasping, the shift of the sofa against the floor and, finally, a moan from deep in my throat as pleasure bursts over me and I explode. He's right behind me, his own release intense but silent. He drops his head, burying it in the curve of my neck, his breathing hot against my throat, spiced rum filling my senses. I run my hands along his back and now the thoughts that refused to be calmed before slice through me, so I wonder at this, at him, at why he's here, why he's been drinking in the middle of the day.

I wonder about everything.

He pulls away from me, straightening and turning his back on me, zipping his jeans up and moving into the kitchen. A second later he returns, presumably having disposed of the contraceptive.

And he stares at me, his eyes dark, his expression impossible to interpret and it's then that I notice his cheek is marked. There's a red line down it and a hint of bruising.

I frown, standing, easing my skirt down around my hips, ignoring the fact my underpants are somewhere under the sofa. 'Holden? What's happened? You're hurt?'

He doesn't say anything, just looks past me to the clock on the wall. My heart turns over in my chest. I have the strangest feeling that he's going to cry. Except he's not, of course, but there's something within him that calls to me and I ache for him.

'Holden?' I lift a hand to his cheek. He pulls away. Concern perforates my gut. 'Has something happened?'

He shakes his head, then reaches for my hand, squeezing it. 'No. I shouldn't have come here. I'm sorry.'

Sorry? My concern grows. 'Tell me what's going on. What's happened?'

'Nothing.' He drops my hand and steps backwards, looks around, then focuses back on me. 'I'll see you later, okay?'

I don't follow him. A part of me wants to, but somehow I know he wouldn't welcome it. He needs space. From what? Has he been in a fight? At the casino? Or with someone he knows? And now a niggling concern stretches through me, growing so I can't ignore it, and I don't want to ignore it.

There is an intensity about him, and a darkness, that I've felt many times. I think back over the course of our relationship and try to picture him laughing, a carefree laugh, happiness, relaxation, and I can't see it.

Worry trips through me. What's going on?

It doesn't matter that this is temporary, I'd be an automaton to not feel worry, to not feel concern for him.

The afternoon bleeds into night and my tummy continues to knot with tension.

Finally, I reach for my phone, load his number up and hesitate for only a moment before pressing 'call'.

It rings and it rings. No answer. My worry grows. I bite on my lip, telling myself not to think about him, telling myself this was meant to be light and fun, just great sex while he's in Australia and before I get on with the rest of my life—he definitely wasn't meant to take up so much of my mental space. And yet I can't stop thinking about him.

So I try to call him again at midnight, and this time he answers. There's a lot of noise behind the call, like he's in a bar or something. When he speaks, his voice is slurred.

'Hey, baby.'

My heart turns over in my chest, but the worry cuts through me. 'Hey.'

'Whatcha doing?'

I rub my toe over the grout of the kitchen tiles. 'Just…about to go to bed.'

'Sounds good.'

I bite down on my lip, choosing my words carefully. He speaks first.

'Want company?'

Do I? I want to know he's okay. I want to know what happened earlier today. And yeah, I want to see him. Knowing he's going back to America makes me want to milk every moment I can with him.

'Sure.' I look around the apartment and, for some reason, decide against inviting him over. 'I'll come to you. The casino?'

'I'm in the VIP bar. Ask for me when you arrive.'

CHAPTER ELEVEN

Four nights left in Sydney

IT'S LOUD. MUSIC IS PLAYING—jazz music, but it's still noisy—and the bar, despite being a VIP space, is busier than I imagined. I probably pictured Holden on his own, sitting in the middle of a huge space, but no. I recognise the crowd as I enter. Not individuals, but the type. I've worked in first class cabins long enough to recognise people who live and breathe money and that's what I'm surrounded by.

I'm under-dressed. A pair of jeans with holes at the knees and a singlet top underneath a red woollen jacket I bought in Hong Kong a couple of years ago; at least I slipped on a pair of stilettos and a coat of lippie before leaving the house. My eyes scan the crowd and ping to him almost instantly.

My heart thumps.

My breath stops.

Everything around me goes silent and all I do—all I want to do—is stare at him. In the midst of the noise he's alone, and still. There is palpable happiness in the atmosphere that makes it easy to spot the contrast in his mood. Something shifts in my gut. A pain, and an awareness. He sits at the bar, unbearably handsome, a tumbler of Scotch cradled in his hands, his eyes fixed straight ahead.

I begin to move towards Holden but before I can reach him I pause again, wanting simply to observe him, to see him like this. I don't know why but I feel like if I look for long enough a piece of the puzzle will fall into place and I'll understand what's bothering him.

As I watch, he lifts the Scotch, bringing it to his lips and hovering it there. I swallow in time with him, so I can almost taste the alcohol, then start to move again, weaving through the last few people until I'm beside him.

'Hey.' My heart *kerthunks* against my chest. He shifts, turning on the bar stool so his legs form a frame around me and I can see his face properly. There's a definite bruise on his cheek. I look at it for a moment, then concentrate on his eyes.

He stares at me for a beat, almost like he's forgotten who I am, or what I'm doing here. Like he's surprised to see me. That makes no sense. I lift a hand to his shoulder. He's wearing a long-sleeve shirt, good-quality cotton. I run my fingers over it a little, feeling his warmth beneath it, feeling him.

'Hey. You came.'

My smile turns quizzical. 'Didn't we agree I would?'

His hand's on my hip, lifting my shirt a little so his fingertips connect with the bare flesh at my side.

'Yeah. I just thought—' He shakes his head. 'Want a drink?'

Do I? Not really. But there's something about the idea of sitting in a bar with Holden that persuades me. We've only been together in private until now. There's a novelty to sitting here with him, so I nod. 'Sure.' I scan the range of liquor bottles against the bar wall. 'Just a soda.'

He lifts one brow and I can't tell if his look is amused, mocking, disapproving, or a combination of all three, but he lifts his hand and a bar guy practically sprints over. 'Yes, Mr Hart?'

'A soda.'

He turns back to me so I'm left to smile at the bar guy and offer a word of thanks.

'Have a seat.' He gestures behind me, to a stool. I pull it nearer, planting my bottom onto it. Holden shifts his seat even closer, so his legs still surround me, his whole body like a frame of warmth and wants.

'What happened?'

He quirks a brow, silent.

'Your face. It's changed colour.'

He shifts his hand, his long fingers running over his cheekbone, his lips a gash, a frown chiselled deep on his face.

'Holden?'

'Nothing. A stupid fight.'

'With whom?'

'It doesn't matter.' He reaches for his Scotch, putting the glass between us and closing his eyes as he throws it back. He holds the empty glass, looking at it a moment.

'I think it does.' I lift a hand, curling it over his cheek, my thumb gentle on his flesh. 'Whoever it was punched you.'

He lifts his gaze to my face; something in his eyes sends a chill along my spine. 'It was a fight. I punched him, he punched me. End of story.'

'I don't think so.' I take his empty glass and put it on the bar, then rest my hand on his. 'I've seen the security you have around you. So this wasn't just some random guy on the street, right? It's someone you know?'

A muscle throbs at the base of his jaw and his eyes are the stormiest shade of grey I've ever seen. 'I said it doesn't matter.'

A fresh Scotch is placed in front of him without Holden needing to ask. I look at it, frown, wondering how often that's happened tonight. He doesn't seem drunk, but he's a big guy; presumably he can handle his liquor.

He had alcohol on his breath when he came to my place this afternoon. Has he been drinking non-stop since then?

'I think it does.'

There's wariness in his expression, like he's a trapped animal and I'm his pursuer, and I don't want him to look at me like that. Even worse, I don't want him to push me away, and I have a strange feeling that if I go too hard at him, ask too many questions, he'll get up and leave. *He's leaving anyway*, a little voice reminds me—unnecessarily. There are only four nights until he's due to fly out of Sydney, and the idea no longer fills me with a sense of relief, like this will come to an end. It fills me with panic.

I try not to show that in my voice. 'We don't have to talk about it.'

He reaches for the Scotch as though he knew it would be there, as though he needs it, and I feel a great welling of sadness.

Inexplicable and absolute.

I've seen compulsive drinking before. I know how to recognise it, and now I recognise it absolutely in Holden. Pain lashes me. Pain at the memories of my father, pain at the idea of Holden—dynamic, intelligent, compelling Holden—being held captive to alcohol.

It's a sadness that almost makes me lose my metaphorical footing. I stare at him, realisation spreading through me, and I'm the one who wants to run away. I want to get up and turn my back on him, because what I absolutely refuse to do is let someone into my life who's battling the same demons that killed my father. I've been so careful on this front, so suspicious of alcohol, so studious to avoid parties and events where alcohol is the main theme. And somehow I let Holden into my life—my soul?—without noticing that he's almost always drinking. He's so overwhelming, that's all. He drowned all my senses from that very first meeting so I couldn't think clearly. He's like a frequency jammer. And now? I'm seeing clearly and doing nothing.

Panic makes it hard to breathe.

'It was Jagger.'

It takes me a second to connect the random threads of information. 'Jagger? Your brother? He hit you?'

He lifts a hand to his cheek. 'Not very well. Fatherhood's made him soft.' His smile lacks humour.

'Why did he hit you?'

'We argued.'

I move closer to him, needing contact. 'What about?' I lift my own fingers to his cheek, tracing the bruise, wincing at the colour there.

He catches my hand, his eyes clashing with mine. 'Life. My choices. His choices.'

It's a suitably vague response. I ignore it. 'You've done something he doesn't agree with?'

His lips shift into a grimace. 'You could say that.'

'What…'

'Just leave it, Cora. It's a family thing.'

My heart stings. A family thing. The words shouldn't have such an impact but they do. I feel as though he's pushed a line between us, reminding me of my place in his life.

As if to underscore that, a second later he leans closer, his lips crushing to mine. 'Come upstairs with me.'

I want to tell him to go to hell, I want to demand he stays right where he is and tells me everything I want to know, but in the midst of that I want to kiss him and hold him, to be held by him and kissed by him, to feel the passion that's capable of sweeping any pain from my mind and heart.

He takes my hand, pulling me to standing, and for a second he simply stares at me as though he's unable to stop. He stares at my eyes and my heart quickens, my insides melt, and then he's pulling me behind him, his hand holding mine, his step long so I have to walk quickly to keep up.

Security guards stand at a roped-off section. They unclip one of the thick burgundy ropes as we approach. We walk through as another guard presses a button for the elevator. The doors open after only a minute and we move inside. As soon as the doors are shut Holden's kissing me, one hand lifting to curve around my throat, his thumb brushing the base of my jaw as though he can't help himself, his tongue probing my mouth, his big, strong body pushing me against the wall, pinning me there so I can't move, can barely breathe, and definitely can't think straight.

His kiss is everything I need—reassurance, promise, hope, everything. I surrender to it even as my brain is screaming at me that he's too big, too much, that I've become too consumed by him. I kiss him back though, trying to lift up against the wall of the elevator, trying to get him closer to me. His head presses to mine, his kiss intense, and then he swears, cocking his head towards the control panel to see how many floors there are to go. Not many and the elevator moves quickly but his urgency sears me. As soon as the doors ping open he's lifting me, carrying me and kissing me through the penthouse. We barely make it to the bedroom. His hands push at my clothes, ripping my shirt as he fumbles it from my body. He utters a guttural oath as he strips himself naked with the same imperative, barely pausing to sheathe himself before lifting me, wrapping my legs around his back and driving into me, making me cry out with pleasure and surprise, with blatant need.

He steps sideways, pushing my back to a wall so I'm supported by it and him, and then he thrusts into me, desperate, hungry, insatiable, mine.

Mine.

The word echoes through me with every shift of his hard cock. Pleasure radiates inside my blood. I'm not conscious of anything except the beauty of this feeling. I run my hands through his hair, kissing him, all of me all of his. His hands roam my body, his hands rough on my breasts, his touch perfect.

He swears, moves his mouth to the side of my throat and buries his lips there, kissing me then nipping his teeth over my flesh, and I groan, pleasure threatening to consume me. My orgasm is so close I can feel every inch of it. I dig my nails into his shoulders and hold on and then I'm screaming his name at the top of my voice, completely overpowered by the way he makes me feel.

He holds me as I explode, his body my comfort. He stands where he is, his breathing ragged, as though he's trying to keep a grip on his own feelings, his own desire rampant and almost impossible to control, and then he carries me to the bed, sitting on the edge of it, positioning me on his lap. His head is the same height as my breasts; he leans forward, drawing a nipple between his teeth as he begins to move again, each thrust of his hips driving him deep inside me, his cock so perfect for me that I wonder how I ever doubted he'd fit. It's as though we're designed for this, him and me.

I tilt my head back, arching my breasts forward, so while his mouth tortures one nipple his hand plays with the other. A thousand butterflies explode through me. I grind my hips down, wanting so much more of this, knowing I'll never grow tired of how he makes me feel, knowing I need this and him, and that life without Holden in it will leave me, in an irredeemable way, empty.

The thought is unwelcome. I ignore it. Tomorrow will come and another tomorrow beyond that, and eventually a day will come that is devoid of Holden, and any prospect of seeing Holden. But it's not today. It's not tomorrow. There's still time, and I intend to utilise it—and him—for as long as I can.

He cries my name out against my breasts. I roll my hips and he swears, and the power I hold thrills through me.

His weakness for me is abundantly clear. I revel in that knowledge, and I revel in this—him—us, even as fear is like a drumbeat pursuing me mercilessly.

I catch his face with my hands, lifting it, and as I feel his control being obliterated I kiss him, my mouth dominating his for a change, my kiss driving us inexorably to a mutual release. He groans my name into my mouth now, breathing the word deep inside of me, and I swallow it, holding it there, not realising that the combination of two syllables are beating a tireless march towards my heart.

It's dark outside. We lie together in silence for so long I wonder if he's fallen asleep. I stare at the ceiling and I contemplate getting up, grabbing my things and going home.

Escaping.

Hours after meeting him in the bar, I am spent, and I'm exhausted and now, with passion satiated, I'm scared.

Yes. I'm scared.

Because I've found myself in exactly the kind of position I wanted to avoid. I don't have a good track record with relationships. In fact, I've come to accept that I have terrible taste in men. That's why this—with Holden—was going to be so perfect! Because it was casual and easy—sex so unbelievably hot it didn't leave room for anything so banal as feelings and emotions.

This isn't the time for me to be getting involved with *anyone*. For once in my life I'm going to do what I need to make my dreams come true, and a broken heart isn't part of that.

But, despite that, I feel.

I feel deep in my soul, my bones, my heart.

I shift a little, just so I can see him better. His eyes are open, staring at the same ceiling I was just studying, his face as serious as mine. My heart plummets.

This isn't easy or uncomplicated, not for either of us.

I push up onto one elbow, a frown on my face. 'I didn't know your brother was in Sydney.'

He turns to face me, his eyes swirling with feelings I don't understand. 'They both are, at the moment.'

'Living here?'

'Jagger lives here.' I lift my fingers to his bruise; his eyes close.

'Not the other one?'

'Theo,' he supplies. 'No. He splits his time between New York and Paris.'

I nod. 'That sounds glamorous.'

He doesn't answer. For a while, there's only the sound of our breathing, and then the rustle of fabric as I shift a bit, lying down beside him, my head on his chest. His heart thumps with mesmerising timing. 'I'm sorry you and Jagger fought.'

'We've been fighting for a long time. Today it just got physical.'

'You don't have a good relationship?'

Fingers that were running the length of my spine stop, perfectly still, between my shoulder blades for a moment before resuming their trajectory. 'No.'

'What about with your other brother?'

'Theo,' he supplies once more.

'Right. Are you close to him?' I lift my chin onto his chest, propping up so I can see into his eyes.

'Not particularly.'

'Why not?'

'Can't you just accept that we're not?'

I frown. 'No.'

His laugh is a dull sound. 'You'd make a great spy.'

'I'm not spying. I'm trying to get to know you.'

I ignore the futility of that, my heart hurting a little inside of me.

'Unless it's some kind of state secret,' I prompt when he doesn't speak. Still, he doesn't answer. 'They're your brothers,' I say gently. 'I don't know what happened between you but I do know that you're lucky to have them. You have family and presumably they love you—why not try to fix whatever's going on between you?'

'That's idealistic.'

'And idealism is bad?'

'It's misplaced in this situation.' He shifts a little, gently, so I move off his chest as he sits on the edge of the bed, his back to me.

'I'm sorry if my idealism offends you.'

He stiffens. 'It's not you.' I'm silent, waiting for him to continue. 'It's the whole situation. It's hopeless.'

'Why?' I try to imagine what could have happened to split three brothers asunder. I have no familiarity with family dynamics. I run through the possibilities, discounting most of them immediately. I don't have enough information but, even if I did, nothing would have prepared me for his next statement.

'They're not my real brothers.' I wait for those words to spread through me, wondering if they'll make any kind of sense. 'I found out a while ago that Jagger and Theo are brothers; I'm not. I'm not really a Hart, Cora. That's what we fought about today. That's what we fight about every day.'

CHAPTER TWELVE

FUCK. FUCK. FUCK. I want to pull the words back as soon as I've said them. It's like the removing of a dam wall—once done, it's impossible to put it back in place. I've said something to Cora I had no intention of saying and yet the words burst from me without my consent, certainly without my forethought.

And now she knows.

She knows what only a handful of people in the world do. Fewer than ten. Jagger, Grace, Theo, Asha, Ryan—dead—my mother—dead—the PI I hired, Barrett, our lawyer and family friend, me... My dad? My real dad? I have no idea if he knows I exist. Did he choose not to know me? Not to love me?

Ice fills my veins.

'What?'

I don't look at her. I can't. But I feel her eyes boring into my back, determined and sharp. I can see them without even looking at her.

'Holden?' A rustle of the sheets. She moves, her hand on my shoulder, her body close. She's warm; I'm not. 'What do you mean?'

I swallow convulsively, stare straight ahead at the twinkling lights of Sydney. 'I was raised a Hart, but I'm not.'

'I don't understand...'

Of course she doesn't.

'Ryan Hart took me in as a kid. He raised me as his son. Told everyone I was, so I thought—*everyone* thought I was. I broke up his marriage to Jagger's mom because I was living proof of his many, many infidelities.' I clamp my mouth shut, disgust filling me. 'I have no idea why he did that, Cora. I mean, I'm not his kid. He didn't have to do that. None of it makes any sense.'

She's frowning. It emanates from her to me, her thoughts spinning loudly. 'How do you know he's not your dad?'

'After Ryan died, a friend of ours, who happens to be a lawyer for the firm we use, approached me. He had some paperwork from years ago—they'd been buried in a heap of other stuff; Barrett only found them by chance, going through Dad's old files. He didn't know about this or he would have told me— we've always been close.'

She's quiet for a moment and then, gently, 'What were the documents?'

'Legal adoption papers.'

'So your dad—Ryan—adopted you?'

'He tried to. My biological dad would have had to give up his custodial rights, and he didn't. I don't know if he couldn't, if he was dead or lost, I don't even know if they were able to contact him, but it never happened.' My expression tightens. 'Which proves only that Ryan knew all along—I'm not his son. He knowingly lied to me.'

She comes to sit beside me, her hand on my thigh. 'To protect you.'

'You don't know Ryan.' I dismiss the very idea. 'He was a self-serving bastard. There's no way he raised me out of the goodness of his heart. Which leaves me to wonder why. Did he know who my father was? Did he hate him? Was raising me some kind of revenge? Was it to punish him? To punish my mother? I'll never know, Cora. In fact, the only thing I know for certain is that I don't belong.'

The words are sharp between us. There's sympathy in her eyes, such sympathy that I want to punch something. I have known this sympathy before and I resent it as much now as I did then.

'Don't.' The word is a warning.

'Don't what?'

'Don't look at me like I'm a kid whose balloon just got popped. It's fine. *I'm* fine. It's just one of those things.'

More sympathy. Fucking great. 'I'm serious, Cora.'

'How can you say that?'

'What?'

'That you're fine. You're obviously not fine; only a sociopath would be.' She stands up, stands right in front of me, hands on her hips, naked and beautiful and like some kind of defiant angel. 'To think you're one thing all your life and then find out you're not? You must feel an incredible sense of betrayal.'

'Must I?' The words are sharper than I intended. I regret that. Cora's completely right, and none of this is her fault. Nonetheless, I hold my pose, rigid and determined.

'Yeah.' She answers my challenge directly. 'Don't you?'

'Feel a sense of betrayal? I couldn't tell you.' I drag a hand through my hair. 'I feel a sense of anger. Blind, all-consuming anger. Like I could strangle Ryan if he wasn't already dead. I feel angry at everyone and everything, all the time. I hate my brothers—I hate them. I hate that they keep wanting me to stop being mad, like one day I'll wake up and be "normal" again, like they don't realise I've never felt normal a day in my life.'

Tears fill her eyes. Just a little—enough to dampen them and make my gut twist. But it feels good. Hurting her, pushing her away, it's the one thing I know I do well, and I do it to everyone who's ever been in my life, to anyone who looks in danger of caring about me.

'Even as a kid I was angry. Different. I was never one of them. At least now I know why.'

'Feeling like you belong is important.' Her voice is quiet, raw, as though she can ever understand what this feels like. I try to tell myself I'm not angry at Cora, except, shit, I'm angry at everyone right now. Everyone.

'Speaking from experience?'

She understands. I'm taking it out on her and her look speaks of annoyance, but also patience. It's such a contradiction, but then that's Cora. Complex, contradictory, beautiful Cora.

'Well, yeah. I guess so. As a kid, I was always different. I didn't have a mum, and my dad was half-loaded most of my life. My clothes often weren't clean, my tummy rumbled in class, my hair was like a bird's nest. I learned how to do a lot of stuff really young. I had to, to take care of him and myself. But those early years, when I was little, six or seven, I got teased mercilessly. I had no friends. I still remember that feeling, hiding under a bush at school so no one would see me and call me names.'

My desire to punch something increases. Cora going through that makes me feel enraged.

'I hate that.' It's honest. It feels good to be honest.

'It's not the same thing, though,' she murmurs, putting her hand on my shoulder, her fingertips somehow breathing into my heart, slowing it down, calming it. 'Your mom turned her back on you. You grew up with that sense of being unwanted, and all the worse because you'd known your mother, you loved her, and so her turning her back on you was an actual choice not to have you in her life.'

She's pressed her finger to the crux of what hurt so damned bad.

'You must have missed her,' she continues, like she has a hotline to my soul.

'I wasn't allowed to miss her. Ryan didn't approve of that.'

She opens her mouth to say something, closes it again, then, after a second, 'Maybe he thought that was better for you. It's misguided, but perhaps he thought it would be easier if you just…forgot your mother.'

'I told you, Ryan wasn't guided by affection for me. I became his possession and he wanted to control me absolutely. I have no idea why, but that motivated everything he did.'

She mulls this over. 'He still chose to raise you, to treat you as his own.'

My spine straightens. 'Yes.' I can't argue with her there. I was raised a Hart in every way—he left a third of the business to me in his will; there was no indication I wasn't one of his children.

'Why did you and Jagger fight today?'

My heart thumps; her eyes narrow. 'I don't even know.'

'You said they want you to be "normal". Have you talked to them? Really talked? Told them all this?'

I jerk my face away, looking towards the windows. 'I've told them I need time.' The words are defensive.

'It sounds like they've given you time.'

I bristle. Cora taking their side? Hell, no.

'And what have you been doing since you found out?' She's relentless.

'What do you mean?'

'Look at me.' A soft challenge. I ignore it at first but slowly lift my head and then stand, so I'm at least several inches taller than her. I don't know what's in her eyes. Sympathy. Sorrow. Affection. Fear? Of me?

She sucks in a deep breath and expels it slowly. 'Are you using alcohol to deal with this, Holden?'

I stare at her, no idea how to answer such a direct question. 'God, Cora. Are you kidding me?'

'Listen to me.' There's urgency in her voice. 'I know about this. I *know*. My dad—he was a genius. I mean a proper, bona fide genius. His IQ was off the charts; he got taken over to Yale on a scholarship when he was fifteen. But the pressure burned him out. The constant activity in his brain was horrifying. He could only silence his thoughts, his intellect, by drinking and smoking weed, and so he did both, and he got so addicted to the blunting of his mind that he couldn't function without alcohol any more. I get it. Alcohol anaesthetises you to the pain you're feeling but it's not a real solution. It might help right now, but you have to get *proper* help. You need to speak to someone. Me. Your brothers. A therapist. Someone who can help you unpack your emotions, who can make you see that, despite what your mother did, and your biological father's absence from your life, you are a worthy person, completely deserving of love, and that needs to start with loving yourself.'

Her voice cracks a little in the last sentence and her words bring me to the edge of reason; they stoke all the fears inside of me, and all the anger too.

'I don't need you to psychoanalyse me, Cora.' I say her name heavily.

'Well, someone needs to. I doubt you ever recovered after your mom left you, and now you have all this to deal with and how can that not take a toll? How could you possibly be a normal guy, looking for normal things in relationships?'

'I don't want a relationship; I told you.'

'So what do you want? What do you need from me?'

'I need you for sex.' The words surprise me. They sure as hell surprise her. Even as I throw them at her, I feel like a fire is being lit in my gut. I'm burning alive and I need to put the fire out but I can't. I can only fan the flames, make it worse.

She stands her ground. But I need her to go. This was a mistake. There's a reason I 'fuck and forget'. I let her get to know me, to know too much about me, and I don't want anyone close to me right now. I need her to go and for this to be over. I wish I'd never met her.

'Like that's all this is?' she challenges, her eyes showing both hurt and scorn.

'What else do you want it to be?'

She frowns, her own uncertainties obviously pulling at her. 'I don't know. But it's more than just sex. Maybe that's what we both thought this would be, going into it, but it's different now. I'm different, and you're different.'

Even if that were true, it wouldn't matter. I have only the ability to hurt Cora, and the sooner she realises that the better. 'I'm the same man I was the day we met and I want the same things from you.'

'And that's sex?'

'Yes.' I'm exasperated. It shows in my voice.

'Damned sex. And soon I'll go back to the States and forget you exist. Because that's what I do.'

She recoils a little but doesn't otherwise move. 'That sounds like a great way to live your life.'

I grind my teeth together.

'And ignoring everyone who cares about you?'

Something in the tone of her voice digs inside of me. 'Are you saying *you* care about me?'

Her eyes flash and it's not until a moment later I realise I've taunted her, the question mocking.

'I didn't say that.' Her skin is pale. God, I'm hurting her and I need her to leave just so I stop. I hate this—I'm too good at ruining things and I don't want to ruin this, to hurt her. I don't want her memories of me to include this night, this argument.

'I was talking about your brothers.'

'So you're saying you *don't* care about me?'

She frowns. 'Why would I be standing here going through this if I didn't care? I care, Holden. I hate seeing you like this. I hate seeing—' She stops and her eyes are suspiciously moist but she blinks quickly and her tears are gone again. 'I hate seeing anyone turn to alcohol as a cure-all, because it's not. You think it's helping? It's destroying you, destroying your life, and if you don't get a hold of yourself you're going to wind up completely alone, or dead. I don't want that for you.'

I don't know how to respond to that. 'I'm not an alcoholic.' The need to reassure her comes out of nowhere. 'I'm not your father.'

'When was the last day you didn't drink?'

I close my eyes for a moment. 'You see everything as so black and white. Haven't you ever done something that was bad for you?'

'Plenty of things! And, what's more, I've had a front row seat to watching someone I love destroy themselves so I know a train crash in motion when I see it.'

'I'm not your father.' The words roar out of me, repeating them important in some way.

She's unflinching, that defiant angel all over again. 'His demons were different to yours, but you're dodging them in the same ways.' And then she puts a hand on my cheek, the gentle touch completely unexpected in the midst of the words we're throwing at each other. 'Don't you think I wanted to put my head in the sand, after the baby?'

I force myself to meet her eyes because she's showing such courage and strength and it feels like the least I can do.

'I would have done anything to help me forget.' Her eyes close for a moment and her face carries the burden of remembering, torment in her features. 'I felt my son move inside me, flipping and flopping, I nourished him and had him measured through my belly at each of my prenatal appointments. I readied a room for him, I chose his name, I imagined him into every picture of my future, and then he died and there was no time to prepare. I delivered my baby but never heard him cry.'

Jesus. Something big clogs my throat. Her words are like acid and electricity. Shocking and sharp, eroding everything inside me, making me feel like I don't know a thing about pain.

'I understand the desire to escape. I left home. I ran away in a sense because everything there reminded me of him, of what I'd lost, and I couldn't face it. I haven't stopped travelling for eight years. I barely stood still because, if I did, the memories were there, filling my dreams, making me catch my breath and remember all over again. Only now, eight years later, do I feel ready to pick up the threads of my life again, to start doing what I've always loved, to settle down and face the fact that those memories will always be a part of me, that what I went through isn't going anywhere.'

She's brave and maybe she's right. But she's also wrong. 'It took you eight years,' I say, when there's so much more I want to add. 'Don't I get more time too?'

Her throat moves as she swallows. 'The difference is, you're destroying yourself in the process. The worst I did was fly away. You're annihilating the relationships in your life, and you're destroying yourself.'

'Should relationships be so easy to annihilate?'

She drops her hand, frowning, a line between her brows. She's quiet for a long time, and I find myself staring at her, wondering at the way we're arguing, wondering how I can stop this, fix it—but fixing is way outside my realm of experience.

'No.' There's been such a lengthy pause it takes me a second to recall what I asked.

'But isn't that your problem? You're trying to push your brothers away and they refuse to budge. That's why you're so angry, right? You just want everyone to go away and leave you in peace? So you can drink yourself into a hole?'

I don't say anything.

'You want me to go away too, right? When you said this is just sex, your implication was that you could have sex with anyone you want, that I'm nothing special. That I don't mean anything to you.'

The ground tilts under my feet because I feel the exact opposite of everything she's said and that terrifies me and catches me completely off-guard. And I know I have to push through the haze of this anger to say the right thing: that this really matters.

'Sex is sex.' Great. *That's perfect, jackass.* 'We agreed to that.'

Her eyes are rebuking me, but she nods slowly. 'We agreed to a week. I don't know if we said it would just be sex.'

Did we? Didn't we? I don't know. I can't remember any more. My own thoughts were loud enough that perhaps I only thought I spoke them. 'It's what I meant.' The words come out gruff, defensive. 'I'm sorry if I wasn't clear, but sex is all I've ever been offering, Cora. One week, and this.' I gesture to the bed.

She blanches visibly but a moment later regains her composure, turning to look at me with steel in her eyes. 'I know what you were offering. I thought I was okay with that. To be honest, I had my own reasons for wanting to keep this simple. But it's not and I don't want it to be. You're hurting and I want to help you.' She moves closer and presses her hand to my heart, her palm flat on my chest. 'I don't want you to leave in four days. I don't want you to leave at all.'

It's my turn to blanch. The idea of what she's offering hurts too much to contemplate. It's a normality and reality that's so completely removed from what I'm capable of. Doesn't she see that?

'You're right.' I force myself to speak with detached coolness. 'I've become obsessed with you. When I'm with you everything feels better somehow. You make me forget, but that's not about you. It has nothing to do with you. It's how you make me feel, that's all.'

'And that's nothing to do with me?' she repeats with obvious disbelief.

My temper is growing. I try to control it. 'What do you want me to say, Cora? Do you want me to say you made your way into my heart? I'm afraid to tell you I don't think I have one.'

She flinches. 'You're wrong. No one without a heart would hurt this bad.'

Her words hurt because of the faith she's showing in me, even now.

'I have spent the last eight years completely on my own.' Her voice is a whisper. 'I've made friends, but I let no one get to know me beyond a surface level, no one I trusted. I know what casual feels like, and that's not this. You and I mean something to each other, something different to normal. God, Holden,

I don't want to watch you destroy your life, but nor can I just walk away from you. I need you to listen to me. Stop fighting me and let me care about you, let me help you…'

But that's the last thing I can do. I know what she went through with her father. Like she needs my basket case issues to deal with now. 'No.' The word is firm, unyielding. I take a breath, standing on the edge of a cliff with a fire raging at my back. There's no option but to jump.

'The day I met you, I'd woken up beside some woman whose name I don't even know. I guess I'd picked her up the night before. I honestly can't remember. Maybe it was the day before that.'

I pause a moment, letting those words sink in. 'I like sex. Sex makes me feel good, and yeah, it makes me forget. And sex with you is better than anything I've ever known, but it's still just sex. Nothing more.'

Her face is pale. I flinch inwardly.

'I want you to be happy, Cora. You're an incredible woman, and you deserve to find someone who makes you smile, all the time. But I'm not a part of that—I'm not a part of your life, and you're not a part of mine.'

'You're—'

I lift a hand to silence her. 'I don't *want* this. We had sex. It was fun. But that's all.'

I didn't want to hurt her but I have. I can see it in the way her face shifts and contorts, even in the way she draws her features back into a mask of cool, but her eyes are vibrant, awash with feeling.

I have to cut the cord. For both of our sakes, I need to end this. I should never have let it get this far.

'You should go.' I move away from her, towards the bedroom door. 'I'll have my driver take you home when you're ready.'

I feel her eyes on me but I don't look at her. I stand just outside the door, waiting. I hear her moving around the bedroom, the rustle of fabric as she dresses, a small sniff that almost slices through me, but I harden my heart to it because ultimately this is the best course of action.

No, scratch that, the best course of action would be going back in time and not letting this get off the plane. We screwed once; I should have left it at that. Why did I go to her place? Why did I let us get involved in this?

She walks across the room and I catch her fragrance. It assaults me, so sweet and familiar, that my gut pulls and every instinct I possess screams at me not to let her go. To tell her I've changed my mind. Instead, I walk to the front door and pull it open quietly.

One look at her face shows me that even if I were to get down on my knees and apologise it would be too late. She's determined. She's furious. She's hurting like hell, because of me.

'In the morning you might regret this.' Her words are gentle. 'You've been drinking all day. You're emotional.' I fight an urge to tell her I don't get emotional. 'You might think about calling me, or texting me, maybe even about apologising. You might wake up and want to fuck me, so let me save you the trouble now. Don't.' Her eyes flash with warning. 'Don't call me. Don't text me. Don't think about me. Don't even remember me. You want to push away the people who love you? Well, congratulations, Holden, you've succeeded. I hope you're happy.'

CHAPTER THIRTEEN

As soon as I left I regretted my tirade. It felt amazing to shove those words at him, to see a look of surprise on his face as he computed my threat, but before the elevator had even reached ground level I was fighting back angry, hopeless tears. I ignored his car, the driver he'd arranged and instead I walked. It was the early hours of the morning but I didn't care. I needed to do something mechanical, like putting one foot in front of the other, until I'd got far away from the casino.

Only then did I pull my phone out and call a rideshare. It arrived almost instantly and fortunately my driver wasn't chatty, leaving me free to sit back in the seat and stare out of the window. And replay every damned thing he'd said, everything I'd said, everything I'd felt.

And now I'm sitting here, watching the sky change colour, morning overtaking night, and I feel like I want to curl up in a ball and cry. I feel like I want to go for a run or a swim or lash out. I feel—too many things.

I feel love.

Yes, I fell in love with Holden Hart, even though I've been telling myself since I met him that this isn't the time to get involved with anyone. I've been saying one thing and doing completely another. I fell in love with him and it's a disaster because he isn't capable of making me happy, and I can't—I refuse—to watch someone else I love destroy himself.

Does that make my love less valid? Shouldn't I want to stay and fight for him? To help him?

Fresh tears fill my eyes and I shake my head in a silent refutation of that. No one person can save another. I would fight his battles at his side, I would stand shoulder to shoulder if he wanted that of me, but I won't—can't—stand by and watch him keep going the way he is.

I should be glad that we've only known each other a short time, but the truth is, that makes no difference. I loved him, even a little bit, the first moment I met him. It's not about minutes shared but the connection built and we connected in the most real sense I've ever known. For the first time in my life, for a brief moment, I didn't feel alone.

But I am alone, completely.

It's a sobering thought but at the same time it galvanises me into action. There are things to do—that new life I wanted is still out there, waiting for me to grab hold of it. I just have to firmly dismantle my old life first. *Running away again?* my inner voice jibes. I ignore it. I'm running towards my future; that's not the same thing.

I pack my things quickly, throwing enough clothes to get me through a week or so into a rucksack, make a coffee and then tidy the apartment, watering the houseplants and vacuuming the dust.

I'm almost ready to leave when there's a knock on the door and my heart leaps into my throat. Despite what I said to him when I left, I am filled with hope. Is it Holden?

I knew it would be, even before I opened the door. Holden bloody Hart, dressed in a leather jacket and jeans, his expression guarded, his eyes watchful.

And I'm angry again—angry at him and how much I love him, angry at the impossibility of this. I'm hurting again too, my heart pounding painfully in my chest. 'What are you doing here?'

He looks past me, to the bag at my side.

'Are you going somewhere?'

I throw a glance towards it, then back to him. 'Does it matter?'

A frown shifts on his face. 'Can I come in?'

My eyes narrow, my heart trips. I want, more than anything, to say yes. To offer him a coffee and a hug, to hold him and stitch his hurts back together, but I know the futility of that. His wounds need to be repaired from inside his own heart, not mine.

'Why?'

He shakes his head. 'To talk. About last night.'

But pain is in that prospect, pain and danger, because it's very possible that he could string together enough of the right-seeming words to make me forget why this won't work, and I can't do that. Because I know it won't. I love him, and he doesn't love me.

'Honestly, Holden, I meant what I said when I left. If you think sleeping with me was just a way to forget, if you think you were just using me for sex, that sex with me could easily have been replaced by sex with any other woman you just happened to pick up, then I suggest you go and do just that. Run away, just like you have been.'

A muscle jerks low in his jaw. 'Isn't that what you're doing?' Again, he looks towards my rucksack.

Heat stains my cheeks. 'I'm not running away.'

'Really?'

'I'm doing the exact opposite. I'm going home, to Sundown Creek. I'm packing up my dad's house so I can finally move on with my life. That's not running away; it's confronting something I've been avoiding for years.'

I'm satisfied by the surprise in his features, the look of frustration too.

'When are you going?'

'Any minute.'

His nod is disjointed.

'So you can move on, guilt-free. If you hook up with some other woman tonight, you don't even need to think I'm in the same city. I won't be here. You're free to do whatever you want.'

'I don't want to sleep with anyone else.' His words still me. 'You're different, Cora, so different.'

I refuse to feel anything at that admission.

'Sure, but it's still just sex.'

'No, I'm trying to tell you—' He shakes his head, his eyes haunted. 'Fuck, Cora, just give me a break for a second, okay?'

'Why?' The word is barely a groan.

'I'm trying to tell you that we have to end this.'

My heart stops.

'I'm trying to tell you that you were right to leave me last night, and you're right to walk away from me, but before you go I need to tell you that this is so much more than sex. I hate that I said that.' His admission is raw. 'At first, I wanted to use you to forget, and Christ, you made me forget even my own name. But then I got addicted to you. Not just because of your ability to push the past out of my head but because I got addicted to everything about you in the present.'

My heart stands still. My blood stops rushing. My knees feel weak.

'You were right about a lot of things last night.'

I close my eyes for a second, breathing deeply, tasting him in my lungs. 'I know that.'

'I can't keep doing what I'm doing. I don't want to keep living like this. You were right.'

'So don't.' I swallow, wishing I could make him see what I'm offering, what I want. 'Stay here, get help, let me help you.'

'No.' His expression is grim. He takes a step backwards, closer to the footpath, and his voice is cold, resolute, as though he feels nothing. 'There's a million reasons I'm not right for you, Cora. Not the least of which is I have no idea if I'm ever going to change, and I won't put you through this.' His eyes hold mine, as if willing me to understand what he's not saying, what he feels deep inside.

'But I—'

I don't know what I was going to say but he interrupts.

'No. I know what I'm capable of, what I've done to my brothers.'

I swallow heavily.

'I'm not going to call you again, and I'm not going to see you, but I needed you to know that this was real. That you mean something to me, and always will. You're the first woman I've kissed in a very long time.' He lifts his thumb to my lips, stroking it across the flesh there, and I shudder because I want to press 'pause' and ignore everything that's happened in the last twenty-four hours.

My eyes sting, my throat hurts. I have no idea what to say.

'I'm so fucked up.' The words are like little bullets, shattering against me. 'But you were—are— the most amazing person I've ever known.' He steps back towards me and hesitates for the briefest moment before pressing a kiss to my lips. So light, so brief, I wonder if I've imagined it. Then, a second later, his hand curls around my cheek. 'Take care of yourself, okay?'

'I'm glad you came back.' Grace pushes out of their door and wraps me in a huge hug—for a tiny person, she has bear-like qualities when it comes to hugs. I'm not generally a hugging type person but Grace doesn't care.

'You sure?' The question is laced with irony but she rolls her eyes, her smile filled with kindness—kindness I don't deserve.

'Yeah, I'm sure. Come in.' She puts her hand on my elbow and drags me in, as much as she's able, as though I might back out at the last moment. When I walk in, it's to see Jagger sitting on the sofa, Felicity in his arms, a bottle up to her mouth. He eyes me warily. His face sports a matching bruise; we did this to each other. It's not the first time we've fought, but it's the first time I've known myself to be almost completely in the wrong.

I stand there, not knowing what to say, where to sit, what to do. And I look at Felicity and find myself thinking about Cora, about her baby, about her loss and grief, her courage and strength. I find myself thinking about fate and life, about Jagger and Grace and the way they found each other, about this baby they have, so sweet, and such a mix of them, and the darkness creeps back in.

Darkness at what I don't have, at what I've never known, darkness at what I've lost.

'Give me a second.' Jagger stands up, his skill at doing that while holding a sleeping baby impressive, and strides across to the crib in the lounge. He places the baby in, pausing to press a hand to her chest and then turns to face me.

'Out here.'

'Do you want a coffee?' Grace doesn't whisper.

Her voice reaches us so I instinctively look towards Felicity—she barely flinches.

'No, thanks. I won't stay long.'

'You sure? We're having crab linguine for lunch.'

My smile feels tight. I could really do with a beer but I don't ask for one.

Jagger leads the way to the balcony and closes the glass doors behind us. Once out there, he gives me the full force of his attention, his look difficult to read. But I know Jagger. I know him as well as I know myself. Our experiences in life are comparable. I get him.

'I was pissed off.'

His lips twist into a grimace. 'Is that an apology?'

I look out over Sydney, my eyes instinctively finding the balcony of my penthouse, visions of Cora wrapped in a blanket populating my vision so for a moment breathing is difficult.

'Look—' Jagger sighs, apparently not waiting for an answer '—I get it. You *were* pissed off. That's how you live your life now, and Theo and I want to help you but I'm fucked if I know how. What do we do, man? What would you do?'

I hear the helplessness in his voice. I hear the same tone Cora used with me last night, frustration at their inability to make me snap out of this and stop giving a shit about the fact Ryan lied to me all my life.

'I don't know.' It's the truth. 'Do you think I want to feel like this?'

'No.'

'I want— I've always known I was different to

you guys, but I thought it was because I wasn't a Hart from birth. I thought it was because I crashed into your family and pushed your mom away. But maybe on some biological level I knew. And now I have no idea if I'll ever get the answers I want. Maybe I'll never know who my dad is. I'll never know why Ryan took me in.'

'You probably won't,' Jagger agrees. But his tone softens when he speaks again. 'But none of that changes who *you* are, or what you mean to us. You're our brother. You're the guy we grew up with, you're the one who remembers everything about every single movie we've ever watched, who can stay up all night and run a marathon the next day, the one who makes us laugh by refusing to laugh at any damned thing.'

'You don't get it.' Though his words do something strange to me, pushing at my insides. 'I feel like I'm missing this huge part of me. I don't know who I am. I don't know where I came from or why I ended up living with you. Everything about my life is either a mystery or a lie. I spend my days working in "our" business feeling like a fucking fraud because Hart Brothers Industries isn't my birthright. Not like it is yours and Theo's. I have no idea why Ryan raised me but I can't keep acting like this is normal.'

'Bullshit. Ryan loved you. He tried to adopt you— that's the one thing we *do* know about this. And you want to talk about something being missing? What do you think Theo and I have felt like this last year or so? You've checked out, disappeared, and it's like we've lost an arm or something. You barely know my wife, my baby, you're never around and when you are you're drunk and aggressive. You're our brother. Did you even stop to think about what you're taking away from us by simply disappearing?'

My chest hurts. I look at him, the earnestness in his face pulling at my senses so I have only grief and regret, and an abiding uncertainty.

'I'm not saying this is easy. We're all grappling with this, but Christ, man, let's grapple with it together. Stop running from us, and let us help you. Please. We love you. Grace and me, Asha and Theo—you're part of our families. Stop disappearing and let us help you.'

None of this is new. Theo and Jagger have both said this to me a lot in the last eighteen months, and yet when I hear Jagger now it's in light of Cora's words.

I'm doing the exact opposite. I'm going home, to Sundown Creek. I'm packing up my dad's house so I can finally move on with my life. That's not running away; it's confronting something I've been avoiding for years.

I have been running, and they've been calling me on it for years, but it's Cora's voice I hear, Cora's courage that forces me to stop and really listen, to understand. I've tried it my way. I've run and I've drunk and I've used every tool at my disposal to ignore what's happening but now I need to try something different or I'm going to wind up like Cora's dad, of that I have no doubt.

* * *

The plane will always remind me of Cora. I see her everywhere I look. I stare at the beer in front of me, open but not yet touched, and reach for my phone instead. I didn't save the photo of her—the one photo I have of Cora, that she sent me via text. I load it up out of our message conversation now, making it the size of the screen.

My heart feels like it's going to tear out of my chest.

I zoom in on her eyes; my gut clenches. I drop my head back against the armchair's headrest, closing my eyes. Her eyes are still there, smiling, teasing. Then hurt, accusing, as I told her we were just sleeping together.

'You want to push away the people who love you? Well, congratulations...you succeeded.'

The meaning of her words was obvious at the time but it's only now, ten hours out of Sydney, closer to the States than I am to Cora, that I feel the importance of what she said, the beauty of the gift she offered, and I feel the fierceness of my rejection.

'Don't call me. Don't text me. Don't think about me. Don't even remember me.'

As if I could ever forget her. I blink my eyes open and stare at the photo once more, pinching out to full size so I can see her whole face, and the airline pyjamas she was wearing that night.

If I'd been punched hard in the stomach it wouldn't have hurt more.

I'll never forget Cora, but will she forget me? Will

she look at someone else like this, make them smile, offer them her beautiful, sweet heart? God, for her sake, I hope so. Cora deserves the best, and that's very far from what I am right now.

For someone like me, who exists partially through the medium of photography, I find it impossible to believe I didn't take a single photo of Holden. There are a heap of him on the internet. About a week after I got back from Sundown Creek I made the mistake of googling him. Mistake because the sheer volume of photos of him with other women, strolling out of nightclubs, made my skin crawl. I promised myself I'd never google him again.

In any event, a photo of him that I took would be so different. A photo that captured his eyes specifically as they looked at me, the shadow on his chin, the unconscious shift of his lips when he was lost in thought.

Why didn't I take a single photo?

It's been six weeks since I saw last him.

Six weeks and neither of us has broken the agreement we brokered that last day. He hasn't called me, he hasn't texted me, for all I know he hasn't even thought of me. And I haven't contacted him either, because nothing has changed. I get the futility of it, the uselessness of trying to make this work.

He has too much to focus on, too much to overcome, and while I desperately want him to be happy, I know that happiness can't come from me. I think about sending him a message, just to see how he's doing, but I don't.

Am I afraid of the answer? That if he's gone downhill I'll blame myself for walking away? Does he have any idea how much I miss him? How often I think about him? Does he know that I love him? In a real way, not just because sex was great, but because he's moved into my heart and will never vacate it.

I wish I'd been clearer on that score. I wish I'd told him that I love him despite the fact I can't be with him. I wish I'd told him that he's worthy of love—my love, his brothers' love, that the man who raised him loved him. I wish I'd pushed that point home to him because the idea of Holden Hart being out there and not feeling like he deserves love makes me want to scream.

My photography course starts. I concentrate on that to the best of my abilities, trying to keep Holden and memories of what we shared locked into a small part of my brain. I wonder if in time I'll come to think of him less.

But, no. That's not love. I love him and therefore he's a part of me—my breath, my thoughts, my smile, my sadness. Holden is in me and he always will be.

CHAPTER FOURTEEN

Three and a half months after meeting Holden

SYDNEY IN SPRING can be a cranky mistress. The sky is an ominous grey, sparks of lightning flashing in the distance, a low rumble of thunder churning in my gut. I push one foot in front of the other, running a little faster, checking my watch. I'm at least a kilometre from home.

The buildings—familiar by virtue of the fact I've been doing this run every night for the past three or so months—lead me down the streets I know well. Past the bakery that—even at night—smells like croissants, across the street to the gym where people are running, just like me, on treadmills though, illuminated by fluorescents rather than streetlights.

I wonder if they're running from something, like I am. I wonder if they're running from loss, sadness. Heartbreak.

Three months ago I came back to Sydney. I left Sundown Creek, my dad's home, my old life, and this time I left it for good.

It was one of the hardest things I ever did—but nothing compares to the pain of losing Holden.

Missing Holden has become an essential part of who I am. In every breath I taste that pain. I ache for him. It is a cruel and awful reality to exist in and yet I hold onto my pain because it's one of the only ways I have to know this is real.

I turn a corner; the streetlight overhead flashes and a moment later lightning does the same. I flinch, drenched to the core and glad for that. I'm glad for anything that makes me feel alive now. Nothing compares to Holden—his touch, his kisses, his possession—but running like this comes close. My blood rushes, my heart races, my legs feel like they're filled with jelly.

I thought about moving out of the apartment. Memories of him are so vivid there, so much a part of everywhere I look, but in the end I stayed for that exact reason. Holden is everywhere I look and here, in some strange way, I can pretend—for a moment—that things ended differently for us.

Now who's running away?

I grind my teeth, dip my head and run the rest of the way like this, pounding up the street and stopping only when I reach my front steps. I drop my head forward, inhaling deeply, trying to ease the pain in my lungs.

Rain lashes my back; I don't care. I stare down at my joggers, breathing in the clay-like air, humid and wet, acrid all the way to the back of my throat, and then begin to straighten right as a car door next to me opens. I turn to it on autopilot, reaching for the key I wear around my neck at the same time.

I'm halfway turning back to my door when Holden steps out and everything inside of me lurches into a cataclysmic kind of life all over again. My heart jolts so hard against my chest I half think it's going to do a Shawshank and burrow out through my ribs.

I do a double-take. It can't be him, right? It can't be Holden. I see him everywhere, all the time. He's burned into my eyes and it's easy to transpose him into my local café, my course, my living room.

Holden moves. I blink again. It's really him. I try to remember to be angry with him, hurt, wary, careful but my heart twists and I know love is the strongest emotion I feel.

Love—despite the fact he disappeared from my life. It's been so long, and I have missed him so much and he's been nowhere.

It takes me a few seconds but I rally, straightening my spine and fixing him with a look that I hope passes for cool and indifferent.

He comes around the car, crossing towards me, pausing frustratingly too far away.

But on the one hand that's good because at this distance I can stare at him and really see every detail. His broad chest, his immaculate dark suit, his handsome face, hair that is much longer than when I last saw him, a traditional guy style, dark and thick so I want to run my hands through it.

'Cora.' His smile is tight, his eyes locked to mine

with an intensity that makes breathing almost impossible. 'How are you?'

Such a formal question! Has time done this to us? Made us feel like strangers? Rain pelts down, landing hard on his head, mine. Thunder rolls. I don't move towards the door.

'I'm...fine.' I'm not fine. I haven't been fine in a long time but if the past has taught me anything it's that pain fades, or at least becomes more manageable. This, I suspect, will become a part of who I am, like a knot on a tree's trunk. I'll never get over Holden but one day I'll become adjusted to living with the hurt he inflicted on me by leaving.

He continues to stare at me without speaking, through the fast-falling rain. He stares at me with a frown on his face and I feel a thousand things in return—I feel anger that he's here, outside my place when I didn't expect him, so I've had no time to mentally prepare, no time to brace for this. My heart is in knots and my stomach too.

Lightning slices the grey sky, some distance away. Thunder cracks. Holden shakes his head a little, as if rousing himself from a dream. 'Sorry. I just...haven't seen you in so long.'

I swallow. It's been three and a half months. Each day has felt like an insurmountable hurdle at the start, and each evening I am exhausted from acting as though I'm fine, my normal self, when I'm shattered into a thousand little pieces.

I've missed him with every breath and I've questioned everything about what we were, what I felt, whether it was genuine or not.

'I've been thinking about you.'

Something like a fever runs through my veins. 'Yeah?'

His eyes flash. 'Have you started your photography course?'

I nod.

His gaze roams my face. I'm completely drenched—the rain no longer bothers me. 'Did you go back to your dad's?'

The line of questioning is odd, as though he has a checklist of things he wants to have answered. And then what? He goes away again? Is it possible he's only seeking the same reassurance I was—that I'm doing okay?

'Yes.'

'Would you…do you want to sit in here?' He gestures behind him, to his SUV. I eye it warily and shake my head impulsively.

'You're getting wet.'

'I know.'

He nods, distracted.

A frown draws at my brows but something shifts inside of me—an anger, an impatience, a frustration that maybe he's here just to chat. 'Holden, what's this about? Why are you here?' It comes out harsher than I intended but crushed hopes and an overflow of emotions make it hard for me to regulate anything.

He looks at me for several seconds without speaking and I feel like I'm tipping off the edge of the earth. I'm so close to snapping; I can't stand seeing him and not touching, standing opposite him as though we're barely civil strangers.

'God, Holden, is this some kind of game to you?'

'No, Cora, Christ. Just…let me speak, okay?'

But anger is humming through my veins, perhaps because it's so much more preferable to anything else.

'Then speak quickly. I don't want to stand here in the rain all afternoon.'

Nothing.

'Holden—' my voice holds a warning '—tell me why you're here or, I swear to you, I will walk away right now.'

'I came to see you,' he blurts out. 'I came to Australia to see you.'

I stare at him, my mouth dry, my pulse firing.

He speaks quickly, perhaps afraid I'll make good on my threat and storm off without giving him a moment to say anything else. The rain begins to fall more heavily so he has to shout to be heard, and he steps closer as well so he's only a few inches from me. 'The thing is, Cora, you were right that night. I've been running away since I found out the truth about my father. I'd been doing everything I could to not feel a damned thing for even longer than that. My whole life I was taught not to feel, not to show emotion, not to let anyone in. Learning that Dad—Ryan—wasn't my father just underscored the importance of that. I was so messed up, and I had no intention of ever changing.'

I stare at him, my heart slamming into my ribs.

'Honestly, if I hadn't met you I don't think I would ever have woken up. So I came here to thank you.' Thunder growls beneath his words. 'I needed you to know that I've changed—or I'm working on changing—and that it's because of you.'

Relief spreads through me, a relaxation of a worry I didn't even realise I've been carrying, but I have no idea what I can say.

'I'm seeing a shrink.' His expression isn't rueful—he's completely serious, and unapologetic. 'I guess I needed to talk it out, to get a different perspective, and it's helping. Just like you said.' He stares at me, his eyes loaded with ferocious strength. 'I'm not drinking. I don't want to drink.'

My stomach squeezes and I close my eyes because, of all things, this I needed to know most. I love Holden Hart and I need to know that he's not wasting his life, that he's not destroying himself.

'I'm working on things with my brothers and I'm working on letting go of the past too. I'm trying to be less messed up.'

There's nothing but the sound of the hammering rain. I clear my throat and try to decide what to say because I feel as though all of this needs some kind of acknowledgement, but the problem is, I just feel too much—how can I distil it into words?

'I'm glad.' Stupid, insufficient acknowledgement is all I offer.

The air crackles. After all that we've shared,

how can there be this kind of awkwardness and uncertainty?

He frowns. I know he's feeling it too.

'Please come and sit in the car.' He gestures to it, his eyes briefly dropping to my body, so sparks lift within my blood. I repress them, ignoring their familiar pull, because sparks and Holden are inevitable but they don't solve anything.

'I'm fine,' I insist. I'm not fine. I'm a mess, my heart, my head, my body, my brain, all at odds, all unsure and hurting and wanting me to say and do completely different things.

'You know you asked me about that tattoo?' He gestures to his chest, where the Greek word is inscribed. I can picture it perfectly, beneath his shirt.

I nod, not quite meeting his eyes, heat spreading through my veins like molten lava.

'It's Greek.'

'I gathered.'

'Theo's half-Greek. He dared us to get the tattoos. We were drunk.' His smile is nostalgic. 'We each got one.'

'Matching ones?'

His eyes trap mine. 'No.'

'So what did they get?'

'Jagger got Zeus because he runs the construction arm of the business. Theo got Poseidon because he deals with our maritime operations.'

'And you?'

There's a haunted quality in his eyes, a pain that's familiar to me because I've seen it on his face before.

And then he exhales and relaxes, offers me a small smile. 'It's Hades. The devil.'

My intake of breath is involuntary. Perhaps he mistakes it for a shiver because he makes a gruff noise of frustration then moves, putting a hand lightly on my elbow, guiding me up the stairs to the small portico that offers some protection from the weather.

'I run the casinos,' he explains once I'm out of the rain. 'The dark side of our empire.' He lifts a hand and draws it across the back of his neck. 'But it's more than that. All my life I've felt like an outsider. I've been angry and lonely, someone who doesn't trust easily. I never fit in with the Harts.'

I consider this. 'You had a far from normal upbringing.'

'True.'

'That leaves marks.'

'Yes, it does.' His nod is slow. 'I've grappled with this darkness inside of me and never wanted to deal with it. Until I met you, Cora, and I realised that the thing I wanted most on earth—you—was so far out of my league it's not funny.'

I press my back hard to the wall, the pressure there necessary to hold me upright.

'God, Cora, I don't know if I have any right to tell you this, but all I could think about, all I've thought about every day since I left Australia, was coming back here when I was like this—sober and facing up to everything I've been dealing with, really facing up to it—and telling you how I feel.'

I brace for this, I brace as though I'm in an aeroplane being dragged towards earth, as though oxygen masks are falling from the ceiling.

But he's quiet, like he's waiting for me to say something again.

'Go on.' The words are raspy, throaty, strangled inside of me.

'My dad—Ryan—was pretty fucked up.'

I want to scream. The disappointment is unending. What the hell does his father have to do with this?

'He married a lot of women. Destroyed even more. He was a bastard. A selfish, arrogant bastard. Which makes his decision to raise me even stranger. But that's not my point.'

'No?'

'No.' He runs his hand over the back of his neck again. Is he nervous? That's ridiculous to contemplate because he's Holden bloody Hart but he seems to be having trouble getting this out.

I wait, breath held.

'I never expected the whole "happily ever after" thing for myself. Hell, I never wanted that. I'm not that kind of guy, right? I'm just like him. It wasn't until I met you that I realised everything I thought I knew—about myself, life, love, everything—was wrong. Everything was wrong, Cora, and you were so right. I fell in love with you and that was the catalyst for every change I made.' He stops talking, stares at me then seems to gather himself, visibly calming. 'And I don't want you to think that I only changed for you. This is about me, and the kind of man I want to be. But you woke me up to that. You made me see

I could be different, that I could be more. You gave me a reason to *want* to be more.'

Tears are thick in my throat. Love floods my veins.

'I told myself three months was long enough—to convince myself that the changes were lasting, and to show you I meant this. I couldn't come back after one month even though, believe me, Cora, I wanted to. I have ached to see you, to talk to you, every day since I left.'

My heart soars and splinters, all at once. 'I've missed you too.' Such a bland way to explain what I've been feeling!

He nods slowly. 'I came here today because I wanted to apologise to you.'

'What for?'

'I was in a really bad place. You were beautiful and kind and I acted like an asshole. I came here because I don't have a lot of friends, and I was hoping we could be. Friends.'

'Friends,' I repeat, nodding when my heart is groaning under the weight of disappointment.

'I miss you. I want you in my life, Cora.' A muscle jerks low in his jaw. 'If you think that's possible.'

I stare at him, confused and lost. 'I want you in my life too,' I say honestly. 'But not as a friend.'

His eyes lock mine and something flares between us. I wouldn't notice a reaction at all if it weren't for the way his chest stills, as though he's holding his breath.

'I fell in love with you, Holden. Messed up, angry, lonely you. I'm glad you're getting help and that you're dealing with all your stuff, but I loved you at your worst. Why the hell do you think I wouldn't love you now?'

He makes a noise that's half-groan, half-laugh. 'Why would I think that? Because I shouted at you and reduced what we were to "sex" and then disappeared out of your life completely.'

'And that hurt, believe me. But you did it for me; I knew that at the time and I know that now. You were protecting me, trying not to hurt me. I got it. It made me love you all the more.'

Another sound of surprise. 'I thought about you every day too, Holden. I didn't want you to disappear from my life and I never wanted you to feel like you had to face your battles on your own. I wanted to—and always will—stand shoulder to shoulder with you, no matter what you're staring down. I just needed you to want to stare it down too. I want to support you, I want to help you, and I want to be with you.' And when he still doesn't say anything I reiterate, 'I love you.'

Now he moves, closing the distance between us completely, our wet bodies melded together, his mouth seeking mine, his kiss so familiar, his body so warm and strong despite the rain, so perfect that I lose myself in his arms—or is it that I find myself right here, with the only man I've ever loved?

'You have term holidays next week, right?'

I blink, surprised by the rapid change of subject. 'Um, yeah. Why?'

He expels a small sigh. 'I was wondering how you'd feel about coming to Alaska with me.'

'Alaska?' I laugh. 'For a little salmon fishing?'

'Sure. And to see the Northern Lights.'

My heart skips a beat. 'You want us to go see the Northern Lights together?'

'Baby, I want us to go everywhere together, but let's start there first.'

I bite down on my lip, happiness bursting through me, brighter than the Aurora Borealis could ever be.

'So?'

'So...' I pretend to consider it for a minute. 'You've got yourself a deal, Holden Hart.'

He grins, a sexy, wolfish smile that lights all my pulse points on fire. 'Remind me to tell you something funny later.'

'Tell me now.'

'Later.' And he kisses me, driving all thoughts of anything else clear from my head.

'You were going to tell me something.' Her fingers are feather-light on my naked torso. I trap them in my grip, lift them to my mouth and kiss them.

'My shrink told me.'

'Told you what?'

'I was talking about you—'

'You talk about me with your shrink?'

'A little.' I run a hand over her hair, closing my eyes and letting myself soak this up. I came here to Australia without a single shred of hope this would ever work, that she'd still love me, but lying here with Cora I honestly wonder why I ever doubted this. Because we fit together; we're meant to be. This is as right as anything I've ever known in life.

'What kinds of things do you tell him?'

'That I love going down on you?' I can't help teasing her and she responds by punching me lightly on the arm. I grin.

'I'm serious.'

'I wasn't.' I return to stroking her hair. 'Why did your dad call you Cora?'

'Oh.' I feel her confusion. 'I'm not really sure.'

'Was he into mythology at all?'

'He did some literature subjects at Yale. Why?'

'Cora is another version of the name Persephone.' She props her chin on my chest, her beautiful eyes tunnelling into mine. 'And Persephone was the much-feared queen of the underworld. Hades' wife.'

Her smile is slow to spread. 'Really?'

'Yeah. He abducted her—as you do—and they lived happily ever after. Hades and Cora, a love for the ages.'

'Well, that seals it then.'

'Hmm?'

'We'll just have to get married after all. It's written in the stars.'

I laugh and I kiss her because, even though she's joking, I believe there's truth in it too. If I were ever going to believe in myths and magic, I would believe Cora was sent to me, that every part of our falling in love was in some way preordained.

'And so we shall.'

EPILOGUE

'I STILL THINK we could have had a double wedding.'

I'm teasing Cora. It's one of my favourite pastimes. She pokes her tongue out at me, pressing her hand to mine. In the three months since getting engaged we've laughed about lots of places to get married, but ultimately decided to wait until after Theo and Asha's wedding.

'I don't know if I'd want to be compared to Asha on my wedding day.' She sighs. 'Doesn't she look amazing?'

I eye Theo and Asha. Their happiness is so apparent—the kind of happiness I would have resented twelve months ago, before I found Cora and my own heart's desire.

'You kidding? She can't hold a candle to you.' I lean closer. 'No one can, Persephone.'

She flips a smile up at me. The day is perfect. Sunshine, clear skies, everything just as it ought to be. The ceremony was simple and short and now, in the grounds of Asha's vineyard in the Loire Valley, it feels as though life is full of all that is good and right.

A little shape hurtles between my legs and I look down to see Felicity there, her tentative steps no encumbrance to speed. I scoop down and pick her up, throwing her into the sky so she giggles, the sound so rich with happiness that I laugh in response—how can I not?

'What are you up to, Mischief?' Cora leans towards her, tickling her tummy so Felicity laughs again and I look at Cora, capturing this moment and trapping it in my mind. It's strange how I didn't think of Felicity as 'mine', a part of me, when she was first born. I got so caught up on the biology of our blood relationship—or lack thereof—that I didn't understand. I love her. She's a part of my family, just as Cora loves her despite the fact they don't share blood.

I find my old thoughts and behaviours completely foreign now. A year with Cora, a year of happiness, has shaped my opinions so differently. They are almost the complete opposite to what they once were. I may never know the truth of my parentage, I may never understand why Ryan chose to raise me, but I can look at his decision with gratitude now. He did love me, in his own selfish way. He gave me a good home but, more importantly, he gave me brothers, and without them I don't know who or where I'd be.

'You're buzzing.' Cora smiles up at me and I'm so wrapped up in my own thoughts it takes me a moment to hear her, let alone comprehend what she's saying.

I reach into my pocket, pulling my phone out.

'Hold her?' But I pause to blow a raspberry on

Felicity's tummy before handing her to Cora. I take a few steps away, lifting the phone to my ear.

'Holden Hart.'

'Holden? It's Dominic.'

I frown, for a moment, forgetting that I even know someone called Dominic. How long has it been since I thought about the investigator I engaged for ever ago to find out about my birth father? But my blood runs cold now because I cancelled his contract almost a year ago, and so for him to be calling...

'What is it?'

I move further away, throwing a look over my shoulder. Cora is talking to Jagger and Grace. My family. I grip the phone more tightly, unsure how I'm going to take the news I'm sure I'm about to receive.

'I've had something come across my desk just now.' His accent is thick Cockney. 'Something I wanted to let you know about.'

It's my father. He's found him.

'Go on.'

'Still no luck on your dad.'

I close my eyes, surprised by the flash of disappointment that overtakes me.

'Have you heard of a woman called Savannah Maxwell?'

I frown, and now when I look at Cora it's with a blade of worry. How many women was I with before her? What if this Savannah is one of them? What if there's something from my past about to reach into my future and grip it by the throat?

But Cora looks at me and smiles at that exact

moment, so I relax, because I know how she loves me—just like I love her. There's nothing from my past that could hurt us. She accepts me—all of my past pitfalls, everything.

'No.'

'I'm not surprised. She died about fifteen years ago.'

'So why are you telling me this?'

'The thing is, she left behind a little girl. A fourteen-year-old called Avery Maxwell. Holden, there's no easy way to tell you this. She's Ryan Hart's daughter.'

All my breath leaves my body. My brain explodes against the inside of my skull. 'What did you say?'

'It's a long story. She submitted to DNA testing for a little girl who needed a bone marrow transplant. I have access to the database. The results pinged—I had an alert set up from when I was working on your case. I did a bit of digging and it's true, beyond a shadow of a doubt. She's Ryan's daughter.'

'Jesus Christ. Does she know?'

My heart is slamming into my ribs. I turn around. All my family are together now. Theo and Asha, Jagger, Grace, Felicity and my reason for being, Cora.

'I don't know. The father's not listed on her birth certificate, and she grew up pretty broke, then went into foster care after Savannah died. I'd have to think if she knew about your family she'd have made contact. Or that someone would have.'

'Jesus Christ,' I repeat, dragging a hand through my hair. I'm aware of Theo's eyes on me and wonder if I look as shocked as I feel. I must, because he says something and they start to walk towards me, all the people I love most in the world.

'Can you email me everything you've got?'

'Already done.'

'Thanks, Dominic. I appreciate it.'

I disconnect the call just as Theo reaches me. 'What is it?' No preamble, no bullshit.

'Where's Barrett?'

Jagger looks around, points to our friend. He's at the bar, two beautiful women talking to him. That figures. The guy never met a woman he couldn't charm.

'I need him.'

'I'll go.' Theo steps away and we stand silently, only Cora moves, putting her hand in the crook of my arm, her eyes scanning my face with concern.

A moment later, Theo and Barrett are back. 'This better be important.' Barrett grins. 'I was having quite a nice conversation with Mandy and Louise.'

Jagger rolls his eyes, but they're relaxed. They don't get this.

'Barrett, have you ever heard of a woman called Savannah Maxwell?'

His expression shifts. He shakes his head, his brows lifting. 'Should I have?'

I expel a soft breath. 'That investigator I hired just called. Apparently, not only am I not your biological sibling, but it turns out Ryan did have another kid. A daughter.'

'What the hell?' Theo's voice is quiet, but deep with anger. 'That can't be right.'

'What are you talking about?'

'The investigator says it's fact, beyond a shadow of a doubt. We have a half-sister out there, and I don't think she knows anything about us.'

'For crying out loud,' Jagger explodes, shaking his head. 'If our father was alive, I'd kill him.'

Grace lifts a hand to his shoulder, her eyes awash with compassion. 'What do you know about her?'

I lift my phone out of my pocket and open the email, scanning it quickly. 'She's twenty-eight, lives in San Francisco.' I keep scanning the email. 'Runs a successful tech start-up and also founded a charity supplying homeless people with sanitary goods.'

'So she has no idea about us?'

'I don't think so.' I turn to Barrett, frowning. 'But I want to find out for sure.'

'So give her a call,' he says, as though it's that simple.

But Theo's on my wavelength. 'No, it can't be one of us. It's too risky.'

'What risk?' Grace prompts.

'Because she might hear she's a Hart and decide she wants to lay claim to a quarter of Hart Brothers Industries,' Asha says gently, her own position as heiress to one of the world's largest textile manufacturers giving her a unique perspective on this.

'She'd have legal grounds,' Barrett adds in a considering tone.

'It's not just that,' I insist. 'If she's Ryan's child

then she has that right.' I square my shoulders. 'Hell, some could argue she has a considerably greater right than I do.'

'Not this again.' Jagger shakes his head.

'We need to know what we're dealing with.' Theo cuts over Jagger, his words echoing my thoughts.

'Agreed.'

'Yeah.' Jagger nods.

We each turn to look at Barrett simultaneously. 'If only there was someone impartial we could send.'

Barrett's eyes widen. 'You can't seriously be suggesting—'

'Come on, Sir Barrett.' We only invoke his title when we want to tease him. 'You're the perfect man for the job.'

'Oh? Why's that?'

'Because you know our family inside and out, you knew Ryan almost as well as we did. Because you're a lawyer, and a damned good one, so you'll know how to protect us. And because we trust you,' I add, the final caveat by far the most important. Trust doesn't come easily to any of us, but Barrett has it in spades.

'Please,' Grace adds, sending us a look of kind admonishment.

'Yeah, right. Please.' I nod. 'Go to San Fran, find out what you can about her and report back. Simple.'

He narrows his eyes for a moment, so I hold my breath, wondering if he might be going to say no. But after a moment he grins, a look of total acceptance. 'Fine. But only because I love you guys like brothers.'

Meanwhile, two weeks later, San Francisco

The music forms a pulse in my veins, the beat deep and throbbing. I look around the exclusive bar, mojito in one hand, clutch purse in the other. The thin strap of my dress drops a little over one shoulder; I don't bother to catch it.

The day has been a stinker. Baking hot, with barely a hint of relief coming in off the Bay. Even a dip in my infinity pool didn't cool me down and here in this club, the press of bodies, the tightness of space combine to make my skin lightly sheened in perspiration.

But I'm not leaving, not yet. I look around, considering my options. A hot guy near the bar lifts his drink, silently inviting me to join him. He's gorgeous but a bit fussy, his hair a little too styled, his look a bit too contrived. Then again, there's the cowboy I was talking to earlier, straight out of Texas, all faded jeans and plaid shirt. It's unusual to find a guy like him in a place like this—but in talking to him I learned his dad's an oil baron. Makes more sense.

I continue to peruse the bar until my eyes skate past someone—at first—and then skim back. A man is watching me. I narrow my eyes, trying to determine if I've met him before.

He's handsome, so it's possible we've hooked up and I've forgotten, but no. I'm sure I'd remember him. His jaw is square, covered in stubble, his face autocratic and symmetrical, his skin has a golden tan and his hair is a deep brown with a slight wave. He has an air of authority in his bearing, from the way he's sitting, so straight and controlled, to the breadth of his shoulders. He's wearing a suit, definitely bespoke, and hand-made shoes.

My lip curls with a hint of derision, because while there's a chance he's self-made there's also a greater probability he's some kind of entitled rich kid, living off his trust fund, wasting money on big boy clothes. Nonetheless, I'm intrigued enough to return his stare dead-on, lifting my drink and draining it until it's empty.

I sashay towards the bar, not taking my eyes off him, and as I draw closer I lift my lips into a slow smile, loaded with sensual promise.

Rich kid or not, I'm not looking for anything more than one night. It's my tradition—how I mark this date every year—and he looks like he'd at least be good in bed. Then again, that's hard to know for sure—lots of hot guys have been total disappointments in the sack.

'Hi there.' I flash him a megawatt smile now and I see the way his expression shifts, speculation in his eyes.

'Hi. How are you?' An English accent, very plummy, very formal. Definitely rich kid.

'Let me guess…' I murmur. 'You're a lord.'

He shoots up one brow and my stomach twists because he's incredibly handsome and, up close, he's also very charming. His skin is tanned but he has some freckles across his nose, freckles that speak of a life spent outdoors. His hair is a deep brown with natural highlights at the side, and there's warmth in his features, a look of complete kindness that I can't help but recognise.

'Close. Earl.'

'Ah.'

'Earl what?' he prompts, expecting me to some- how intuit his title.

'Well…' I purr in response. 'Now, that's a little harder.'

'Have a drink and I'll drop some hints.'

He gestures to the seat beside him but I don't take it. Instead, I move closer, so I'm standing within the void created by his legs. 'I'll have another mojito.'

A frown flashes across his face but then he smiles, lifts a hand and orders our drinks. I don't know what his name is or why he's here in San Fran, in this bar talking to me, but before midnight I'm going to have my wicked way with him—Happy birthday to me.

* * * * *

LOSING CONTROL

RACHAEL STEWART

MILLS & BOON

For my husband.

I never had any control over my feelings for you.
They just were.

Dublin will always have a special place in our hearts,
as does the location of the ending,
which marries with our own HEA.

Love always,

Rachael xxx

PROLOGUE

Things you should know about me.

I don't do trust.

I don't do love.

I don't do family.

I am me and I stand alone.

I run a billion-dollar empire and nothing can shake it.

Nothing can shake me.

Only I'm standing here at a double funeral, my brother and father both dead, and my collar is too restrictive, my chest too tight.

I shouldn't care. Not when they pushed me out years ago. Took all that mattered to me in one fell swoop. The family business, and her. Alexa Harrington. My ex-fiancée. The only woman I have ever loved. Now my brother's widow.

I run my finger along the inside of my collar, wishing the entire thing over. Wishing away the anger that still fizzes in my blood, the regret that shouldn't exist, the feelings that should have died a death seven years ago.

I'm standing at the back of the church while the priest commands the room. Far enough away from my family—my mother and *her*. Far enough away not to cause a scene. Far enough away to remain anonymous, should I choose to. The room is full to the brim, row upon row of pews crammed with people. No one need know I am here—not if I'm quick enough.

Why I came is anyone's guess.

A choked sob echoes through the rafters and I hone in on its source. My mother. She's hunched forward, head bowed, body shaking in tune to her cries. In response my own body shudders and I tighten against it. I can't breathe. I can't swallow. My eyes burn—

Fuck this!

I am not going to cry.

I am not going to care.

Only, Mum is the reason I came. Her plea. Her message full of regret, begging that I at least pay my respects, say a last goodbye. And for what? My father didn't deserve it—not when he made it so clear in life what a disappointment I'd been.

Well, screw you, Dad. I did it all and more.

She places a soothing hand upon my mother's shoulder. I can see her perfect French-tipped fingers gently rub, can imagine her whispered words designed to calm. My gut twists and I plunge my fists inside my pockets, tearing my eyes away.

She plays the part well enough, dear sweet Alexa. Behaves as if she cares. But how can she really, when she simply followed the money after I left. Swapped me for my greater counterpart. It doesn't matter what I've achieved since then. I will always feel inferior when presented with the past.

And that's why I shouldn't have come. Being weak is as alien to me now as the sentiment of love. I have no place for either in my life.

I have no place here.

I bow my head and start to move along the pew. I'm only four people away from the end, only a few strides from the exit, but it feels like a mile. It's hard to breathe, to see straight. In my mind's eye, the two coffins side by side at the front taunt me, my father and my brother's bond surviving even in death, pushing me out, leaving the two women to suffer— one I've missed more than I care to admit, and one I loathe myself for ever having loved.

I feel suffocated, unstable, and something catches my leg. There's a thud and I focus through the blur to see a hassock at my feet, a steadying hand upon my elbow that I can barely feel. I follow the arm, lift my gaze to meet an old man's eyes.

He's vaguely familiar. We lived in a small village growing up, the village in which my parents still live—no, my *mother* still lives. He's likely part of the community, and he'll know everything there is to know about us. There were never any secrets. So it's a surprise when I see sympathy shining back at me. Sympathy and compassion.

I feel as if I'm choking. I don't need his sympathy— not when the cause of all my pain is so far removed from what he suspects. I give a brief nod and withdraw, my focus once more on the door. On sanctuary.

I push it open and break out into the pouring rain, the Irish weather the perfect accompaniment to my mood. All I need now is thunder to meet my anger and I'd almost believe God was on my side. Not that I believe.

What kind of God would take away not only a woman's husband, but her son too? The better son? The worthy one?

I laugh at my cynicism, my twisted logic. My parents and my ex both deemed him better. I was almost ready to return, almost ready to prove my worth and face their disappointment, make them admit they were wrong.

I drag air into my lungs and look to the heavens. *Why?*

The rain beats my eyes closed and I blink against it, seeking out the sun in the looming grey above. *Why now?*

Is it the ultimate punishment for walking away? Is this what I deserve? No amends, no peace, no nothing?

I stagger forward. I can't bear it any longer. I never should have come.

'Damn you, Dad, for not believing in me.' I rake my fingers through my sodden hair, feel the weight of my rain-laden jacket and the fabric of my shirt clinging to me like a second skin. I throw my head back and curse the heavens. 'Damn you, Liam, for taking my all!'

'And damn *you* for coming back at all.'

I stagger back. I don't need to turn to know who it is. I'd know that voice anywhere. It haunts my dreams. My nightmares too.

I feel her presence as though it were the sun's rays beating down my back, feel the hairs upon my neck prickling to greet it.

The door swings shut. I hear her footfall on the path amidst the pounding beat of the rain and I urge my body to move. My car is at the end of the path, my driver ready and waiting.

Damn you for coming back at all...

Her words echo through my hangover-ridden skull, each syllable chiming with the emerging headache.

'Don't you walk away from me, Cain. Not this time.'

I spin on my heel to confront the angel who ruined me. *Angel?* Demon, more like. My lungs contract on a rush of air. She is beautiful—blindingly so. Her skin is pale against the dark grey stone of the centuries-old church standing tall behind her, her auburn hair like a comforting shroud of warmth as it falls around a face that is far too hollow and drawn, her eyes too big within it.

She's lost so much weight—too much. Just the slightest gust of wind and I fear she'll be gone. She's so far removed from the carefree, curvaceous woman I left behind, and right now she looks shocked into stillness, when seconds before she was the one commanding me to pause.

'You should go back inside.'

I say it, but I'm barely aware of the words. My voice sounds distant with the effort to ignore the racing of my heart, the twist to my gut, the pain.

Rain beads on her lashes, framing eyes that are so blue and look as haunted as I feel. She holds my own eyes trapped, her lips parted as rain rushes freely over them.

'You're getting soaked.'

Her eyes flicker, as though I've woken her up, and I can almost feel the shaky breath she takes, her chest shuddering in her simple black dress.

'Where are you going?'

The strength has gone from her whisper-soft voice and she presses her hands to her abdomen in a strange gesture that leaves her looking every bit as fragile as her slight frame suggests. The urge to offer her comfort, to sweep the rain from her lashes, her face, burns through me—instinctive, possessive, and wholly unacceptable.

She's not mine to warrant such care. She hasn't been for so long.

'I'm leaving.' I clear my throat and reinstate the wall around my heart. 'I never should have come back. Isn't that what you were trying to say just now?'

'I...'

She runs her teeth over her lower lip and I'm a prisoner to the move. Sent back in time. She used to do that when I teased her, when I turned her on. To remember it now is wrong—plain wrong—and yet my body reacts all the same. It seems my wall is not as solid as I'd like, and I don't need that realisation to tell me it's time I got the hell out of there.

'You should at least speak to your mother before you leave.'

'And say what?'

She shakes her head. 'She's just lost her son and her husband; don't you think she needs you now more than ever?'

What can I say? It's been seven years with barely a word spoken. My mother's plea to return has come from her grief. Her forgiveness has come from the same place. My eyes sting. I'm on shaky ground. Any moment now the tumult of emotion will out and I'll crumble.

But I can't.

I won't be weak—least of all in front of her.

'I'll call on her tomorrow…when we can talk in private.'

She gives a shaky nod and I drag my eyes away, force my feet to move once more.

My unspoken warning is clear: *Make sure you're not there.*

I watch him walk away, my shoulders easing with every step he takes. The rain is pounding down, streaming off my face. It's a welcome distraction from the pain that swells inside. It mingles with the grief, the hurt of losing Liam, of losing his father too. I wish I could be numb to it; heaven knows I've had enough thrown at me over the years.

My hands throb and I tear my gaze from his retreating form to stare at where my palms press tight against my abdomen, nursing the invisible wound beneath.

I've always known this day would come—part of me hoping for it, the other dreading it like the plague. But it *is* good he's returned—for his mother's sake. Marie has lost everything; he's all the blood family she has left.

And then there's me. An orphan, an outsider. Welcomed into the loving arms of the O'Connors when Cain brought me home to meet them all those years ago. I was fifteen and alone. And they took me under their wing, gave me a place to run to, a place where I felt loved, and that love never waned.

His did, though. Cain's. The boy who became the man I believed myself in love with, was destined to marry, have a family with.

My hands clutch tighter. He's the man who gave me the family I always wanted and then crushed me by walking away.

I look back up and see him stumble as he reaches the kerb, the downpour making the ancient path from the church unstable. I feel my hand reach out on instinct and snatch it back. He doesn't deserve my worry, my aid, and he certainly doesn't deserve the flicker of awareness that rippled through me the moment his glittering grey gaze collided with mine.

I felt his presence the second he walked into the church. It was the same as always—the strange flutter, the sudden awakening in my body. Almost as though I've been programmed from birth to detect him, to seek him out, with the rows upon rows of people between us doing nothing to douse it.

And Marie felt it too, in her own way. I saw her turn, saw the hope spark in her eye, a flash of something other than the grief she'd worn for the last few weeks. Waiting for the bodies to be fished from the sea, the plane crash to be investigated, the confirmation that the freak weather was to blame.

I couldn't stop myself chasing after him. It didn't matter that the service was still underway, that Marie needed my comfort. The fear that he would walk away and leave her with nothing, not even a word, drove me to follow him.

She deserved something, anything—no matter the cost to me of coming face to face with him again.

Seven years ago, he broke my heart, ripped it from my chest and left me with nothing…

No, that's not true.

He left me with a child—*our* child.

My hands are claw-like on my belly now, the nausea swelling thick and fast as the reminder rips through me. More death, more grief, more pain.

Thunder rumbles overhead, the sound vibrating through my skull, waking me up. At least I made my feelings clear, my curse falling easily from my lips on the tail-end of his. But then he turned and I was incapacitated with the rush of…of love, anger, betrayal, pain—more than anything, the pain.

A pain that he reflected back at me, blazing from him so strong I couldn't breathe through it. His masculine beauty, only intensified by his torment.

I think of the last time I saw him. Seven years ago. The lines etched in his face, nothing to do with age back then and everything to do with his anger. At life, his family…me.

I look at him now and a movement further down the pavement draws my eye. There's a driver waiting, the rear door of a sleek black car open. I know it's for Cain. I know of his wealth—hell, everyone knows of his success. Not many know the price he paid for it, though. The price we all paid.

But I do.

And that's why he doesn't deserve my attention. I've done what I came to do. I have his assurance that he will visit his mother tomorrow.

So go back inside and say goodbye to those who've always stuck by you...

I take a breath and smooth my shaky fingers over my face to sweep away the rain that I know is mixed with tears, then turn back.

Maybe he has a heart after all.

Shame it's taken him seven years to find it.

Not that I care.

I will never care for him again.

CHAPTER ONE

Three months later

'ISN'T IT TIME you went home, Alexa?'

I squint up at Janice, who's currently frowning at me as if she's my concerned counsellor and not my super-practical PA.

'I'm fine. I need to reply to Matthews before I call it quits today.'

She shakes her head at me, her frown deepening. 'Whatever you need to say, it can wait until tomorrow. It isn't going to change things right this second.'

No, it's not. She's right. But our investors are on edge. They have been since the plane crash that took out the company founder and his equally impressive son. And it's getting to me more and more. Making me feel helpless, ineffective, practically a failure. I can't bear it much longer.

Don't get me wrong—I *know* I'm worthy of this role, of being CEO. I was always Liam's equal. We graduated from Oxford together, top of the class, and companies were vying to take us on. But our hearts were in this firm. The one his father built up from nothing and dreamed his sons would take on. Together.

No one could have foreseen what had happened.

Least of all the investors.

But no amount of reassurance from my lips will convince them, and I feel every bit the disadvantaged female when I sit with the board. All male, bar me. Their greying hair and condescension make it clear they don't believe in me. Not that I take it personally. I get the impression they don't think *any* woman should be at the helm of a *Fortune 500* company.

But I'll prove them wrong if it kills me.

Not for the first time I wonder... Would this be happening if Cain had inherited the shares? If he'd been forced to come back, to get involved? What if I'd taken him up on his departing offer of calling on him if we needed anything?

Not that he'd made that offer to *me*. No, it was what he told Marie on his one and only visit, the day after the funeral. At least I think there's only been one—the one she's spoken to me about. But then, would she have told me if there had been more? Would she have wanted to risk any more upset, any more pain...?

And there you go, thinking about him when you should be focusing on what matters...

'Maybe you should call him, you know. Just...'

I know Janice means Cain. It's not just me thinking about him; the majority of the company are.

His success knows no bounds, even when compared to ours.

'I don't need anyone's help, least of all his.' I smile to soften the acidity of my words.

She nods as she clutches her tablet to her chest. 'Forget I said anything.'

'I will.' I go back to my screen.

'Night, then.'

I don't look at her, only nod. There's too much emotion in my face, in my voice. I can't bring myself to speak any further. I'm tired and far too bitter not to say something about Cain that I'll later regret.

She leaves, closing the door softly behind her, and I feel a stab of guilt at my brusque treatment of her. It's not her fault I'm tetchy. It's all Cain's.

We're supposed to be ancient history, our relationship a whole other lifetime ago. So why, three months after the funeral, does his reappearance still have me reeling? And not just with shock, but with a multitude of feelings that I'd thought long since dead?

I rub at my face, my eyes, try to focus through the burning haze to read my computer screen. But it's no use. I've been staring at it for almost twelve hours and my eyes are protesting now. It really is time for home.

Matthews, my head of technology, can wait—just as Janice tried to tell me.

And as though I've conjured her back, there's a tap at my door.

'Yes?' I push out of my seat, start to rise, then

freeze, my hands clutching the chair-arms for support. *'Cain?'*

He fills the doorway to my right, the precise cut of his dark suit speaking of its price tag, the flint shade of his shirt an exact match for his eyes, which seem to glint at me from across the room. There's not a black hair out of place in its brushed-back style. His face is clean-shaven, his collar open—even his hands are relaxed inside his pockets. He's so at ease, in control… Nothing like the broken man I saw three months ago.

'We need to talk.'

I swallow, a shiver of fear running down my spine. It's not rational. This is *my* domain—my office, my company.

What can I possibly be afraid of when it comes to him?

Nothing can hurt me more than he already has. *Nothing.*

'I was about to leave for the night.'

'For the *night*? Hell, Alexa…'

And there it is—a slight crack to his calm exterior. He rakes his fingers through his perfect hair, a heavy sigh leaving his lips—lips I don't want to remember as though I devoured them only yesterday when over seven years have passed. But my body remembers. The rush of warmth low in my abdomen tells me so.

'You might as well stay a little longer and you'll be on a new day.'

'What's that supposed to mean?'

His hands are back in his pockets as he pins me

with a glare, half-censorial, half-something else that I don't understand and don't dare analyse. I got him so wrong before that I don't trust my instincts where he's concerned now. I won't even risk trying to read him.

'It means you should have left hours ago.'

I settle back into my seat, refusing to rise to the anger that flares at his surprising concern.

Yeah, it's anger that has you so worried...

'You gave up any right to have a say in my working hours long ago, Cain—or do I need to remind you that you walked out on me seven years ago?'

Too personal, Alexa.

But at least he can't see my insides wince at the revealing nature of my anger.

'You walked out on us all.'

There, that sounded better.

'I did what I felt I had to...at the time.'

'And now?'

For the briefest of seconds his lashes flutter, as though I've inflicted a physical blow, but then it's gone and I realise I imagined it. I also realise that whatever glimpse I thought I had three months ago of a man in pain, or just now of a man who cares about the working hours I keep, he doesn't really exist.

This is Cain.

And he only cares for himself.

'Going over old ground isn't the reason I'm here.'

I'm disappointed with his evasive answer. The rejected part of me—the part left to survive after he fled, the part that gave birth to our stillborn child without him—wants to have that argument. Wants him to acknowledge what he did and to see him beg forgiveness.

But only a fool would expect such humanity from Cain, and I'm no longer that fool.

'So, what *is* the reason you're here?'

I cross my legs and turn my chair slightly, angling it to face him. I don't miss how his eyes sweep my length. I'm wearing a teal satin blouse, buttoned almost to the collar, and a black skirt to the knee. All perfectly respectable, but I swear I see the flicker of what I know is dangerous, what I should ignore… Only the ache kickstarting down low has other ideas.

I watch his throat bob. His eyes strike mine, a second's fire, and then nothing. The mask slips back into place.

Cold Cain. Composed Cain. Downright callous Cain.

This is the man I can deal with.

'I haven't got all night and, as you so rightly pointed out, I should have left hours ago,' I remind him, sickly-sweet. And then I have to wonder… 'How did you know I was here, anyway?'

'My mother. I paid her a visit first.'

My mouth quirks up. 'You *paid* her a visit—how awfully dashing of you.'

His eyes flash, and his annoyance is like catnip to me. We never argued, Cain and I—not really. Unless you count that one occasion. The occasion that ended it all. And it's oddly thrilling to do it now, when I owe him nothing—no love, no respect, no loyalty.

'She told me you're often here until the early hours of the morning.'

He looks to my desk, the spread-out papers, the mess, and I fight the urge to scoop it all up into something orderly. He has no right to judge me. And I'm a scientist through and through—ordered chaos is how I live my life.

'Although I have to admit...' his eyes come back to me with some hidden question burning deep '...I'm surprised to see you here. I half expected it to be some cover for your extra-curricular activities.'

His words spike both ice and fire into my blood. 'Are you insinuating I've lied to Marie to cover up an affair?'

He shrugs. 'Can you blame me? The second I left you jumped into bed with my brother. Why shouldn't I think the worst?'

My stomach lurches. 'What would *you* know of it? You were long gone—completely off-grid, no contact number, nothing.'

'Oh, I came back. To see a ring on your finger and my brother at your side.'

'You...?' I can't even swallow. I feel dizzy, sick. 'When?'

'Three months later. Can you imagine my surprise at returning home only to find you were all out at the registry office, of all places? Of course I had to go there myself to truly believe it. And there you were, the blushing bride, all innocent and happy.'

A laugh chokes out of him and the blood leaves

my face, my pulse slowing down as I piece the night-mare together.

'It didn't take you long at all, did it?' he says.

I don't want to believe he truly witnessed that scene, but his anger is so visceral, so real... 'Why didn't you say anything?'

'Like what?'

His mouth is a grim line, his eyes hard, unread-able. And, Christ, do I want to read them now.

'Congratulations on your *fucking* marriage. I'm so happy for you both!'

I jump at his profanity, the force of it, and shake my head. The movement is negligible, but it's all I can manage as I'm transported back seven years to the life his brother offered me. Me and my unborn child. He was my best friend, my rock, offering me everything I could wish for to give my child a stable, loving home. Everything I didn't have growing up.

'And what do you know, Alexa?' His tone is hard, scathing. 'It's been three months since Liam died, which means you likely have someone else lined up to take his place by now.'

I can't speak. I can't breathe. His insult sends fire through my bloodstream. My ears are ringing with its pounding beat. I force in a breath, two, feel my eyes sting as I stare him down.

Don't let him win. Don't sink to his level.

I rise out of my seat and turn my focus to the computer screen, shutting it down. The silence in the room stretches...heavy, loaded...but I don't trust my voice. Not yet.

And then he moves and he's standing beside me, his proximity like a drug I can't resist, can't get enough of even now.

'Now I think about it, Lexi…' His voice is low, and the use of the name he gave me all those years ago is purposely teasing, crushing, cruel. 'Maybe I've come back at just the right time to take on that role.'

I twist on my heel, my hand gliding through the air to make for his cheek—*of all the goddamn nerve*—but he's quicker than me. He grabs my wrist a split-second before it collides with his arrogant, self-assured face and I'm panting, the ragged sound the only thing I can hear.

He's so close, I can feel his breath brush against my forehead, feel the heat of his body through his shirt, the old familiar scent of his cologne invading my senses.

I breathe him in—just a second's weakness—as my lashes lower and I'm transported back to a time *before*. A time when I didn't have to resist this persistent pull, this inherent need, this impulsive ache.

'*Lexi…*'

His voice is husky and it grazes over me like sandpaper, calling to the very heart of me. I wet my lips and look up, scared of what I'll see, hungry for it all the same.

His eyes burn into mine, his desire etched in every hard line of his face. And then his gaze falls to my fingers in his grasp, to the ring still on my finger, and I remember who he is—what this is. I clamp my eyes shut and shake my head, as though that will rid me of him.

'Don't touch me.' I pull my hand from his grasp and back away. 'Don't ever touch me again.'

I force my focus onto my desk, shoving papers into my bag and praying he doesn't spy how my fingers tremble, how my entire body quakes.

'Why don't you do us all a favour and disappear off again, Cain?' I don't look at him as I say it. I don't dare. 'It's what you do best.'

'I'm not going anywhere.'

I still, my hands deep inside my bag as I process what he means. I can feel my pulse beating in my neck, my lips drying up and my throat clamping tight.

I chance a look. 'What do you mean?'

'It means I'm here to stay.'

He walks away, over to the window that stretches along one wall of my office, but it does nothing to ease my panic.

'Stay?' I fight to keep the tremor out of my voice. 'Stay where?'

He doesn't say anything, simply stares out at Dublin's Liffey River and the bustling Beckett Bridge. It's as though I've lost him to the view as its myriad of lights dance in his darkened gaze and form shadows across his face.

I part my lips to speak, to draw him back and get answers, but then he turns to me and the intensity of his eyes alone dries up my words. My knees weaken and I lock them tight, forcing my mouth closed again as I wait for what he has to say.

'I'm back, Alexa, and this time nothing can stop me taking all that I'm owed.'

I wait for her to erupt, to demand my explanation and tell me to go to hell.

Instead she frowns, her brows drawing together as her hand—the one that still bears my brother's ring—rises to her neck. It taunts me. Fires my blood with the need to possess, to take back what was once mine. But she's no object. I have no hold over her.

Only, my body can't be told so easily.

She wets her lips, and when she speaks it's with a calmness I'm sure she can't feel. 'What, *exactly*, do you think you're owed, Cain?'

Her question chimes with my mental rampage. Calls my mind back to my choice of words seconds before. The double meaning is glaringly obvious to me and I wonder if she has any idea of it.

If I'd thought about it first maybe I would have been more careful, masked the personal entirely with business—just business.

But I was angry, bitter, my mind lost to how different things might have been—no, *should* have been.

Her by my side, wearing my ring.

My younger brother still alive and working alongside me.

My father proud, my mother prouder.

But, no. I'm back as the black sheep, half my family gone, and now... Now what?

Now I'm staking my claim to the business and...

I look to the single gold band around her finger. 'You don't wear an engagement ring.'

Her frown deepens. 'What does that have to do with anything?'

Hell, I have no idea. I came to discuss business. Instead I'm caught up in *her*, in the personal. In what we once had and what I lost.

'I'm just curious.'

She lowers her hand and rotates the gleaming metal between her thumb and forefinger, brandishing her love for another man with every twist. 'I didn't need one.'

I laugh; it's a bark. Harsh. Brutal. 'No one *needs* an engagement ring, Alexa. It's just expected...a loving gesture—' My voice catches and I mask it in a barren smile. 'It's tradition.'

'It was enough that he proposed.'

'Enough?' I stare at her, incredulous, my anger getting the better of me. 'How very romantic. You science folk really are clinical, through and through.'

Her eyes snap to mine, bright and fierce. 'If you've come here to lay into me and rip apart Liam's memory, you can leave right now. You don't get to speak ill of us—especially not him.'

'Why? Because he was so talented at everything? So good? The proper little Catholic boy my parents always wanted but had to wait two extra years for?'

She releases the ring and flexes her fingers. I

know she's itching to swing for me again. Funny, I've never thought her capable of violence.

Shows how much I knew her then.

And how little I probably know her now.

Or is her love for my brother so strong even in death that she just can't bear it…?

Ice pierces my heart, rebuilds my defences, reminds me of why I hate her.

'He was a better man than you'll ever know or understand.'

Her soft-spoken words cut deep, her meaning clear.

'Of course.' The words thrum out of me. 'I couldn't possibly know because I wouldn't know what it takes to be a truly good man.'

I raise a brow at her in challenge. I want her to refute it, tell me I'm wrong…

'Yes.'

The simple syllable vibrates with budding fury, making her affirmation all the more powerful, and I cling to it. To her honesty. To the fact that there is nothing between us any more. Only a mutual hatred that I can use. I need all the hatred I can get to keep my guard up. To resist this crazy pull that won't quit.

But what right does she have to be angry with me, when all is said and done? She's the one who betrayed me. Yes, I walked away—but I came back for her. *She* was the one who moved on. With my brother, of all people.

'And you think I should've just rolled over and accepted your relationship with him, the better man?'

She looks at me and I see her anger waver.

'Don't hesitate now, Alexa. You've stuck the boot in—you might as well keep on going.'

'I didn't... I don't...'

'You don't what?'

She says nothing, and my patience for this conversation is over. I never should've let it start in the first place.

'I'm sorry if you find me critical of your marriage to my brother but, given the circumstances, I would have thought it understandable. Even for someone like you.'

'Someone *like me*?'

'Did the affair start before I left? Or did you wait until a few days after I left?'

Her hands clench and her cheeks flare. 'We never had an affair.'

I pocket my fists and ignore the way my gut writhes at the idea, at the conjured-up images of the two of them together that I don't want to see and am powerless to prevent.

Maybe this *is* what I need.

Answers to the past before I can move on.

We're going to be working together—that's a given. My mother has already handed over my father's shares, and Alexa can't change the fact that we'll be equals as far as this business is concerned. I'll need my head clear to do what's needed, what's right for the company. Not enshrouded in anger, jealousy...intolerable desire.

'We *didn't* have an affair, Cain.'

'So you say.'

She shakes her head. Her cheeks are streaked with colour. She looks guilty as sin to me. It should make me despise her, but instead I'm thinking of how much she looks like she used to in my bed— the same colour in her cheeks, her eyes bright, her hair wild about her bare shoulders as she called out my name in sheer ecstasy.

Fuck.

I ram the thought out of my mind. It has no place in the present. It was so long ago. But I have no control over my dreams and they've teased me with it far too often.

'You only have yourself to blame for all this.'

She declares it as fact and I let out a harsh laugh— more to fend off the unwelcome heat plaguing my veins than at her words.

'You were the one who left, Cain.'

'Tell yourself whatever you like, if it makes you feel better, but it doesn't change the truth of it.'

'That *is* the truth.'

I suck in a breath, my lungs fighting my body's stillness to take in air. I shouldn't feel like this. She shouldn't have this power over me. And yet the tell-tale pressure building behind my fly knows otherwise.

Remember the pain.

Remember how she hurt you.

How *they* hurt you.

'Did you ever wonder why I left?' I ask, clinging to the memory as a lifeline.

'Are you serious?' Her eyes widen. 'You walk out without a word, go completely off-grid, where no one can reach you. Christ—of *course* I wondered. We all bloody did! It was only the fact you spoke to Marie that stopped us calling the police and sending out a search party!'

She's trembling from head to toe, her voice shaking, her eyes watering. I could almost believe she'd cared. Really cared.

'I had my reasons to leave.'

'Oh, yes, of course you did—and they all revolved around looking after *numero uno*. Yourself. And to hell with the rest of us.'

'I cared, Alexa, believe me. I cared more than you can possibly know.'

She laughs, and the manic sound drives me crazy. Pain collides with something more fierce, something more treacherous, and I move without thinking.

I'm across the room and pulling her against me. Her startled moan is drowned out by a growl I cannot contain and I realise my folly the second my lips claim hers.

Folly because she's not fighting me. She's on fire with me, her lips meeting me halfway and leaving me in no doubt as to how much she wants this too.

Fireworks erupt inside me—an explosion of sensation wrapped up in a warning so powerful it makes me dizzy. Drunk on her. On what's right. What's wrong.

I try to see sense even as my lips move with hers. Remembering. Reacquainting. But there's nothing soft or loving about this. It's harsh, demanding. Each of us taking what we want, what we need.

Her hands are pressed against my chest. I feel their heat burn a path to my heart beneath. And then she's lifting them to my hair, holding me, her body melding to mine. She's giving herself over to me. It should be enough. I should stop now. I should be the one to stop it. The one in control.

Instead I'm kissing her back like a drowning man on a quest for air. My hands are in her hair, and its softness is so familiar, her impassioned surrender so pure. It's pulling me under. It's not air I want—it's this sea of sensation, of incandescent need that she's always instilled in me.

I want to use it to obliterate my brother's touch with my own.

I want to use it to obliterate the past, the pain, the ache of loss.

But at what cost?

Do I really want to succumb? To lay down my defences? To be weak?

CHAPTER TWO

Don't do this, Alexa.

The mantra is on repeat, playing at the back of my mind, but I can't listen. I don't want to listen. It's been so long since I've felt this way. Alive. The heat pulsating between my legs, robbing me of any coherent sense and making me feel again.

I'd started to think I was immune, that nothing would bring this feeling back.

But I'm not numb. I'm not dead inside. I'm thriving, flourishing, abuzz with it.

He's the reason you feel like that. And he's the reason you shouldn't be giving in to it now.

I kiss him harder, forcing out the dawning sense, the voice of reason. I only want to feed this budding ache, to go with it until it consumes me, and it's all I'm capable of thinking of.

I know he feels it too. I can feel his need pressing between us, his breath hitching in tune to mine, his hands fierce as they fork through my hair.

Our teeth clash as our pace outruns us and I laugh. I'm delirious at letting go, at not being in control.

I don't feel like myself. Or rather I feel like my younger self, with no cares, no worries. He pulls back and I look up at him. He's grinning, his eyes alive with mischief, and I *am* that young again. So is he.

But you're not.

The realisation ripples through my system, the chill contending with the heat as the past seven years rapidly replay and I'm in freefall. Lost to it.

The sudden burn of tears is my wake-up call.

Oh, God, no.

I try to draw a breath, my fingers freezing in his hair as I close my eyes to block him out until I can see straight again. I cling to the chill within my belly, the echo of my pain, of my loss.

'*Lexi...*'

It's part-groan, part-plea, and then his mouth is back, travelling along my jaw, his shadowed stubble teasing a rough path to my earlobe. The ice is melting. My fingers are softening in his hair...my disobedient deprived body is curving into him and letting his heat burn out the cold. This is better. This feeling. I don't want the chill. The grief that will overcome me if I let it.

'*Lexi...*'

The way he says my name is a tortured sound that meets my inner torment head-on. He knows we shouldn't do this. He knows it's wrong. He has his reasons and I have mine. Yet we are both losing it. Letting it win. And the battle makes it all the more powerful. All the more desperate.

I cling to his head as his teeth graze the delicate

flesh of my earlobe, shiver as his hot breath invades my ear and moan my approval. Not that he needs it. He knows my every erogenous zone and is using that knowledge to push me.

But I know his too.

And I'm eager to remind him of it.

I tug his shirt from his waistband, slip my hands beneath and feel the heat of his skin under my palms. He's harder than I remember. Hot, lean, chiselled.

My mouth waters anew and I trail my fingers up his back, feel his skin prickle, his body shudder against me, and I smile. Still the same Cain. The one who can't determine if he's ticklish, turned on, or both.

Confident, I rake my nails down his shoulder blades and he grinds his hips against me with a hiss against my throat. I want more than a hiss, though; I want him out of his mind. I want the controlled man of minutes before surrendering to the wild man of old.

I drop my hands to his waistband, go to pop the button, and his hands drop to my wrists, stilling me.

'Not yet.'

When? I want to ask, but I can't speak.

His mouth is moving down over my blouse, the light fabric allowing just enough sensation to draw my nipples through both it and the lace of my bra, betraying exactly what I want, what I need. He pulls my arms behind my back, clasps my wrists in one hand as he walks me backwards against my desk.

I'm restrained, captive, and all his. It shouldn't turn me on like it does.

He shouldn't.

But, hell, I'm turned on and willing to lay myself bare just to feel the completion of this. The promise of the climax to come. That height of bliss, of ecstasy, of what I've not had in over seven years. Ever since… Ever since…

He thrusts my skirt up my thighs and my breath hitches, my mind quits. His palms are hot and hurried against my skin, frantic—and, *fuck*, I am too. It's like a long overdue homecoming. Being here, like this, with him.

The breadth of his palm covers the front of my thigh, his thumb is so close to the heart of me, and then he skims over my underwear, a gentle brush that has me bucking and crying, arching my back to plead for more.

He makes a sound—half-laugh, half-groan—and then his mouth is covering one nipple, his teeth biting through the fabric. I curse the very existence of my clothing. Of any barrier. I want it all gone. Hell, I want the last seven years gone. A rewrite of every painful second. If only…

I'm too close to sanity again. Too close to ending this before I've had my fill—

No. No. No.

I don't need slow and steady. I don't need him savouring me. I don't need time to reconsider.

I want it hard and fast—no thought permitted.

I pull at my wrists, still encased in his grip, drop

my head forward. But my lips are silenced by what I see. Cain. He is heaven and hell all rolled into one. All strength and sinew, carnal and lascivious. His chiselled jawline emphasised as his mouth works over me, his eyes darkly intense as he focuses on drawing out my nipples, making them beg, making *me* beg.

I whimper and his eyes shoot to my face, their fierce intensity making my belly contract. The heated swell down low, so rampant I bite down on my bottom lip and watch his eyes flare in response.

I feel like he's testing me, pushing me, silently asking: *can we do this?*

I have no answer. Hell, he hasn't even put a voice to the question. But I feel it all the same. The question pulses through me, urging me to decide.

Can we?

Yes.

Should we?

No.

My fingers clutch the back of his head, his thumb rolls over me, and I want to cry and moan and say to hell with it. He keeps his eyes locked on mine, that question still blazing as he scrapes one protruding nipple with the edges of his teeth. Heat surges to meet his bite, pleasure on its tail. Pleasure and pain, desire and need. Then he launches back up to my mouth, his tongue delving inside, twisting with my own, making me whimper, making me fight back. Fencing, entwining…

Oh, God, yes.

He's back at my throat, my breast, my mouth again. I follow his every caress, and now I'm the one savouring every single touch as if it will suddenly expire—because it will. I know it will. There is no future here. Just like seven years ago, it will be whisked away. There'll be no warning. No nothing.

I claw his skull as pain spears me.

Stop thinking. Just feel.

He's crazy over me. His movements are frantic, as though he can't get enough of every part of me and he wants me all at once. I know that feeling. My lower body is grinding against his hardness, pleading for release, and he's meeting me. The hard length of his cock joins me at every rise and fall...our climaxes build as one. Like teenagers dry-humping for the very first time. Christ, just like our first time.

He was my one and only. In heart and in body. Not that he will know that—not unless I tell him the truth of my marriage to his brother.

I clamp my eyes shut as reality invades—another glimpse of pain threatening to destroy this moment, to take it all away. I can't have that. I won't. I have suffered for so long. Not even my own fingers are able to give me this heady, mind-obliterating pleasure.

There are so many reasons I shouldn't cave. So many reasons we shouldn't do this. But I can deal with those later. When I'm alone.

'Cain.'

It's the first time his name has left my lips like

this, and so much is loaded into that pleasure-filled tone I want to take it back. It gives up so much of me and I fear the exposure. But it only ramps up his tension, his need.

'I want you.'

He claims my mouth and releases my wrists in one movement. His hands grip my hips as he thrusts me back over the desk and lifts my legs around him. He's tight against my slick heat, his fingers vibrating as he holds me, his breathing ragged.

'Say you want me too.'

Oh, God.

His request is strained, gruff. But I can't do it. I can't. I do want him—but I don't.

He stares down into my eyes, our noses almost touching. I can see how much he needs the words. I close my eyes and kiss him instead. He caves for seconds, but he's no fool.

'Tell me you want me, Lexi.'

It's a command now, his entire body still as he waits on me.

'Say it.'

I risk a look into his face and the air catches in my lungs. So much pain tangled up with desire.

My fingers curl around his neck as I hold him to me. I part my lips, but nothing will come.

'You can't say it, can you?'

'I...'

He's Cain. He broke your heart. He'll break it again if you let him.

'No. No, I can't.'

It comes out as a whisper. I take a breath, then another, and watch his eyes flicker and his jaw clamp shut. I wonder if he'll come back to me anyway. I start to rise to meet his lips, but he's already gone, averting his gaze and stepping back, releasing me so quickly I almost fall.

I plant my palms onto the desk to steady myself and push myself to stand before he can turn and see the state I'm in.

His words come back to me: *'Nothing can stop me taking all that I'm owed.'*

'Is this why you're here?' I ask quietly. 'Is this what you mean by taking all that you're owed?'

He's tucking his shirt into his trousers as he sends me a look I can't decipher and my anger flares twice as strong, powered by my fevered pulse, by his demand, by his rejection.

'You just had to hear me tell you I want you? Just to win one over on Liam?'

I can't believe it, but at the same time I'm convinced it's true.

'It may surprise you, Alexa, but I don't make a habit of sleeping with women who don't want me.'

I laugh, the sound shuddering out of me. 'I think you know how much my body wanted you.'

He studies me intently, his eyes raking over me, exposing me. I fold my arms high on my chest, wanting to conceal the damp path created by his mouth, to block out the slickness between my legs that tells me how close I've come to making a mistake.

His eyes lift to my mouth, dark, intense, and he

takes a step forward, closing the distance between us. 'You and me both.'

He reaches out and I lift my chin, eyeing him warily. His palm comes to rest against my cheek, his thumb smoothing over my cheekbone, and I'm captivated by his sudden softness.

'I cared, Lexi—about you, about us.'

His eyes are fixed on my lips as he says it, his sincerity as bewitching as his touch.

'I loved you once.'

His eyes lift to mine.

'Don't ever question that.'

A lump rises in my throat, and my eyes burn as tears well.

'I loved you once.'

If he loved me, how could he have left? How could he have abandoned me and the unborn child I didn't know I carried?

I stare into his eyes, desperate for answers, and swallow down the lump to speak. 'But—'

'But nothing. It's in the past.'

Not when it still has the power to hurt. I need answers, I need to understand.

'How can it be?'

'Because it was a mistake I'll never make again. Ever.' His jaw pulses, his eyes harden and his thumb stills its caress. 'I won't love you. I won't mourn you. I won't be that fool again.'

He walks away, back to the window, and I stare after him. Cold. Confused.

'Then why kiss me?'

His eyes come back to me, his face set hard. 'It seems no amount of hatred can stop this fire between us.'

I feel sick. Sick to know he speaks the truth. Sick to know I almost caved.

'Well, I beg to differ.' I smooth down my skirt, ignore the damp cling of my blouse where his mouth has been, and face him down. I won't let him win this.

'It's a bit late to deny its existence now. That little display was enough to convince us both. We just established that.'

There is no answer I can give to that, so I go with my gut. 'Go to hell, Cain.'

I turn to start stuffing the rest of my belongings into my bag. The sooner I leave, the sooner I can get away from him and—

'I'd have a pretty hard time running the company from there.'

I freeze. My heart thuds in my chest. I can't have heard him right.

I glare at him. 'What's that supposed to mean?'

'When I said I was coming back to take what I'm owed…'

He faces me head-on now and I can see his power visibly seeping into every pore, his ease returning, his control.

'I wasn't referring to you—appealing as that idea is. I was referring to the company…to Dad's shares.'

I swallow. 'You're not serious?'

'Deadly.'

'But Marie wouldn't... She would have discussed it with me first. She would have at least mentioned it.'

'Be that as it may, they are mine.'

I shake my head at him. This can't be happening. It just *can't*.

He pockets his fists as he holds my eye. 'You need to practise looking happy about it. My personal assistant, Sheila, will be arranging a function in a fortnight, for the investors and some acquaintances of mine—a kind of welcome back into the fold, so to speak. It'll be good to make the right impression. Don't you think?'

'You can't do this...*we* can't do this.'

'Correction. We *need* to do this if the business is to survive and our investors are to be happy once more.'

'How do you know about the investors?'

'Everyone in the industry knows, Alexa. You can't keep that kind of thing a secret.'

My hand presses into my abdomen, the empty ache beneath increasing tenfold as I ask, 'How long will you be here?'

'Who's to say I won't make it a permanent thing?'

Is he goading me on purpose? Rubbing salt into the wound? There's no way he would come back permanently.

He can't.

'Because you have your business, your commitments... Ireland is hardly a convenient location for you. You have no presence here.'

He shrugs. 'Maybe it's time I changed that. A new

headquarters, a new operation—it'll be great for the local economy and it's time I had a base, a home.'

'A *home*?' I'm going to be sick.

'Are you not feeling well?'

My eyes narrow on him. Have I gone green? Then he gestures to where my hand clutches at my stomach and I snatch it away. It's too incriminating, too revealing of the painful secret I hold from him.

'How can you ask me that when you've just dumped this news on me?'

He has the audacity to almost smile as he nods. 'Fair enough—but the sooner we move past this and get started on presenting a united front, the sooner the investors will get off your back—*our* backs.' He straightens and clears his throat. 'We can talk properly on Monday morning. Eight work for you?'

'Monday?'

Try never.

But what choice do I have? If Marie has passed on those shares, she has done it because she has faith in her son. Faith she didn't have in me to pull the investors back onside.

Or maybe it's her way of getting her son back?

'Yes, I have to fly back to London for a few days. It'll give you plenty of time to get used to the idea.'

Whether it's for her son or for the company, I can't fight Marie's decision, and so I nod as I pull my bag up off the desk. 'Eight o' clock, Monday.'

I expect him to leave. Instead he hovers.

'You can go now.'

'How are you getting home?'

He looks and sounds as if he cares. But I know better—hell, he's told me he doesn't—and I resent having to give an answer. I do it in the hope he will then leave, giving me the space I so desperately need.

'I have a car in the basement.'

'Good.'

Thankfully, he heads for the door, and my resentment gives rise to strength. I call out. 'Cain?'

He pauses and looks at me over his shoulder.

'If we do this,' I say, square on, 'we're equals. You are *not* my boss, and you don't *tell* me what to do. We agree together. Is that understood?'

His lips quirk. 'Agreed.'

I swear I can see admiration in his gaze before he turns away again. Well, he can keep his fucking admiration.

'And Cain?'

Another look.

'I was a fool to love you once too. I won't make that mistake again either.'

His brow lifts. 'Tit for tat? Really, Alexa? I would have thought that beneath even you.'

Argh! I want to scream at him, pound at his chest until he acknowledges that *he* was the one in the wrong. Not me. And not Liam. *Never* Liam.

But I can't make him see that without telling him the whole truth, and I fear that more.

'If you want to see it that way, then fine.'

He's still, his eyes searing into mine, as if he can see all the way inside me to the truth. But I don't back down. I don't even flinch.

And then he's gone as quickly as he appeared and I succumb to the scream, fisting my hands and then flinging them out as I let it go. It feels so good that I do it again and again, and then I slump into my chair, my head in my hands, and breathe.

Just. Breathe.

It'll be okay. You just need to keep your guard up and all will be well. A piece of cake.

'Some cake…' I mutter into my palms.

CHAPTER THREE

ISN'T IT STRANGE how you can be someone to the outside world, even believe you *are* that someone, but the second you walk into the home you grew up in, with the same smells, the same furnishings, practically the same décor, you're transported back to the person you used to be? Exposed.

I don't feel like a successful billionaire who knows his own mind, who makes critical decisions on a daily basis.

I feel like a child.

Vulnerable. Angry. On edge.

I roll my head on my shoulders and shift back in the armchair my mother has set before the roaring fire especially. Dad's chair.

'Tough week?'

I smile at her, wanting to put her at ease. 'You could say that.'

She frowns at me from her own seat, angled like mine to face into the fire, but her soft green gaze is all for me and it's concerned. I really could be that schoolboy again, just come home after a run-in with his best mate. Or the teen who's just fallen out with his girlfriend and doesn't know how to feel.

She's much the same as she always was. Her long hair is woven into the same plait she's always favoured, only now it's greying at the temples. Her voice still possesses that melodic ring that Dad was so fond of and Liam and I were comforted by as children.

My stomach lurches. It happens every time I think of Dad, of Liam. And I know the added lines on my mother's face, the extra grey in her hair, have come in the last few months since the funeral. That the weight of facing life without them is taking its toll. But there's still a strength to her, a spark to her eyes when she smiles at me, that tells me I've done the right thing. That having me here has helped to ease that burden.

Yes, coming back was the right decision—even if it's brought me face to face again with Alexa and the unfinished business between us.

My mind replays the scene in her office. The crazy heat. The even crazier words that came out of my mouth. Out of hers. They burn through me even now, four days later, far more effective than the fire roaring before us.

I drag my eyes to the flames and watch them crackle and flicker.

'Do you want to talk about it?' Mum asks. 'A problem shared and all that…'

My fist pulses around the arm of Dad's chair and

I take a deep breath—only to have the scent of my family home attack my defences further. I don't even know where I'd start. Seven years ago? Three months ago? A week? And even so I'm not willing to voice the chaos underway in my head. To put words to it will only make it more real.

'It's nothing I can't handle.'

My own conscience mocks me, laughing at my projected confidence.

I want to be confident, though. I want to be in control.

But in Alexa's office I lost both, succumbing to the weakness of emotion, hormones, endorphins... I played myself for a fool.

'It can't be easy for you...coming back and working with Alexa—'

She breaks off, struggling for the right words, and I can't find any to stop her, to put an end to this conversation before it starts.

'I have a good feeling about this, though.' She nods, sounding far more certain. 'She needs you. She needs your help, your business acumen and your reputation.'

She reaches across to place her hand on my arm, her expression softening.

'She can be stubborn, but she'll see that eventually. She can't continue like she has been, and neither can the company. To see it pulled apart, failing... It's your father's legacy.'

Her voice is transformed with her grief, her concern. Just as it was a month ago, when she asked me to consider doing this. I balked then, but the more I heard about the company, the more I couldn't ignore what was happening.

And I trust myself to keep it all contained. The last seven years have taught me to think before speaking, to always be in control of myself, that it doesn't pay to act on emotion. It's how I've achieved all I have. I'm not the same man who left seven years ago.

Now, with hindsight, do I regret leaving? *Yes*.

But regret doesn't help me.

I have to look to the future.

So why did I lose sight of that in Alexa's office? Why did I allow my emotions to take the driving seat when I should have been focusing on the business? On what matters?

Why? my conscience mocks me again. *Because you're not over her. Because you love—no, loved her. And now you want her.*

Fuck—I do.

I don't love her. Not any more. How can I possibly love her when I hate her for what she did? I still can't believe the audacity of her parting words.

'I loved you too.'

How could she possibly have loved me, only to marry my brother within months of my departure? It was sick. Twisted.

And still I want her.

Maybe I'm the twisted one, for wanting what was taken from me.

Just like the business was taken from me when

my father decided to give a portion of it to Liam instead of me.

He said it was my wake-up call—that if I truly wanted to be a part of the business then I needed to demonstrate I was worth it.

'Knuckle down,' he said. 'Give up the sport, the mates, the fun. Grow up.'

I've definitely done all that.

And look at me now. Everything my father would have wanted. Only he's not here to witness it.

'I'm so glad you've come home, that you've agreed to help Alexa and the company,' Mum suddenly gushes, patting my arm. 'Your father would be glad too.'

And there it is: the confirmation I definitely want but don't feel prepared to hear. No matter that my thoughts had been going down that path seconds before.

'I hope so.'

'No hope about it, love.'

Her voice cracks with emotion and my stomach twists.

'He spoke about you often, you know. Liam did too. They always hoped… Well, you know…'

Oh, God. I don't want this conversation. I don't feel prepared for it. Emotionally or physically. I came for Sunday dinner—not to be emotionally battered by the past and my mistakes.

'We can't change the past, Mum.'

'No, no, you're right. And it doesn't help to dwell, does it?'

She reaches over to squeeze my hand, her smile bright even as her eyes glisten with unshed tears.

'I've made your favourite—shepherd's pie.'

I swallow. 'Brown sauce?'

'Always.'

And just like that the mood lifts, as it has every time I've returned over these last few months.

Every visit is an emotional rollercoaster that will get smoother as time goes by and will continue to get easier, I tell myself.

It will.

I open the wrought-iron gate and smile as it gives its familiar little squeak. I already feel calmer. The welcoming charm of the O'Connors' nineteenth-century cottage and its pretty little rose garden out front never fails to work its magic over me.

It's funny, really. You'd have thought with all the wealth they accumulated over the years Marie and Robert would have moved out—bought somewhere bigger, more impressive. But, no, Marie loved it, and therefore Robert loved it too.

My smile turns bittersweet as I let myself in, dropping my handbag in the hallway and toeing off my shoes. At least Marie still has me, and vice versa.

And now she has Cain too.

And that's just fine.

Absolutely.

Fine.

I push him out of my mind, though I know he'll make his way back in again soon—like he has done practically every minute of every waking hour these last four days.

I dip to pull from my handbag the bottle of wine I've brought and tell myself that this is mine and Marie's time and no one else can encroach on that. The wine is Marie's favourite red, and I bring it every Sunday. It's our weekly routine. We don our comfies—which for me means leggings, a big fluffy jumper and equally fluffy socks—and put the world to rights over good food and good vino.

'Only me, Marie!' I call down the hallway—as if it would be anyone else—and follow the sounds of crockery to the kitchen.

The house smells delicious, of comfort in all its glory. Marie's a terrific cook—something she's always been keen to pass onto me—and the homemade sticky toffee pudding I have hooked under one arm is all thanks to her teaching.

I kick open the kitchen door and walk on in, my smile wide. 'Hey, I hope you're up for something naughty—'

My eyes land on the tall, dark figure standing before the window and my smile dies. *No, it can't be.*

But of course it is. Cain's her son. This is her home. How naïve I've been to think things wouldn't change, that our easy routine wouldn't be upended with his arrival.

'Something naughty sounds thrilling.'

He pushes away from the window as he says it and stalks towards me. For one half-crazed second I think he's going to embrace me...kiss me, even...

Something naughty.

My mind races. Why did *those* have to be the words I used?

'Sounds perfect, love.' Marie is talking to her prized cast iron range as she finishes serving up some steaming veg. At least I think it's veg, but my eyes are hooked on Cain, my lips parted, my heart pulsing in my chest.

He pauses in front of me, his smile so warm I wonder if I've imagined the way we left things. And then I meet his eye and, no, it's there. The war blazing between us.

I can see it in the tightness around his eyes, the way his neck cords with tension. Tension and strength. I felt that strength first-hand four days ago, when I'd explored him in my office—and, damn it all to hell, that ache swells at the juncture of my thighs, my body reliving that scene in one vivid sweep.

Oh, fuck. Swallow.

He lifts his brow.

Shit—did I curse out loud?

Oh, please, God, no.

But Marie is still pottering, and my mouth is still gaping; it's so dry I don't think words could have formed even if I'd tried.

Then his finger is under my chin, and to my horror he pushes my jaw to close my mouth for me. I look away, but not before I spy the open amusement dancing in his gaze, and I want to slap myself. He's read me like an open book. But, hell, I didn't expect this. I'm unprepared, ill-equipped.

Excuses, excuses... I can practically hear him saying it.

I quit the mental rambling and say what I'm thinking—or close enough. 'I wasn't expecting you.'

I try to keep my voice neutral, but it's hard. So hard. I think of Marie, within earshot, and use it to claw back control.

'That makes two of us. Allow me.' He reaches out for the bottle and the glass-lidded dish, eyeing the dessert with open speculation. 'You cooked this?'

I thrust them into his hands, glad Marie can't see the aggressive manoeuvre, and make my voice sweet—sickly, even. 'I've been taught by the best.'

Marie's easy laugh breaks through the tension as she turns and sweeps me into a hug. 'I wouldn't say I'm the best—more that you're a good student.'

I embrace her, give her a kiss to the cheek. 'How are you?'

She releases me and steps back, her gaze sweeping us both. I don't miss the sheepish glint in her eye, the flush to her cheeks. The minx.

'Better now I have you both under this roof again.'
Marie. Don't push this.

I glare at her in warning and she purposely ignores it.

'Now, come on, I don't want dinner getting cold.'

One look at Cain and I know he hasn't missed his mother's guilt either. But we do as she instructs, carrying the food and the wine through to the dining room.

Marie sits at the head of the table and we sit either side of her, facing one another—far too close for comfort. I stare at the bottle I brought, not at him, but he's lifting it and my eyes follow.

He's wearing a simple sweater and jeans. At least it should be simple, but on him it's practically indecent. The jumper is thin, and it clings to his chest to the point that I can just make out the pearls of his nipples beneath, the pecs that surround them, the muscles of his arms flexing as he uncorks the bottle.

And then I remember what I'm wearing and my cheeks flush crimson. I look like Bridget Jones on a crying-into-a-tub-of-ice-cream night. Not the capable CEO I need to prove to him I am.

'Wine?'

Oh, God, he's looking right into my eyes— probably clocking my heightened colour and thinking it's all down to him and his damned appeal, rather than the fluffy bunnies adorning my equally fluffy socks. I plaster a smile on my face and nod, immediately questioning the decision. I'm going to need my wits about me to keep this chaos in hand and get through this meal unscathed.

'Ah, I've forgotten the brown sauce...' Marie pushes out of her seat.

'I'll go,' I say. Any excuse to leave and get my head straight.

The way his lips pull at the corners in a suppressed grin, I know he knows why I want to flee. And he thinks it highly entertaining.

I'm instantly irritated—to the point that I have the

most ridiculous urge to stick my tongue out at him. Very un-CEO-like. Very unlike me.

'Don't be silly.'

She's already heading for the door, and any moment now we'll be alone. No one to keep the peace—no one to stop me losing it.

'Stop looking at me like that.' I say it under my breath, but my cheeks are blazing crimson under his dancing gaze. His continued amusement is provoking me to the point that I can't zip it.

'I should tell you the same. You could have stripped me bare with your X-ray vision just now.'

Fuck!

My cheeks, my entire body, are flushing like a lobster. 'Don't mistake civility for anything more, Cain.'

'Oh, I know civility, all right, Lexi. But your thoughts were less civil and more of the X-rated variety—'

'Cain!'

My eyes flick to the door, the very idea of Marie overhearing him sending my blood pressure up another few notches. Not to mention his use of that pet name again. No one else uses it—ever. It was his endearment. His name for me. When he loved me… before…before…

God, woman, get it together.

'Your ego can tell you what it likes,' I say, grateful that my tone is hard, steady. 'But I'm being *civil*, Cain, for Marie's sake. And I will continue to be so for the company's sake too.'

His eyes flicker over my face, pause at my lips, and hell if I don't feel that heat from the inside now, burning low down. I cross my legs, fending off the dull throb that beats there.

'On that we can also agree.'

His voice is thick, his eyes dark. The table for eight feels small all of a sudden, as if the whole room is closing in around us and drawing us together. I can feel myself leaning, floating, drawn into his magnetic pull… And then I hear movement at the door and Marie is back.

I snap upright—*fucking smooth, Alexa*—and grab the chilled water jug, pouring myself a generous helping. It'll balance the alcohol and chill my insides. I hope.

I fill Marie's and Cain's glasses too, without asking. I think my voice would squeak if I spoke, and in truth I need something to do with my hands, which seem determined to wring themselves raw in my lap.

Four days. Four days I've had to come to terms with his return, to prepare for our meeting tomorrow, and I am no more ready now than I was when he first walked in.

'I'd like to raise a toast.'

My eyes flick to Marie as she raises her wine glass and I try to keep my expression neutral. A toast? Really?

'To new beginnings.'

I swallow and I swear it's audible. 'New beginnings,' I mutter, taking up my own glass.

I don't dare look at Cain as I drink. I don't want to see what he's thinking.

'New beginnings.'

There's that speculation again, ringing in his voice, and I'm pulled back to him, unwilling. He's studying me intently over his wine glass and I can't look away. I want to, I do...

'I'm sorry I didn't tell you both that the two of you were coming, but...' Marie shrugs merrily '...I figured it was best to face the music head-on, so to speak. It's so much better that way.'

I smother a startled cough, the remnants of wine catching. *Head on, indeed.*

'Cain, I am so glad to have you back here.' She reaches over to pat his hand, doing a good job of pretending not to notice anything amiss in the room. 'And Alexa...' She places her other hand on mine now. 'You have been running yourself ragged these past few months. Now you have someone to share that burden. Someone who will care for the company like you do.'

She smiles at us both, her hands resting on ours.

'So, please, indulge me with this.'

'There's nothing to indulge, Mum.'

He is so perfectly calm, and I envy him for that.

'You're right—it makes perfect sense for me to come back and help.' He places his hand over his mother's and smiles at her. 'I'm happy to be home too.'

My breath catches at what I see, what I hear. For the first time since he's been back he's completely unguarded, open, his face full of love—relief, even. I feel a stab of guilt. This is why I need to get myself in hand. To put on a front and make everything just so. Because he belongs here far more than I ever did or will again.

I wet my lips and squeeze Marie's fingers gently, my smile aimed to reassure. 'What Cain said...'

She studies me for a second longer and then she nods, her beam so full of relief, happiness. 'Good. Good.' And then she picks up her cutlery. 'In that case, let's eat.'

She looks as if a weight has been lifted. For the first time since the crash I see a glimpse of the old her and my smile is genuine, filled with the love I feel for this woman who has treated me as her own for fifteen years.

My eyes drift back to Cain and my smile dies a swift death. He's watching me, eyes intense, brooding, and so many emotions cross his face I can't latch on to a single one. I just know they centre on me. All me.

Where has the composed Cain from seconds before gone?

I pull my eyes away and lift my fork, preparing to eat, hoping he'll do the same.

He doesn't.

What have I done? Did I say something, do something, to put him on edge?

'This looks lovely, Marie.'

I stare pointedly at his plate and his lashes flicker.

He gives a slight shake of his head and then finally he follows suit.

'Smells as good as ever,' he says.

'Well, it always was your favourite. A mother never forgets.'

Shepherd's pie. I should have remembered. Should have realised. I want to kick myself over my stupidity.

Marie hasn't made this dish in over seven years. Not since that last family meal when his father announced the redistribution of his shares, cutting Cain out of the business. Not since Cain and I fell out in the O'Connors' front garden, of all places, straight afterwards, both flinging accusations that neither of us could come back from.

But we might have stood a chance if Cain had only stuck around. Instead he'd fled. Leaving not just me but the O'Connors too. A hate-filled goodbye, all he'd deemed us worthy of…

Jesus, Marie, you really are facing the past head-on.

I glance at her, seeing the hope in her bright green gaze, and I wonder if maybe, just maybe, she's right to do this. Maybe it's exactly what I should be doing too?

My hand goes to my stomach, stroking back and forth. There's so much he doesn't know. So much I need to confess in order to truly face the past. So much pain to dredge up.

Can I really go there and come out whole again?

Do I have a choice?

Now he's back, doesn't he deserve to know?

My skin prickles beneath my jumper as a cold sweat breaks across my back, down my front. I wish I'd worn a vest, so I could take off my suffocating fur-ball of a jumper, but even then I'd feel like this.

It has nothing to do with the warmth of the room and everything to do with the pain of past, of the memories I try to bury but not to forget, all at the same time. Because Rose shouldn't be forgotten. I gave birth to her. Held her. Her small body fragile and still.

My eyes sting and I avert my gaze, blink, reaching for my water glass and hoping they don't notice how my fingers quake.

Yes, telling him is the right thing to do.

In my heart I know that.

But confessing will also rip my heart in two, and I'm not sure I'll be able to piece it back together again.

Not this time.

CHAPTER FOUR

I EAT EVERY last mouthful of shepherd's pie and go in for seconds. I do it for Mum. To see the pleasure on her face as she dishes out another helping.

I give her a smile of thanks, then force my eyes back to my plate and away from Alexa.

I know why Mum made this meal. Yes, it's my favourite. But, more than that, she's doing just what she said she would: she's getting us to face up to the past head-on, in the hope that we can all move on.

Move on?

I manage to prevent the shake of my head as I take a forkful of food and chew it. My eyes drift back to Alexa, as they seem determined to do at every opportunity, and the past comes back to haunt me... The night we last had this meal. The night I let my anger get the better of me and made the decision to leave both my family *and* my fiancée.

It was the night Dad made his announcement regarding the company, confirming my ingrained suspicion that I would never stack up, that Liam would always outshine me. There'd been no discussion, no warning, no three strikes and you're out. He'd just gone and done it—written me out of the company as he wrote my brother in.

The food sticks in my throat and I force it down. I'm not angry about my dad's decision any more. I'm not bitter about it.

The past seven years have taught me about graft—the real hard graft of putting in the hours and proving your worth. Something my brother had done in spades back then and I had not. I've also had the last three months with Mum, talking to her, seeing it through my father's eyes, and although I may not agree with how my father went about it, I can forgive his reasoning now.

What I can't forgive is Liam. Liam and Alexa.

Their betrayal. *Hers.*

I glare at her now, and resent that my anger eases at the sight of her looking so pale. She's gone from flushed pink to deathly white, the smattering of freckles along her nose and cheeks striking out against the pallor of her skin. And I shouldn't care, I shouldn't be concerned with her discomfort. I hate that she makes me feel anything, but she does.

It will never be forgiveness, though, never love.

She wears no make-up today, and it riles me to admit that she looks all the more appealing for it. The reddish tone of her feather-like lashes setting off the blue of her eyes. Eyes which look even bigger with her auburn waves pulled back, her ponytail softened by the strands that fall free, all casual and sweet.

And her freckles—God, those freckles. They tease me, making my fingers itch with the need to trace their pattern like I've done a thousand times before. It was a lifetime ago, but I remember that path like it was only yesterday.

Does she have more now? More to discover, more to trace, more to kiss and tease?

My cock pulses, but so too does my heart. I bite back a curse and look for safety in my dish instead, only I have no stomach for food now.

She chose Liam. She married Liam. You weren't good enough for her. Remember that.

'How was your park run this morning, Alexa?'

Mum's been trying to get us to talk, and now that Alexa's plate is cleared and she can't stuff her mouth full she has to answer. I know this has been her tactic, because it's been mine too.

She smiles at Mum, but this time it doesn't quite reach her eyes. Not like earlier, when her smile shone with such love and affection for my mother that it lit me up from head to toe, strangling any warning my brain tried to give.

'I managed to get a PB…although I think that had more to do with Ed dictating the pace than me.'

Ed? Now my ears prick up.

'Quite eager, was he?'

Eager?

Alexa laughs softly, and the easy sound has my heart dancing in my chest.

'Very. I haven't the heart to rein him in either; he's too irresistible by far.'

Are they seriously talking about a guy? In front of me? Do they have no shame? No feelings? *Fuck.* Maybe three months really is all it takes for Alexa…

'Ed?'

They both look to me, and I see a faint flush of colour in Alexa's cheeks.

'Why, yes, love. Alexa takes Ed out for a run every Saturday and Sunday,' she announces proudly. 'Her neighbour works weekends, so it helps them out.'

'Ed's a Labrador.'

Alexa fills in the last blank, and although I don't want to feel it, relief washes over me all the same— even though it's none of my business…none at all.

'So you've taken up running?' I say with polite interest. 'Since when?'

I know straight away I've put my foot in it. The hint of colour in Alexa's face vanishes and my mother looks at her with a definite wince.

I know the answer already.

But it's too late to take it back.

Alexa clears her throat. Her fingers play with her cutlery and then she looks back at me, her face admirably still. 'A few years ago.'

Try seven, my brain supplies for her.

I stuff a fork full of shepherd's pie into my mouth and chew it with a nod, wishing for a rapid change in subject. My mother thankfully comes to my aid.

'So, how was your trip to London, Cain?' she rushes out, her smile forced as she looks at me. 'Was the event a success?'

I take a sip of wine to help the food go down. I can't remember ever having endured a meal as tense as this one. The second my father made his announcement seven years ago I ran. But there would be no running now. I'm not the same man I was then, and I don't run. Not any more.

I put down my glass and give another nod. Christ, if I keep on like this I'm going to come across like one of those ridiculous nodding dogs you get in the back of vehicles.

I force my head to still. 'I believe so.'

'Event?' Alexa asks, jumping on the change in topic too.

'I sponsor a youth centre back in London—'

'Don't be so modest, love.' My mother shakes her head at me before looking to Alexa. 'He *launched* that youth centre; without him it wouldn't exist.'

It's my turn to pink up. And I don't blush. *Ever.*

'It would have eventually,' I say. 'The proposal was already in place.'

'Yes—and you took that proposal, built on it, and made it a reality.'

I couldn't exactly deny it, but boasting about it…

I rub the back of my neck, which sure as hell feels hot. My cheeks burn.

I do these things to help people. Kids. Teens. People who need an outlet—somewhere to go to feel safe, less alone, to vent and let off steam.

'What does this youth centre do?' Alexa looks at me, and her interest seems so genuine I struggle to quash the spark of pride it triggers.

'It's a place for kids to hang out, play sport, study…
or just get help.'

'Help?'

'We have counsellors on hand.' I shrug. 'Sometimes they just need to talk to someone who won't
judge, won't hit back… It's a safe environment for
them to work off steam and make something of themselves.'

'He funded it, and he helps to run it too. Tell Alexa
what you were doing this weekend.' Mum smiles at
me indulgently and then says to Alexa, 'You will
love this!'

My cheeks burn deeper and I pick up my glass for
another swig. At least I'm not nodding now. I can see
what Mum's doing. She's trying to big me up in front
of Alexa. No doubt looking for us to make amends,
to get Alexa to accept that I may have walked out
but, hey, I'm a good man really.

Well, screw that. I have no amends to make.

She moved on. I didn't.

'Cain?'

Alexa's soft prompt pulls me up sharp and I know
I need to escape soon, that it's getting too much, but
I can answer this question easily enough. I can talk
about the youth centre in my sleep. It's my passion
to help those that need it. To make sure they have
a place to go to, to belong, when they don't have a
home of their own or home is part of the problem. I
know it chimes a chord with me—Alexa even more
so, when I really think about it.

'We have a youth entrepreneur scheme. Once a year they get to pitch to investors and I always sit in.'

I look at my plate, which is almost empty, and I can't stomach any more. I roll my shoulders and try to think up an excuse to leave that won't disappoint Mum.

There isn't one.

'And do they get investment?'

I look at Alexa, note her continued interest and feel a sudden pull to tell her more, to share the importance of this venture and why I care about it so much.

But sharing with Alexa…it opens me up, makes me vulnerable. This past week—these last three months, even—have proved just how much I'm not over her. That no amount of hate will protect me from her.

'The ones that are ready, yes,' I say. 'The others get invaluable advice from the best in the business. It gives them drive and confidence in their abilities to succeed.'

'As well as giving them a place to call home when they don't have a real one to go to,' Mum chips in.

I don't know whether she realises it, but she's just described me. The man I was when I set up the centre. I wasn't a kid, or a teen with good reason to feel how I did. I was a man who should have known better—who had thrown it all away because I was jealous, obsessed with being pushed out and not feeling good enough.

Something that had only been reinforced when

I returned after those first three months, hoping to make amends, to win Alexa back, only to find they'd all moved on quite happily without me.

My body burns with the memory—the sight of them on the steps of the registry office, taking photos, laughing, smiling. I never should have gone. The second I learned of their location—from my father's PA, of all people—I should have bolted, put myself on a plane to America and not looked back.

Instead I stood there in the shadows, a frozen statue, incapable of moving until they disappeared out of sight.

And now I've come back again, when it's all too late and that family is irrevocably broken…lost.

No, not completely lost. You still have Mum. And she needs you as much as you need her.

But what of Alexa?

It seems she's part of the package, thanks to her closeness to Mum—a bond that only seems to have grown over the years. Hell, she's even taught her to cook, something I never thought Lexi would take to or show an interest in. And they have such an easy awareness of one another's routines, an obvious fondness in their eyes when they look at one another.

Yes, she's definitely part of the package.

I meet Alexa's eye and I don't want to see the admiration she's directing at me now. I don't want to react to it with the warmth that's spreading inside, soothing the hurt with scary ease.

'It sounds great.'

I know she means it. I know that in spite of our past she's praising me.

It's the kind of youth centre she could have done with when I first stumbled across her, lost in the corridor of our crowded school, wide-eyed and alone. She was the epitome of a troubled teen, tossed from foster home to foster home, school to school, as they struggled to tame her. And I, the sports hero, fell for her hook, line and sinker.

I took her under my wing, brought her home, gave her everything I could. And my family took to her too, her intellect making her the perfect study buddy for my brother. They were the same age, after all.

It didn't matter then. They studied together, but I got to date her, and our relationship grew over the years. But then so did theirs. They finished school together, graduated from university together, worked in the family company together...

My gut twists with that old familiar pang, but as I look at her now, in that oversized sweater, with those ridiculous socks covered in bunnies beneath the table, the last seven years evaporate. I'm transported back to cosy nights on the sofa when she'd lie with her legs across my lap, book in hand, while I'd catch up on the football. Occasionally she'd shake her head at me as I shouted at the screen, but her eyes would be filled with love, all for me.

The reimagined scene flickers to life inside me, and as I continue to watch her I feel that old protective need come alive once more, the desire to have back what we lost growing out of my control.

And if I can't depend on my control to keep those feelings at bay then I know I'm in trouble.

Heart, mind and soul.

'That was incredible, love.'

Marie smiles at me, having just finished the last of her dessert, and wipes her lips with her napkin.

'I told you—I've been taught by the best.'

I feel Cain's eyes on me and wish I hadn't finished that second glass of wine, let alone the dessert wine Marie insisted on pouring. I can feel its heady warmth soothing away my tension, blurring the boundaries I've worked so hard to draw up.

The problem is that I can stay angry at the Cain who left seven years ago. I can even detest *him*.

But the man opposite me... He's the same, and yet...

I sense so much is different.

He's more measured, less likely to jump in before thinking, less fun-loving too. He used to be quick to laugh—quick to act the fool, even—but I can't see that in him now.

If he hadn't broken my heart I might even feel sad that he's hardened over the years. But that youth centre initiative... If there was ever a way to soften my defences, that would be it. Wine or no wine.

Not that I *am* softening. He left once—there's nothing to say he won't do it again. In fact, he's even more likely to do it now he has a life to go back to. Regardless of his threats to stick around, to set up home. I'm convinced he only said those things to goad me.

And what of his life elsewhere? Does he actually have people to go back to? A woman? A family, even?

I realise I know so little about him and my stomach writhes over those missing years. There must have been women. Plenty of women. No one can look like Cain and keep an empty bed.

And, oh, God, why am I thinking like this?

The blasted wine.

Marie eyes us both. Our silence is heavy even to her, I'm sure. 'How about a spot of brandy?'

'No!'

It blurts out of us both and for a second our eyes meet. A smile—hell, almost a laugh—erupts, but I shake free of the weird connection.

'No, thank you,' I say, softer now as I look back to her. 'I could murder a coffee, though.'

An injection of caffeine. Sobriety—that's what I need to see the rest of this meal through. And then I can go home, take a bath and read a good book.

Anything to distract myself from this. From *him*.

Despite Marie's best efforts, I'm not ready to address the past head-on, and I hate that his return has put me in this position. If only he hadn't upped and left in the first place there wouldn't be this colossal secret between us. A secret with the power to cause so much more pain.

And, if I'm honest, I don't want to dredge up that last argument, the words that were said, the things that can't be taken back, no matter how wrong or twisted they were.

'Coffee it is. You head into the living room and I'll bring it through.'

We rise and she looks at Cain as he moves to follow her. 'Shoo, shoo—I can manage coffee on my own.'

If ever there was an order, that *is* one, and without thinking I raise my brows at Cain, who's pulling the same expression at me. And there it is again— that connection, our eyes dancing into each other's as Marie's shameless orchestration of 'alone time' unites us.

He clears his throat and gestures to the doorway. 'Shall we?'

'We best had.'

I try not to look at him as I pass him by. I even hold my breath so I can't get a hit of his cologne. But my body warms over the memory of it anyway. It's musky, welcoming, all male. And it took over my senses four days ago, when he kissed me—when *we* kissed. The intensity of it, the old familiar versus the new…

No, there's no way Cain has lived a life of celibacy these last seven years and I shouldn't care.

I want to blame his power over me on my abstinence. On the fact that while he was burning me out of his system with many a willing woman, I spent seven years with nothing more than a peck on the cheek, an awkward kiss to the lips…mine and Liam's one attempt at consummating our marriage, icky at best, and halting before we got anywhere close.

But is it really to blame?

The fire's crackling in the grate as we enter, its

glow the only light in the cosy room and making it feel even smaller. I immediately head to the lamps dotted around, knowing that Marie favours their soft lighting to the brightness of the overhead one, and start switching them on, keeping myself busy.

My ears are attuned to Cain, though. I can hear him tending to the fire, adding logs, stoking it, but I avoid looking at him. If I'm lucky Marie will return before I have to.

I walk to the glass doors that open up onto Marie's courtyard garden and watch as the various solar lights flutter in the wind. Their glow lends a magical, fairy-like feel to the pretty pots, the garden wall and the climbers she's planted. I try to empty my mind, focus on the soothing scene—until a sudden stillness in the room draws me back.

The spit and roar of the fire is the only sound I can make out, and as I turn I see Cain is standing rigid before it. He has something in his hand. Something...

Oh, God...

I feel my skin pale, the cold sweat returning. I've forgotten about the photo. Or at least I haven't had the foresight to recall it. It's just a feature of the room, blending in with the many other ornaments, pictures and paintings.

Why hasn't Marie put it away?

And why should she? my conscience berates. It was our wedding, for Christ's sake—of course she would keep it on display. It's also one of the nicest photos of the four of us—Liam and me, Marie and Robert—taken on the steps of the registry office by a passer-by. We're smiling, happy—though I know the truth is more skewed than that. Each one of us is missing the man who now holds the picture as if it's an instrument of torture.

I look away before he can see me watching, waiting for him to speak and dreading what he'll say all the same.

I hear the gentle knock of the wooden frame as he places it back on the mantelpiece, hear him take a ragged breath against the crackle of the fire at his feet.

'Taking the let's-be-civil act a bit far, don't you think?'

My eyes flick to his. He's facing me now, his hands deep in his pockets, his expression hard. I don't know what I expected him to say, but it isn't that.

'How do you mean?' I'm hesitant—confused, even—and I wrap my arms around my middle.

'"*It sounds great.*"'

It's practically a sneer, and I know he's referring to my comment regarding his Youth Centre.

'It does. I'm impressed.'

He looks away and shakes his head on a short laugh.

'What?' I ask.

His eyes come back to me, but he says nothing. There's no hint of that easy connection now. We're back to how we were when we parted four days ago.

The silence stretches and I'm so aware of everything about him. I can feel his anger, his hurt… And, hell, guilt is what *I* feel. Guilt for the photo. Guilt at what I did. *Guilt!*

It's unbelievable. Why should I feel guilty when everything that happened was down to *him*? It was *his* blasted fault.

But even as I think it I know the truth is more complicated, that there were things I could have done differently seven years ago—things I shouldn't have said, things I could have said and didn't.

But he was the one who left, not me.

'Why don't you say what's really on your mind?' I ask.

He says nothing and I lose it, striding across the room towards him. He's no innocent in this and I'm going to make him answer.

'This is what you're thinking about!' I snatch the photo from the mantelpiece and thrust it out, making him look at it. 'This is what you're angry about. Not the fact that I dared compliment you on your youth initiative.'

His jaw pulses. He's so close now. Not even a foot between us. And as I drag in a breath his scent invades my senses…my head swims with it. The heat spreading through my body, nothing to do with the fire beside us and everything to do with my anger and the persistent need, the lust I just can't shake.

'It's *your* fault, Cain—can't you see that?' I force the words out, refusing to listen to the guilt, to the simmering heat, as I glare up at him.

'What's my fault, Lexi?' He leans closer, his eyes raking over my face, the flames from the fire flickering in their depths. 'How you feel this second?'

He reaches out, his fingers surprisingly soft beneath my chin, his eyes falling to my lips that I now wet and wish I hadn't. 'Don't, Cain.'

'Don't what?'

He traces my lower lip with the pad of his thumb and I shiver—too much heat, too much need. I feel the frame start to slip in my hand.

No.

I back away, out of his reach and tighten my grip on the photo.

'*Everything's* your bloody fault!' I throw at him, my body thrumming with it all. Frustration at myself for being attracted to him. Anger at him for not accepting the part he played. Desire. The carnal ache calling for satisfaction—*No.* I try and burry it with more words, more accusations. 'The whole damn lot is your fault! If you hadn't left…if you hadn't abandoned us all then…then…'

I shake my head, squeeze my eyes shut, haunted by the old, tortured by the new—the plane crash, losing my best friend, my father figure… Would they have even been on that plane together if Cain had never left?

Christ!

I open my eyes. Would Cain have been on it as well? Or instead of them?

My whisper is almost ghost-like. 'The plane crash…'

His eyes flicker dangerously. 'You may see me as some kind of God, Alexa, but even *I* can't conjure up a storm worthy of taking out an aircraft.'

'That's not what I meant, and you know it.'

He closes the gap that I've created. 'No, what you mean is if I hadn't left seven years ago then maybe there's a chance it would have been *me* on that plane instead of *Liam*.'

His lips curve into a smile that is all the more chilling, all the more immobilising for the pain I know it masks. And the hatred it doesn't.

'How tragic for you that I'm the one you're left with…'

'Right, I've brought both! Brandy and coff—'

Marie is halfway in the room when she freezes, a laden tray outstretched before her. Her eyes fall to the picture still in my hand and I see her skin pale beneath her make-up.

Damn you, Cain.

'Everything okay?' she says, her voice unnaturally high.

I move quickly, placing the photo back where it belongs and going to help her with the tray. I take it from her hands with a smile. 'Coffee smells lovely.'

She doesn't respond. Her eyes are on her son and I curse him again.

Say something, I urge him with a look alone.

'It does,' he says finally. 'But I'm going to have to give it a miss. I've an early meeting tomorrow and I need to get back.'

'But…' Marie wavers, her eyes wide with disappointment. 'Don't you want to call a taxi first? You can at least wait here for it.'

'No need. I can walk.'

'But you live miles away.'

He strides across the room and kisses his mother on the cheek. 'I could do with the air. Goodnight, Mum, and thank you for the meal.' He looks to me now. 'The pudding too.'

'Our meeting's not until eight—surely you can stay a little longer.'

For your mother's sake, I add silently.

'You're not my first meeting.'

And then he's gone, leaving an aching silence in the room that neither of us seems able to fill. I put the tray down on the table that sits between the two armchairs before the fire and drop down into one of them.

'You're going to have to tell him, you know.'

I hear Marie's words and I know exactly what she means. But, Christ…

'How can I? After all this time?'

'You just need to be honest with him.'

She moves to sit in the other chair, pressing down the plunger in the cafetière before picking up the bottle of brandy and pouring two glasses. She passes me one.

'I was just having coff—'

'Humour me.' Her smile is small. 'You look like you need it. The coffee can wait.'

I shake my head. 'You're incorrigible.'

But I sip it anyway. It's not as if I need my wits about me any more. He's gone. And instead of feeling relieved, I feel… I don't know how I feel.

I shake my head, not ready to examine it any closer.

'I know it's not going to be easy, love.'

Marie sips at her own brandy, her eyes not once leaving me, their sympathetic quality making tears prick.

'But he deserves the—'

'Don't say he deserves the truth, Marie. I know he's your son, but *he* was the one who left…he was the one who ran…he was the one who…who…'

'Broke your heart.' Her lips pull back into a tight line, but dimples appear in her cheeks as she nods. 'Yes, I know, love. I know. But he has to know the truth or it'll eat away at you, destroy any chance you have of being able to move past this together.'

'Who says I want to move past it together?'

Silently she studies me, her assertive gaze reading me far too well.

'You think you can carry on like this? With this secret between you?'

'I don't know.' My empty hand goes to my stomach; the other pulses around the brandy glass as I struggle to even think on it, let alone speak. 'I just know I'm scared—scared of telling him and not knowing how he will react. Of leaving myself open…bare…having him crush me like he did before.'

Her eyes glisten in the firelight. 'I know, and I understand. But you need to do this and trust that he'll do right by you. He's not the same man who ran away.'

'You say that like you know him now.'

'I know him well enough.'

'How can you? He's hardly been here.'

She doesn't answer me, and I get the sudden impression there's something she's not telling me.

'Marie?'

'He's been in touch a lot over the past few months…visited too, ever since the funeral. I didn't say anything because… Well, I guess it's been a habit for so long—none of us mentioning his name for fear of upsetting one another, and I guess more so with you.'

'With me?'

'Yes, love…' She looks at me, guilty now. 'Because every time he came up that look would come over you and…'

Her eyes fall briefly to where my hand still presses against my abdomen and I know what look she means. I know then that she's been protecting me. That while I've been trying to look out for her, she's been doing the same right back. And so the guilt returns.

'I didn't want to hurt you,' she finishes.

'I'm sorry.'

'Don't apologise.'

'You shouldn't feel like you can't talk about your son to me.'

She shakes her head. 'You've had enough pain, that's all.'

'And you haven't?' I raise my brows.

Her smile is soft, wistful. 'I love you like a

daughter—you know that—and I just want you to be happy. I want both of you to be happy.'

My heart squeezes tight in my chest. *Happy.* I just can't imagine it. Not with Cain back in my life as a constant reminder of what I've lost, of what *we've* lost—only he doesn't know it.

Our daughter, our little Rose, is a burden I carry alone. Yes, I had his family, all of whom suffered her loss with me. But they hadn't felt the pain of a mother, of a parent.

Liam would have loved her. He would have brought her up as his own. And, no matter how twisted, how messed-up that would have been, it had been our plan. To give her everything I'd lacked growing up: a stable, loving home, a mother and a father...grandparents.

I swallow as the brandy rises in my throat, the rolling of my belly meeting the pain in my heart. Would Cain feel it like this? This sickness? This empty hole inside? The skin-prickling grief that you don't want to believe it has happened to you, to your precious little bundle?

'Have you said anything to him?'

My voice is distant as I ask the question, my head still filled with images of being in that hospital bed, her frail body unmoving in my arms, my body in a weird state of post-labour numbness.

'No—good heavens, no.' Marie's eyes are wide with her insistence. 'It's not my place. Don't get me wrong, I hate keeping it from him—especially know-ing how much the past haunts him. But—'

I scoff. I can't help it.

'It *does*, Alexa, and you know that deep down.'

I'm quiet. I can hardly deny it.

I wrap an arm across my stomach and lean forward, staring into my brandy as if the amber liquid will have all the answers. 'What if he can't forgive me?'

'Forgive you?' She frowns. 'For what?'

'For not telling him sooner.'

'He left you no choice. None of us could reach him. And by the time we could it was in the past and you had moved on with Liam. He didn't want to be reached. Not until he was ready.'

'Would he ever have been ready?' I wonder aloud, needing to speak my mind. 'If not for the plane crash, I can't help thinking he may never have come back at all.'

'He would.'

She says it like she knows for sure, but I'm not convinced. It's been seven years, for Christ's sake—plenty of time for him to get over it and return if he was going to.

But he did come back, my conscience reminds me. *He came back, saw you and Liam together, married, and he ran.*

His declaration in my office comes back to me.

'I loved you once.'

Were we the reason he stayed away? Liam and I? Did we leave him so broken he couldn't face returning?

'I loved you once...'

I hear those tortured words as though he's speaking them in the room now, and I shake my head to empty it.

He *left* me. He *left* us.

Whatever he felt, it wasn't love—not the kind I felt for him. Because if it had been then he would have stayed. He would have fought it out. And telling him the truth of our baby will be easier if he's the villain of the piece, the person who abandoned us and broke my heart.

But what if it's all skewed? What if I'm more to blame than I know? What if the words I threw at him that fateful night cut deeper than I could ever have imagined? What if my marriage—a marriage I have to accept was driven by my anger and pain at losing him as much as it was my lonely childhood and wanting more for my child—kept him away?

Do I run the risk of casting myself in the role of villain?

Am I the villain deep down?

The one to be hated, despised, cast out?

Alone again?

CHAPTER FIVE

I DIDN'T REALLY have a meeting before my eight o'clock with Alexa. I was making excuses, covering my need to get the hell out of there before I lost what scrap of control I had left.

Seeing that photo last night…having the memory of that day in full colour before me…

I don't know how I missed it when I was in there previously. I sure as hell wish I'd gone on missing it.

I rake my hands through my hair and grip my skull, hoping the pressure will somehow stop the incessant noise inside. The noise, the emotion, the inability to think straight…

It's useless. Nothing will rid me of her, of our messed-up past and our even more messed-up future.

Because it *will* be messed up if we can't get a handle on this. We need to be able to work together. To separate the personal from the business.

But I can't even look at her now without that photo taunting me. They looked happy. All four of them smiling in front of the registry office, her in a simple white dress, hooked on the arm of my brother, my parents beaming as they toss confetti over their heads.

Seeing it was like being an observer again, watching the scene of happiness unfold from across the street, feeling the pain that ripped through me and having it return twice as hard, twice as fierce, along with the grief I've yet to deal with.

I shove myself back from my desk—no, *Dad's* desk. This was his office, his space, up until three months ago.

I launch myself to my feet and stride to the window as I feel the familiar churning in my gut, the cold sweat pricking against the collar of my shirt.

I'm surprised to see the windows have latches and I push one open, breathe in the crisp morning air and let it calm my skin. A definite perk to being in a low-rise city, I guess. Something I rarely ever get to be.

I have bases all over the world. But they're just that—bases. Penthouse apartments in skyscrapers that dominate the streets beneath, hovering above ground level and keeping me apart…distant.

Nothing like this.

Everything feels smaller here, more intimate, and rather than feeling a part of it I feel ever more out of place…on edge. Yet I was born here—lived here for twenty-five years. The building in which I stand is owned by my family's company—the company I dreamed of being a part of and of which I now own a controlling share.

And still I don't belong.

Why?

Because Dad didn't give it to you... Fate handed it over...

And now, more than ever, I need to prove myself, to make myself fit.

I look at the harp-shaped bridge, rising proud over the river, at the early-morning rush starting in earnest now, and take another breath.

It doesn't matter how I feel—insider or outsider, fate or not—now I'm here at Dad's company, and that means leaving the past behind enough to be able to work alongside Alexa and convince the outside world, the investors—Mum, even—that all is well.

And all *is* well.

I close my eyes, feel the sun trying to break through the clouds and warm my face...

All will be well.

Movement inside the outer office has me turning sharply on my heel. It's six-thirty a.m.—hardly a time I would expect anyone to be in—and I'm already opening my office door before I think better of it. Before I acknowledge that there's only one person who'd be here at this time...

'Lexi?'

I want to wince as her name comes out in its pet form. It's as if I'm exposing the old me—the one who loved her—each time I do it. But she hasn't even heard me, and I'm too surprised at what I'm seeing to try again.

She's dressed for a run: skin-tight Lycra from head to toe, showing off every curve, hot pink earphones dangling from her ears and her hair swinging in a ponytail. She's obviously just finished, judging by the flushed sheen to her skin, and she's singing under her breath, practically skipping as she moves on, unaware of my presence.

I lean into the doorframe and watch as she goes to the water cooler. She bends forward to fill the bottle in her hand. Her perfect behind, round and full, hugged in black Lycra, is offered out to me, and I feel an unwelcome surge of heat rush south.

Her voice inches higher as she hits the chorus of a song I can only just about recognise from her high-pitched rendition and I feel my lips quirk upwards. I've not seen her like this—relaxed, happy even—in so long. Her hips start to rock back and forth to the music as she carries on filling the bottle—*Christ, how much does that bottle take?*—and I feel my cock pulsing, getting harder, hotter, with each sway.

Jesus.

I adjust myself, and to my horror she spins and falters and freezes as her eyes hit mine. Water erupts out of the bottle as she clenches it too tightly, her other hand still holding the lid.

'Cain!'

She's the picture of embarrassment, and *damn* if that doesn't make her sexier still, with her lips parted in a provocative O, her colour high. My gaze travels lower, to where the water from the bottle meets the sweat that runs down the unzipped V of her running top, which she's clearly yanked down, thinking no one will be in yet. And then there are her breasts, the teasing curve of each as she pants for breath—

Holy Mother of...

I drag my eyes up to her mouth, which is still parted, to her cheeks flushing darker still, to her eyes, which are bright... And then she blinks and the shutter falls into place, her easy spirit evaporating as if it never existed.

She yanks the earbuds out. 'You could have warned me you were here.'

'I tried.'

'Well, I...'

She opens and closes her mouth. When she does it again I'm hit with the oddest desire to laugh and I can't stop it. It erupts out of me. And I haven't laughed in so long my head spins with it. She glares at me, and that only makes me laugh harder. Maybe I'm starting to lose my mind a little. Is this what grief does when you don't let it out?

'What's so funny?'

I push off the doorframe and close the distance between us, my eyes on the earphones now dangling from her clenched fist.

'Still your favourite band, huh?'

She closes her eyes and shakes her head. 'You heard all that?'

'Yup.'

I take the bottle from her weakening grip and bend to fill it up once more. It keeps me busy and it's a nice gesture. I'm hoping that with enough nice gestures we can start the day on neutral ground. Do what needs to be done for the company's sake.

'Lucky for you, you have a well-paid day-job.'

She takes the bottle from me and screws the lid on. 'Thanks.'

'No, thank *you*—that little scene brightened up an otherwise shitty morning.'

'It's only six-thirty—what could possibly have gone wrong already?'

I run my teeth over my bottom lip, look down into her face, so near, and wish to God things were different—another life kind of different.

'Do you need to talk it through?' She takes a swig from her bottle and I can tell she's putting on a front, following my lead. 'I'm just going to take a shower and I'll be right out.'

She starts to move off.

'Wait! You have a shower in your office?'

Not even Dad's office has one.

Her eyes flick away, and I wonder what I've hit upon now.

'Liam had it installed so we wouldn't need to go home after our morning run.'

Of course he did.

I nod, try to appear uninterested, and know I'm failing miserably. 'No need to rush. It's not something you can help with.'

No, that mess is all me... Unless she suddenly wants to go another round in her office. This time I won't be fool enough to demand her verbal confirmation. I'll happily take the confirmation from her body. Because *that* had definitely wanted me.

Like mine wants her now.

'Okay.' She's walking away again, and I swear

she's purposely teasing me with the sway of her arse. 'I'll be in my office if you change your mind.'

Her office...

I'm treated to a mental replay: her leaning back over her desk, her blouse damp from my mouth, her legs tight around me, my ears filled with the heady moans she gave.

A truce. That's what you need. That's what the company needs.

A fuck I could go elsewhere for—because she would never be just a fuck.

It's seven-thirty, and I'm itching to cross over the outer office and get this started. Whatever *this* is. I have no idea what Cain intends to take on—what role he's going to play—but if he has some grand idea of pushing me out he has a fight on his hands.

I drum my fingernails against the desk and look at my computer screen. My calendar is open, today's schedule stares back at me, and my heart sinks further in my chest.

Back-to-back meetings. Another day of getting no real work done.

I want to go and brainstorm with our techies—I want to feel the buzz of innovation, of fixing problems people don't even know they have yet. And instead here I am, suited and booted, ready to talk the talk...but I can forget the walk...the doing.

Although come to think of it, now Cain is here maybe it doesn't have to be that way. The idea sparks

a hopeful flutter inside me. Can I relinquish enough
control to go back to what I really want to be doing?

And have him slowly push you out?

No way.

I immediately quash the idea. I don't know what
his intentions are, and on top of that do I really trust
him? Do I really believe he won't run again? What
if this is some fleeting interruption for him, during which he shakes things up and then bails? What
then?

There's movement in the outer office and I see
the early birds are starting to arrive. I give a small
smile through the glass in acknowledgment and push
up out of my seat. He said eight, but he's here, I'm
here, and I can't stand this stomach-churning wait
any longer.

I leave my office, taking my coffee with me,
and my pulse starts to thrum in my veins. Nerves.
Dogged lust. I'm not sure which, but my mouth is
dry. I sip my coffee and try to tell myself this is just
like any other meeting.

His door is ajar, but as I go to rap on it my hand
stills in mid-air. The last time I crossed this threshold it was shortly after the crash. Marie wanted Robert's personal effects to be taken home, and I didn't
want to put anyone else through the pain of doing it.

His PA had served him for thirty years; she'd suffered his loss like a family member. And as for me…
Well, it was something I could do to be useful—anything to distract myself from my own grief.

But it wraps around me now…a chilling blanket

that I have to straighten my body against as I force my knuckles to strike against the door.

'Yes, it's good to be back,' I hear him say.

I peer through the gap. He's on the phone, standing behind his desk. His eyes shift to me as I enter and I mouth an apology, turn to leave, but he raises his hand, stopping me.

'Yes, a week Friday, Ethan… Glad you can make it…'

His eyes are hooked on mine and I feel his attention on the call slip. Mine doesn't, though. I know exactly who he's talking to and my blood fires.

'Dinner? Let me check the diary and get back to you…' A frown mars his brow and I wonder if he's read the eruption that's coming. 'Look, I have to go… Will do…bye.'

I turn and close the door, telling myself to count to ten and remember that these walls are thick, but not entirely soundproof. Especially in an office building that isn't at full steam yet and lacks the usual background hum.

'Hey,' he says to me now.

'Ethan Tennant, I take it?' I drop the pleasantry of a greeting as I face him.

But his eyes are busy sweeping over me, his attention off my words and totally on my appearance.

What the…? And then I remember what I'm wearing. *Damn silly move.*

'You choose that outfit on purpose?'

He drags his eyes back to mine and they are dark, intense, openly feasting on what he can see, what he can remember from the last time I wore it. In my office, just last week. My stomach contracts, and the heat he injects is as visceral as if he's stroked the pad of his thumb over my clit.

I bite the inside of my cheek, stave off the betraying whimper that climbs my throat. 'I asked you a question first.'

His mouth quirks up to one side. 'Yes, it was Ethan.'

'You seem very...*chummy.*'

He pockets his hands and steps out from behind the desk as he considers me. 'He was Dad's best friend.'

'Yes... And you've not been around for seven years, but now you're best buds?'

He shrugs, the movement slow as he steps closer and leans his head to one side, narrowing his eyes.

'Tell me...' I wet my lips, my mouth once again parched. 'How long have you and Ethan been planning this?'

His eyes widen and he shakes his head. 'I don't know what you're talking about.'

'No?'

I step towards him, ignoring the buzz our growing proximity gives to my eager body. I'm not turned on. I'm angry. One hundred percent livid. And if the ache between my legs would just quit, I'd believe it wholeheartedly too.

'So, the company's most influential board member—the man I consider responsible for sowing the seeds of doubt about me, the *doubts* that brought *you*

back here—' I stab him in the chest with one finger '—just happens to be on great terms with you?'

He holds my eye, doesn't blink.

'I'm here to help regain the board's confidence.'
His voice is smooth as silk, brushing over my skin.
'And, as you so correctly state, he *is* the most influential board member—which means I'm starting with him.'

He catches my finger in his hand and the contact
zings along my arm.

'It's good business sense…nothing more.'

I laugh, but it's high-pitched—either from his
touch or my continued disbelief. I hope he sees it
as the latter.

'Are you sure you didn't start with him three
months ago? Start sowing those seeds of doubt yourself?'

I stare resolutely up into his face, refusing to let
him catch a glimpse of what he's doing to me.

'I don't like what you're insinuating, Lexi.'

My stance softens at the pet name and I feel my
temper soar, angry at my body's betrayal. 'Quit with
calling me Lexi. It's Alexa.'

'No… To me, you're Lexi.'

I inhale, to fend off the dizzying dance his insistence creates, but instead his familiar scent invades
me, cocoons me.

When will I learn my lesson? Don't get too close.
Don't breathe him in. And, above all, don't fucking
touch him!

I try to pull out of his grasp, but he has me held fast. 'That was a long time ago,' I say.

'Was it?' he murmurs.

Too close. Far too close. His free hand snakes around me, curving my frustratingly pliant body into his.

'Because right now I want you every bit as much as I wanted you then.'

'Cain…' It's a whisper, and my body trembles with it. The pent-up desire, the continued fight. My good sense battling my neglected libido.

He's the only man to have made me feel this way, and I have this irrational fear that he's the only man who ever will. It doesn't matter what we've been through, what he put me through.

I shake my head, try to kill the thought dead, and I feel the splash of something on my ankle. It forces me to focus on the coffee cup still in my unsteady hand, and I stare at it rather than him.

'How about some honesty?'

His voice is gruff and my eyes snap to his, surprise making me forget that there's a reason I don't want to look up at him this close.

'Shall I start?'

My tongue is tied, caged by an overwhelming urge to pull him down and form a tryst with his.

'What do you say?'

I nod. It's all I can manage when my lower body is pressed against his. And I know it's not his hand that's holding me there. I know it's my own treacherous need to feel his desire straining between us.

To have that heady reassurance that this is no lie. He wants me. Regardless of everything else, he wants me as I want him.

His gaze darkens as it falls to my lips and I realise I've wet them on impulse. I can feel their sheen in the cool air-conditioned room, feel how they're slightly parted and demanding what I won't dare to.

'This morning is the first time I've spoken to Ethan,' he says.

I go to respond but he stops me.

'Let me finish.'

I oblige and his hold around my fingers relaxes, no longer gripping as he starts to caress them, the gentle touch as hypnotic as his gaze.

'I haven't spoken to Ethan in over seven years.' His voice is soft, earnest. 'Yes, when I returned last week he soon learned of it, and he reached out to me. What you just overheard was me returning his call.'

I want to say I don't believe him. I want to throw his words back in his face. And he must know it, because his fingers over mine still and his jaw flexes.

'Lexi...'

He sounds pained now, and his eyes, staring down into mine, are just as tortured.

'I am not the enemy. I'm here to help you. Regardless of the past.'

'But...'

I give another shake of my head. Because if Cain isn't the enemy, then how can I protect myself? How can I protect myself from him and a future with him in it?

'It would be so much easier if you didn't fight me...if you just trusted me.'

I feel tears prick and curse my own weakness. 'How can I trust you? I loved you, Cain, and you left. You didn't stay and fight—you ran.'

'It was all I was capable of doing back then. I couldn't cope with my father's decision... I couldn't cope with...'

His eyes glisten and—*oh, my God*. He can't be. Cain doesn't cry. I've never seen him suffer the weakness of mere mortals and I feel a fundamental shift inside me—a shift I can't prevent and that's far too close to my heart.

Is he reliving that last argument? Is that why he can't bring himself to finish his sentence? And do I really want him to? Do I really want him to dredge it all up?

'I'm not the same man I was then,' he says eventually. The glisten is all but blinked away, but his voice is still thick. 'And I'm not going anywhere now. Just let me help you...*please*.'

I can't speak. I can't move. It's taking all I have just to stop my own tears from falling, to stop my toes from lifting, from my lips meeting his.

'Let me help the company my father created...the company my brother loved.'

Oh, Jesus.

It's a low blow. He knows I can't say no to that. I just can't. It doesn't matter what risk it poses to me, to my heart that has never healed, to my baby...our baby...the truth...

I can feel myself nodding—even though deep down I'm still tormented by the past, by what's still left unsaid.

'Good.' He breathes out. 'Now it's your turn.'

'My turn?' I frown, confused.

'For honesty?' He reminds me of our pact.

Oh, God. Oh, no.

He releases his grip on my hand, my lower body, but he doesn't release me. Instead his hands rise to my face, gently cupping my cheeks as his eyes burn into mine.

'Can you deny you still feel this?'

'Don't, Cain. Don't do this,' I whisper. 'You want a place in this company. You want to see faith in it restored. That's fine. But don't bring our connection into it.'

His lashes flutter. 'You're denying it, then?'

'No. I won't lie to you. I want you. I want you more than I've ever wanted another soul. But that doesn't make it okay. It doesn't mean I'm willing to go there again.'

I take his hands in mine and gently press them down and away.

My body pines even as I step back, but I lift my chin, ignoring it. 'Where do we start?'

'Alexa?'

At least he has my name right this time, and that helps rebuild my strength. I've given him my honesty and now it's time to focus on what we should be.

'Please, Cain, the business is what matters now. Let's just concentrate on that.'

* * *

I want to curse. I want to grab her, pull her to me and kiss the rejection out of her.

She wants me. She admitted it.

'I want you more than I've ever wanted another soul.'

Which puts me above Liam...

I'm instantly chilled, goosebumps rife across my skin. To think it is bad enough: getting one up on my younger brother...my younger and very dead brother. My gut clenches tight and I can't breathe. The grief I haven't yet surrendered to is building with force.

'Cain?'

Her voice sounds distant, miles away, as I swim in a misery of my own making. I feel my fingers shake as I rake them through my hair and turn away from her.

'*Please*,' I force out, 'can you go?'

'Cain...?'

I spin on my heel. 'Lexi, just go. I'll find you shortly.'

'But...'

I stare at her, my pain, my past, my present all in one. *'Please.'*

And she does exactly as I ask, quietly, with no more sound—nothing but the click of the door as she closes it behind her.

I turn a full three-sixty and I'm surrounded by Dad. But both Dad and Liam are gone. Dead. There's nothing bringing them back. Nothing.

I sink to the floor in a crouch, a winded, wounded

mess. I heave in a breath. Another. I slow it down until I can get my breathing under control.

I stay like that until my skin cools, my head quits and the sickness passes.

All better. Almost.

I head to my desk, straightening my tie, my hair. Another deep breath and I'm calmer now.

One day I'll mourn. One day I'll feel strong enough to let it out. But not now.

I have a job to do and I'll get it done.

I will.

CHAPTER SIX

THREE MONTHS OF working alone—or rather, working without an O'Connor alongside me—has been hard. Lonely, even. And the pressure—I don't mean the pressure of the workload, I mean the pressure from my peers and from the board—has been unbearable.

It doesn't matter what I say or do, nothing can convince them I have this. I don't need help. They just need faith. And I'm convinced that doubt stems from my gender—my gender and my age: a combination it seems no amount of hard work on my part can fix.

But, of course, the second I caught that whiff of a conspiracy between Cain and the board via Ethan I pounced on it, desperate to blame someone other than myself. It came from my frustration, my anger, my dwindling motivation as I struggled to hang on under the constant weight of having to prove myself while keeping my grief private.

Days given to work, nights to tears. That was my routine for so long I'm finding it difficult to adjust to this new state of affairs.

Two weeks Cain has been back. Two weeks since he officially re-joined the fold and the transformation within the firm is marked. I wasn't enough, but Cain, it seems, is plenty.

News of his return rippled out swiftly, with calls coming in from investors and clients alike, the office abuzz with it. He already has Sheila, his PA, in position outside his office. John, his second-in-command, is in the office next to him; and a whole host of others are infiltrating my teams, gleaning what they can, helping rather than taking over.

No one is pissed off.

No one except me.

Although 'pissed off' isn't the right term to use. Don't get me wrong—I'm pissed off that all he has to do is walk back in and suddenly everyone feels safe again, confident, with the kind of faith in him that's something I've failed to earn, no matter how hard I've tried. But I have to acknowledge that my work life has eased. I'm starting to enjoy my job again, focusing on the things I'm good at rather than paying lip service to nervous board members, investors, peers, all of whom should've had faith in me from the off.

As for Cain and I, we seem to have found a way to function that doesn't involve sniping at each other one minute and ripping each other's clothes off the next... Although the desire to do the latter is there, simmering under the surface. It's a constant recognition that all it will take is one moment of weakness and we'll be re-enacting his first visit to my office and this time there'll be no stopping.

It's a dangerous tease that I try not to think about, but I have no power over my dreams, and it seems my mind is happy playing out a multitude of teasing scenarios that often leave me breathless and panting before I wake with a start.

And, as though my dreams aren't enough, working with Cain does the rest: watching him command a room, discussing ideas, strategy, debating next steps and ultimately coming to an agreement that we are both happy with. I never thought it possible.

Liam and I had a working relationship that stemmed from our love of programming, of software, of building something and having it do what you need.

Cain has never shared that love. He's always been a sports fanatic, intelligent, but fun-loving. When he was younger he wanted to live a little before getting serious with his career. That had been fine by me—until that fun-loving side had cut him out of the business and sent him running.

He obviously learned some hard lessons fast, because within five years of leaving us behind his start-up hit the headlines. Its record-breaking market capitalisation made sure everyone knew the name Cain O'Connor, but his own family were forced to read about it second-hand.

I shouldn't be surprised, therefore, that he can command a room, a board, an edgy investor or two. I shouldn't be surprised at his marketing skill, his seemingly off-the-cuff competitive analysis, his strategic decision-making, his even hand.

But I am.

The Cain of old contends with the Cain of today, and I'm struggling to merge the two, to keep my wits about me and my heart intact. He's the man who crushed me seven years ago. Who left without a backward glance.

But all I see now is the man he has become—and his charisma isn't just winning over the people who matter to the business, it's winning *me* over. It's getting under my skin and messing with my head.

And that brings me to this evening: the night of the function he asked Sheila to arrange. His welcome back do.

He's using it—*we're* using it—as an opportunity to present the company's roadmap and put to bed any remaining doubts over the company's future. I'm doing most of the talking—at his insistence— and I'm a nervous bundle of energy.

I know I'm up to the task but I argued that people would rather hear it all from him. His response had been a sharp 'no' as he insisted that *I* was the face of the company, the one who'd given it their all for so long and above all, it was what Liam and Robert would want.

He made me feel alive with his words, his faith, his belief. The fact he could say it all, say it all and mean it, without the bitterness Cain-of-old would have possessed is eye opening.

Eye opening and ever more threatening to my heart and head.

So here I am, fluttering. Nervous about what's at stake—nervous about what to say, how to say it. And most of all I'm nervous about being with *him*. Standing by his side for a whole evening. Providing a united front that is starting to feel less front and far too real.

I eye my reflection in the hall mirror. Scan my outfit which has taken too long to choose. I've gone with a deep purple dress down to the knee. It fits like a second skin, the square neckline not too revealing, the stiletto heels classic black patent. Perfectly professional and one hundred percent feminine. I'm going to rub my gender in their faces whether they like it or not.

And then I spy my unadorned ears. We can't have that.

I turn to walk down the hall, back towards my bedroom, and my apartment buzzer breaks through the quiet. *Shit.* I check my watch. Seven-fifty. He's early.

My heart flutters in my chest—an uncontrollable reaction I've come to expect every time he's near.

I head back towards the door and press the intercom. 'You're early, Cain,' I say, trying to resist the urge to gaze into his face as he looks up at the camera.

It's too tempting to watch him unobserved, to indulge in the need to enjoy his appearance when I know I need to keep my distance. Our non-verbal agreement to stick to business at work and 'safe' topics when in the presence of Marie, is working too well to crush it now.

He grins—and too late I realise I'm looking, feeling, enjoying…

'So sue me…' He shrugs, his hands casual in the pockets of his dinner jacket, a move he does a lot around me…and I wonder…is it because he struggles to hold himself back, just as I do. 'I'm eager to get tonight done and dusted.'

I shake my head, but can't resist grinning back—which is ridiculous, because he can't even see me.

'You want to come up and wait? I'm almost ready.'

'Sounds great.'

I buzz him in and force my smile to dampen.

Feeling excited about seeing him is one thing.

To let him know it is another.

And to feel it in the first place is just plain dangerous.

I take the stairs to Lexi's penthouse, admiring the converted Georgian home as I go. It's full of character, impressive and bold, and definitely Lexi all over. The vibrant colour in the paintings and the contemporary sculptures that feature on every white-walled floor remind me of her fiery hair and alabaster skin.

It's a foolish comparative, born of a long-forgotten romantic streak, and I scorn it even as I think it. But, hell, that streak is getting stronger, coming back with a vengeance the more I'm around her. The more time I spend with her and try to control it.

My stomach ramps up another gear in its chaotic fluttering as I get closer to her floor. *Gut-flutters, for fuck's sake.* My hand practically trembles as I rake it through my hair and I try to breathe through it. This doesn't work for me. This constant state of nervous energy, of anticipation, of arousal.

I live for our every meeting. Even a fleeting glimpse across the office and I'm there, watching until she passes out of sight again. It's as if seven years of absence have only made this connection stronger, all the more consuming, and I'm powerless to stop it.

Something has to give.

I mean, *Christ*, I've not banged one out with my fist in years. I haven't needed to. I date. I fuck. I move on. The women I see have a similar ethos. Sex is sex. Nothing more.

Only I haven't wanted just sex since I came back here. I've only wanted *her*. And she's forbidden.

She doesn't want me.

I don't want her.

That's what our sense dictates—what our past determines. Except I'm starting to listen less to reason and more to my aching cock, which fears a case of blue balls if something doesn't change soon.

Yes, it's all about your aching manhood. Nothing to with your heart that's never quite healed.

'Shit.'

I'm on her landing, staring at her door. For all I know she's staring back at me through the peephole and wondering why I'm standing here frozen to the spot and swearing to myself. It's enough to shake me out of it and I stride forward. A quick rap of my knuckles and the door's swinging inwards and…

Oh. My. God.

I lose my tongue. It's hanging somewhere in my mouth. The only reason it's not hanging out is that my jaw is clamped so tightly there's no escaping it.

'You going to come in?'

She cocks her head at me, her words slow, her smile oh, so curious and her eyes dancing. She's wondering why I'm dumb, mute… What would she say if I told her the truth? That her beauty, her appeal, has me wanting to forgo our plans for the evening—plans that are critical to the company—and slake this thirst.

Would she say *Go to hell*?

Or would it be *Come on in*?

Would we screw until neither of us can walk straight? Until the past is a distant memory and our present is all that matters?

Hell, it would work for me. But then life isn't that simple, kind or easy.

I step forward and resist the urge to touch her, giving her a wide—*safe*—berth.

'Nice place you have here,' I say as she closes the door and proceeds to walk me through into what appears to be an open-plan arrangement: a kitchen, a diner, a living room and a study area… A study for *two*.

I swallow.

'We liked it.'

Her words merge with the sight I'm seeing. Two

desks at right angles to one another, sleek monitors, stationery, even matching charger cables. It's as if at any moment Liam could walk back in and I'm frozen to the spot, my body chilled, my throat seizing up.

'Can I get you a quick drink? I just need to find my earrings.'

She's moving off. I try to say no, but I can't speak. I can't break away from the scene building in my mind. This was *their* space, where they worked and lived together every day. Did they share a pot of coffee, a bottle of wine, between desks? Did they laugh, joke, design together just there?

I sense her pause.

'Cain? Are you okay?'

She comes up alongside me, her eyes following the direction of mine.

She takes a small breath. 'I haven't had the heart to change it. It's exactly how he left it.'

And there it is. The confirmation of how much she loved him, of how much she's lost—hell, how much *I've* lost. My only brother.

My insides feel as if they're being crushed, my lungs are incapable of drawing breath—and then I feel it: the burn behind my eyes, the need to cry. Again.

I can't stand here any longer. I need to go. I need to get air and empty my head. My heart. The lot.

'Cain?'

Her hand is on my arm, soft and warm even through my shirt and jacket, and still I can't speak. I shake my head and walk away.

'Cain…?'

I force down the lump in my throat just enough to say, 'I'll meet you outside.'

'Cain!'

She calls after me, but I can't stop… I won't.

I race down the stairs. Floor after floor. My breath comes faster and faster and I fight the urge to run back up the whole lot, to seek the burn that will take this pain away.

Idiot. You should've known you were walking into their space and yet you went in, pumped up on your dick. You absolute heartless fuckwit. You deserve the pain, the grief—

I break out onto the pavement and heave in air, heave until my pulse calms…

No, not heartless. I loved her first. She was mine first. I—

'Sir?'

I focus through the haze to see Chris, my driver, a few strides away, his frown telling me I'm far from composed. Far enough that I'm worrying him.

And I never worry my employees. I never warrant concern. I'm a man who prides himself for his control—the control I lacked when I ran away seven years ago rather than face up to my emotions.

I've been back two weeks and I'm losing it more and more with each passing day.

I nod at him. 'We'll be along shortly.'

'Very well, sir.' He moves back to the driver's door, respectfully giving me the space I haven't asked for but so obviously need, and my head starts to clear. The apartment evaporates, the desk, *his* desk...

Breathe...

It took me by surprise, I try and reason. The sudden swing from desire to grief. It would make anyone weak.

But to feel someone's presence and know they're not there and can never be again... To know Lexi passes that space day in, day out.

Her husband. My brother. Gone.

Stop it, Cain. You haven't time for this now. You have a company to save. For Liam. For Dad.

I rake my hands through my hair, stare up at the stars and swear I'll do right by them. I'll see their company back to full strength. To hell with my own hurt and the part they played in it.

And this time I will be above reproach.

Lexi will be grateful.

Mum will be grateful.

And my conscience will be clear.

CHAPTER SEVEN

THE EVENING IS going swimmingly. The food was excellent, the presentation perfect, the response better than I could've hoped for.

Yes, swimmingly—so long as I discount the bit beforehand, back at the flat.

I know I should be glad—should be happy that the investors have lapped up my words, are paying me and the company the attention it deserves. But I'm too focused on Cain.

I can't get his expression out of my head. His pain. His anguish. I wanted to press. I wanted him to let me in, to open up and tell me exactly what he was thinking. Christ, I *wanted* him to show me the true grief I'd glimpsed at the funeral. Instead he'd run. Again.

I should be glad of that too. I should be glad that he left before I could feel any more than I already do. Because seeing Cain in pain—it breaks me. It breaks my resolve…it breaks everything I've fought so hard to keep in place for the last seven years. Even now my hand goes to my stomach, to soothe, to take away the chilling ache.

'I'm impressed, Alexa. I can't deny it.'

I look to Ethan Tennant, our most influential board member, and smile my most dazzling smile— the one that masks it all. Because he's the biggest reason I have worries at all; he's the one whose negativity has spread through the ranks and brought Cain back to my door.

'I'm pleased to hear it.'

I've only told the room the exact same things I've been saying for months—but in a presentation with Cain by my side. And it's not the presentation that's made the difference.

We're now in wrap mode…sipping the finest champagne before going our separate ways for the evening…and I'm ready to do just that. I'm tired. I'm sick of delivering platitudes when really I want to rant and rave at what they've put me through these last few months.

'Excuse me a moment while I pop to the restroom, Ethan.'

While I pop to the rest room and scream blue murder, releasing the words I so desperately want to lay at your feet, Ethan.

'Am I intruding?'

I feel a heated palm through the fabric of my dress, hear his voice trickle like honey down my spine, and just like that I am no longer chilled.

'Not at all.' I look up at Cain with a smile, and it's genuine. I don't need to force anything. And it's strange, the warning siren—the one that says there's no future here, the past will always stand between us—is quiet.

'I was just telling Alexa how impressed I am with the roadmap.' Ethan gestures to the presentation slides cycling through on the big screen—a mini-promo video of what we're proposing.

'It is. You seem surprised, though, Ethan?'

I send Cain a warning glare. I can't believe he'd say such a thing—especially in front of me.

'What can I say?' Ethan clears his throat, his awkwardness clear and making my skin flush. 'It's all down to the exceptional delivery.'

Exceptional delivery. I can't stand here for this. 'Excuse me gentlemen.'

They both nod in my direction and I feel their eyes on me as I leave. I force my stride to remain steady, measured, my ears burn though. *Please drop it, Cain.* If I can drop it for the sake of the company then he sure as hell can.

But will he?

'I can honestly say I'm impressed, Cain.'

I study Ethan Tennant's weathered face. He's aged over the years since I saw him last, filled out too. He was my father's best friend. His biggest backer. He's also the man to blame for the loss of faith in the company, the man who sparked the spread of scepticism about Lexi's ability to lead.

And it boils my blood.

I take a sip of champagne, keep my cool on the

surface. 'She's an exceptional CEO; the company's lucky to have her.'

He eagerly nods his agreement.

'So, tell me, Ethan, why the surprise? Why the negativity? Why the unease spreading through the board that she's not up to the job?'

He frowns at me, a cough rumbling at his double chin. 'Why, I don't... I'm not sure what you mean...'

'Come on, Ethan.' Both my smile and tone are purposely conspiratorial. 'You know exactly what I mean.'

'Well, I...' He clears his throat, his cheeks taking on a ruddy glow. 'Look, you can't blame us.'

'I don't blame "us". I blame you.'

I can't keep the menacing tone out of my voice now. I'm too angry, too disappointed in him—a man I've always respected, believed to be wise, honest, loyal. Hell, he's known Lexi almost as long as me.

'Now, hang on, Ethan.' He waves a hand at me, but he doesn't meet my eye. 'I don't know what you've heard, but I can assure—'

'It's not just what I've heard—it's who you are. You keep these board members in check. What you say goes. It's been like that since I was a boy and I'm sure it'll be like that for a long time yet...'

My tone is back to being level now. I want him to know I'm serious, and that means taking the emotion out of it. Making it about the business.

'Unless, of course, I have something to say about it. Maybe it's time the board had a shake-up.'

I know the power I wield. My money and my influence buy me the ability to deal with things as I see fit—and even someone of Ethan's reach and influence can't fight that.

I can't deny that using my power to address his treatment of Lexi feels exhilarating. Far too satisfying to be purely business-driven.

'Seriously, Ethan, you can hardly blame me.' To my surprise he visibly relaxes. 'You'd have done exactly the same in my position.'

I can't believe he has the audacity to say it, let alone believe it. And I know he does believe it. It's written all over his face.

'Look, Alexa and Liam were a team,' he continues. 'United, they were a force to be reckoned with. Apart…'

I grit my teeth as I bear the weight of his words, wait for the familiar stab of jealousy, the grief that I can't afford to succumb to…

'She's a force on her own,' I say.

'I agree. But you can't blame us for having doubts.'

Christ. I'm not jealous—I'm angry. Angry at their lack of faith in her.

'She has given the company everything to ensure its success, to ensure Dad and Liam's legacy lives on. You should have trusted her.'

He faces me head-on now, his forehead crinkling as he raises his brows. 'Okay, I'm going to level with you—but you may want to be careful what you report back to Alexa.'

It's my turn to frown. I'm completely thrown, flummoxed. 'What the hell are you talking about?'

'Yes, she's an intelligent, talented programmer; yes, the employees and the clients love her; yes, she leads and people will follow,' he says. 'But you're forgetting that she's lost the only father figure she has ever known *and* her husband, her best friend, her business partner in one fell swoop. Losing just one is hard enough. Christ, I took a month off when my wife passed—'

He breaks off, his eyes flicking away, and when they come back to me they glisten with such sorrow, such heartache, that I'm lost for words, guilt crushing me. It isn't that I've forgotten, but it isn't like I was here either. I haven't even paid my respects.

'I was so sorry to hear about Louisa,' I say, when I can manage it.

He shakes his head at me. 'Two years and still it hurts like hell. But what I'm saying is, even that month wasn't enough. I couldn't think straight. I had to pull in extra support. Alexa…' He shrugs. 'She was like a woman possessed—back in the office within a week, like nothing had happened, issuing directives, taking control… I know she was proving she could do it, proving that your father's faith in her, your brother's too, hadn't been misplaced. I tried to tell her to let it go, to be with Marie, to take some time, that we would organise interim support.'

'But she was too stubborn?'

His lips thin into a tight smile as he avoids giving me the answer I know he's thinking. But I'm not letting him get out of it so easily—not when it hurts Lexi.

'So—what? You worked behind her back to see her pushed out?'

'It wasn't like that.'

'It's how it seems.'

'Why do you think Marie came to you?'

I'm taken aback, thrown once more, and my brain reels, trying to process where this is going and what it means.

'She came to me because she was worried about Alexa's health,' I say. 'The fact that she was working so hard. She knew things in the company were unsettled and...' Suddenly it all clicks into place. '*You* spoke to her?'

He takes a second to respond, and then he acknowledges it with a nod of his head. 'I did. I had to. She had her own grief to come to terms with. She couldn't see what was happening to Alexa under her nose. How exhausted she was. How overworked, under-rested... Not to mention she wasn't grieving. Not properly, at any rate. She was too busy protecting your mother from seeing anything bad.'

Now I truly am lost for words. It makes sense now—so much sense I can't believe I didn't see it for what it was. How did I not guess Ethan's motivations from the off?

But it was a risky strategy. Using the company to do it, risking its reputation—not to mention he played *me*.

'I'm sorry if you thought it backhanded,' he says, as I quietly process it all, my conflicted emotions likely playing out in my face. 'But Alexa needed someone to break through that exterior of hers, make her realise that it's not a weakness to accept help, and that someone was you.' He shrugs again, and this time his eyes sparkle, a true smile playing about his lips. 'Judging by the two of you this evening, I think I called it quite well.'

His suggestive comment has those gut-flutters taking off again and I cover them with a stern statement of fact. 'You risked the company to do it.'

'No, Cain.' It's his turn to be severe. 'Alexa needed help, and Alexa is the company. You both are.'

I don't want to dwell on whether he's right or not—whether I *want* him to be right or not, I'm still reeling from the fact he set us up and I was blind to it.

'So you played us?'

'Don't sound so defeated about it. I was playing these games when the pair of you were still in nappies.'

A surprising laugh erupts from within me. Shock, I guess. Shock and a sea of other emotions I can't begin to identify.

I take a swig of champagne, my eyes sweeping the room, looking at the people who have welcomed me back with open arms. But the only person I want to greet me in that way is currently in the ladies', and all I want to do is go to her and tell her I'm sorry. Which is madness when I think about the past and all she's done to me. It doesn't stop the urge, though.

'And it wasn't just for the good of the company...'

Ethan's voice is thick with emotion once more and I look back to him, my eyes narrowed. 'No?'

'It was for your father too.'

The drink catches somewhere between my stomach and my throat, burning like acid. 'What do you mean?'

'It was always his dream to have you come back, to have both his boys at the helm. He never realised his first step in that direction would send you running...'

He has the good grace to look apologetic about raising what my father did, cutting me out, but he carries on anyway.

'And then, when you got so big all on your own, he knew he could hardly go asking you to return. He never gave up hope that you would to do it of your own accord, though... One day.'

My stomach churns and my ears whirr as blood races too fast through my system. I need to breathe, but I can't pull in air. Dad was right. I always intended to come back. I even had a house built—a home not far from theirs, made ready for when that day came.

Only I waited far too long and fate stepped in. And their deaths brought an anger that I've clung to in order to avoid this crippling force inside me, this desolation, this agonising loss.

Mum has helped me to understand my father's motives—helped me forgive, even. And Ethan's words only reiterate what she's told me many a time.

The regret I feel at never being able to fix it, to make amends...it's crushing. But Liam... My head shakes. My battle with him is about so much more. It's about *her*. Lexi. My twisted heart taunts me with my age-old feelings for her—feelings that no amount of jealousy or hatred have been able to quash.

How can I forgive them?

But do I really want to hold this grudge for ever?

I can't make amends with Liam, but I can with her.

And do I truly want to? Is it even possible?

I think of our relationship now, when we put aside the past. I think of how easy it is, how right it feels— how my need to be with her is as real as my need to breathe. And then I think of *them* together, of that shared kiss on the registry office steps, and my stomach lurches just as it did then.

'She's coming back, Cain.' Ethan says it under his breath. 'Look, let's not be morbid. Let's look to the future, hey? With you and Alexa taking the company forward, no one will stand in your way.'

I'm not really hearing him. I'm already lost in the sight of her gliding through the room. My heart pulses in my chest, telling me exactly how I feel about her regardless of it all. As if she hasn't tortured me enough already…as if I'm willing to go back for more.

I'm a bloody fool. I know it even as I say to Ethan, 'You're right—we should be focusing on the future, a fresh start.'

And there's another thing I know: *this* Lexi—the one who has worked so hard to reach this point— deserves to end the night on a high, to know how exceptional she is, and she needs that truth from me just as much as the rest of the room.

They've done their bit. Now it's my turn.

'Thank you for being honest with me, Ethan.' I turn to place my drink on the side. 'Now, if you'll excuse me, I have someone I need to celebrate with.'

I feel his smile against my back as I head straight for her.

Christ, she's stunning—all elegance and sophistication, but with a hint of awkwardness that's always lured me in. A geek-like edge that tells me she wishes she were in her jeans and an oversized hoody, pinned to her computer screen, her nose wrinkling as she concentrates.

The image grips me, conjured up from the recesses of my brain.

Fuck, why didn't I stay and fight? Fight for her? For the life I wanted for us?

I have to stop my fingers reaching for her when she's close enough. I have to remember who she is, where we are, and that she's not mine. The presence of that ring on the hand now resting over her abdomen reminds me of that.

I cock my head and gesture to her tummy. She does this move a lot—it's like a nervous tic, but it's not one I ever noticed when we were younger. 'Are you feeling okay?'

'Absolutely.'

She's all breathy as she says it and my eyes lift to her face, to the flush of colour in her cheeks, the darkening in her eyes.

'You want to get something to drink?'

'I thought we already were?'

She turns and takes a champagne flute from a passing waitress, raises it to me before taking a sip. A sip that seems to be full of teasing, although I know it's just my mind that sees it that way. My twisted desire to have her want me like I want—

'I mean a real drink.'

She smiles around the rim of the glass. 'Too fancy for you?'

'You could say that. So, a drink? My place?'

'With you?'

The hint of a line appears between her brows and I have the ridiculous urge to kiss it away.

'No, with the Queen—she's staying for a few days.'

She surprises me with a playful punch. 'Funny.'

'So, what do you say?'

Her eyes waver over my face and she pinches her bottom lip with her teeth.

'Your place?'

'Or a bar, if you prefer?'

I see her hesitate, and then she kicks back a gulp of champagne.

'Your place is fine.'

I let go of a breath. 'Great, let's go.'

Her eyes widen. 'Now? But we have all these people. We have—'

'You've done enough. I promise.'

'You mean, we have.'

'No, you have. Now, come on—before Ethan insists on joining us.'

She rolls her eyes. 'Don't mention his name. I've not forgiven him yet.'

I take her gently by the arm and start to manoeuvre us towards the door, nodding respectful goodbyes as we pass people.

'You may want to go easy on him, you know,' I say between my teeth.

She glances at me sharply. 'What's that supposed to mean?'

'It means things aren't always what they seem.'

'You're going to need to do better than that.'

'I will,' I say. 'Later.'

'When, later?'

'Do you always have to question everything?'

'Do you always have to act so mysterious?'

I laugh and shake my head. 'You are a pain in my arse. You know that, right?'

'Takes one to know one.'

But she's laughing now, and the sound is so easy, so happy, so very different from how things have been between us. I know what I'm risking, I've been there and done that, but there's no putting the brakes on, not now.

'Cain?'

My name is a soft request from her lips and I pause to look down at her. She's so close I can smell her perfume, see the tiny flecks of black in the blue of her eyes.

'Thank you for tonight.'

I want to kiss her. I want to so badly my lips thrum with it.

'The night isn't over yet, Lexi.'

CHAPTER EIGHT

'YOU WERE REALLY impressive tonight.'

He's sitting on one side of the car, me on the other, and his voice is filling the space between us and drawing me in. I want to scoot over, curl up against him and rest my head on his shoulder. I want to close my eyes and empty my head.

It's what I would have done years ago. It's what I would do now if there weren't this chasm of hurt between us.

'Thank you.'

I keep my eyes on the window, my hands clenched in my lap. I can't bring myself to look at him. I'm wary of the admiration warming his voice, the admiration that's shone in his gaze all evening.

I can almost forget the fact that he ran from me hours before. That pain, that anguish, so obvious in his face.

Maybe this is a foolish idea.

What do I hope to achieve by going back to his place?

Do I think that he'll open up, tell me how he's

truly feeling, and we can go some way to repair the damage of the past? Am I hoping this will be my chance to tell him the truth? Get it all out in the open and face whatever comes my way? Whatever I deserve? Am I really ready for that?

I wet my lips and ask, 'How far is it to your place?'

'Ten minutes.'

I nod. I can still change my mind. Ask that he take me home.

I grip my fingers together tightly. *No. Get it done now, before too much time passes.*

Too much time with him back in my life. Too much time when I've had the opportunity to be honest and haven't been.

Because, let's face it, I could have told him the truth years ago. Once I knew how to reach him I could have tracked him down, made him listen and dealt with it head-on. When Liam and Robert were still alive...when there was a chance for him to make amends.

Oh, my God. The realisation hits me like a slug to the stomach, the air leaving my lungs on a rush and my eyes tearing up. It's my fault it's too late. *Mine.*

'Lexi?'

I hear the frown in his voice.

'Are you feeling okay?'

'Yes.'

My lie is obvious in the pained whisper, but he doesn't press, and I stare unseeing at the passing world outside, knowing that this is it. It's time to tell him everything. He deserves the truth. I owe it to him and I owe it to Liam. I owe it to Rose, too. Her father should know she existed—*still* exists as a part of me, of us.

He doesn't talk again and I'm grateful. My nerves are shot, my head and heart a mess. All he needs do is ask if I've changed my mind and I'll be going home instead.

But then I'd be the one running.

And I refuse to run.

I'm nervous.

It's a weird state of mind.

After everything we've achieved these past two weeks I should be used to her, to this, to the whole chaotic lot. But this is different. This is my home. The home whose existence I only recently disclosed to Mum, and she was stunned.

No surprise, really, since it took almost a year to build and was completed well before the plane crash. It's helped convince her I was serious about return- ing, and I guess it'll do the same for Lexi.

'So, you had this built?'

Her eyes are wide as she literally twirls on the spot to take it all in.

'Yes.'

'When?'

Here we go...

'The contractors finished last year.'

And there it is. She stops, the tip of one heel clip- ping the polished marble floor of the hallway as she asks, 'An investment?'

'A home.'

'But you… When we talked you suggested…made it sound like it wasn't a done deal—that you were *considering* living here, not *actually* living here.'

'I know. I guess I wasn't sure myself—not entirely.'

'But you had this built before—?'

She breaks off and I know she can't mention the crash. I'm not sure I want to either, so I say, 'Yes.'

Her smile is laced with sadness. 'It's amazing.'

'You like it, then?'

My ego is waiting for her answer. Hell, it was designed to my own specification, every last centimetre agonised over. As if I wanted to create perfection to lure me home, to make that transition easier.

She frowns at me and I can see the question in her eyes before she even asks it. 'Does it matter to you if I do?'

Does it? *Yes.* Regardless of my ego, I want her to like it for reasons I don't want to explore—just as I don't want to examine my real reasoning for bringing her back here.

'Yes.'

Her eyes glisten and she looks away, moving through the hallway under the pretence of exploring. But I know she's trying to hide from me. I follow her, captivated by every brush of her fingers over the surfaces, the sweep of her eyes. She looks through doorways, takes in the vaulted ceiling high above, the occasional piece of art. There isn't much of 'me' here in terms of possessions—not yet—but the shell, the fixtures and fittings…that's all me, thanks to my design team.

'It really is incredible,' she says softly.

My heart soars more than I'd like. 'I'm glad you approve.'

She walks into the open-plan kitchen, with its sleek black work surfaces, the white units that show no handles, the range cooker that I wouldn't know how to use…much to Mum's chagrin.

Lexi would, though. The thought is impulsive, and now it's there I can't let it go. I imagine her…fluffy jumper, silly socks, all casual and baking, earphones in, singing…the idea warms me from the inside out.

'Is that a swim spa?'

'Hmm?'

I pull my eyes from the stove, back to her. The real her, not the imaginary version. And it's just as appealing, just as damaged, and just as perfect with it.

She's in front of the glass that runs the full length of the room. Outside, the hard-landscaped garden is illuminated with subtle lights that enhance rather than glare and, as she so rightly surmised, there's my steaming swim spa, just waiting for its lid to be rolled back and enjoyed.

Beyond that is the open sea.

It's private, secluded—a real oasis.

An oasis in which I could lie her back in the bubbling water, her flushed skin bare to my gaze, my hands, my tongue… The image plays out, my body overheating with it.

She turns to look at me and I realise I haven't answered her.

'Yes,' I say.

The simple word is gruff, and I wonder if she can spy the cause. I can sure feel it. The tension building, the anticipation of where this night could be heading…

'A bit James Bond, don't you think?'

She cocks a mocking brow, but I know she's teasing—and, hell, she's right. What boy didn't want to grow up to have a Bond house? I sure did.

'Built into the craggy cliff face…dark and sleek… fully pimped-up.'

'Does that make me double-oh-seven or a villain?'

'Why don't you tell me?'

She runs her teeth over her bottom lip and I swear she's flipped from sad to flirtatious. I want it to be the latter. I want her to flirt with me.

Her eyes flick back to the spa and there's a definite longing in her gaze that I can't miss.

'You're welcome to come here any time you like,' I say thickly, without thinking, and now that the offer is out there, I can't take it back. 'There's an indoor pool downstairs too, protected from the onslaught of the Irish coastal weather.'

'A pool?' She lets out a hushed laugh and it feels wistful, distant.

'What is it, Lexi?'

She doesn't speak. I don't even feel like she's heard me. I walk up to her, about to ask again, when she takes a breath and turns to me.

'So, about that *real* drink...?' she says.

There's a sudden strength to her voice, to her smile, but I know it's all front.

'A Jameson's?'

Her lashes flutter and I know she's remembering. It was *our* drink, *our* whiskey. On a night after all was said and done, when I'd pulled her away from work—*from Liam*—we would lie back on the sofa, switch on the TV and crack open a bottle.

'Perfect.'

It rasps out of her. There's so much we aren't saying, so much that needs to be said, and I feel like we're dancing around it, neither willing to go first.

I turn and head back into the kitchen. The clip of her footsteps follows me, beating in tune to the pulse in my ears. I take out two crystal-cut glasses and place them on the side, the sound of them hitting marble loud in our silence.

I lift up the whiskey that's already there, waiting, as if it's always been waiting for this moment, and I pour a healthy measure in each, the slosh of the liquid echoing around us.

As I lift both glasses I turn to face her and she's even closer than I expect, her proximity stunning me still. Then she offers a small smile, her hand reaching out for one, and I smile with her.

'Cheers.'

She clinks her glass against mine and takes a sip, her eyes closing, her hum of appreciation almost provoking the same from me.

'Cheers…' I murmur, my eyes locked on her as I raise the glass to my lips.

She gives a small sigh of pleasure, her eyes opening and glowing against the pink creeping into her cheeks.

'Still like a real drink, then?' I ask.

'It has its place.'

We stay like that, our eyes hooked on one another, our drinks halfway to our lips, and say nothing. The silence is heavy, weighted.

'I wish you'd never left.'

Her admission has me sucking in a breath—not just because of what she's said, but because of the raw emotion in her voice, in her eyes. I throw back a gulp of whiskey, feel it burn as the words resonate within me, hammering home how much I feel the same. I know I do.

'You and me both.'

Her eyes waver and then they look up at me, searching my gaze, looking for answers.

'Then *why* did you? *How* could you?'

Her eyes glisten, and the desperation in her words rips through the heart of me.

'You know why I left, Lexi.'

She takes a shuddery breath, the hand holding the glass before her lips trembling. 'No—no, I don't.'

'You were there when Dad announced his intentions,' I say slowly, my voice low with warning. I don't want to relive that night, but she's forcing me to do so now. 'You were there when I told you how much it had hurt, how much I needed you to side with me, how much I loved you and needed your support.'

'No.'

She's shaking her head at me vehemently, anger sparking in her glistening blue eyes.

'Don't you *dare* throw love into this. That night had nothing to do with your love for me and everything to do with your own selfish expectations.'

I stagger back a step, shocked that she would throw the same words at me now as she did then, when she knows the damage they caused. 'How can you say that?'

'Because it's the *truth*. You left us sitting at the dinner table...your mum in tears, your father mad, Liam... Christ, Liam didn't know *what* to do. He'd earned that position with your father—he'd worked hard for it and he deserved it. And you—you just expected to be *given* the same because you were blood.'

She's shaking from top to toe now, and I can't even speak. Her argument is something that's gone around and around in my head for so long.

'You expected me to walk out on them—on your *entire* family, *my* family too—because you felt hard done by.'

'You were my partner,' I say coolly, trying to keep my anger at bay. 'They were only your family because of me.'

She gives a harsh laugh, 'You said the same that night, if you remember?'

I remember, all right. I remember accusing her of playing brother off against brother, hedging her bets until she settled on the one who would give her the most.

Wasn't that why I turned up at the registry office? To see for myself that I'd been right to leave? That she was just as scheming as I'd accused her of being?

'I said a lot of things that night, Lexi, and all of them still hold true.'

She pales, her lips parted in shock. 'How can you *say* that?'

'How?' I shake my head and walk away. I need air that's not tainted with her perfume…space without her body's warmth in it. 'Because you did exactly what I accused you of. You went and *married* him, for fuck's sake! For years I watched the two of you getting closer and closer, huddled together in the lab, working on project after project. I used to come in, try and coax you out for dinner, drinks—anything but work. And you'd spare me the merest of smiles and tell me, *"Later, Cain, later."'*

She drags in a breath and then she laughs, the sound high and grating.

'Spare me the *woe-is-me* tale, Cain. I *loved* you. Loved you so much your accusations crushed me. You made me feel like a dirty whore who would sleep her way to getting what she wanted.'

I flinch. My entire body trying to deflect the harsh vulgarity of it. A whore—no, never. But… 'You got to keep my family. Hell, you even got to be CEO of the family firm when all was said and done.'

She clutches her stomach with her free hand, her

skin ashen now. But *she* brought the past into this and I can't stop the words from coming now.

'You see, the thing is, Lexi, I can forgive my father. Yes, I'm still hurt that he didn't even consult me, didn't even offer me a chance to prove my worth before doing what he did. That he didn't seem to care how it would affect me, how pushed out I would feel. But I can understand his motives—sympathise with them, even. I've had years of building up my business, understanding the graft that goes into it, understanding how hard Liam must have worked and why he was worthy—why *he* deserved it and I did not. But you and Liam…together…'

I shake my head, nausea swelling at the sight of them in my mind's eye.

'How can I *ever* forgive that?'

'*Jesus*, Cain!' She shakes her head fiercely. 'Your brother and I were geeks. We understood each other…shared the same love for programming. He was *my best friend*. We didn't care that we weren't popular, or cool, or part of the "in" crowd… We weren't like you. We—'

'You think the fact I was popular with a bunch of idiots at school made me invincible? Stopped me feeling insecure within my own family? With you?'

She slams her glass down on the side, the liquid sloshing over the side, over her hand. 'I never once gave you reason to doubt me. Your own jealousy did that for you.'

'And after?' I say, ignoring the seed of doubt she's sowed. 'When you walked up the aisle with him?'

I place my own glass on the side, feel a toxic mix of jealousy, anger and desire raging like a storm within me. I stalk towards her, half expecting her to back away, but she doesn't.

'Or are you saying you married my brother in some reckless move of your own just to get back at me?'

It's a ridiculous notion. She would never...

But her eyes flare as I pause before her. Her lips are silent. No, she wouldn't have done that. She loved Liam; I know that. She even told me so that fateful night. She loved him as a friend, as a brother, she claimed.

But that doesn't stop my eyes burning down into hers, seeking an answer. I see how she looks at my mouth, how her pupils swell with the need I so easily trigger in her, but she's not getting out of this.

I raise her chin with my fingers, brush her lips with my thumb and feel the air she sucks in pass over it. 'Tell me Lexi, did he make you feel like this?'

Her eyes snap to mine. She gives an infinitesimal shake of her head and my heart soars even as my chest tightens with the twisted question.

'No...?'

'That's not... I mean... Don't do this, Cain.'

I press her back against the kitchen counter, her breasts crushed against my chest, and the carnal sensation is bittersweet in its intensity. I look at her mouth, parted beneath me, and I lower my head. My tongue teases inside, sampling the hot whiskey taste of her. She whimpers, the sound small and clamped inside her throat.

'I want to know, Lexi…' I brush the words against her lips, my fingers lifting to caress her neck, just like she used to ask me to. 'Did he kiss you like this…?'

My fingers start to trail down as I slant my mouth over hers, feel the softness of her lips. And the ease with which she lets me tells me I have her. She's mine.

I circle my fingers over her breasts, feel their hardened nubs press against the fabric of her dress as she rocks into me.

'Did he make your breath catch and your body ache like I do?'

I rotate my hand over one nipple and raise my head to look down at her. She's all wanton, swaying into every touch, every sweep of my lips, and I'm losing control. I can feel it shuddering out of me.

Did he make her feel like this? Did he make her wanton, lustful, desperate?

The twisted questions sear my brain, my body, push me, goad me. I want them gone. I want her begging me. I want her demanding that I fuck her. Demanding that all trace of any man, be it my brother or another, be gone from her mind.

'Are you wet for me, Lexi?'

Her lashes flutter open.

'*Are* you?'

'Yes.'

The admission is small, a whisper, and the colour rushing back to her cheeks is an added confirmation.

I stroke my fingers down her belly. 'Show me.'

She wets her lips. My brother would never have done this. He would have had her on a pedestal, all perfect and pristine. But I want the Lexi I know that's inside her—the one who would perform for me, drive herself crazy while I watched.

'Show me.'

She lowers her hands from where they grip the counter-top and strokes them down her thighs. I step back—just enough to give her room, to give myself a better view. *Fuck*, she's exquisite. Desire thrums through me, tightening up my muscles; my cock straining against my zipper, painful, ready.

Slowly she ruches up the fabric of her dress, taking it higher and higher, until the black lace of her knickers comes into view.

'Show me.' The repeated command scrapes out of me, hoarse with need and the worry that at any moment she will stop. I don't want her to. I don't want this crazy state of need ever to ebb.

She hooks her fingers into the waistband of her knickers and eases them down her thighs.

'That's enough.'

She pauses mid-thigh, her eyes lifting to mine, the burn of her need blazing in their depths.

'Step wider.'

She straightens, and the sight of her spreading her legs is almost my undoing. I groan as my cock bucks painfully inside my trousers.

'Now show me.'

She lowers her fingers to part herself for me, those fingers delving in deep and coming out coated in her wetness. I drag in a breath and watch as she pulls her fingers back over her clit, her hips rolling into the move. She moans softly, her eyes fluttering closed.

'*No*, Lexi, no… *Look* at me.'

I want no other man to be in her head. I want it to be me. Always me.

Her breathing is erratic, hitched like my own, but she does exactly as I command, her eyes locking with mine as her climax builds with the tempo of her fingers. The lace band of her knickers bites into her thighs as her legs widen and lock, her other hand flying out to grip the marble top.

'*Cain… Cain…*'

My name pants from her lips. She's close, so close, and I realise I want to taste her. I want to capture her release with my tongue, my mouth.

I'm already stepping forward and dropping to my knees. I urge away her fingers so that I can surround her with my mouth. *Fuck*, she tastes so damn good. So perfect. So right.

Seven years fall away. There's no pain, no hurt… only this. Our bond.

She cries out above me, the pleasure-filled sound ringing through the room, her hands forking through my hair, harried, desperate.

'Yes, Cain, *yes*.'

I look up, see her eyes on me, the flush to her skin, the waves as they roll through her body. And I know this is all for me. That no matter our past, no matter what *they* shared together, we have this. We *still* have this.

And now I want so much more.

CHAPTER NINE

'TELL ME, LEXI, did he make you feel like this...?'

I rock back against the counter, my body and mind shaken by what's just happened—what I *let* happen and what I *did*, driven by his perverse questioning, his need to compare and contrast.

I should have stopped him.

I should have come clean there and then, in the midst of our argument.

Instead I became lost in his lascivious game, his words, his command.

And where does it leave us now? Where does it leave me and what I need to tell him?

Slowly, he slips my underwear back into place, his stubble grazing against the inside of my thighs as he traces sweet kisses over the sensitive skin. My legs tremble, my body quakes. I daren't snap my legs together, or moan at his continued touch. Because, no matter the torment inside me, I still want him. So much it hurts.

He smooths my dress back down over my thighs and rises up, but he's as close as ever. His chest brushes against mine, teasing over my nipples which are sensitised in the aftermath and willing him to do more.

I look up into his eyes, scared of what I'll see, and I wet my lips—as a result of nerves rather than desire.

'I'm sorry I used my brother like that.'

His apology surprises me, as does his guilt, his remorse, but the passion is still there. The fire in his gaze... He cups my jaw softly and lowers his lips to mine. His breath is all whiskey and me as he brushes his mouth over my parted lips.

'I just...it's tortured me for years...' He squeezes his eyes closed. 'The idea of you and him...what you did together...him replacing me, surpassing me.'

I silence him with my lips. I can't bear him talking of those years—not when he doesn't have the full story. I want to tell him. I do. But now is not the time.

When will it be? I ask myself.

I kiss him harder, forcing out the questions, the doubt, the worry. But he breaks away, lifts his head to rake his eyes over my face.

'I hate it that he gave you everything I could not, that he took the most important thing in my life...'

His eyes soften into mine, his love of old as obvious as his desire, and I'm caught in it, unable to breathe.

'I know I left you, that I have a part to play, but you went to him. He asked you and you went. And all it took was three months.'

His voice is raw, his pain as real as if it were yesterday, and my heart squeezes inside my chest.

I reach for his face, cupping it in my hands as I stare up into his tortured gaze and tell him what matters in that second. 'We *never* had an affair. I *loved* you. I promise that I loved you with every part of me.'

And then I kiss him. I seal my vow with it. I can't rewind history and write a better path. I can't change the fact that I still haven't told him the full truth.

And when I do, will he hate me all the more? Will he see it as the greatest betrayal of all?

My stomach rolls with the thought of it even as he lifts his hands to my face, mimics my hold on him, his eyes searching mine as his thumbs stroke against my cheeks.

'I loved you,' I say again, desperate for him to see the truth of it.

His groan is half-anguish, half-desire, and he kisses me. Slow, savouring this time. It's not like the kiss in my office, or his seduction born of anger just now. It's something far more intense, far more powerful. And it's this *something* that binds us, that's stood the test of time.

I'm so tired of fighting it—tired of being alone, tired of feeling nothing but emptiness and grief. Grief for Robert, for Liam, for Rose—

Rose.

I kiss him back. Kiss him until there's a combating force strong enough to smother the pain. My tongue slides against his, rough, probing, sinking deeper. I lower my hands to his chest and feel the heat, feel the muscles flexing through his shirt, the race of his heart beneath.

'Cain…' I whimper against his mouth.

And he answers with a groan that's all desire, his hands urgent as they tug me against his hardness. The feel of his need, the evidence of his desire, has me burning up inside. That throbbing ache returns tenfold as my hips writhe and my hands rake over him.

I need this. *We* need this.

But he's tearing away again, his head shifting to one side, his body totally still. I open my eyes and he's looking away, his shoulders heaving for breath, for control. But I don't want control. Not any more. I'm sick of it.

I reach for his face and pull him back to me. 'Kiss me,' I urge.

Kiss me before I say something that we can't come back from. Kiss me before the truth brings this to an end.

I nudge his mouth open, dipping my tongue inside to gently coax his own, and a shiver runs through his body. I feel it beneath my palms, hear it in his shaky breath.

'I need to know you want this,' he rasps out, his eyes dark and glittering into mine. 'I need to know that you want *me*.'

I go to kiss him again, to show him how much I do, but he presses me away.

'Walking away from you in your office…'

He closes his eyes and shakes his head. When

he opens them again, they're blazing with hurt and need, pain and desire.

'It all but killed me. But I can't play second fiddle in your bed, Lexi. I won't.'

My heart aches inside my chest. His vulnerability is raw, honest, and all the more powerful as it breaks through the controlled, commanding exterior I've been accustomed to these last two weeks, knowing it's all because of me...

But my heart has no place in this. This is sex. Primal. Safe.

Don't confuse it. I recall our conversation in Marie's living room, but so much has happened, so much has changed...

'I want *you*,' I stress, 'like I've never wanted anyone in my whole life.'

It's the truth, and it's more than he's asked for. I'm making myself vulnerable by admitting that he's always been the one, but it's impulsive and it's driven by his honesty.

It's also the perfect time to tell him everything... not to shy away from it for fear of the damage it will cause.

'Tell me, again.' He presses his forehead to mine, his eyes staring down at me.

'I want you, Cain.'

Now. Tell him now. Tell him it wasn't a real marriage. Tell him why Liam married you. Tell him about Rose.

But his lips are already crushing mine as he turns me away from the counter and propels me back against the glass doors to the terrace. I can't think any more. It's dizzying, disorientating, discombobulating. His body covers mine from head to toe, hot, urgent, and I'm on fire, the delicious throb of pleasure whipping up inside me all the stronger for my recent release.

I take the onslaught of his kiss and return it just as fiercely, just as desperately.

Seven years without anything coming close to this. Seven years of feeling empty, of being alone. And now this—mere minutes after I lost it under his mouth.

I fork my fingers through his hair, down his neck, inside his jacket as I shove it from his shoulders.

A seven-year wait—for this. I can't trust him with my heart. I won't. I can't survive that pain again. But this—*oh, yes, this*—I can trust him enough for this.

It isn't about love—it's about need.

And I need him more than I need my next breath.

His jacket hits the floor as his hands force my dress up my thighs. His fingers against my skin are rough—shaking, even. Or is it me who trembles?

'*Lexi.*'

My name vibrates out of him and I realise we're both trembling, both unsteady as we try and slake this hunger.

I yank at his tie and nip at his bottom lip, delivering a sharp hit that has the breath hissing out of him. He growls and kisses me harder, almost punishing me in return, and I'm losing it. Desperate to have him naked and not able to summon the skill, the wit, to do it.

Buttons are too fiddly, zips catch. I moan in frustration as I claw at his shoulders instead, one leg lifting to curve around him. I draw him close, shamelessly riding his hardness as his tongue plunders deeper and deeper still.

Our kiss is suffocating, neither wanting to break it to draw breath, neither wanting to create any space between us at all, and the friction is so goddamn perfect. My clit is getting the continual grind of his cock as he strains against the confines of his trousers.

'Oh, my God, Cain…'

I start to pant, my ability to kiss him back breaking as my mouth turns slack, my movements stilted. I'm going to come. I can feel it curling up from my toes, pulling at my core. My body tenses as the delicious heat swells rapidly around me, through me. I try and stave it off, talk it down—*not yet, not yet*. And then Cain takes the driving seat. He knows and he grinds against me, pressing me back into the glass. His mouth returns to my neck and then his hands are on my breasts, rough, groping…

I want more…so much more… I want his hands on my bare skin…his mouth on my nipples.

'Damn this dress.'

It's Cain who says it, as though he's in my mind, seeing what I want. He finds the zipper at the back and yanks it down. I think I hear it tear but I don't care.

He parts it over my shoulders and I wriggle to help.

My exposed back meets the cool glass and I buck away. But his hand is there, curving me against him. I lower my leg to let my dress fall to the floor and my bra swiftly follows. My bare nipples brush against his shirt, the accidental caress as erotic, as charged as anything, and then his palms are there, weighing, caressing, thumb and forefinger rolling, plucking.

'*Fuck.*' I'm going out of my mind. I clutch him tighter, whimper more.

'*Lexi.*'

He says my name as if he can scarcely believe this is happening. Hell, *I* can't. It's too intense, too dreamlike, too heady.

He twists my hair around his fist, pulls my head back against the glass as his hot mouth trails across the exposed skin of my neck, sucking, devouring. He cups the back of my knee to lift my leg around him once more, delivering that perfect hit of friction again, each grind taking me higher and higher.

My nails bite into his shoulders. I'm unable to move, rigid with the spiralling heat, the knowledge that I'm close…so close. He pinches my nipple, squeezes it tight, almost painfully, and my clit pulses. He does it again. And again.

And then his hand is between us, slipping inside the elastic of my knickers. I bite into my bottom lip, hold my breath, and then he's there, slipping down into my wetness, the brush of his fingers circling over me.

'*Cain!*' It bursts out of me—a warning? A plea? I don't know.

'You're so wet,' he says against my collarbone, his kiss feverish upon my skin.

And then he drops lower, sucks in one pert nipple, the hot cavern of his mouth surrounding it, his tongue rolling over it, and I tremble in my rigid state, my body not knowing which sensation to focus on more: his fingers over my clit, his mouth, or his hand over my breast.

'I need to taste you again, Lexi.'

The heat pulses between my legs, my belly contracts and I drop my head forward, look down into eyes that gaze up at me imploringly. His tongue flicks out to tease at the nipple jutting at him, begging for more. He keeps my eyes trapped in his gaze as he tongues the sensitive flesh, his fingers picking up their pace inside my knickers…the same dizzying pace of his tongue.

'Yes, Cain…*yes*.'

His hand slips out of my underwear and he drops to his knees. My legs lock tight as I fear I'm going to collapse, but then he's cupping one of my ankles, coaxing me into bending my leg to step out of the dress, which is pooled at my feet. He returns my foot to the floor and does the same with the other, purposely widening my stance as he does so.

Cool air sweeps over the dampness of my knickers, arousing and shocking in one, and then his hands are easing softly upwards, stroking up the skin at the backs of my calves, my thighs, my bum… He leans forward, his nose nudging against my clothed seam and—God help me—I jerk into the simple touch.

He smiles up at me and does it again…slowly… very slowly…

He breathes over me. 'Tell me again.'

I don't even have to ask to know what he wants to hear. And then I realise he *needs* to hear it—he needs to be the one and only. Not because he's staking his claim, or possessing me. It's because of the same vulnerability that drove him away seven years ago. The fear of being the outsider.

For all his confident, outwardly arrogant persona back then, he was vulnerable. And for all the man he is now, he still has that fear deep down. It crushes me. I should have realised back then. I should have seen it for what it was and talked him round. But instead I pushed him away. I made it worse.

My throat closes over. Tears prick. The heat of desire and the burn of my failure, intensifies everything as I bury my fingers in his hair.

'I want you.'

It's a whisper, but it's there, and then his hands are easing the fabric aside, his tongue is flicking out and he's pressing it against me, parting me. The merest hint of friction sends me rigid, straining for more. My knees quake, my thighs tremble and, as if he senses my weakness, he palms my arse, holding me fast against him.

'I want you…' I moan again, grateful for the sensation that's overtaking the pain of all that lies between us.

He groans over me, the rumble working its way through my body. *Oh, yes.* His fingers curl into the waistband at my hips and slowly he drags it down, over my thighs, my knees. I step out for the time it takes to strip it away, and then he's on me again, wasting no time. His fingers part me for the arrival of his mouth and he sucks me…

Oh, God, yes.

'You taste so good,' he says over my clit, his lips brushing, his breath caressing, and then he dips his fingers inside me and runs the flat of his tongue upwards.

'Cain…'

'I love hearing my name from your lips…your Irish lilt…' His fingers delve in deeper, pressing on my G-spot, his words separated by the sweet circle of his tongue 'It's so fucking hot… It's like coming home.'

And I haven't got time to process his words because he's driving me to the precipice of release, with fingers and mouth and tongue. It's a dizzying dance that he knows of old and I'm lost to it, ecstasy rolling through me as I let go.

I rock against the glass, against him, as the waves ricochet through me. I cling to the pleasurable heat, wanting to make it last, to feed it, to have it go on for ever, and I stave off reality because I'm content to stay like this always.

'Cain…'

Another breathy whisper, and slowly he releases me, his mouth trailing kisses from the tip of my pubic bone to my belly button to my clavicle. And then he's there, face to face, and I'm gazing into those eyes which are so familiar, and yet not, and I want to cry. Both pain and happiness are merging into one.

'Yes?'

I shake my head. How can I speak when I don't even know what I'm asking? I don't know how to make sense of what I feel, how to tell him what I must. What I *do* know is that I need him. I need him inside me, filling me so completely that it wipes out this age-old pain, even for a short spell.

And maybe that's all I need to ask of him.

'Make love to me.'

His smile is slow, seductive, and it triggers another sweep of ecstasy through my overactive body that hasn't had its fill.

'Your wish is my command.'

He scoops me up in his arms as if I weigh nothing, and I hear the soft whirr of the glass door sliding open behind us. I have no idea how—a secret panel on the wall? Some psychic connection to its owner?—but I'm impressed... Until I register the cold night air over my bare skin.

'Don't worry,' he says, holding me tighter as I tense. 'No one can see us here... There's not even a boat close to shore.'

I look out into the darkness. He's right. There's nothing but the sound of the rolling sea, the sight of the waves breaking and the salty sea breeze that rushes over my skin. I curve into his body, seeking his heat, and then I feel steam at my back. Warm, alluring steam. And, just as the door slid open, the cover of the swim spa rolls back.

'Is there anything this house doesn't have?'

I laugh as I say it, and look up into his gaze, but my laugh freezes with my breath. The intense sincerity in his face, his eyes, pulls me up short.

'You, Lexi. It doesn't have you.'

He didn't… He can't… He can't possibly mean it, but my heart throbs longingly all the same. Do I dare to believe, dare to hope…?

No, you were fool enough to hope once. You can't do it again—you can't risk it again. No matter the role you played in his departure. How can you trust him not to run again?

'Well, I'm here now.' I make it jovial, as light-hearted as I can.

'True.' He grins as he lowers me to my feet. 'Step in.'

I do as he asks, my hand in his as I feel for the steps with my toes. The heat of the water seeps into my skin, warm, tantalising, soothing my goose-pimpled flesh.

'I'll get our drinks.'

He walks away and I tie my hair high on my head before settling back. It's heavenly, almost otherworldly, being cocooned in this delicious bubbling warmth while looking out on blackness, on the never-ending sea. I can feel my mind threatening to wander into risky territory, into fanciful what-ifs, and I claw it back, focus on the immediate present and indulge in the fantasy for what it is—*temporary.*

I hear his step behind me and turn my head. It immediately empties. He's naked, with two glasses of whiskey in his hand. I raise my brow—it's about the only outward response I can muster, even though my tongue wants to flick out and wet my lips like some sex-starved vixen. Because all I can think about is how I want to devour the thick, hard length of him that's protruding, proud and unashamed.

I'm like a woman possessed. A woman seeking her younger self and clinging to it desperately. A woman who never went through pain, who has never suffered between then and now.

'Nice to see you appreciate the finer things in life.'

My eyes snap to his, which are glittering with laughter and a far more carnal, overriding urge.

I almost say, *It's been a while*, but it's too close to the truth—the truth he has yet to learn—so I laugh softly instead.

He slips into the water beside me, his bare leg brushing against mine and setting off a frisson of excitement in its wake. He leans back and passes me one of the glasses, offering up his own in toast.

'To us.'

My throat tightens. Hope and fear collide.

I want there to be an 'us'—my heart pulses with the very thought—but can there really be an us when all is said and done?

His eyes narrow as he lifts his glass higher. 'And to the O'Connor firm.'

I want to breathe a sigh of relief, but I mask it in a smile. It's a toast I can agree to.

'Yes,' I say, raising my glass. 'To the O'Connors.'

We drink, and I force myself to hold his eye, even

though the fear of what's to come hangs over me, endangering it all.

Now we have this moment, this closeness, I don't want to break it. It's selfish—but, hell, I've lived my life for others for so long. Just for one night…a few hours, even… I want to let it go.

And I *will* tell him.

Very, very soon.

I can't take my eyes off her.

She's glowing, the light from the water reflecting off her skin, glittering in her eyes. She has droplets of water clinging to her cheeks, her neck, her collarbone. I reach out and trail a path along her skin, sweeping some away, and I love how her lips part and she leans into my caress.

'You are beautiful, Lexi.'

She looks at me, her smile small, thoughtful, and I wonder what she's thinking. She's been quiet since I joined her in the water and made that impulsive toast. The toast that had her eyes flaring in what I can only interpret as alarm.

I thought I'd recovered the situation well enough, but the last few minutes have passed by in silence, only the bubbling water and the sound of the ocean breaking up the quiet.

Is it my toast that has her so contemplative? My suggestion of an 'us'? Or is it more than that?

I find her hand in the water and pull her towards me. To my relief her smile slinks higher and her body comes willingly, gliding through the water.

'Lonely over there?' she teases.

'Positively isolated.'

I bring her across my lap, feel her body brush over my eager cock as it bucks to meet her. I'm still hard from making her come, from the taste of her, the feel of her coming apart for me. Twice over. If I recall it in enough detail I could come on the memory alone, and it's that which has me clamping my jaw shut and trying to think of something off-putting—anything to stave off the heat.

My old science teacher—she's perfect. She hated me. She wore insipid green, wrinkled-up tights around her ankles, and had the most fascinating wart on the tip of her nose. Yes, perfect.

'Why so tense?'

She strokes my jawline as she says it, one finger brushing over my stubble, teasing, provoking, and I dip my head to surround it with my mouth. The move is impulsive, necessary—payback. I circle it with my tongue and watch her eyes glitter, dark and needy, before I release it.

'I'm not sure… Could it be that all I want right now is to sink myself inside you and never let you go again?'

It's raw. It's honest. And it makes her eyes flare—but not with alarm this time, thank fuck.

She wriggles her arse, and I don't know whether it's intentional or not, but my cock isn't fussy.

'You feel so big,' she rasps, her cheeks blushing with her observation, so bashful.

I want to choke. What man wouldn't love to hear

those words? But when she says it like that she isn't saying it to boost me. She says it because she's genuinely thinking it.

'Carry on like that and I'll be taking you here and now.'

'Here?' Her eyes narrow, as though the thought hadn't occurred to her. It's been seven years—has she really not *lived* in seven years?

'You've never done that?'

She shakes her head and bites into her bottom lip, excitement sparking in her gaze.

I want to focus on the thrill of being another first for her, want to get caught up in those pools of blue, but instead I'm caught up in those missing years. In Liam and Alexa and what they must have done. What new experiences they must have shared. Hell, they must have done plenty, and the idea chills me.

I used him as a game earlier—a game driven by anger, by jealousy, by the need to be the one in control—but I want none of that now.

'Never,' she says in verbal confirmation, trapping her lip once more as her eyes fall to my mouth.

I force my focus on that look, on the hunger in her eyes and the feel of my cock pulsing between us. *Better.*

I raise my fingers to her chin and drag her bottom lip from between her teeth. It's plump, swollen from our kisses, from her teeth, and I'm about to kiss her when she dips to take my thumb inside her mouth. She sucks over it, her tongue rotating, doing exactly what I did with her finger, and Holy Mother of—

I feel like it's my cock she's sucking.

Her cheeks are hollow with the move, her eyes alive with suggestion.

'Lexi...' I croak.

I'm not about to come like a horny teen—but, *Jesus*, if she keeps doing that, with her arse massaging my cock, I might. Shame or no.

She does it again, and I drag my eyes lower, to where her breasts bob on the surface of the water, the bubbles teasing nipples which are taut and ready. *Oh, fuck.* A thrilling shiver runs through me, my hips buck, and I snap my eyes to hers just as she slides my thumb from her mouth.

'It's my turn to taste you...' she purrs.

'Lexi...' I'm shaking my head and I don't know why.

'It's only fair.'

She gives me a pout and it's so goddamn sexy that my body bucks again.

'Just the idea of you...' I rub her lips with the pad of my thumb, my head already imagining it, and lustful heat rips through me. My words are tight as I admit, 'I'll lose it.'

She gives a soft laugh. 'Isn't that the point?'

Yes.

So why am I hesitating?

Because you want her, you want to be inside her. As much as you want her mouth, you want her.

So why not have both?

'Stay the night with me?' I say, before I can over-think it.

Her frown is instant.

'If you stay the night, I get to have you in all the ways I want.'

She searches my gaze. 'I…'

I drop my hand beneath the water, curve it over her thigh, smooth it higher and higher. 'You…?'

She whimpers low in her throat as I slip one finger between her legs and then pull it back to find her taut little nub.

'You…?' I ask again as she gives a breathy moan. 'Hmm?'

'Cain.'

She rocks into my touch, her cheeks flushing pink, and the sign of her so turned on washes through me like an aphrodisiac.

'That's a dirty trick,' she pants, but she doesn't stop rocking and I don't stop circling.

'I like to play dirty.'

I lean forward to nip the delicate skin of her throat, feeling the tension slip from her body, feeling her clit swell beneath my touch. I know I have her.

'Will you stay?' I ask.

'Yes, Cain…*yes.*'

She hangs her arms around my shoulders, rides my fingers like I'm her everything—and, my God, how I want to be. It's a terrifying realisation but I can't shift it. The need for her to be mine, for us to be together again—it's all I can care about, all I can think about in this second.

'You'll stay?'

She grinds down on my cock and stares at me in determination. *'Yes.'*

'Good.'

I claim her mouth with mine, sup from her as she rocks and explodes against me. Her abandon pushes me ever closer to my own release. And then she's turning into me, her body still quaking, and I think she's about to settle down, rest her head into the curve of my neck. But instead her teeth scrape at my earlobe, her lips lift to my ear.

'My turn.'

I shiver as the words send her breath rippling down my ear canal. Never have two words sounded more sexual, more filled with promise.

'Up,' she commands, coming to her feet with a certainty that has me surprised as much as turned on.

I rise up with a lopsided grin.

'Now, sit.'

Sit? I raise my brow at her bossy demeanour— but, hell, I'm loving it, and my cock is standing proud and waiting.

'Happy?' I say as I sit back on the cushioned edge of the spa.

'Like I said,' she practically purrs, 'it's most definitely my turn.'

And then she's sinking to her knees in the water, the steam rising around her. The cold night air wraps around me from the knees up, but I don't feel it. I'm only concerned with her hands wrapping around my cock, her grip tight, her eyes locking with mine.

'Do you taste the same?' she murmurs around my tip, her lips brushing against the head.

I grip the edge either side of me as I drag in a breath. 'You'll have to tell me.'

I'm rewarded with a smile, and then she's sinking me inside her mouth, her blushing pink lips wrapping around me and taking me so far in I'm shaking with the effort to restrain. But I need to hold out.

I'm not fighting it to be a man, to delay my own satisfaction. I'm fighting it to *show* her. I don't want to be that weak. I don't want her to control me so easily. But, hell, I wish to God someone would tell my body that. Because she's sucking me back so hard, her tongue caressing me, her lips playing with my tip as she stares up at me.

Oh, God.

'Nice?'

Did she really just ask me that?

Then she licks at the slit, at the pre-cum forming there, and I grasp at her hair, my words choked. 'You have no idea…'

She laughs, her tongue flicking out to repeat the move. Jesus, she has me so easily.

And then she takes me in deep, her mouth wrapped around me, her suck so powerful I see stars. My fingers in her hair claw more than I want them to but, hell, she's making me tremble, and my release is so close…

'*Christ*, Lexi…' I groan the words and I'm transported back over a decade, to when she perfected the same move, and the old merges with the new. 'Like that…just like that.'

She smiles around my tip. 'I know—I remember.'

She's with me in my bedroom at my family home, having sneaked in during the hour before dinner. We're learning what makes each other tick, what tips each other over the edge. Christ, so many firsts, so many mind-obliterating experiences—is it any wonder I never moved on from her? Any wonder that she is my life, my soul, my everything?

And then my mind quits as my balls contract, tingling with my imminent release. I'm trying to warn her with the tightening of my fingers in her hair, my body clenching as I struggle to speak, but she doesn't let me go. She does what she always did. She drinks me down, every euphoric pulse disappearing into her, and it's like no other pleasure I have known.

I haven't been a saint. She knows that, I'm sure, and I know it. But no one has ever come close to her, and as I caress her hair and gaze down into her triumphant gaze I believe she knows that too.

'You are a minx,' I whisper.

'Better the minx you know, right?'

Oh, my God, yes.

I shake my head and stand, pulling her up against me, breast to breast, cheek to cheek. 'You will stay?'

She nods. 'For now.'

I don't know what 'for now' means, but it's enough for me. In this second, it has to be. I comb my fingers deep into her hair and clutch her closer as I kiss her shoulder and inhale.

It has to be enough.

CHAPTER TEN

JUST AS HE carried me to his hot tub, Cain carries me to his bed, and despite every warning in my brain telling me to leave, that it's gone far enough, I'm too loved up. And I use 'loved up' in the loosest sense of the term—because I can't be *in love* with him again.

I'm just emotional because of all that he's said, raking up the past, the role I unwittingly played in it. Not to mention the crazy rush of desire and endorphins that have lain dormant all these years.

He lowers me to his bed and I'm surrounded by luxury: soft sheets that welcome me in, envelop me; low, deep music that plays a strumming rhythm in tune to my heart, and him—oh, God, *him*.

He's naked and striding towards me, a filled champagne flute in hand.

'Cain…' I shake my head at the glass. I don't need any more alcohol. I only need him. His mouth, his fingers, his—

'Drunk too much already?'

I laugh. 'No, but I only need *you*.'

He smiles, and it's so full of feeling my breath catches.

'Indulge me.'

Oh, God, how can I not? He's my past, my present…*my future?*

It doesn't matter how locked-down my heart is—he still has the power to crack it open and break it if I let him.

He leans over me on the bed, the glass hovering between us. 'Drink.'

It's a command, not a question, and I raise my mouth and angle my head to take a sip. It's cold… ice-cold. The tiny bubbles fizz over my tongue in a sensation far more powerful than it was at the presentation meal, and I wonder if it's because this is the real deal—the best money can buy—or if it's just that my senses are heightened, desperate to cling to any sensation he delivers?

'My turn…'

He takes a swig, but I don't see him swallow. Instead he lowers his head—not to my lips, but to my breast. He surrounds the peak with his mouth, ice-cold bubbles fizzing over the sensitised flesh, and I cry out, my hands flying to his hair.

Oh, yes.

How can it feel so good? So intense? So soon?

But I'm still tender from his earlier attentions, so the delicate fizz, his flicking tongue, his grazing teeth are all enough to send erotic shudders running through me.

He moves to the other breast, does the same, and

I cling to him, watching his every move, my mouth slack with unrestrained need.

What you should be asking is how you walk away from this? How, Lexi? How?

I whimper. Sex. Fear. Need. A mix that I can't get a handle on. I just know I want this crazy, almost delirious heat to continue, to overpower all the rest, to stop the past from breaking in.

But it's there—haunting me, taunting me.

I cry out, frustrated that my brain won't quit, and he gazes up at me, his teeth sharp over one taut peak, his fingers sinking low. There's a question in the depths of his eyes, a question I can't answer, and I throw my head back onto the pillow, beckon with my hand in his hair for him to continue.

And he does, but I feel the question still hanging, burning into his every caress: *What aren't you telling me?*

I grind against his fingers as they slip between my legs. I won't let the pain back in. I have lived with it for so long and right now I feel alive, born again. Let me lose it...let us lose it together.

He parts my legs with his body and rises onto his knees, the glass still in his hand as his eyes trail over me, coming back to mine. No question now, only desire.

'You are stunning.'

His voice is rough, setting my skin alight as he watches me. He tips the glass and dribbles a path of champagne from my breasts to my belly button... I suck in a breath as the liquid pools and trickles either side of me. Then he moves lower still. His fingers part me to the flow of liquid and I arch my back, whimpering as it seeps between my legs, a cold caress.

'Lexi and champagne…the perfect cocktail.'

He bends forward to cover me with his mouth. The heat after the cold liquid is a striking contrast that has my hands clawing into his bedsheets, my body arching further.

'Yes—God, yes.'

He groans over my clit, the vibrations firing spasms through my body.

'I want… I want…'

I'm trying to articulate my thoughts, but I can't keep my breath long enough to finish. I'm panting, gasping for air as my climax builds, and Cain is unrelenting, the tip of his tongue stroking me in a fierce dance that has my toes curling, my legs tensing. I can't believe I'm going to…again…already, but I'm going, I'm going—I'm gone, roll after roll of pleasure shaking me to the core.

He dips down to tongue my wetness, to take all that he has milked from me, until my body twinges in its hyper-sensitivity and I'm pulling his body up to me. He lets the glass of champagne, now empty, roll off the bed onto the plush grey rug beside it, and covers me from head to toe.

'I don't think I can ever tire of making you come,' he says.

'You and me both.' And oh, how I wish that could

be the case, that we could stay like this always. Close, connected, happy.

I rake my hands down his back and pull him closer.

'I'll crush you,' he warns, but I can't speak.

I don't trust my voice not to betray my inner turmoil. Instead I continue to tighten my arms around him, feeling the reassuring weight of his body on mine before he plants his elbows either side of me and eases up onto them.

He looks down at me and I feel his hardness pressing urgently into my thigh, telling me that although his hands are soft as they sweep over my cheeks, his face calm, satisfied, he still wants me.

I haven't let anyone make love to me since Cain— since the night we made Rose. Not even Liam and I could ever get that far. I want to tell myself it's okay, that this is what I want, but the pain has me clamping my eyes shut, my teeth biting into my lip.

'Hey, I told you I'd crush you.'

He tries to move off me but I pull him back, my eyes flying open and pleading with his.

'Don't go.'

I want Cain. I want him to replace that memory with a new one. And I want it now.

'Make love to me?'

The request chokes out of me—a thousand memories, a thousand spasms of pain and want—and as he searches my gaze I'm convinced he's read them all.

'I want nothing more.'

I curve my legs around him, urging him closer,

telling him with my actions that I feel the same. The tip of his cock nudges inside my opening and I hold my breath, ready…so ready.

And then he freezes. His entire body is rigid.

I open my eyes and see his are squeezed shut now, his breathing ragged.

'Don't move.'

His command is gruff.

'But—'

'I need to get a condom,' he explains.

I'm relieved and stunned in one. How could I be so stupid, so wrapped up in the moment, not to think…?

He drags in another breath and withdraws, and the effort it takes for him to do so is etched in every hard line of his face, his corded neck, his straining cock.

My body pines for the loss of his, but he doesn't leave the bed.

He stretches across to the sleek white bedside table and pulls out a small foil packet. He tears it open with his teeth and sheaths himself in a way that tells me he's done this a thousand times before. Not only that, but the presence of condoms in his bedside drawer tells me he's always prepared—even here. And surely that means I'm not the first woman he's brought back to this amazing house and I won't be the last?

I close my eyes, wanting to block out the unwelcome truth, wanting only to care about the here and now.

'It has only ever been you, Lexi.'

I open my eyes and he's there, lying on his side, gazing down at me. He lifts a strand of hair from my face, twisting it around his finger.

'You don't need to say that,' I whisper. 'I don't need you to say things to make me feel better.'

'I'm not saying it to make you feel better...'

I cock an eyebrow at him.

'Okay, I am...but it doesn't mean it's not the truth.'

I raise a hand to his hair and pull his mouth towards mine. 'Less talk, more action.'

He shakes his head, but then he's kissing me back with all the passion, all the need, I know he feels. I wrap my arms around him and pull him on top of me. He nudges my legs apart with his knees, his tip pressing into me once more. I curve my legs around his hips, encasing him, welcoming him, and he drives into me, forcing my unaccustomed body to adjust to his size.

I cry out as the intense sensation rips through me.

He stills and I stare up at him. 'Don't stop.'

His eyes penetrate me. 'Are you okay?'

I nod fiercely but he frowns, his eyes locked to mine. 'Are you sure?'

I can hardly announce that seven years of celibacy is to blame. It feels foolish. Inadequate. And, yes, it hurts to be made love to again, but more than that is the overwhelming pleasure of being filled so completely, so perfectly, by him.

'Did I hurt you?'

His cock pulses inside me, buried so deep, but he's refusing to move, refusing to do anything without my assurance. And his concern is killing me, exposing me, breaking me.

'No, Cain, no…please, I want you.'

Still he frowns, and his sincerity is reaching inside me and chipping away at every defensive wall I've put in place. I squeeze my thighs around him and wriggle my body to get comfortable.

'Please.'

His eyes flicker and slowly, so slowly, he eases out of me, tension pulsing in his jaw. 'Stop me if it hurts.'

He looks so serious, torn between taking his own pleasure and looking out for mine. I love him for it. *No, not love—desire.* I desire him all the more for it.

'It's only ever been you,' he repeats softly, and my wetness is slick along his length as he re-enters me, my body taking more and more of him with each gentle thrust until he's striking at the very heart of me and I can feel the tension vibrating through his body.

'Only *you*,' he stresses emphatically.

The spasm of pleasure as he enters me is all the more powerful for his words and I don't know how to respond. My messed-up thoughts merge into each other and I keep quiet, losing myself in sensation, in every heartfelt thrust of his body. I match his tempo and as it turns jagged, I grip around him, keep him where I want him, where I need him and I don't think any more. I say what's in my heart and let go. 'It's only ever been you, Cain.'

* * *

'It's only ever been you...only ever been you...only you...'

I'm between sleeping and waking, her words replaying through my mind, and I grin as warmth spreads through me. I roll over, blindly seeking her out, and wake with a start. I'm alone. Very much alone.

I launch bolt upright up in bed, my palms pressing into the mattress either side of me as I scan the room.

Where the hell is she?

I blink through a sleep-induced haze to see the sun is only just creeping through the blinds, and as I sweep my palm over the space next to me I can feel her residual body heat still there.

Is she in the kitchen making coffee? Making breakfast?

My heart soars and then immediately plummets, my fingers clawing at the bedsheets where she lay. There is no distant sound of movement, no smell of coffee in the air, and I know in my heart that she has gone.

I fall onto my back and stare up at the ceiling, replaying the night in all its glory—everything we did, everything that was said. We were desperate to sate our thirst, eager to fill the gap of seven years apart. Hell, we were eager to show one another how much we'd cared, how much we still cared for one another... Or so I thought.

Why didn't she at least wake me? Say goodbye?

I throw off the quilt, push off the bed and pull on my gym gear, keen to sweat every answer out of me.

Because there's only one reason. No, two…

Either she's still in love with Liam or she can't move on from the past… And that means she can't love me back…

Love me back?

My throat convulses. I am in love with her. I never stopped being in love with her. Despite the betrayal, the years apart, I love her more now than ever.

And she's gone.

CHAPTER ELEVEN

I'M RUNNING SO FAST that my lungs are burning and my heart is thumping like crazy in my ears, but I press my earphones in tighter and up my pace. I can't let the guilt in, the pain, the pleasure...the incredible, intoxicating pleasure of being back in his bed. I can't be that weak again. I won't be.

But you love him—you know you do—that's why it hurts all the more.

I pound the trail harder, my tear-streaked face looking out to sea, grateful that Howth Head is quiet at this time of the morning. Dawn is only just breaking over the horizon and it's virtually just me and my four-legged Ed against the world. It's a liberating time of day. Where nothing can encroach and there are no time pressures—just us and the track, the sea and the birds.

But today my gut is weighted, my legs threatening to slow against the burden of it all.

Even now I can hardly bear to think of Rose, to face the pain head-on and cry—because it terrifies me how much it hurts, how I can't feel whole again without her, how I feel as if something is always missing.

And now with Liam gone, and Robert too, it's just too much.

The very idea of passing that grief on to Cain, of it haunting him like it does me...

But I have to. I know I do. He deserves to know it all.

It was hard enough thinking about telling him before. Now that we've slept together—now that he's shared so much with me and opened up...now I know how much I've failed him—how do I break it to him?

I fell asleep in his arms so readily—only to wake up in the early hours with my hand clutched to my abdomen and a cold sweat across my skin. I could hardly wake him to tell him something of that magnitude. I could hardly lie back and go to sleep either. Not with the reason for my guilt so very present.

And so I left, like the broken, nasty piece of work I feel I am, and now he'll be waking up with me gone.

I didn't even leave a note—something to thank him for the night, something to make him realise I wasn't running from him. Not for the reason he would think, anyway.

I left because we had a child—a child he knows nothing about—and she died.

How do I even begin to tell him that?

I'm so sorry I didn't tell you, but you weren't around. And when you were back on the scene too much time had passed, too much stuff had happened.

'Christ!' I shake my head against the chilling wind and Ed looks at me over his shoulder, his tongue hanging out. 'Don't look at me like that... you have it simple.'

He gives me a bark that I take to be agreement and I smile at my own madness. Talking to animals? What will I be doing next?

I run harder, for longer than my body or Ed can take, and it's him that has me reining myself back in, forcing myself to return before I'm ready. But then, I don't think I'll ever be ready to face up to the reality I've created for myself.

I take Ed back to his house, fill up his water bowl and then head back to mine. It feels quieter than usual, but then I'm earlier than usual. My neighbours in the building are still making the most of their Saturday lie-in.

I set the coffee machine going and take a shower, hoping that when I come back to the kitchen the soothing aroma of caffeine will help to ease the cloud that's hanging over me.

But it doesn't work.

I stand before the window, my mug cupped in my hands, my nose hovering just above the rim as I breathe it in.

And nothing.

Outside the sun is shining, streaming down on me in all its warming glory, but I don't feel it. I only have to close my eyes for a second and Cain is there, looking down at me as he fills me so completely.

'Only ever you.'

It's so strong I can sense him in the room with me and my eyes shoot open.

Of course he isn't here.

The street is quiet below. Save for the odd car moving, the city is still quiet. And that's when I see it, glinting at me in my reflection. The ring on my left hand.

I hold it out, admiring the simple band, and a bittersweet smile lifts my face. Liam. Dear, sweet, intelligent, Liam. We had a pact, after Rose, that should either of us ever meet someone, fall in love, we would divorce and give each other our blessing. It just never happened. Our arrangement was so easy, so comfortable, with work filling our days, and our nights quite often too. It filled the void…helped to keep the pain of loss at bay.

I lower my mug to the desk, where our monitors still face one another, and I know it's time. I know that in order to move on I have to accept that he's gone—my best friend, my husband in all the ways that mattered to us at the time. No matter what happens with Cain going forward, I can't hang on to the past any longer.

And, as per the pact I had with Liam, I can't wear his ring when I love another.

I twist the band on my finger, ease it over my knuckle and with a tug it's off. I stare at it in my palm and a single tear drops to meet it.

'I'm sorry, Liam.'

I don't know why I'm saying sorry. We were never in love in that sense—never boyfriend and girlfriend before we became husband and wife. It was always about being a mum and dad to Rose…being a family.

I clutch the ring in my palm and raise it to my lips as the sobs rack through my body.

'I miss you.'

I don't know whether I'm saying that to Rose, to Liam, or to both, but I do know I need to move on. To take control of my life again and start afresh. To look forward rather than back and hope that in some way I can take Cain with me, make him a part of it…

It's eight in the evening and I know I shouldn't be here. I know that chasing her down when she so obviously wants space is wrong. But after everything we've shared she owes me something. *Anything.*

I've had no call, no text, nothing. I'd say it was wounded pride, but I'd be lying. I know it's my heart that's breaking.

I press her buzzer and step back, gaze up at the ancient building to the sash windows that I know belong to her and the soft glow of a lamp or two that tells me she's home. Not that she's answering.

I press it again, looking for movement even though I know that unless she steps right up to the window I'll see nothing. It's not like I can yell up at her. She has no windows open and I'm likely to disturb all the other residents before she even hears.

But I want to. I want to yell until my lungs hurt— until I can't feel my panic-ridden heart any more and she speaks to me, tells me what the hell is going on.

'Lex—'

My outburst is cut off by the door release. I stare at it for a second, disbelieving, and then rush forward before it clicks shut.

I take the stairs two at a time and ignore the weird angst inside me because I have to face Liam again by coming back here. I have to accept their past together to be able to move on. And I will.

I'll do anything to be given another chance at happiness and I need her to see that. There's nothing we can't get through together, I'm sure of it, and whatever made her run, it can't be bigger than my love for her.

'Lexi—' Her name rushes out of me as I exit the final flight of stairs and see her standing in her doorway.

Her skin is pale, her blue eyes glittering in the overhead lights. I slow down, not wanting to spook her. She looks like a frightened bird, about to take flight, and as she cradles her belly I see her hands are shaking. I reach out as I near, wanting to offer comfort for whatever this is, and as I close my hands around hers, I squeeze them softly.

'Can I come in?'

She looks up at me with a nod, wets her lips as if she's going to speak, but drags in a breath instead. She pulls her hands away as she turns, and that's when I feel it—the obvious difference on her finger…

'You've taken off your ring.'

She pauses, nods. 'It was time.'

Oh, God, is that why she ran? Was it guilt? Guilt that she'd slept with me when her heart…?

I can't even finish the thought.

'I'm sorry.'

She shakes her head. I follow her through into the kitchen area and watch as she pours water into the kettle and switches it on.

'Can I get you a drink?' she asks. 'Tea, coffee, wine?'

Her voice is expressionless and the panic inside me swells.

'I really am sorry, Lexi. I don't want to cause you more pain… Hell, I don't want to hurt you at—'

I stop. She's looking at me as if she's seen a ghost and I know I've called this so wrong.

'There's something I need to tell you,' she says, and she takes a shaky breath that has a chill sweeping over me. 'Something I should have told you a long time ago, but…but it was never the right moment.'

She trembles on the last words, her hands falling to her stomach in that gesture I've become so familiar with over the last few weeks.

Weeks? Christ. Has it really only been weeks?

I quickly count. Not even three full weeks since I came back. Since I acknowledged my love for her has never really waned. Since I accepted that she's what I've been missing for the last seven years.

I take my jacket off and place it on the side. I want to comfort her, reassure her, and I step forward.

'Whatever it is, baby, you can tell me.'

She raises one trembling hand between us, her

finger wagging, her eyes widen and spill over, a steady stream of tears that has the panic building within me.

'We had a child.'

It's quiet, so quiet. I can't have heard her right.

'A child?' I say, wary, disbelieving.

But she nods, rapidly, her pallor, her tears all the more severe. 'She died.'

No— *No, no, no.* My stomach lurches. I feel goosebumps pricking all over my skin as my body chills. I could never have imagined…never have guessed…even for a second…

'You and Liam had a…' I take a choked breath '…a child?' She says nothing and desperately I push. 'When? How? No one said…no one called…'

My ears ring as I strain to hear her answer, and yet I don't want her to all the same. I had a nephew? A niece? And no one told me? Not even when they died?

'No, Cain. Not Liam and I. *You* and I.'

Her trembling hand goes to her mouth. Her other hand clutches at her stomach, at the fabric of the simple navy sweater that she wears, and I can't blink, I can't process, I can't…

'What are you saying?'

She lowers her hand to her throat, the skin around her fingernails turning white as she claws into her skin.

'I'm saying…' She swallows and winces in one. 'I'm saying…'

But my mind is racing ahead now. I know what

she's saying and I can't believe it—I won't. Is this how she thinks she'll get rid of me? Does she loathe me that much?

'Spit it out, Lexi.' It's low, menacing, my fury lacing every word as I say it between my teeth.

'When you left, I was pregnant...'

She whispers, but in my head the words are loud and getting louder, reverberating through my skull.

'I didn't know for a few weeks, and when I found out...when I found out I was almost three months gone.'

'Three months...?' I don't want to believe her. 'What makes you think it was mine? You were so quick to hop into Liam's arms, it could have—'

'I never slept with Liam.'

'Come on, Lexi, drop the act,' I say desperately. 'You married him within three months of my departure—how can you expect me to believe that?'

'Because Liam and I never slept together. *Ever.*'

I stare at her, dumbfounded. None of this is making any sense. Lexi, pregnant? A child, dead?

My child.

No, just no...

My head is shaking but I'm barely aware of it.

'Liam married me because I was pregnant and you—' she sucks in a breath '—you were gone... He knew I'd never want to bring a child into this world alone, how much it pained me to think of a child growing up without a family, without a mother and a father, like I did.'

My head is shaking and spinning all at once, and

the griping sensation in my gut is making it roll until I'm sure I'm going to be sick.

'He married you…' it's barely audible '…to be my baby's father?'

'I know how it sounds,' she rushes out. 'Believe me, I know! But I was so confused, so emotional, so heartbroken and abandoned. And the idea of doing it alone…' She shakes her head. 'He was my best friend. He understood. He had no interest in relationships at the time. He was married to his job and that suited me. It suited us both.'

I say nothing. I can't.

'I loved him, Cain, but not in the way I love you.'

'Love?' I repeat on autopilot, catching the present tense and not knowing how to feel.

I'm too many things in that second. Confused. Devastated. Bereaved… Fucking betrayed. Lied to.

'Sit down, Cain.'

I stare at her, my eyes widening. 'Sit down?'

'You look like you might fall down.'

She takes a hesitant step towards me and I spin away. And that's when I see it. The empty desk. Liam's desk. His equipment is in a box on the floor next to it, ready to be packed up. I grip the kitchen counter, heave in a breath, and another, my eyes seeing, my heart disbelieving.

'I wanted to tell you I was pregnant. Of course I did. But you were gone. We had no way of reaching you. Not even Marie had any way of contacting you, not for that first year, and by then…'

Her hand is gentle on my shoulder, the warmth of her touch at odds with the chill beneath.

'By then there was nothing to tell.'

'What happened?'

Silence. I look at her, ignoring the devastation in her haunted gaze.

'What happened, Alexa?'

Her lashes flutter and I know she's reliving it, but I can't care. I *won't* care. I need to know. Christ, I *should* know. I should have been there.

'I was eight months pregnant when Rose stopped moving…'

Rose? My child was called Rose?

I drag in a breath, but I can't seem to fill my lungs. I feel like my vision is tunnelling, the world closing in, my chest suffocating.

'I tried to tell myself it was okay, that she was just getting too big, too snug to kick out. Liam was so supportive. He told me not to worry—that the midwife would check and all would be okay…'

Her hand falls away from me to clutch at her stomach and then I understand it—the gesture I've become so used to. I understand it and it crushes me.

'But it wasn't okay. There was no heartbeat, no sound other than my own body. She was lifeless, gone… My body killed her.'

Her cry of anguish is like a slap to the face and I spin to pull her against me, burying her head beneath my chin and holding her against my rigid body. I ignore the swelling sickness in my throat.

'I should have *known*,' she stresses. 'I should have

known something was wrong and told them sooner, so they could get her out, make her better... I had to give birth to her. I had to go through labour knowing I was bringing her into the world just to say goodbye.'

She's shaking in my arms, her whole body racked with sobs, her tears soaking through my T-shirt. But I feel dead. Frozen solid. Unmoving.

'Do they know what happened?'

She shakes her head. 'Not with any certainty. A problem with the placenta that stopped her...stopped her getting what she needed.'

I clear my throat and ask the question that burns through me. 'What did you...? What did you do with the body?

'We scattered her ashes.'

'At Howth Head?'

She nods against me. Of course they did. It's where Dad is now. Liam too.

'You should have told me.'

I can't keep the anger, the hurt, from vibrating through my voice, but I can't release her either.

'I know. But reliving the pain of her death, reliving it and having to tell you, having you suffer too... To what end? It doesn't change the fact she's gone.'

'You stayed married, though. You and Liam. Even after...'

'I needed his strength more than ever. I couldn't have you, so I had the next best thing.'

'He was second fiddle.' *Not me.*

'Don't say that.'

I see red. I thrust her away from me and stare down into her anguished face, wet with tears. I see her hair clinging to her cheeks and my heart shatters inside me.

'I thought *I* was second fiddle, Lexi. For years I hated my brother for taking everything that was mine, for taking you… I *hated* him, Lexi, and it was all a lie. It was *your* lie.'

She grips her stomach and that breaks me even more. She drops to her knees on the floor, her body rocking back and forth. 'I know. I know. *I know.*'

'How could you do that to me?' I force it out, making myself ignore her harrowed state. 'How could you let me believe you loved him? How could you give birth to my child without me there? How could you rob me of the chance to say goodbye?'

I retch and cover my mouth in horror. I need to leave. I need air. Space. I need to be anywhere but here.

She says nothing, only rocks, and I'm done. I can't stay here and witness this. I can't stay here and come to terms with it all.

I run. Just like I did after watching them on the registry office steps all those years ago.

Only this time I have the facts, and the reality is far more crushing than the fabricated world I've spent the last seven years believing in.

Half an hour ago I'd believed there was nothing to come between us and the future I so desperately wanted.

But nothing had prepared me for this. *Nothing.*

I think of my mother, think of her easy acceptance of their marriage, and I know that she must have known the truth. They all did. All except me.

The outsider.

And now I have nowhere to go. I can't go to Mum. I can't go back to Lexi.

I walk and walk, until I can't walk any more, and then the lights of a bar lure me in.

A drink. Something to numb the pain…

Then maybe I can start to make sense of this mess…of my whole goddamned life.

CHAPTER TWELVE

I DON'T KNOW how long I stay on the floor after Cain leaves. I only know that the water in the kettle is stone-cold when I go to pour it and the sounds of the people on the street, in the flats below me and next to me, have tapered off. It's just me and the flat, which feels far too big and empty now that Cain has gone.

Oh, God, what have I done?

I grip the kettle tighter as I place it back on its rest and switch it on.

You've told the truth. No more secrets. No more omissions.

Whatever the future holds, at least it's all out there now. That has to count for something. But his face, his departure, his…

I don't realise I'm crying again until my knees give way and I'm on the floor once more.

It hurts. It *really* hurts.

Cain, Rose, Liam, Robert. The O'Connors. The whole heart-wrenching lot of them…

I wake to the sound of buzzing in my ear, my body

stiff and uncomfortable. I'm curled into a tight ball, the floor beneath me hard and cold.

What the...?

My eyes protest as I try to open them, crusted with dried on tears, and I wince as I rub at them. I see my kitchen sideways on and I realise where I am and why. *Oh, God.* My stomach starts to churn and I wrap my arms around my knees, squeezing tight.

The buzzing starts up again and I remember why I woke. I look towards the hallway. Someone is eager to see me.

The clock on the oven tells me it's past midnight and I feel a flutter of hope rise up in my chest. *Cain.* It can only be him.

I push myself to stand, ignore my protesting muscles and head to the intercom. The second I see him on the screen the tears are back, and I cover my hand with my mouth to trap the sob that wants to come out.

His lips are moving, as if he's saying something on repeat, but there's no sound forthcoming.

I don't know whether to buzz him straight in or speak to him first, but I'm conscious of disturbing the whole building.

'Cain?'

It's so quiet I'm surprised he hears me, but he does. His whole body tenses, and his eyes are wide as he leans into the camera.

'Lexi, thank God. Please...let me in.'

I press the button and swiftly he disappears through the door. I head into my bathroom and splash my face with water, towelling it dry. I glance at the mirror. I look like hell. My eyes are puffy, my face blotchy and my hair… I pull it out of the ponytail it's in and shake it out as I go back into the hall.

I take a breath and open the front door. My stomach is an anxious knot, my heartbeat wild as hope upon hope builds.

He appears on my landing and then freezes. 'Lexi.'

His voice is raw, thick, and I can't say anything. I can't even swallow to shift the wedge in my throat as the tears are threatening to make a return.

He steps towards me and I back away to let him enter the apartment. His fingers tremble as he rakes them through his hair, and as he passes me by I get the scent of cold night air mixed with the strong scent of beer. He's been drinking.

My senses sharpen. Cain sober and hurt was crushing. Cain drunk and hurt…

I close the front door and press my palms against it, my head bowed as I take a breath.

It'll be okay. Whatever he's here to say, it'll be okay.

I lock the door and keep my head bowed as I walk past him into the kitchen and put the kettle on again. I can hear him follow in a silence that's strained and stretching to the point where my nerves can't take it any more.

I snap. 'Why are you…?'

I turn around and the question dies on my lips. He's staring at the box by the desk. Liam's desk…

Liam's things. His eyes are so filled with anguish that I'm chilled to the bone.

'Marry me, Lexi.'

My heart skips a beat; my eyes narrow. I can't have heard him right. I can't have.

I raise unsteady fingers to my face. 'What did you say?'

He turns to me now, his eyes ablaze. 'You heard me. I want you to marry me.'

I shake my head. 'You don't mean that.'

'Don't I?'

My heart is screaming at me to shut the hell up. To say yes and live the life I always dreamed of with him. But, no—not like this.

'You don't know what you're saying…'

'I'm not a child, Lexi. Credit me with knowing my own mind.'

'You've been drinking,' I say quietly, my arms falling to wrap around my middle.

'And?' He laughs, but it's deranged. His eyes are dark and glittering as he pins me with their glare. 'After the news I've just received, I think I deserve a drink, don't you?'

I don't say anything. I can't.

One second passes. Two.

The bubbling kettle fills the void.

He looks away and takes a ragged breath, rubbing his hand over his face as if that will somehow sober him up.

'I'm sorry, Cain.'

It's all I can think to say, and the words come from the very heart of me, quiet but no less earnest.

'I'm sorry I didn't do more to reassure you, to understand you, to convince you of my love for you all those years ago, and I'm sorry I didn't tell you the truth—that I didn't tell you about…about Rose sooner. I'm sorry. I truly am.'

'I don't want your apologies,' he says, his eyes coming back to me. 'I want you to be my wife.'

'Why?'

'Because you should have been my wife seven years ago. You should have married me. We should have had our child together. We should have…'

His eyes fall to my stomach and I see him quiver. Tears well in his eyes and I can't bear it any more. I close the distance between us, wrap my arms around him and hug him to me. He doesn't move, doesn't react. He's like a statue in my hold.

'We should have said goodbye together.'

I squeeze my eyes shut over his whispered words, hear his heartbeat under my ear and the air that shudders through his lungs.

'I'm so sorry.'

He grips my arms and sets me away from him so that he can look into my eyes.

'Then marry me. Help me fix this.'

Fix this? I shake my head, my voice cracking. 'It can't be fixed. Not this kind of pain.'

'Let me try.'

I remove myself from his hold, knowing I need to be strong, knowing that no matter how much it hurts, this isn't right; it isn't the answer. Not when the reason is guilt, an act of desperation.

'I married for the wrong reasons once. I won't make that mistake again.'

'We belong together, Lexi. We always have. I should have made you mine seven years ago. I never should have left.'

'Made you mine.'

It's all I can hear—and his words from my office all those weeks ago come back to me.

'I'm back to take all that I'm owed.'

I shiver. Have I got this wrong again? Does it really boil down to possession rather than love?

'I'm not some possession you can lay claim to, Cain.'

'No? My brother got to do that, though, didn't he? He got you *and* my child.'

His tormented words stab through the very heart of me and I straighten against them. I put my hurt into strength. I know he's speaking through his pain, through the drink. If I can sober him up maybe we can have a real conversation, a real future.

'Let me make you a coffee and then we can talk properly.'

'Save it, Lexi. I came to ask you to marry me.'

I want you to tell me you love me, my heart screams. *That you want to marry me because you love me.*

'And what about love, Cain?'

He goes very still, very quiet, his eyes fixed on me for the longest time.

'What about it?'

'Don't you want to marry for love?'

His skin pales, his eyes flash. 'You didn't love my brother in that way, yet you still married *him*.'

My world plummets. He doesn't love me.

'And, like I said,' I say quietly, 'I won't marry without love again.'

He hesitates, the pulse in his jaw working to a rhythmic beat, and the kettle chooses that moment to click off. The room is so silent, so cold.

'Then there's nothing left to say. Goodnight, Lexi.'

He turns and walks away, taking my hope, my heart, my world with him.

There's a banging in my skull—incessant, painful. I try and cover my ears, but the movement makes my stomach lurch.

I groan as I roll onto my side and my body suddenly falls. I swing backwards to regain the ground beneath me and realise I'm not in bed. I'm not even at home. The air smells different. It smells of...

Mum.

I'm on Mum's sofa.

'Oh, hell.'

The night comes back to me in broken snippets. Lexi's confession, the pub, my—*my proposal*.

'Fuck.'

I press my fingers into my throbbing temples as the nausea swims inside me.

'Oh, you're awake, then?'

I squint through the haze to see Mum leaning over me, a steaming mug in her hand.

'Mum…' It's a croak. My throat feels like sandpaper, my tongue too thick for my mouth.

She harrumphs and places the mug on the coffee table. 'There's a fresh coffee. Black, two sugars. Drink it and then maybe you'll talk some sense.'

Every noisy syllable sends a shooting pain through my head and my gut lurches again. I fight against it, pushing myself to sit up and placing my head in my hands as I lean forward.

'I'll be amazed if she ever talks to you again. In truth, *I'm* only speaking to you because you're my son and I have to.'

I grimace. In my hunched position, all I can see are her slipper-clad feet, tapping as she looms over me, and I can tell she's pissed off with me. Really pissed off.

'I told you what happened…?' I manage to say eventually.

'I think you gave me the edited highlights; Alexa supplied the rest when I called her this morning to apologise on your behalf.'

I groan. 'It was really that bad?'

'Worse.'

'She shouldn't have let me in. Why did she let me in?'

I shake my head. It's a bad move because it sends my stomach on another roll.

'Oh, I don't know… The fact that you were buzzing her apartment at midnight and she has neighbours to consider? Or maybe, just maybe, she did it because she loves you?'

'She doesn't love me.' I say it quietly, and the pain of it hurts me all the more now that I no longer have the numbing effects of alcohol in me. In fact I have the exact opposite—the morning-bloody-after effect to accompany her crushing rejection.

'Is that so?' Mum chirrups. 'For a clever man, you really are stupid at times.'

'Mum!'

'Don't "Mum" me. That girl has loved you for as long as she's known you.'

I fling my head back to stare up at her, my emotional pain obliterating the physical effect of the move. 'If that was the case then she would have said yes.'

'To your marriage proposal?'

'What else?'

'That was no marriage proposal, Cain. That was you staking your claim—competing with Liam.'

I shake my head, not wanting to hear her, not wanting to think about it. 'You don't know what you're talking about…'

'I know *exactly* what I'm talking about. You were so angry when you came here. Do you remember what you said?'

I rack my brain, trying to fill in the blanks. I rub my temples and stare at her painfully bright slippers so hard I could burn a hole through them.

'I was angry to learn that you were complicit in keeping my daughter—'

Oh, God, my daughter.

I swallow and try to breathe. It doesn't feel real. It can't be…only it is.

'We made a mistake, love, your father and I,' she says, quietly now. 'But it wasn't our place to tell you.'

'You let them get married…'

'I know we did. We stood by them because it was what they wanted and because they loved each other in their own way. They were best friends. They stood as good a chance as any to make it work and provide a stable home for…for Rose.'

Rose. My heart squeezes tight.

'But what about me?'

'What *about* you? You were gone, Cain—who knew how long for? Life didn't just go on hold when you walked out. And when they lost her…when they had to go through all that…they had each other. And I was glad of it because you were still gone. No word, nothing. We lost you and then we lost Rose too. And now your father and Liam.'

Her voice trembles and guilt swamps me. I abandoned them all for my own selfish reasons. It was unforgivable.

'I came back, months later, but I came back.'

Mum sighs and drops down onto the sofa beside me. 'I know you did. Alexa told me. She explained that you saw us…'

I look up to the mantelpiece on autopilot, but the picture isn't there.

'I've put it away,' she says softly, guessing at my focus. 'We've all made mistakes, Cain, but the truth is that Alexa loves you—and I think you love her too.'

She places her hand on my back and I realise I'm crying. I wipe my hand over my face as I turn to look at her.

'But she said she wouldn't marry without love again?'

She stares at me until realisation dawns—Lexi wasn't talking about her lack of love for me, she was questioning my love for her.

'Oh, God. I didn't tell her. I didn't say.'

Mum gives me a gentle nod; her smile one of understanding, of love and sympathy.

'But how could she even doubt it,' I say, 'when I love her so much it hurts?'

'After everything you've been through? You need to hear it from her lips as much as she needs to hear it from yours.'

Her words sink in and I replay my actual proposal, and Lexi's reaction, again and again. I can't believe how stupid I've been.

'How the hell do I fix this?'

'I don't know, son.' She leans into me, her head coning to rest on my shoulder. 'But you two belong together. You'll think of something.'

CHAPTER THIRTEEN

MONDAY MORNING COMES around all too soon, and the idea of walking into the office and knowing Cain will be there has me dragging my feet.

I've heard nothing from him since Saturday night—unless you count the apology Marie gave me on his behalf—and I have no idea how this is going to play out. But we have a job to do, a company to run, and that's what gets me across the threshold.

He's nowhere to be seen, though, and I'm hardly early. I figured arriving at nine would mean the office would be abuzz with people—an audience, a reason for me to act normal.

I dump my bag on my desk and then hesitate. Do I ask where he is? Or will that look like I'm checking up on him and arouse suspicion among the staff?

I turn on my computer and open up my email, my eyes flitting to the door in my continuing debate. I could ask Janice in passing if she's seen him… Ask Sheila, perhaps…

My emails roll in and then I see it. His name. Sent at six-thirty this morning.

I stare at it, my cursor hovering, and then I open it, heart in mouth.

Alexa,
I have some business to take care of in the States. I'll be gone a couple of weeks.
It will do us good to have some space.
I have left John with you. Please use him. He is excellent at what he does, and you can trust him to share the load. Please let him help.
I am sorry.
Yours,
Cain

I stare and stare until my eyes sting and water. He's run away. Just like he did seven years ago. My gut sinks and I don't want to believe it.

He says he's sorry, though. He says he's coming back.

A couple of weeks...

He will come back, won't he?

I want to believe him. I want to believe he'll return. But the past taints everything.

He might not love me back, but the idea of never seeing him again...

No, just no.

I click to reply and my fingers hover over the keyboard, the blank email glaring back at me. What do I say?

A rap on the door makes me jump.

'Yes?'

My voice cracks a little and I clear my throat as the door opens. It's John.

I force a smile. 'Hi.'

'Morning.'

He returns my smile, although his shows none of the strain I'm sure to be showing.

'I thought we could schedule some time to work out a plan of attack for the next few weeks?'

I nod. He's clearly up to speed on Cain's disappearance but his polite expression gives nothing away.

'Sounds great.' I'm relieved it comes out normal. 'Just give me ten minutes.'

'Sure. Coffee?'

'Please.'

He heads off and I look back to the screen and type my reply.

Safe trip. Thank you for John. And the apology. I'm sorry too. More than you can know.

See you in two weeks.
Lexi

I stop myself adding Don't run, although I type it and delete it several times over before I hit 'send' and pull myself away to focus on the only part of this I can control: the business.

Two weeks since Cain left and not a word. I know he's talking to John, though, and that he's keeping abreast of company matters. Maybe even me too.

I wonder if he asks about me. I wonder if he asks Marie too. But I don't dare ask either of them, refusing to acknowledge my weakness so openly.

Work is busy, as always, even with John's assistance, and I'm grateful for it. It gives me less time to dwell, less time to drive myself crazy wondering if I made a huge mistake in saying no.

So many times, I've wanted to go back on my refusal…and if it hadn't been for him leaving the country, I likely would have.

Three weeks since he left and still no word. It's also a week past his promised return date.

I don't want to feel the sadness that accompanies that thought, the crushing disappointment, the realisation that he likely won't return.

That he has run.

What will happen to his beautiful house? Will he sell it? Rent it out?

Will he ask John to stay on permanently? Wash his hands of everything but the shares? Wash his hands of me?

'Alexa, what do you think?'

'Hmm?'

John is looking at me expectantly and I realise I've not listened to a damn thing he's said for at least the last ten minutes.

'Sorry.' I shake my head. 'My mind was elsewhere.'

'No problem.' He gives me a smile that smacks

of sympathy and I wonder just how much he knows; how much he's learned in these last few weeks.

'Do you think we can take this up later? I have a migraine coming on.'

I feel bad for feeding him a lie, but it's not entirely untrue. I do feel under the weather. It just has more to do with my heart than my head.

'Sure.'

He picks up his papers, but doesn't move to leave. Instead he looks at me, and I swear his cheeks colour.

'There's just one more thing.'

I look at him expectantly and wonder what could have got such an unflappable man turning pink.

'Cain has asked that you fly to New York this week. He has a meeting lined up with some investors and thinks your presence is essential.'

Even his name has my pulse skittering. 'And he didn't think to ask me himself?'

John gives a shrug. 'He's pretty busy out there, and I said I didn't mind passing on the message.'

It's been weeks—*weeks!* And he uses John as a go between. He can't even give me the time of day. I'm mad. I'm hurt. I'm... I don't know what I am, but I'm not taking this lying down.

'Well, when you speak to him next, can you tell him I'm too busy *here* to jump to his beck and call and make arrangements on such short notice.'

How *dare* he do this? How *dare* he not ask me himself?

'He's made all the arrangements,' says John, his voice steady in spite of what he must perceive as an overreaction on my part. 'He cleared it with Janice, so your diary is being updated as we speak. Your flights and accommodation are all—'

'Janice!'

He shuts up at my shouted call and within seconds Janice is rushing into my office.

'Yes?'

'Have you and Cain rearranged my dairy for this week?'

Now she's turning pink, and this time John definitely colours. The pair of them are looking at me as if I've just caught them snogging behind the bleeding bike sheds.

'Yes,' she blurts, her lips returning to a zipped-up line almost immediately.

'And didn't you think to check it with me first?'

'Well, I… It's… I… It's important…'

'Very important,' John adds for her.

I'm a simmering pot of rage, but I know it's not them I should be angry at. No, it's Cain. And when I get my hands on him I'll make sure he knows *never* to pull such a stunt again.

But at least he's not running…

No, he's not—he's asking me to come to him. For business. But still…

And if I'm honest, it's not *all* rage that has my body overheating.

CHAPTER FOURTEEN

I AM NERVOUS. More nervous than I can ever remember. I wasn't even this nervous when I played in the big football matches at school, when I took my driving test—hell, at my first corporate job interview without the family name to help me.

In fact what I felt then was excitement—overwhelming excitement. Because I knew I was going to succeed. I was going to get what it was I had my heart set on.

Now I have no clue.

The biggest gamble of my life and I have no idea which way it's going to go.

Lexi is either going to kill me, and go to great lengths to make me suffer while she's at it, or she'll make me the happiest man alive.

I cast my eye over the room one last time. The penthouse suite is the finest New York has to offer, both inside and out. The towering view over Central Park beyond the expanse of glass—beautiful by day, atmospheric by night—will soon be cast in the soft glow of the setting sun. Perfect. I hope.

The scene is set and this time I won't get it wrong.

I can't.

* * *

By the time I'm Stateside I'm not just a simmering pot of rage. I'm bubbling over and steaming.

I'm angry that I've had no chance to prepare for this meeting, that I don't even know who the investor is—least of all why they're so important.

John and Janice would give nothing else away. They just insisted on me coming, showing the kind of fear that would make you think their jobs were at stake. And Cain didn't respond to a single email or phone call.

I'm angry that he's wasted good company money on first-class plane tickets—an expense too far, in my book—and then topped it off with a private chauffeur-driven car to get me from the airport to *this* place. Which brings me to another reason why I'm fuming. The hotel is ridiculously OTT. Every stretch of glass, gold and perfectly polished wood floor tells me that those plane tickets were a mere drop in the ocean when compared to my accommodation fees.

But more than all that I'm angry that he hasn't even shown his face yet. Not even another email to explain the purpose of this visit in detail, or a *Hey, no hard feelings, right? Work is work...* message.

I would have taken that. I would have taken any personal contact over the last three weeks in preference to this.

'Here you go, Ms O'Connor,' the receptionist says to me, her smile perfectly polite. 'Andrew will take you to your room.'

'I can take my—'

'Ma'am.' Andrew is beside me, one hand already on my suitcase, the other gesturing towards the grand lifts.

I feel my cheeks colour, as if my mental tantrum has been outed, and I force a smile through my teeth as I fall into step.

Hopefully I'll see Cain soon and I can wring his bloody neck.

The lift is as smooth as the hotel staff, arriving within seconds of being called and taking us to the relevant floor without giving me too much time to think. I don't even register the room number, simply follow Andrew blindly until he comes to the end of the corridor and we're presented with double doors into what I know is going to be a suite.

A bloody suite? Really, Cain?

And…

Oh, my God.

The doors slide open and I'm gazing at glass walls far ahead, with a view that has me walking towards it, mesmerised. Forgetting Andrew. Forgetting Cain. Forgetting everything as Central Park stretches out before me, bigger than I could ever have imagined.

'I hope you enjoy your stay, ma'am.'

'Oh, yes—sorry, thank you.'

It's beautiful, truly beautiful, and it's not until I hear the door click shut that I turn away and remind myself that I'm here for work. Not to stand around all day, gazing at the amazing view which must have cost the company a fortune.

Another reason to have a go at Cain.

Determined, I head for my suitcase and freeze midstride. I'm in the living area; to my right is a curved sofa, designed to make the most of the floor-to-ceiling view, and on the table, in its centre, is the most beautiful arrangement of burnt orange roses.

I can't ignore it.

I step closer and their fragrance reaches me. Closer still and I realise it isn't an arrangement of cut flowers. It's an actual rose bush.

This really is taking luxury a step too far, but I'm still lured by their beauty, my fingers reaching out to cup one bud as I lean in, close my eyes and take a deeper breath. Their scent is delicate, as beautiful as they look.

My eyes open and I spy an envelope among the buds with a solitary handwritten name: *Lexi*.

Flowers—*no, an actual rose bush*—to welcome me on a business trip?

No.

I find my hand is shaking as I bend to pluck the stark white rectangle from the vivid burst of colour and open it, anticipation coursing through me even though I know it's foolhardy.

I step back towards the window and let the sunlight warm me as I read:

I wanted to do something special to remember our Rose. I know I can't turn back the clock and be there for you when you needed me most, but I can be there from this day forth.

Love always,
Cain x

I'm stunned. Hot and cold at once. This isn't about business. This is about us. About us and Rose.

Our Rose.

I look back at the flowers, find my legs moving towards them, and then I see the label protruding from a stick at its base and its name.

Little Rose O'Connor

I choke back a sob, my eyes overflowing, disbelieving. I pull out the label, stare at it some more, and then realise it's official. He's had a variety of rose named after our daughter. And I know the colour is no accident.

'Mum told me she had hair like yours.'

Cain.

I spin towards his voice and almost feel as if he's a figment of my imagination. He's there beside my suitcase, wearing a navy sweater and jeans, the epitome of casual. But the intensity of his eyes takes my breath away. He steps forward, just a few strides before he pauses. He's hesitant.

'Do you like them?'

'Do I…?' I say dumbly, the card and the label clutched to my chest, my eyes flickering towards the rose bush and back to him. I don't think I've blinked. They're watering that much. I feel starved of oxygen and have to heave in a breath.

'But I… I don't understand…' I wave my hands at the roses, my suitcase, the whole room. 'I thought… I thought I was here…we were here…for business… for…'

I can't speak any more. I'm shaking. I clutch my arms around me and look back at him.

'I'm sorry. I didn't like having to lie. I didn't like making John and Janice do it either. But…'

He pockets his hands, his uncertainty so obvious and only adding to his appeal.

'I was scared if you knew the truth you might not come, and I wanted to get it right this time. I wanted to be honest with you regardless of how scared it makes me feel. I needed to see you face to face and tell you.'

Anticipation has my heart beating out of control, and my words are hard to form. 'Tell me what?'

'That I love you, Lexi.' His eyes glisten as he says it. 'I've loved you ever since I came across you in that school corridor, lost and alone. I've loved you every single day of those seven years apart, even when I thought I hated you… I wish to God I'd never left, and I'm sorry for the time we lost, the time I lost with my family. I regret it so much. But I don't think I'd be the same man now if I hadn't gone. In truth, I don't think I deserved you then, but I hope I'm the man to deserve you now…if you'll have me.'

I'm listening to him, and I can see the sincerity in his face, feel his love filling the air between us.

'But when I told you I would only marry for love, you said nothing.'

'I said nothing because I was a fool. I thought you didn't love me—that it was your way of telling me it could never be.'

I'm shaking my head now. 'You wanted to own me?'

'No, I wanted to marry you and spend the rest of my life loving you.'

He steps forward, his arms reaching out, but I instinctively step back.

'How can I trust that this is real? That you won't run away again when life gets hard? When…when things outside of our control crush us?'

I look to the flowers and I know he knows what I mean. I don't need to spell it out.

'Because I know we're stronger together. Because I've learned from the mistakes of our past. I should have been there for you then, Lexi. I should have been there for both of you.'

Slowly I bend to place the card and the label back on the table. 'So, what…?' It's not accusatory, it's soft, inquisitive. I'm trying to understand. 'You had a rose named in our daughter's honour?'

He gives a soft laugh that's shaky with sadness. 'Don't say it like that if you ever meet Peter—which I hope you will. He's certainly eager to meet you.'

'Peter?'

'He's the rose breeder who created her. She's been years in the making—almost a decade, in fact.'

'And he just happened to let *you* name her?'

His smile is slow. 'For a price. But when I told

him the reason I wanted to name it…when I told him
about you and our Rose—'

His voice breaks a little, his smile falters, and I
want to run to him. But I feel rooted, my heels stuck
in the luxurious rug beneath me.

'I think he let me haggle him down.' He looks
to the flowers. 'She's worth every penny, though.'

I don't know whether he means the rose or our
daughter, and I can't trap the tiny sob that erupts.

'Oh, God, Lexi, please don't cry.'

He rushes towards me, pulls me into his arms
and his warmth envelops me, his scent, his comfort, his love.

'Shh, baby, shh…'

'It's just so beautiful.'

I sniff, and it's so unladylike, but I'm incapable
of caring. I can't believe this is happening. That I'm
standing in the most beautiful suite, with the most
beautiful man, and the most beautiful rose named
after our beautiful daughter.

'I can't even begin to understand what's going on.'

'It's simple,' he says, his hand soft on my hair. 'I
love you, Lexi.'

I push up off his chest and he looks down into my
eyes, his hands stroking my face as his eyes rake over
me. 'And if you love me too you only have to say it.
You don't have to marry me. You—'

'I don't *have* to marry you?'

He looks at me quietly for a moment, so serious.
'No, not if you don't want to. It's enough to know
you love me.'

'And if I do want to marry you?' I say.

He lets out a soft laugh, his expression lifting. 'I'll be taking you to Tiffany's in a few hours.'

'Tiffany's…?' Realisation dawns and brings tiny flutters of excitement rising in my chest. 'You mean, you haven't bought a ring yet?'

'I thought that would be too presumptuous.'

'And bringing me to New York *isn't*?'

'No, that was about making my proposal perfect… this time.'

My lips curve into a grin I can't contain.

'What?' He frowns and goes from sexy to nervous to cute—and so utterly mine. 'Too clichéd?'

'No—no, it's perfect,' I say, looking towards the window and the glorious view of Central Park. The sky is pink and peachy in the setting sun and the room glows with it, setting off the roses in all their colourful glory. 'But what if I'd said no? All this effort and…?'

'You would have had a few days' holiday—something you haven't done in a long time.'

'How do you know?'

'Janice.'

'Janice.'

We say it in unison, our smiles matching.

'Why a few hours, then?' I tease, my smile becoming a mock pout.

'A few hours…?'

'Before we go to Tiffany's?'

The happiness inside me is bubbling up so much I fear I'm going to burst if I don't tell him I love him soon. But I'm holding out. I've waited so long to say it without fear hanging over me.

'Won't it be closed then?' I ask.

'Not for us, my love. They've been forewarned that they may have some late-night shoppers.'

'You're kidding?'

'Not at all.'

He hooks his hands low down my back, his blazing eyes falling to my lips. I know exactly where this is going.

'But I have three weeks of absence to make up for—not to mention seven years—and I plan to start immediately.'

He lowers his head, and his lips are almost on mine when I press my index finger against them. 'You're insatiable.'

'Sue me,' he murmurs against my finger, and I laugh, shaking my head at him even as I know the time has come.

I curve one hand around to cup his cheek and raise the other to do the same. I gaze up into his eyes, holding him just where I want him.

'I do love you Cain.' I brush my lips against his. 'I've always loved you.'

And then I kiss him with everything I have. No more holding back, no more fear. No secrets, no lies. Just us and our love for one another and our dear sweet Rose.

EPILOGUE

Five years later

THERE'S ONLY ONE THING you need to know about me.

I love my family.

Even when they're driving me to absolute distraction.

'Liam Robert O'Connor—if you don't put those wellies back on this instant…'

I'm using my 'boardroom voice', as Lexi calls it, but it's having zero effect, and I look to her imploringly as our three-year-old monkey swings his footwear around like two propellers and heads for the biggest puddle on the trail.

'Please can you sort him out?'

Lexi merely laughs as she squeezes Bella, who's on her hip, and presses a kiss to our daughter's rosy cheek. 'Mummy needs to go and take care of your brother before Daddy has a tantrum.'

Bella giggles and Lexi bends to put her down, straightening out her bright red jacket as she does so, her auburn curls escaping its hood and blowing in the wind.

'At least you have the sense to keep your wellies on, Bella.' I take hold of her chubby little hand and smile down at her. 'It's a mud pit out here.'

'Their favourite kind,' Lexi murmurs, placing a kiss on my cheek before heading off after Liam.

I watch her go, feeling the warmth, the love inside me, swell. It's not raining now. The clouds have cleared, the sky is blue and the seagulls are circling. It's picture-postcard-perfect—even with my rogue little man front and centre.

How anyone copes with twins is beyond me. Even with three adults to their two I feel outnumbered. Not that I'd change it—not in the slightest.

I smile as I watch Lexi tackle Liam, watch Mum trying to help, but she has Ed pulling her in circles.

And in the distance I see the waves crashing around the Bailey Lighthouse and feel the presence of Dad, Liam and Rose.

This is our Sunday routine now—a walk around Howth Head with all of us together. Sometimes we talk about them, sometimes we don't, but they're there in our thoughts and that's enough.

I feel a tug on my hand and Bella pulls out of my grasp. I lower my gaze just in time to see her drop promptly to her bottom, her hands going to the muddy heel of one welly…

'*Bella Rose*, don't even think about it…'

* * * * *

COMING SOON!

We really hope you enjoyed reading this book. If you're looking for more romance, be sure to head to the shops when new books are available on

Thursday 17th September

LET'S TALK
Romance

For exclusive extracts, competitions
and special offers, find us online:

 facebook.com/millsandboon

 @MillsandBoon

 @MillsandBoonUK

Get in touch on 01413 063232

MILLS & BOON
A ROMANCE FOR EVERY READER

- **FREE** delivery direct to your door

- **EXCLUSIVE** offers every month

- **SAVE** up to 25% on pre-paid subscriptions

SUBSCRIBE AND SAVE

millsandboon.co.uk/Subscribe

MILLS & BOON

THE HEART OF ROMANCE

A ROMANCE FOR EVERY KIND OF READER

ODERN

Prepare to be swept off your feet by sophisticated, sexy and seductive heroes, in some of the world's most glamourous and romantic locations, where power and passion collide.
8 stories per month.

STORICAL

Escape with historical heroes from time gone by. Whether your passion is for wicked Regency Rakes, muscled Vikings or rugged Highlanders, awaken the romance of the past.
6 stories per month.

EDICAL

Set your pulse racing with dedicated, delectable doctors in the high-pressure world of medicine, where emotions run high and passion, comfort and love are the best medicine.
6 stories per month.

ue Love

Celebrate true love with tender stories of heartfelt romance, from the rush of falling in love to the joy a new baby can bring, and a focus on the emotional heart of a relationship.
8 stories per month.

Desire

Indulge in secrets and scandal, intense drama and plenty of sizzling hot action with powerful and passionate heroes who have it all: wealth, status, good looks…everything but the right woman.
6 stories per month.

EROES

Experience all the excitement of a gripping thriller, with an intense romance at its heart. Resourceful, true-to-life women and strong, fearless men face danger and desire - a killer combination!
8 stories per month.

DARE

Sensual love stories featuring smart, sassy heroines you'd want as a best friend, and compelling intense heroes who are worthy of them.
4 stories per month.

To see which titles are coming soon, please visit

millsandboon.co.uk/nextmonth

JOIN US ON SOCIAL MEDIA!

Stay up to date with our latest releases, author news and gossip, special offers and discounts, and all the behind-the-scenes action from Mills & Boon...

 millsandboon

 millsandboonuk

 millsandboon

It might just be true love...